FATAL CLINCH

Terry's hands caressed his chest. She breathed heavily in his ear, and lightly nipped his neck. With a sigh, John relaxed in her arms.

Suddenly, her hands shot up under his arms and behind his neck.

"What?" he gasped before she tightened the full nelson. His head bent forward as she increased the pressure. Her knee slammed into the middle of his back, driving him into the seat.

Confused, John struggled feebly.

"I'm so sorry, lover," she said in a deep voice that wasn't her own. "It has nothing to do with your money." He heard her laugh just before his neck snapped.

Terry shook him like a rag doll, enjoying the sound of grinding bones. Certain he was dead, she released her grip. John's lifeless body slumped to the floor.

The thing inside Terry whetted its lips; it was so hungry, but the others were still waiting. . . .

DAWN OF THE VAMPIRE

WILLIAM HILL

PINNACLE BOOKS
WINDSOR PUBLISHING CORP.

PINNACLE BOOKS

are published by

Windsor Publishing Corp.
475 Park Avenue South
New York, NY 10016

First printing: January, 1991

Printed in the United States of America

Prologue
A Fallen Soul, Found

John Traylor slammed into the water back first, his metal tank digging into dark blue neoprene. Then he sank. Silvery bubbles of air thrashed about him. Escaping from his body, they fled for the surface. Fish scattered, disturbed by his entry.

Lead weights pulled on John, slowly drawing him deeper into the olive-colored lake. He relaxed and stared above. The circle of sunlight slowly closed, its brightness dimming. The water's color deepened as Traylor slipped to ten feet below the surface.

Except for John's slow breathing, the watery world was silent. Being underwater was second nature to him, so he felt at home in the element. It was an easy adjustment, and as always, the second dive of the day was even more comfortable than the first.

John loved being near water and scuba diving thrilled him — nothing made him feel more alive.

Testing the resiliency of his mortality made his soul sing. Danger was intoxicating. Just the thought of exploring the sunken town of Wreythville excited him almost as much as his lovely companion. As if on cue, Terry Bray's lithe form exploded into the water above.

John watched Terry's long black mane weave about, contrasting with the bright blue of her skintight wet suit. As she sank, her hair stretched out like tendrils. John clicked on his light and flashed it at Terry to catch her attention. She returned the favor. Her beam surrounded him, then flashed off.

Terry's long legs kicked in a circle. She faced him, then swam downward. Silhouetted, her shadowy figure only served to accentuate her shapely figure. Terry quickly caught up with John. Clasping hands for a moment, they smiled. His brown eyes locked on her crystal blue ones. John was glad that he'd met such a woman — one that loved the thrills of life as much as he.

Terry pushed away, shifted her flashlight to her left hand, then gave John the "thumbs up" sign with one gloved hand. The orange streaks along her fingers seemed to glow. With the other hand she shook her stick and flashlight.

John knew she was ready to go exploring once more. He pointed to his watch, reminding her that their afternoon dive, the second of the day would be short. They could only spend twenty minutes maximum along the bottom. Understanding, she nodded. They both turned on their diving light and dove head first.

Following the anchored rope, they swam deeper into encroaching shades of darker green. John grabbed his nose, squeezed, and blew. The pressure left his ears.

Their lights led them but weren't necessary at this depth. John silently marveled at the range of vision. Although the drought had becalmed South Holston Lake, allowing the sediment to settle and improving visibility, it was still a far cry from crystal clear. At twenty-five feet down he could see twenty feet around him without a light. They continued equalizing. When they reached thirty-five feet, John could hardly see ten feet without the brilliant beam. Catfish and crappie slipped silently by the couple.

With probing shafts of light to guide them, John and Terry continued following the rope which led them to the water-entombed town. As if waiting to greet them, shadowy shapes wavered ahead. Cans, wrappers, and plastic bags were strewn before them. At forty-five feet the divers eased through the layer of trash that floated above the colder water. John shivered as he passed through the thermocline.

Suddenly he felt a slight resistance—something tugging on his air hose. He swam ahead, attempting to pull free, but was held fast. A tinge of fear swelled in his thoughts.

As John quickly turned around, the regulator was ripped from his mouth. Panicking, he grabbed at it. A glint of light, the flashing of a knife caught his eye. Terry swiped at him.

The slash cut the water before him, and John

felt his regulator come free. He shoved it back into his mouth and regained control of his emotions. With care, Terry loosened three rusted hooks from his air hose and untangled a length of fishing line. She smiled at him, signaled "okay," and then cleared water from her mask.

John nodded, mentally laughing at his momentary panic. He thought he'd reasoned away the unnerving sensations from their morning dive. He was surprised that peace of mind was still eluding him. That had never happened before. John couldn't remember ever being uncomfortable while diving.

As they moved farther below the thermocline, their range of vision amazingly improved to thirty feet within the illuminating beam. Despite the colder water closing in, John grew more comfortable as his body heated the neoprene-held water. Regaining his composure, John picked up the pace. He didn't want to waste any more dive time. Besides, action made him forget the nagging thoughts which haunted his consciousness.

Larger fish began to appear, signaling their nearness to the lake floor. John hoped the visibility was still fair at the bottom. He hated to admit it, but today he felt a little claustrophobic — it was chilling the way Wreythville's buildings seemed to stride forth from the murky gloom. The shadowy structures always hung just beyond the reach of clarity, no matter how near one swam. John concluded that he would be happy as long as he didn't run into one of the lake's legendary catfish. The six-foot monsters usually stayed near the dam and deeper waters.

The rotted remnants of a short, empty bell tower materialized, then grew slightly clearer as they neared Wreythville. The paint had peeled away and the wooden slats had warped and frayed, giving the building a fuzzy appearance. Having already explored the small structure, they moved on. Shortly, another buckling rooftop appeared. They passed it too.

They hadn't explored the house which sat just ahead. Terry had discovered it just prior to surfacing that morning. John didn't understand why, but the house had given him the creeps. He shook his head. Just thinking about it made him shiver.

This morning's events flashed through his mind. He and Terry were trying to keep their first dive short, and it was time to return to the surface. John pointed up, but Terry shook her head. Swimming to him, she insistently pulled him along. Suddenly, an ornate building appeared from the darkness, centered in her light.

Surprised, John shook his head. He swore that he'd already swum through that area and found it deserted—or so he thought. The limited visibility made it difficult to be sure. It wasn't like diving in Maui; that was next month. This was a warm-up dive, and John thought that a chance to explore underwater dwellings shouldn't be squandered.

Floating before the building, John felt chills dance along his spine. He noticed that the water felt colder here than anywhere else. Terry didn't even seem to feel the temperature change. She wanted to enter and explore, but John checked his air and shook his head. Grudgingly, she followed him to the surface.

On the surface, Terry mentioned feeling drawn to the place. She claimed that she had almost collided with a corner of the copper roof before seeing it. John saw she was anxious to go back. With her eyes alight, she laughingly told him that a fabulous diamond necklace was drawing her to the spot. With dreams of treasure hot in her head, Terry asked him several times to cut their respite short and return to the house. A stickler for safety, John wouldn't. They waited until the afternoon for their second dive.

John's mind came back to the present. Just thinking about their morning visit to the ornate house elicited chills. Now they were almost there. Traylor forced himself to bury the sensations and focus on the present.

As he swam, John envisioned finding fabulous antiques or treasure—maybe a pre-World War II relic or coins from the 1800s. He wondered how many times this area had been explored—he hoped very little. The church and the previous house had both been rotten and barren, but maybe earlier divers had overlooked something in the other dwellings. The structure Terry had discovered, the ornate building with the copper roof, was partly made of stone. It might be in better shape.

Terry tugged on his arm and pointed ahead. As if slowly drifting out from a coiling black cloud, the chalky green roof appeared in their light. The corroded tubing which had once formed the chimney stretched toward them. John still didn't understand how he'd swum by the house the first time without noticing it. He shook his head; he must have confused this area with another. Often areas of sea and lake beds looked very much alike.

They floated alongside the chimney and crawled across the roof. Once again, he noticed the considerably colder water. Thinking that the building groaned under their touch, John strained his ears but heard nothing unusual. The underwater world was silent except for the gurgling release of bubbles from their regulators. John stilled his irrational fears — his imagination was running amok.

Grabbing the gutter, Terry pulled herself off the roof and over the edge. John followed. This time he noticed that the structure had two stories. A heavy buildup of sediment had settled to just below the warped and shuttered windows of the first floor.

As Terry approached a second-floor window, she absently traced the grooves in the shutters with her fingertips. The window was open and inviting. Surprisingly, Terry waited for John. From the way she had acted earlier, he thought she would have bolted inside. He felt relieved.

John pushed away from the building and floated alongside the wall. As he drifted toward the open window, he pointed his light inside and peered within.

The beam danced across strangely contorted walls, swaying as if alive. Undulating slowly, wispy white tentacles stretched out. Startled, John kicked away. He gulped down air, sucking heavily on his regulator. John thrashed about for a moment, then realized that the wallpaper and sections of dry wall were shredded and loosely floated in the water. He took another deep breath and calmed himself. What was it, he wondered, that unnerved him about this house? There was the feeling of death — something long dead. It stirred within the place. John passed it off as paranoia and an over-active imagination.

He looked around, expecting to find Terry curiously staring at him and wondering about his frantic reactions . . . but she was gone! He looked about wildly. Only moments ago she'd been stroking the intricate carvings in the shutters which surrounded the windows.

Trying to find Terry, John waved his light back and forth. To his right, he spotted her disappearing fins. She was entering the house through another window. His worry turned to annoyance — she knew better than to leave her dive buddy without notification. They weren't supposed to leave each other's sight. Safety was priority when diving. So many things could go wrong.

With powerful kicks, John quickly approached the window. Reaching it, he peered within. He recoiled as a burst of light surrounded him, and then was gone. Darkness recaptured the room. Blinking, John cursed and pointed his flashlight ahead to guide his entrance.

Large, shiny white teeth appeared from the darkness. An amorphous shape swayed behind the double row of daggers. Flailing at the needle-nosed monster with his flashlight and kicking backwards, John swam away from the open window. He pressed himself tightly against the wall and waited. His heart pounded, sounding like a jackhammer in his ears.

Sharp teeth forming a vanguard, the huge gar slowly drifted out the window. John's eyes bulged at the five-foot creature. At least a quarter of its length was made of deadly looking teeth. As if it didn't notice him, the gar slowly swam off. John closed his eyes, letting out a long slow breath.

He didn't believe in omens and wasn't superstitious, but after a head-on meeting with a huge gar, John didn't really want to enter the building. Only his concern for Terry drove him forward. She was acting oddly, and he didn't want her to be alone. Taking another deep breath, John forced himself to relax and entered the house.

His guide light searched the interior but found only small carp and a gray catfish. They darted for safety as John pulled himself inside. Part of the window frame crumbled in his hand and he fell forward. He righted himself quickly, his eyes searching the room. The paneled walls were warped but held steady. He shivered. The water was even colder inside the house, cutting through his wetsuit to the core of his being. His muscles stiffened.

John spotted a dim, greenish glow emanating from beyond the doorway. It seemed to alternate in intensity growing brighter, then fading, like the pulses of a heartbeat. John swam toward it.

The door he passed was rotted and appeared ready to fall off its hinges at any moment. As he entered the hallway, his air tank thudded against the frame. He followed the light, somehow knowing it would lead him to Terry. The glow emanated from around a corner just down the hallway. Still feeling uneasy, he scrutinized the corridor. It was devoid of any furnishings or pictures. Only a tattered carpet covered the floor.

John checked his dive watch. Its luminescent hands indicated that he was at sixty-five feet. He figured they had less than fifteen minutes of bottom time left. Then he looked at his air gauge . . . he was already below fifteen hundred pounds! His fear was causing him to use more oxygen than usual. Little things were annoying him, like the water seeping into his mask. John tilted his head back, pressed on his mask, and blew out through his nose. His mask cleared and he turned his attention back to his search. He carefully finned onward.

Suddenly, the green glow disappeared. Except for his light, the darkness closed in around him. As Traylor advanced, he continued searching and probing. The blood pounding in his ears and the bubbling release of air from his regulator were the only sounds keeping him company.

Then his flashlight died, and darkness surrounded John. His heart skipped a beat, then rampaged as his breathing sped up. John shook his light. He didn't understand—he'd just changed the batteries. The depth pressure shouldn't have caused this. He fumbled for his extra flashlight and felt the loop on his belt empty. Damn! It must have fallen off.

Then John thought he felt something swirl

about him. Did something just brush by him? He shook the light again. His other hand searched for a wall. Finding it, John backed against it. Again, the water churned. His heart hammered inside the wet suit.

Cursing, John banged the light against the palm of the hand. Nothing happened. The second time, he hit it harder. It remained dark. John struck it against the wall and light sprayed forth, piercing the ebony waters. He relaxed and sighed.

John rested, calming himself and recovering his wits, then continued down the hallway. As he rounded the corner, he wondered about the absence of fish. There were none present once he'd left the first room. Maybe, he thought, Terry had already scared most of them off. He wondered what the hell was wrong with her.

A staircase and balcony greeted him at the end of the short hallway. John swam forward, passing by a cabinet. Out of the corner of his eye he caught a movement. He whirled to face his distorted reflection in a tall mirror. It hung just above the cabinet. Disgusted with himself, he continued. To his left was a small but elegant chandelier that still hung over the entryway. Rotted tapestries of indistinguishable color lined the wall along the stairway.

John waited, drifting at the top of the steps in hopes of finding some clue to Terry's whereabouts. He silently cursed. There wasn't any sign of Terry's light and he was getting very cold. The tension and temperature were draining him of energy.

Unexpectedly, dizziness assailed him. The disorientation was so powerful that John wasn't sure which way was up. He closed his eyes and clenched his jaw to keep from vomiting. He bumped into something . . . maybe the banister. John opened his eyes and the room spun. He blacked out.

He awoke still disoriented. Surely, he thought, he must have only been out a few seconds. He looked around to get his bearings . . . how did he get on the first floor? John stared up at the overhang of the balcony. To his right, he found the elusive glow once more. It slipped out from under a set of crooked double doors. John wondered if he'd find Terry behind them.

How much time? John checked his watch . . . lord, he'd been out much longer than he suspected. They had only ten minutes of bottom time left before needing decompression. His pressure gauge read around eleven hundred psi.

John headed for the doors. As he moved closer, they seemed to waver and the light shimmered. He wiped his mask as if trying to rub his eyes.

With apprehension, he reached out and grabbed the knob on the right. He turned it and found the door locked. Traylor tried the left one. It pulled open slowly as if ushering him inward. As John entered the room, his body was bathed in an olive light. He'd found his lover, but she didn't notice him.

With her flashlight set on wide luminescence and sitting on its side, Terry was thoroughly engrossed in her search of an old mahogany desk. She opened a lower drawer and knelt, nearly disappearing from sight. Air bubbles slowly rose from her regulator to coalesce into a cloud and dance along the ceiling. All but empty shelves covered three of the walls. A few saturated books had collapsed, falling on their sides. To his left, a single painting of a mountainous landscape hung on the wall. John almost expected to find a skull on the desk, but nothing appeared menacing.

He drifted toward Terry and waited on the other side of the desk. Her attention was so focused that she still didn't notice him. She continued searching the drawers, pulling them free, then turning them upside down. He thought she was oddly obsessed. He'd never thought her a treasure whore.

Impatiently, John tapped the desk top with his stick. Terry looked up at him and smiled as if he'd always been there. He pointed to his watch. They had nine minutes left of bottom time. She nodded, made a looping motion around her neck and pointed to the desk. John just shook his head — she was looking for her imaginary necklace.

A sudden movement to his left caught his eye. He swung his flashlight towards it, capturing the object in the beam. Both divers watched in amazement as the painting slowly slid down the wall. The bottom of the frame hit the waist-high wall trim and halted for a minute, then the top tilted forward and it tumbled downward.

They both stared at the safe door. It appeared slightly ajar. John felt a new wave of uneasiness. Why had the painting chosen just now to fall?

Terry moved toward it. John tapped the desk

once more, but she paid him no heed. He shook his head in aggravation and cautiously followed her across the room.

The picture had just about settled on the floor when John caught it. While he lifted the painting to examine it more closely, Terry slid her stick inside the safe and pushed the door fully open. John turned the painting over and saw that the wire hanger was corroded and had finally snapped. The painting seemed to slowly disintegrate in his grasp. Before it fell to pieces, he noted a castle tucked within the mountains. The remnants of the painting fell from the frame and drifted to the floor.

Moving excitedly, Terry reached inside the safe and removed something. Under the light, she held a flat, wooden box. The silver clasp, hinges, and trim were tarnished. It appeared to be a jewelry case. She marveled at her treasure, then turned to show it to John.

The box slipped from Terry's grasp. She suddenly jerked her hand backwards, leaving a swirling trail of dark blood. She quickly clamped her right hand over her left.

John focused his flashlight on her hand. The glove was torn and an ugly gash greeted his eyes. A reddish cloud formed in the water around her wounded hand.

Pointing at her injury and then to the ceiling, Traylor let her know it was time to surface. He didn't like this place and he wanted out. Immediately. She nodded, then stooped to pick up the jewelry case. John halted her, then pulled a fishnet bag from his belt. He unrolled it, then scooped up the box and pushed it into the bag. As if resisting, it snagged an edge. Traylor poked it in with his stick.

John caught Terry's eyes, then motioned with his head towards the door. She began swimming. He followed her, noticing that she moved erratically. Her injury seemed to have disoriented her. John shivered again. They needed to have a long talk once they were topside.

Without incident, they retraced their earlier path. Again, John noticed the lack of life within the structure. They exited the same way that they had entered and headed for the surface. He was greatly relieved as the building disappeared into the murky depths. Terry never looked back.

Just below the surface, John pressed the button which released air into his Buoyancy Compensator. His BC slowly expanded and his head broke the surface. John stuck his snorkel in his mouth. It felt good to breath "real" air again. He noticed that the water was still calm. The sun's radiance was like a tonic to him.

John swam the last few feet to the boat and grabbed onto the ski platform. Behind him, he heard Terry break the surface, then paddle to the boat. He set the bag and box onto the wooden slats.

Terry reached the boat and John helped her remove her tank. As he hung on with one hand, he boosted her onto the rear of the boat. He watched as Terry removed her weight belt, mask, and fins. He took the snorkel from his mouth and asked, "Are you all right? You look out of sorts."

"It's a nasty cut and the sight of blood always makes me queasy," Terry told him. She set her tank against the side of the boat, and then pitched her equipment into the back. "Just float for a minute while I bandage it. I'll be right back to help you with your tank."

"Sure," he agreed.

Terry climbed forward and disappeared. He heard the radio come on and music drifted from the boat. Suddenly, the motor whined, signaling that it was being lowered. "What are you doing?" The motor continued for a long moment, then stopped.

"Sorry, love, I leaned against the tilt switch. You hid the first-aid kit in the compartment below the steering wheel."

"Yeah, I did. Sorry," John replied. Lazily, Traylor removed his weights, dive belt, fins, and mask. Complacent, he floated on his back and relaxed. The sunshine warmed his bones. The bottom of Holston probably never grew warm, he thought, and that house . . . John shivered.

He heard Terry slide across the back of the boat and crawl onto the platform. John opened his eyes and released the buckle on his scuba tank. In spite of her injured hand, Terry still helped him remove his tank. With a heave, she pulled it onto the platform. John followed.

"Let's check out our find," Terry suggested, her crystal blue eyes sparkling with excitement.

"You sure you don't need to see a doctor? That gash looked nasty. Doesn't it hurt?"

"It hurts a little, but I don't think I'll need stitches. I'll just keep it clean and dry. So why don't we open our treasure chest?"

"In a minute. Lord, Terry, find some patience. What's wrong with you?" John asked, nearly exploding. He fixed her with a burning stare. She didn't reply. "How could you take off on your own, without even notifying me, and enter that house? You know better than to leave your dive buddy. It's not safe. Something could have happened. You could have died. I could have died. Dammit, I was worried about you!"

"I don't understand," Terry responded in a quiet voice. "You were with me the whole time. From the moment I entered the window, you were right behind me. You touched me several times to let me know that everything was all right."

"You're joking, right?"

Terry faltered a bit when she saw his disbelief. "I . . . I remembered you felt uneasy about the house. I didn't, so I led the way. Something seemed to be calling me. You know I have a nose for money as well as adventure." John couldn't argue with that statement.

She continued, "You know I wouldn't leave you in such a situation. I'm a stickler for safety. Leaving a dive buddy is a sin. How could you say I left you?"

John's anger built, then he remembered her expression when he tapped his stick on the top of the desk she was searching. Terry thought he'd been there all along. Closing his mouth on a sharp retort, he let the hot emotions drain away. He didn't understand it—maybe a touch of nitrogen narcosis had affected her. Suddenly, John was unsure. By the look on Terry's face, he saw it pointless to try and discuss it now. She believed she was telling him the truth. Something at the house had affected them both.

"John, are you feeling all right? You look a little pale."

He remembered blacking out in the entry hall. "Yes, I'm fine, forget it. I'll explain the confusion later, I promise." She gave him a pouting look, but he continued, "If your hand feels okay, let's load all the equipment into the boat, then cruise over to that small island and relax." Her gaze followed the nod of his head. "You can clean up, and then we'll have lunch. Later we'll see if we can open that jewelry box of yours."

"It does look like a jewelry box, doesn't it?" Terry said with a beaming smile. "I wonder if there's hand-cut diamonds or gems inside? Maybe—"

"Honey, we'll know soon. Don't get your hopes up too much. That place looked pretty picked over. Anyway, we are finished for the day; I don't think you should dive again with your injury." He unzipped his wet suit.

"Sounds like a good plan, my man," she responded, kissing him on the top of the head, then climbing back into the boat.

"How's the dizziness?" he asked.

"Much better. Eating will probably help." Together they strapped the air tanks to the padded section near the covered engine. Terry turned off the air and removed the attached regulators, stacking them with the rest of the paraphernalia.

John moved to the front of the craft and began hauling the anchor up.

"I love to watch you work. Such fine muscle tone. Hard to believe you're nearly forty," Terry teased.

"Be nice now. I promise to give you an opportunity for a closeup examination real soon," he responded. She laughed. "I've almost got the anchor. Go ahead and start up the engine." Terry did and with a powerful surge it roared to life.

John continued reeling the rope in for a minute, then pulled the anchor from the water. He placed it in the bow compartment and said, "Let's go." As they pulled away, Traylor felt relieved. The farther they got away from the ornate building, the better he felt.

They cruised several hundred yards across the glassy smooth cove and headed for the bare redrock island. "Swing around to the other side and pull ashore. The sun's in the southwest. I got real cold on the second dive and I'd like to bake my bones."

She smiled widely, her tongue dancing over her teeth, and the boat swung around the westward end. "Isn't this the high point of an old graveyard?" Terry asked as she turned off the motor. They coasted toward shore.

John jumped out with a rope and slowed their landing. "You're right. I think it's called Cemetery

Ridge," he replied as he tied the rope to a large rock. "It was part of Wreythville's graveyard until the TVA purchased the area and flooded it. It's no longer a cemetery since the law required that they relocate all the coffins."

"I've been on Holston many, many times and I don't remember seeing it," Terry stated.

"Between the drought and lowering the water level to make repairs on the dam, I think Holston's at a record low. Look at Cliff Island. It's nearly one hundred and fifty feet easy." He set the cooler and picnic basket on shore. "I've jumped from the top before, but not at this level. Last year at this time, it was only a twenty-foot drop from the top. In fact, in most years we probably couldn't have explored Wreythville. The water would have been too deep and the visibility would have been terrible."

Terry picked up the fishnet bag containing the box. "This before lunch," she said. "Sometimes after you're fed I can't get you to do anything." She smiled, but there was an intensity in her eyes.

He decided to appease her. "Okay, I give in. I'll open the box if you'll open a bottle of wine." Her head quickly bobbed up and down in happy agreement. He took the bag from her and set it on the rocks.

Terry dug into the cooler. "Where's the corkscrew?" she asked.

"It's in there, just keep looking. It's probably frozen to a chunk of ice." John tried to dump, then shake, the wooden box out of the net. The silver edges caught several times and it wouldn't fall free. He cursed under his breath, then reached in and pulled it out.

Rolling it over in his hands, John examined the box. Although the silver had tarnished, the wood still looked healthy. He noticed grooves in the surface, so he rubbed it down with a towel. Traylor discovered intricately carved patterns all over the box. The ornate trim was crafted into tiny claws which gripped the corners and pulled the two halves together. The clasp reminded him of fangs tightly snapped shut over a bit. His curiosity aroused, he attempted to open it.

The clasp turned, but it wouldn't open. "It's stuck," he told Terry.

"Do you want a screwdriver?" Terry asked. There was a popping sound as she pulled the cork free.

"No," John replied as he reached for the sheath strapped to his calf. "I've got my knife. It will probably work better anyway."

"Try not to scratch it too bad, lover," Terry requested. "The box looks handcrafted. It might be worth something."

John slid the knife along the groove, scrapping free some of the tarnish. He scaled both sides, then tried to open the box once more. It stubbornly refused. Sticking the point between the silver fangs, John tried to pry it open.

The knife suddenly slipped, scraping along the silver, and cutting into his flesh. "Ow! Dammit!" John dropped the box, shook his left hand, and let go a string of curses. Blood dripped from two fingers.

"Are you all right?" Terry called in concern. She jumped out of the boat, still carrying the bottle of wine and two glasses. She set them down, then examined his wounded fingers. "It's about the same size as mine, but doesn't look as deep. I don't think you'll need stitches."

"Damn, that was stupid!" He kicked the box, then looked to the sky. After a moment, he said, "Where'd you leave the first-aid kit?"

"I put it back where it's supposed to be, under the glove box. Do you want help?"

"No, pour me a glass of wine and I'll be right back." Traylor headed for the boat.

While John attended to his injury, Terry retrieved the jewelry box. It was even more beautiful than she remembered; the silver seemed to regain its shine before her eyes. Terry could only stare. John's blood had seeped into the grooves and seemed to be slowly drying. The patterns wove and twisted, drawing her attention like a whirlpool. It fascinated her—she had to see what was inside!

Picking up the knife, Terry began to pry the clasp. To her surprise, the halves parted easily. She flipped the top back with the knife and gazed inside. Her mouth dropped open and her eyes widened.

Two brilliant fire opals stared back at her like burning eyes. The sunlight made them flare with a warmth and life that she could feel on her face. Her breath was taken away by their enchanted luster and beauty. The gems were coin sized and attached to a silver mesh chain.

The necklace lay coiled, just waiting for someone to handle it. Obliging, Terry gathered up the fiery gems. She had to wear it! It was made for her!

Looking around, she saw that John was still busy wrapping his wound. Terry set the box down, then placed the chain over her head. Pushing her hair aside, she felt the cool metal settle around her neck. It seemed to fit perfectly. The gems felt warm on her breasts.

Terry smiled to herself, wishing that she had a mirror. Her hands caressed the gems and they grew warmer with her touch. She turned to proudly display them to John . . . then dizziness struck her.

The world spun wildly in a kaleidoscope of colors. Sparks flared before her eyes. Terry tried to speak, but her tongue was thick — her lips leaden. Suddenly, she wanted to scream.

Cold chills danced along her skin, but the red orbs grew ever hotter. They burned her breasts, searing flesh. Terry clawed at the necklace, but her hands failed to find it. Her knees grew weak, her eyelids heavy. She staggered forward and collapsed against a large rock.

Sweat poured from her flesh and her eyes shut as if her lids had melted closed. Terry tried to call out, but coherent thought slipped away. Her limbs went limp and she felt herself losing consciousness.

As the darkness closed around her, something wrenched at her consciousness, a hunger . . . for life . . . for blood . . . for freedom. Terry tried to fight it, but the evil presence was too strong. The pressure in her head increased and her mind drifted away from her body. Laughter echoed in her head as she lost consciousness.

Her flailing hand collided with the wine glasses and bottle. They shattered on the rocks, catching Traylor's attention. "Honey, are you all right?" John asked, glancing over his shoulder.

His voice snapped her to attention. "Uh, yes, I'm fine. I think I just stood up too fast. I was a little dizzy, but I'm fine now. How are your fingers?" Terry stood and wrapped a towel around her shoulders, covering the necklace. She wiped the sweat from her brow and walked over to the boat.

"It looks okay. I've cleaned it with hydrogen peroxide and rubbed some antibiotic cream into it. I'm almost through wrapping it. Actually, I could use a hand."

"I'm on my way." Terry climbed into the boat and stood behind him.

"I think I'd better get a tetanus shot tomorrow. It's been a while since I had one. How about you?"

"Last year, I think. Maybe the year before." Terry's hands softly slid across his back and around his chest. Her lips danced across his neck. She whispered in her ear, "You look just fine, a healthy specimen of a man."

"If you keep that up I'll be feeling no pain at all."

Terry's hands caressed his chest. Fingers played in his hair. She breathed heavily into his ear, and lightly nipped at his neck. With a sigh, Traylor relaxed in her arms.

Suddenly, her hands shot up under his arms and behind his neck. "What?" he gasped before she tightened the full nelson. His head bent forward as she increased the pressure. Her knee slammed into the middle of his back, driving him into the seat. She put all her weight and newfound strength into the hold.

Confused, John struggled feebly. He didn't understand—her strength was incredible. His breath came in short, ragged spurts. His threw his weight back at Terry, but she didn't budge. "I'm so sorry, lover," she said in a deep voice that wasn't her own.

He grew weaker. The tremendous pressure on his neck was killing him. John panicked. *He was going to die*. How'd she get so strong? Why? He tried to plead, but could only gurgle. He bit his tongue. Red spittle ran down his chin. "It has nothing to do with your money," she told him. He heard her laugh just before his neck snapped.

Terry shook him like a rag doll, enjoying the sound of grinding bones. Certain he was dead, she released her grip. John's lifeless body slumped to the floor. The thing inside Terry whetted its lips . . . it was so hungry, but the others were still waiting. He would sate his hunger after his friends were freed.

His companions, his true followers, had waited so long for him to return . . . and now *Viktor Von Damme was free!* Her body, his vessel—he leaned back and laughed, the sound echoing between the mountains and carrying along the water. Soon, his followers would be free to live in the light. The time of darkness had passed. It was their time. It was time for revenge. Leaving Traylor's corpse behind, Von Damme climbed out of the boat and onto Cemetery Ridge.

Chapter One
Boys' Reunion

Fading light greeted Dillon Urich as he abruptly awoke from a disturbing dream. Disoriented and slightly unnerved, he lay quietly on his gently bobbing raft. His pulse still raced, and he could feel cool sweat on his skin. Dillon wondered how long he'd slept. The last he remembered the sun had been bright and the music loud. Now the only sounds were the hush of nature as the sun set behind the Appalachians.

All day long Dillon had partied on South Holston Lake, half in Virginia and half in Tennessee. He was enjoying the reunion with his boyhood friends. He breathed deeply, the air alive with the covert sounds of the wilderness. Dillon soaked in the fresh, elemental nature of the mountains. The air mattress shifted beneath him, and the water was warm against his flesh.

Despite the pleasant surroundings, shadows of the nightmare kept returning. He was running down a hill towards water, possibly a stream. It was just after sundown and the crescent moon was on the rise. There was no sound from the beast that pursued him, even

31

the woods were deathly silent, as if a hunter had entered its realm. White fangs — or were they claws? — flashed in the diffused moonlight.

Dillon rubbed his eyes and shook off the nightmare. Obviously last night's film festival of *American Werewolf in London, Serpent and the Rainbow,* and *Wolfen* had played with his subconscious. He laughed at himself, thinking a reporter should have nightmares about deadlines, demanding editors, police chases, and hostage situations . . . or maybe that was too realistic.

Dillon rolled off his raft, stood up, and stretched. He stared across the hot pink colored water towards "Bug Island" aptly named by his friends after one memorable campout when the place had been invaded by thousands of insects. Removing his sunglasses, Dillon surveyed the lake and smiled. Holston Valley was truly beautiful. The setting sun draped the mountains in shadow, hiding the heavily forested Appalachians. The rocky isle stood starkly outlined against the dying red sky. Not far behind the first oasis of land, a second towering island jutted from the water.

For a long time, residents of the Smoky Mountains had called this "God's Country." There was no doubt in his mind that God had blessed it with his enchanting touch. The lake itself was always so quiet and peaceful, rarely crowded even on holidays. Wonderful boyhood memories of summertime carousing, skiing, boating, and tubing returned to him, along with the young ladies in their skimpy bikinis. He was glad he could make this year's reunion. He was sorry Troy couldn't. He was one of the few blood brothers missing. Well, working was always a viable excuse.

Interrupting the serenity, Dillon called to shore, "Is it time?!" His voice carried across the water. The word

32

time echoed through the valleys and coves.

"Hell *yes,* it's *time!*" Tom Marader answered as he leaped out of his beach chair. He whipped off his red "Roll Tide" cap and shook it in the air. "Let's party!"

As Dillon moved towards shore, he saw that a huge, used-car salesman smile was plastered on his friend's sunburned face. "I feel the need, yes, I say, the need for speed," Tom continued, then broke out in maniacal laughter.

Dillon's friend jumped up and down. "I thought you were gonna sleep all day. I was gonna leave you for dead, but Denny said the motor would have awakened you. And we know you need your beauty sleep." Absently, Tom dabbed at the bright yellow zinc oxide protecting his nose, then ran a hand through his thinning greenish-blond hair.

"Why didn't you wake me earlier?" Dillon asked, staring eye to eye with his six-foot friend.

"I know how hard they work you in Dallas. In light of that, remember that my job offer still stands."

"You mean become a partner in running your boat dock and seducing high school girls?" Dillon asked as he laid the raft gently on the rocky shore.

"Exactly! Someone has to do it, why not me and you?" Tom's blue eyes sparkled with mischievous delight. Dillon could see that his friend was inebriated. Tom started laughing again, rubbed his hands together with glee, then turned and gingerly picked his way up the slope to camp. The reddish shale dug into his bare feet. Dillon stopped at the shore, donned his flipflops, and followed his friend.

Denny greeted them with a wide, blocky smile. He was lean, large boned, and taller than both Tom and Dillon. Denny peeked out from under his multicolored sunglasses and said, "Whoa, Dillon, you look a little crisp. That prominent snout of yours could have used some of Marader's neon nose coat. Well, folks, the lobster twins look ready, who wants to go for a night cruise?"

Eight guys all spoke at once. "Wait, wait," Denny said, holding up his hands and staggering back towards his tent. "Such enthusiasm, I'm almost blown over," he said, a small smile touching his lips. He tossed his sunglasses into the tent and put on his horn-rimmed spectacles.

As Denny Rentzel surveyed the expectant faces of his friends, his brown eyes twinkled. Dillon knew his friend enjoyed teasing them. An associate at the *Dallas Morning News* who'd seen a photo of Denny mentioned that his face looked like a Walt Disney creation. Dillon laughed, finally understanding why Denny had successfully gotten away with so much mischief over the years. He looked innocent no matter how guilty in truth.

"We're gonna be here for a couple of nights, and everyone will have a chance to go." Denny raised his large, bony hands in a patient gesture.

"But I wanna be first!" Marader interjected. He gave them all a wide, "eat shit" smile.

"I don't mind staying here," a deep voice called from beneath a tree. "I can use some beauty rest. The sun really drains me." Without opening his eyes, Jamie "Jambo" McGillis stretched his long, bronze body and folded his hands across his T-shirt which read "Wild Bill Phantom's Cars." Instantly, he dozed off again.

"Thanks, Jambo. Continue to do what you do best," Denny said. "Guys, the boat will only hold six," he reminded them. Marader was already moving toward the gray-and-white speedboat. Extra lights lined the sides, bow, and stern.

"I wanna make sure it'll work," Jay "J-Man" Beck said. He rubbed the stubble along his sunburned and slightly jowled jaw. "Remember, I assembled it and am the only licensed pilot here."

"That's helicopters," Dillon reminded J-Man.

"Go ahead, J-Man, we'll let you drive. You did all the work," Denny told him.

Jay raised both palms to the sky. "Great. The gods have once again smiled upon me. Besides, someone has to be there to pick up the pieces when Marader goes splat." He pulled an orange "Vols" T-shirt over his slight paunch and followed Tom.

"Guys, guys, I say listen," Bob St. Martin spoke loudly as he stood up from his chess game. His long-haired opponent watched him rise. "I mean, seriously, are we sure we want to do this?"

"YES!" Tom, Denny, and J-Man chimed.

Bob staggered back. "Whoa, let me try this again. Uh, you guys have never done this, right?" They all nodded. "You don't know if this will work."

"What does that have to do with anything?" Denny asked. "We didn't know that snow skiing at night with mining helmets would work either." He cocked his head to look at Bob through the corner of his glasses.

"And that was an amazing experience," Spider Adder's voice joined the discussion. He stepped out of his canvas tent. His brown eyes locked on Bob. Spider's dark hair stood straight up, then curled over a tie-dyed bandana. Pointing a finger at his bespectacled friend, Spider said, "You were the first to let J-Man rig your car for electrical missile release in the fireworks war."

"Well, that was different," Bob mumbled, readjusting his glasses and nervously running a hand through jet black hair.

"How so?" Spider asked, plopping down and crossing his long, spindly legs. He rubbed his narrow chin as he thought. Dillon noticed that Spider was already deeply, if not evenly, tanned.

"We were younger and less wise then," Bob responded.

"Jay could have blown the electrical system in your car," Denny pointed out. "You didn't know if that would work."

"That car was a heap," J-Man called from the boat. "Ask Knives, he drove it a few times."

"If I'd known that Jay was going to wreck a motorcycle, two cars, and a glider, I never would have let him touch my car," Bob responded.

"Hey, I finally found something I can fly safely," Beck retorted.

"Bob, where has your sense of adventure gone?" Dillon asked.

"It's been replaced by common sense. I'd prefer not to count on prayer to keep me safe. I use my head nowadays," Bob told them.

"Bob, you'll soon be a minister; have a little faith in your friends. We went to college to learn how to do this kind of thing," Denny Rentzel told him.

"Right, Denny. What course was it? Reckless one-oh-one." Bob's voice contained a sharp edge.

"No, it was an advanced course, three hundred level. I took it in med school," Dr. Stephen "Knives" Curran teased, ganging up on Bob.

"Doesn't this go against your Hippocratic oath or something?" Bob asked.

"Actually," Knives started, then took a swig of wine

from a perspiring bottle, "the eradication of disease and the end of human suffering is the primary goal of any doctor." A wide smile created pronounced cheekbones, then his face went stonily serious. "And Marader is about as disease ridden as they come. Think of all the human suffering that would be prevented if he were eradicated. I'm only following my sworn oath to the medical profession and humanity." His blue eyes sparkled in their attempt to hide his amusement.

"Real funny, Stephen, you lil' shit," Marader called from the boat.

"You guys are still as headstrong as bulls. I think I'll stay," Bob said, looking down at the chessboard. He pushed his glasses into place and focused his dark eyes on Denny. "Peter and I want to finish our game. Y'all go ahead and go."

"You sure?" Dillon asked.

Bob gave a short, high-pitched laugh, "Well, I would like to see Marader crash, but I'll wait for daylight. Unfortunately, I'm not exactly in the same shape I used to be. Not everyone is a hard body like Tom and Dillon." He patted his abundant belly.

"Uh, we noticed," Peter told Bob, looking up from across the magnetic chess board.

Tom yelled to them, "I'm ready! Let's go. Par-tee!! What's taking you guys so long?" He stared at them from atop the sun deck, then continued fiddling with the blinking light on his ski vest. The orange beacon pulsed like a rapid heartbeat.

"Chill out, will ya, Marader?" Spider glared at him, then grunted and gave all a satisfied smile as Tom quieted. He turned back to his friends. "There."

Spider quickly sobered. "With Jambo doing what he does best, we have six, so let's go. Pete said he'd fix a fire and start dinner in an hour or so. I know I'll be hungry by then." Spider wrapped his blue-and-white towel around his neck and marched toward the craft as if that officially ended the discussion—and it did.

Dillon grabbed his binoculars, camera, and flashlight. He couldn't wait to see this. "Hey, Denny, do you need help with the videorecorder?"

"No, Knives already has the extra battery pack and cassettes in his duffel bag, don't you, Dr. Curran?" The trio walked down the short slope to the boat.

"Absolutely," the blond-haired man replied. Knives took another swig of wine, then wiped his moustache clean. "I'll bring my first-aid kit too, just in case the idiot hits a large turtle or a dead fish." As they began descending the slope, Knives held up a black satchel.

"How traditional," Dillon commented. He held the Baja cruiser steady as Denny climbed in, then followed. J-Man turned on the regulation lights. Red and green radiance spilled out across the water's surface.

With an angry roar, the motor immediately kicked to life, drowning out all of nature's chirps and croaks. White water churned about the stern. "A little less choke," Denny suggested. J-Man nodded and throttled back on the shift. The motor responded with a muffled purr.

"Let's rock and roll!" Marader yelled over the motor.

Knives set his bags down in front, and pushed the boat from shore. With a shuffle and a hop, he climbed aboard, settling next to Tom. Meanwhile, J-Man put the boat into reverse. Backwards, they slowly glided into dark water.

"Nothing like South Holston Lake for beauty, be it day or night," Dillon told his friends. "Every time I return to Texas, I miss the Appalachians more and more."

Denny leaned forward. "I can't believe you still live there. It's too hot and flat and brown for me. I can't believe that Troy didn't come back with you," Denny said, looking around at the five guys.

"I hope he has fun in Seattle," Knives said.

"He doesn't know what he's missing!" Marader laughed.

"Jambo, Bob, and Pete don't know what they're missing right now!" J-Man told them all in a loud voice. "Our first night skiing attempt! We should have done this long ago. Ah, a symphony of light . . ." he said as he flicked a switch. On the front of the craft, four wide-beamed halogens snapped to brilliance, illuminating the island in a harsh light. The other lights along the side and rear sprayed over the water.

"Hey, shut that off!" Bob yelled.

". . . sound," J-Man continued, tugging on his black cap as he hit a second switch. There was a loud, momentary hum, then music exploded from the black plastic-bagged speakers strapped to the rear sun platform. ZZ Top's Texas sound filled the air. J-Man smiled at Dillon, then mouthed the words, ". . . and speed."

The boat leaped forward, its bow springing high, then flattening as they quickly planed out. Dillon absorbed the music, the sensation of water flying by and the thrill of the wind whipping about him. He could barely hear Tom repeatedly yelling "Yeah, yeah, yeah!"

They cruised along, enjoying every moment. The boat lights cut a swath through the deepening darkness. The lake appeared deserted. Dillon's dark eyes danced along the edge of the forward lights as if he expected to see something suddenly appear.

Despite having already skied the area several times earlier in the day, he was a little paranoid, thinking an obstacle might drift into their path. He shooed the feelings away. They had already scoured the area thoroughly. Without winds, rains, or storms, the lake stayed clear of debris.

Dillon was pleased with the visibility Jay had attained with the modified boat lights. He could see at least five hundred feet in every direction. They worked even better than the headlights of his Mustang. Dillon turned and shouted to his friend, "Excellent job, J-Man." Jay Beck gave him a thumbs-up gesture.

The test run completed, J-Man slowed the boat. He also turned down the volume on the stereo. "Sounds kick ass!" Tom screamed. "Where's the rope? I'm ready, I'm ready, I'm ready. Boy, am I gonna love this." Knives handed him a white coil of rope. "Gloves, I need some gloves. I can't ski without my magic gloves. Check in the glove box, please?"

"Don't be in a hurry, Marader. I swear, Thomas, you're always in a hurry," Denny told him. "I have to get the viddy ready. I want to make sure I catch you when you bite it. Nothing I enjoy more than a good bust," he solemnly pronounced. His blocked jaw was seriously set. He looked through the viewfinder. "Jay, the lighting is superb."

"Thanks."

"Nothing we can do about Marader now. We all know he's hyper with a hormonal imbalance," Spider explained as he searched the crowded glove box. Long fingers found Tom's neoprene gloves tangled in wiring. "Here." He tossed Marader the soggy pair.

"This is gonna be so, so, so much fun. Woo-ee, am I glad I had a few beers. I feel invincible. Yes, yes, I am invincible. J-Man cut the motor. I'm going in." Jay complied and the engine stopped. They silently slid forward. The rope pulled taut. "Hey, could you guys play "Back in Black?" Knives, throw me the ski . . . please." Marader ran a gloved hand through his hair, hesitated, smiled, and then dove into the water.

Knives shook his head. "He's been like this since he was four." He picked up the yellow slalom ski and sent it skidding across the water's surface.

"I'm ready," Denny told Jay from the swivel chair. He held the camera up to his eye. "He's in focus. Truly amazing."

"Hey guys, I'm ready. Can you turn the speakers around so I can hear?" Marader called.

"You were born ready, Marader," J-Man called to him. He started up the motor, then put it into gear. The boat eased forward. The rope grew taut once more.

"PULL!!" Tom yelled.

J-Man jammed the throttle fully forward. The motor growled, roared, and then the boat leaped forward. The bow shot high into the air as they pulled away. As Tom began to rise, the bow began to lower. Tom rose majestically from the white foam.

J-Man eased back on the lever. He had a satisfied smile on his face. "I just love two-hundred-fifty horsepower and eight cylinders. The best engine inheritance money can buy."

"Ah, I was hoping he'd lose it," Denny said with mild disgust.

Tom jerked his thumb into the air.

"Faster," Spider told Jay.

"I thought that was the international signal for

41

swing me into a tree," Knives wisecracked.

"I'm doing thirty-two," J-Man responded.

"Try thirty-six or so," Denny told him. "He's a tough guy, he can take it."

"I like it louder," J-Man said and turned up the stereo. Jay steered them south. As it grew darker, only a few lights provided a hint that shore existed.

Dillon reclined and let all his cares slip away. He reveled in the elemental feel of the wind as it caught his dark hair. Without a doubt, there were few things he enjoyed more than speeding across a lake. He loved the water, especially Holston's glassy surface. At almost any time of day, a skier could find a mirror-smooth finish on some part of the lake.

"Did you see that cut! Wowie! He's still one-hundred-percent ham," Knives told them. "Put him in front of a camera and he's a daredevil. He almost touched his elbow to the water that time."

Dillon closed his eyes for a moment. At night, he missed the beauty of the Smoky Mountains, but he could still feel them. Even over the booming stereo, there was a majesty in the air about him. Nature was fully alive, caressing him with its healing balm. He didn't miss the concrete, highways, or skyscrapers at all.

"He's really kicking butt," Denny chimed in.

Every time he returned to Bristol, Dillon wondered how he had managed to stay away for nine years. Yes, this was God's country alright.

"Go for it, Marader!" Denny screamed.

"Men, I think the boy enjoys skiing more then sex," J-Man called out.

Dillon let his friends' voices fall away and pondered the sensation that he felt. Since before he could swim, he'd been visiting Holston. Yet for some reason that he couldn't place, today it felt vaguely different. The drought had left the area looking barren. Red shale rock instead of lush trees towered around the waters. He thought it was worse than when they lowered the lake to repair the dam in the late seventies.

"I'm going to cruise by Cemetery Ridge. Marader said that it surfaced about two weeks ago. I've never seen it," J-Man told his friends.

"We haven't patrolled that area," Spider interjected, barely making himself heard over the music.

"So?" Denny countered. "This area is as dead as it is dry. Nothing's drifted about in weeks. Besides, it'll make a great addition to the video — Marader skies graveyard."

"He wants to go faster, again," Knives yelled at J-Man.

"I'm already going thirty-eight."

"It's okay. Marader bounces real well," Denny said with a smile. "C'mon, Marader," he called as he watched through the video camera, "crash and burn."

Dillon felt the boat accelerate. The motor's whine heightened, blending with the music. For a moment, the boat floundered slightly, then J-Man adjusted the trim. The craft sliced smoothly through the plane of glassy water.

Spider tapped Knives on the shoulder, "Hey, check out the moon."

"What?" Knives asked.

"The moon, that red thing rising over there."

"Where?" Denny asked, swinging his camera around.

"Guys, c'mon," Jay said, "it's above and behind Cemetery . . . hey, did you see that?"

Dillon opened his eyes. They immediately focused on the advancing edge of their guiding beam. Just beyond, Dillon thought he saw a large dark shape floating in the water. It seemed to slowly shift and roll.

J-Man said something that the wind snatched away. "What?!" Spider yelled.

"I saw something large and black fly from the island. It looked like a large b—"

"Tree!!" Dillon yelled as he jumped up, pointing at the bobbing mass. They sped closer to the floating object. The light struck an edge. Dillon almost instantly changed his mind. The edge was straight, geometric, as if it were a box or a crate.

J-Man stood and peered over the windshield. His eyes narrowed and he immediately yanked the wheel to the right. The hull carved deeply and the boat tilted sharply. Dillon tightly clung to the railing. The craft continued turning. It nearly stood on its side.

Spider lost his balance and tumbled to the floor. "Jay!" Denny yelled, struggling with the shifting video camera. Knives was slammed against a wall compartment. A ski tumbled free. The speakers thrashed against the straps as the boat sliced away from the flotsam.

J-Man played with switches. The lights flickered, then the music abruptly died. He straightened the wheel and they began to level off.

Regaining his balance, Dillon peered forward once more. "Another one ahead," he warned.

"What is this, a minefield?" Jay let out a string of curses as he guided the boat right once more.

"Jay, just cut the motor, for Christ's sake," Spider advised.

"Marader's flipping you off," Denny told J-Man.

Having regained his balance, he was still filming. "Nothing like some drama . . ."

Still catering to the right, the boat raced forward. Another obstacle seemed to appear from nowhere. "Shit! There's a third one," J-Man shouted. He yanked the wheel left.

The craft briefly thrashed, then swung left. Barely hanging onto the railing, Dillon was stretched out across the front cushions.

"This is great stuff!!" Denny glowed. His eyes were alight with excitement.

"Those things looked like crates," Dillon said as he leaned towards his friends.

"More like coffins," J-Man offered.

"Let's stop before we hit something," Knives suggested.

"Marader wants to go faster," Denny told them as he watched Tom swing out to the left.

"Who cares? Stop this thing, I wanna get off," Spider said with exasperation. He touched his forehead, then looked at his fingers. "I'm bleeding. Jay . . ."

As they slowed, Dillon's eyes were on Marader. Tom continued jerking his thumb in the air. Just as he shifted to flip them a bird, his eyes widened.

Marader leaned left, then right, then seemed to catapult out of the water. A hollow noise carried to the boat as Marader sailed out of his ski. Arms spread wide, Tom yelled. Head over heels, Marader somersaulted once before catching a shoulder. He crashed, burying himself. Water sprayed far and wide.

"I've got it on viddy," Denny celebrated, then added, "I hope he's all right. Jay, swing around."

J-Man spun the wheel and the boat turned sharply, returning to the spot of the crash. The lights found

Marader — he was motionless.

As they coasted in, Dillon stared at the form of his friend. Head thrown back, arms and legs spread wide, Tom looked stunned — or dead. The blinking light outlined his immobility. "Hey, he's not moving!" Knives stated the obvious.

Watching intently, they all leaned over the edge of the boat. "Tom, are you all right?" J-Man yelled. Tom didn't move. The ripples began to settle around him.

"Lord no," Spider whispered. Everyone was too stunned to move, to think. All eyes stayed on Marader. Something floated next to him.

"Get in closer," Dillon said. "I think I saw him move."

Marader groaned. Spider and Knives gave a sigh of relief. Denny smiled widely and continued filming. "Hey, what's in the water with Marader?" he asked. "I thought I saw something."

Tom tried to move, but every muscle screamed in pain. He tried to spit water, but his jaw was locked. His face was numb, and water filled his eyes.

God, Marader thought, I must have landed face first — a face plant. He didn't remember it. One moment he was skiing along fine, surviving Jay's stunt driving, and dodging crap in the water, the next instant he hurt like hell.

All Marader could feel were his fingertips. He thought he heard voices, but there wasn't any music. Was he imagining things? Had they left him? he wondered in dazed thought.

As a bit of feeling returned to his limbs, so did sanity. The buzzing quieted and his ears cleared, allowing him to hear the boat's humming motor.

The rescue crew was arriving. Fortunately, he wasn't

badly injured, just stunned. Still, time seemed to crawl. Marader felt like he'd lain there for an eternity. He hadn't hit that hard in a long time; it totally knocked the buzz out of him. What a waste of a good drunk, he thought.

Marader felt something warm on his face. He licked his lips. Blood! he tasted blood. Oh God, maybe he was wrong . . . maybe he was really hurt after all. Tom tried to touch his face but was still too stiff. Something nudged his foot, then his leg, moving up his body. It felt too large to be a fish.

In pain, Marader opened his stinging eyes. He spotted his ski to the left. Again, he felt something nudge him. This time it bumped his arm. It felt cold and clammy. Tom looked down. A white hand rested next to his forearm.

Seized by panic, adrenaline rushed through him. Gasping and stammering, Tom found the strength to throw himself backwards. The hand followed, reaching for him. It appeared to move closer. Tom flailed, splashing about. "Hep, hep . . . help me!" he called.

Everyone looked startled. "What's he doing?" J-Man asked.

"Oh no, he's going into convulsions," Knives said. He immediately rummaged among the towels and found his satchel.

"There's something in the water," Dillon said. It looked man sized to him, but most of it was under the water. The hairs stood up on the back of his neck as his imagination ran wild. "Jay, cruise next to him, but don't run over him."

"I'm going in," Spider told them as he pulled off his shirt. Denny readied a throwable float.

"Wait!" Knives yelled and grabbed Spider.

47

They looked into the water. Marader wheezed as he back stroked. "It's got me! Help me, please! It's . . . it's . . ." Illuminated in the white light, Tom thrashed like a drowning man.

Dillon squinted. "He's bleeding, probably hit his head." There was a flash of something pale and fleshy near Tom. It rolled over and Dillon thought he saw a bloated face, dark hair, and an arm. Quietly he said to Knives, "He's not in convulsions, there's a second body in the water with him."

"What?!" Knives exclaimed. Dillon pointed to the right of Marader.

Tom met the boat just before it glided to a stop. He slid along its side and grabbed the ski platform. They could hear him panting.

Spider crawled onto the platform. "Are you all right? Tom, speak up!"

For a moment all they heard was rapid breathing. Streaks of watery blood ran down Tom's face. His eyes were still wild, his complexion ghostly. "I'm all right. I'm all right." Spider helped pull Tom onto the boat. Despite the warmth of the July night, he was shaking. Marader tried to stand, then collapsed to his knees. "I just scared the crap out of myself . . . oh, lord. I thought something was grabbing me. I must have hit my head harder than I thought. I saw a hand . . ."

"What?" Spider asked. He gave Tom a towel.

"You did," Dillon said, pointing to the corpse. It was floating face down, arms and legs spread wide.

"What?" Tom and Spider exclaimed. Dillon felt everyone tense. Only Knives appeared calm. As a doctor, Curran had seen plenty of corpses.

"Look for yourself," Dillon told them. "It's a man." They crowded to the front of the boat.

"I hit a dead man," Marader said incredulously.

"Denny, keep rolling," Dillon suggested.

Denny dropped the cushion and grabbed the recorder. In moments, he was videotaping.

Chapter Two
Welcome Home

When the phone rang, Troy Bane's hands were poised over his word processor. His weekly sports column was due, and he was contemplating how best to express the latest plight of the Texas Rangers. *Brrring. Brrring.* He shook his head in disgust as the phone continued ringing. Troy hoped someone else would answer so he could order his thoughts. His unscheduled trip to Seattle had left him with jet lag. He was tired and hadn't felt well for days. He rubbed his red-rimmed blue eyes.

Brrring. Brrring. Just another interruption, Troy thought. Oh well, he hadn't been able to think clearly for the past several days. What difference did another distraction make? Maybe he was coming down with something.

"Hello, *Dallas Morning News* sports desk, you have Troy Bane."

"Hello. Oh Troy, I'm so glad it's you. I was hoping to reach you. This is Ida Urich."

"Hi, Mrs. U. This is a surprise. How are things in

Bristol?" he asked. Troy pressed a button on his keyboard. The screen told him that his script was being saved.

"Not good. Not good at all, dear. Umm, have you heard from Dillon?"

"No, in fact I've been wondering about him all morning. I heard he didn't show up for work yesterday . . . and he never misses work. As far as I know, he hasn't called in either. I'm kinda in the dark, though. I flew in late last night from Seattle, and Dillon hadn't left a message my machine. I figured he was having so much fun at the reunion that he lost track of time. Why, is anything wrong?"

"I . . . I don't know. The recent news reports have been very upsetting. There's been so many tragedies, people disappearing, a man murdered—it's gotten so bad that I've quit listening to the news or reading the paper. Bristol used to be such a peaceful place. What is the world coming to?"

"Uh, Mrs. U, how does this involve Dillon? He was supposed to be on vacation." Troy had a sinking feeling. He ran his hand through his dark wavy hair.

"Well, you know Dillon, if he senses a story, leisure time is forgotten. John Traylor's murder sort of fell into his lap."

"John Traylor was murdered!? Good lord! How did that fall into his lap?"

"Strange as it may sound, Dillon and the boys were out waterskiing at night and Tom Marader collided with a body. It was John Traylor's. You do remember John Traylor?"

"Of course. I worked for Traylor's father, James. So did Dillon. What makes them think he was murdered?"

"Papers say his neck was broken, but there weren't

51

any blows to the head. Dillon disagrees, although he didn't offer any theories. Anyway, Traylor was left in South Holston. The boys found several coffins floating in the water and some open graves on Cemetery Ridge."

"That sounds crazy. I thought that Cemetery Ridge was underwater."

"We haven't had rain in over three months, and while the water's low, the TVA is repairing the dam."

"And you think Dillon is investigating Traylor's murder?"

"When I saw him last Thursday morning, he was sort of obsessed by it all. He claimed that all the area's troubles were related to the murder."

"Troubles? Like what?"

"For starters, Mr. Traylor's body was stolen from the morgue."

"Who would . . . What else?" Troy was beginning to see why Dillon had become involved. He couldn't resist a mystery.

"Several people are missing. There has been a rash of robberies. Even stranger, there have been several reports of animal attacks around Holston."

"Mrs. U, besides Tom Marader, who was Dillon with the night they found Traylor's body?"

"Oh, I'm not sure. All the boys."

"All the boys, okay. Tell me if I leave anyone out. Stephen Curran, Jay Beck, Denny Rentzel, Jambo McGillis, Aaron Ackles—"

"No, Aaron wasn't with them, although I think Peter was."

"Okay, how about Spider Adder and Bill Glazier?"

"Detective Glazier wasn't there, he had to work, but I know Dillon has spoken to him."

"Am I missing anyone?"

"Bob St. Martin."

"Ah yes, how could I forget Mr. St. Martin. Tell you what, Mrs. U, I'm going to make some phone calls. If I can swing it, I'll come visit, poke around, and see what I can find out. I have vacation time, and things are sorta slow around here," he lied. His editor was going to hit the ceiling.

"That would make me feel better, dear. Dillon always thought that you were wasting your talents by reporting sports instead of doing investigative reporting," she told him. Troy laughed. "Anyway, I would feel better if you'd check on him. You know how much trouble Dillon can get into." Troy knew; he'd been with him on several occasions.

"I'll do what I can. I'll come see you when I visit. How's Silke doing?"

"She's almost completed her internship at the clinic. I'm so glad she decided not to be a lawyer. The world has enough of those."

"Do you have her phone number?"

"Not yet, dear, she's changing apartments and moving out of San Francisco."

"Thanks anyway, and don't worry, Dillon can take care of himself. I'll see you soon."

Troy immediately speed dialed Knives Curran in Richmond and got his answering service; Knives was in surgery. He tried Jambo at Wild Bill Phantom's and discovered that he was out running errands. Bob was out of the office. J-Man was flying coal executives to Asheville. Frustrated, Troy didn't know where to get hold of Peter or Spider. He refused to call Marader. Disgusted, he left a message on Denny's answering machine.

Over the next few hours, everything ran together. He booked a flight, talked to his editor, rushed home to pack, and drove to the airport in record time. When he arrived at the terminal, Troy stepped out of the taxi and paid the driver.

Troy stopped for a moment. Something was wrong. *He'd driven himself to the airport*. He remembered parking in long term. He hadn't taken a cab. Troy turned to look at the cabby.

The driver tipped his cap and smiled. Troy blanched as the flesh on the driver's face tightened, revealing the skull beneath. With a laugh, he drove off leaving Troy in . . . in a graveyard.

Now Troy was thoroughly confused. He dropped his luggage and stared at the misty surroundings. The cemetery stood on a hill. A wrought-iron fence, painted blindingly white, surrounded the scattered headstones. Sunlight streamed through the fog, highlighting the trees and brilliant green grass. Dew covered, everything glistened. Several small structures stood in the background.

Suddenly, the ground rumbled and shook. The trees quaked and the tombstones wobbled. The fence grated and shrieked as metal chafed against metal. A second, stronger, shock hit, and Troy lost his balance. He landed hard, knocking the breath from him.

A chilly wind blew, carrying a familiar mechanical sound. Troy tried to identify it when the grave before him exploded, spewing earth. The eruption threw dirt far and wide, falling like earthen rain. Small stones pelted him. The onslaught increased, and Troy covered his head.

Long seconds later, Troy coughed, clearing the dust from his lungs. A hand touched him. A terrible, rotten smell accosted him. He nearly gagged.

"May I take your bags, sir?" a harsh voice asked.

Rolling onto his back, Dillon looked up. He stared into the sun through the haze created by the airborne earth. A cloaked figure stood above, punching a hole in the light. Troy's spine crawled and the hair rose on his neck. He felt paralyzed as it extended a pale hand. Dead flesh clung to the bone.

It reached for its cowl and again asked, "May, I take your bags. You won't be needing them where you're going, sir."

"Sir, excuse me, sir?" A feminine voice cut into Troy's dream. The dark figure disappeared. "We have landed at Tri-Cities Airport," the blond flight attendant informed him. "Everyone else has deplaned." Her brown eyes showed concern.

Troy wiped the sweat from his brow. "Oh, thanks. I must have been dead to the world," he told her. She gave him a sympathetic smile. "Let me gather my wits a minute and I'll be out of your way."

"Thank you, sir. I hope you enjoy your stay in the area and catch up on your rest. If you'll pardon me for saying, you look a bit pale."

"Thanks. It's amazing what a bad dream can do to your heart." Troy closed his eyes and attempted to regain his composure. He couldn't shake the feeling that something was wrong. He and Dillon were closer than twin brothers. If Dillon could have called, he would have called. The man didn't forget anything, ever. Besides, Dillon always called into work. It was ritual, a reporter's habit.

Troy reflected on conversations they'd had on several occasions. Dillon claimed that the two shared a special rapport—that they each knew when the other was in trouble. Troy didn't believe in the paranormal. In fact, he all but poo-pooed it. And yet, there were circumstances that were hard to explain, times when they had unexplainable knowledge about each other; his crippling knee injury, Dillon's car crash . . .

Could that be why he hadn't felt right or been able to think straight for the past several days? Was Dillon in danger? Did that nightmare have anything to do with it . . . or was it a figment of his imagination contorted by anxiety and jet lag? Mrs. Urich had mentioned coffins and graves. His subconscious was liable to latch onto anything and play it back. Troy shook his head. He must be tired to even contemplate the possibility of ESP or a psychic link, let alone precognition.

Yet, the nightmare had heightened the feeling of impending doom that had struck him during his conversation with Mrs. Urich. As usual, his mind was probably stretching things a bit. Still, it was based upon his gut feelings that he had made the immediate decision to book a flight to the Tri-Cities. He only wondered if Denny had gotten his second message and was waiting at the airport.

Troy gathered his carry-on bag and briefcase, then deplaned. The sunlight seemed excessively bright for evening, but the days were long this time of year. He put on his sunglasses. As he walked down the metal stairway and left Piedmont Flight 242 from Charlotte, Troy wondered if the Tri-Cities airport would ever be advanced enough to allow exit directly into the terminal. Fortunately, today was a typical July day in northeast Tennessee—partly cloudy, hot, and humid. Actually, it seemed dryer than usual. He noticed that the surrounding trees and grass weren't their normal verdant green. At least it was cooler than Dallas, he thought.

As Troy walked across the runway to the terminal, he stared at the observation deck. A crowd still lingered, watching a flight taxi. For a moment, Troy thought he recognized someone, but she was gone before he was sure. He didn't see Denny.

Troy stepped through the door and into the terminal. The short narrow hallway was all but deserted. He gathered that most of the people were already waiting for baggage. Troy stopped to stare at his reflection in the window. His dark, wavy hair was out of control, even his heavy eyebrows had gone wild. Troy shook his head. The lines around his bloodshot blue eyes had deepend, and he already had beard stubble. I look awful, Troy thought. With a sigh he ran a hand through his unruly hair and continued toward the terminal.

Although Troy entered through the last gate, it only took him a minute to reach the all-flights waiting area. He pushed through the double doors and walked up the short flight of steps to the main terminal. The place reminded him of a large bus station.

As Troy stood at the top of the steps, he tried to remember the last time he had visited Bristol. It was probably three years ago, still nothing had changed. The people in this area didn't want change—well, maybe some in Johnson City, Kingsport, or Bristol did, but the people with the money and power were happy with the status quo.

Everything a metropolitan airport needed was here: the video arcade, insurance booth, post office, coffee lounge, newsstand, gift shop, two airlines, and four rental car agencies, all within less than a city block. Comparing it to the multiple terminals, concrete ramps, tram railways, and on-site hotel of the Dallas-Ft. Worth airport made him smile. Yes, he missed his hometown. Times were simpler and slower in the Appalachians.

As Troy moved toward the baggage claim area, he pondered how he could find Dillon. It didn't appear that Denny received his message, so he'd need to rent a car. He'd also need a place to stay. His parents had retired to Florida some five years ago. Surely he could warm the couch at one of the guys' place.

Taken by surprise, two thin arms wrapped themselves around Troy's neck. The warm embrace was brief. A wave of dark, fragrant hair caressed Troy's face and warm lips lightly kissed him on the cheek, lingered, then pulled away.

The tall woman leaned back to gauge his reaction. As she did, her smile widened, touching her amber eyes. They danced behind her glasses as she hugged Troy again. "You don't recognize me, do you, Troy? Have I grown up that much?"

"Silke, Silke Urich?" He held her at arm's length. The beautiful young woman was long and lean, nearly six foot in height. She was dressed in snug jeans and a simple white shirt. Her hips were almost nonexistent. Long ebony hair poured freely over her shoulders down to her slim waist. Thin framed glasses sat on high cheekbones nearly hiding her golden brown eyes. Troy always thought it was a face more likely to be found on a magazine cover than working in a hospital.

Silke's smile widened as she nodded. "Ah, yes, my broken heart is mended. You do recognize me. It's only been—"

"Six years. Last time I saw you was at Squaw Valley." Troy shook his head a bit, "You've let your hair grow and the glasses confused me. Okay, I confess that I'm not hitting on all cylinders right now. I flew the red-eye from Seattle to Dallas last night before rushing here."

Silke took off her glasses with one hand, and pulled at a handful of her raven's mane behind her neck. "You do look a little worn, but even then you're a sight for sore eyes. Take the red out and your eyes are even bluer than I remembered. So, do you like my hair this long?" she asked, already seeing the answer in his eyes.

"I like it, but is it a good idea to have it that long while working your internship?"

"I just put it up and wear glasses whenever I want to be taken more seriously," Silke replied. One arm slipped around his waist.

"I was thinking more in the line of one of your mental patients grabbing it," Troy told her with a devious smile. He tried to hide it by stroking his two-day growth.

Her smile glowed once more, "You're being silly. What has Dillon been telling you?" Silke's smile left. Thoughts about her brother saddened her.

Troy also became serious. "That you were working in the mental ward of a clinic."

"I'm a psychologist in a pain clinic, not a psychiatrist for the mentally unstable . . . or deranged as Dillon so tactfully phrases it."

"Why are you at the airport?"

"Just after I arrived early this afternoon, I spoke with Mother. She said you would probably be coming to Bristol to look for Dillon. I guessed that you might arrive on this flight. I'm a good guesser."

"Yes, you always have been. When did you last hear from Dillon?" He shifted his luggage to his right hand and took her under his left arm. They began to walk. A small crowd still hovered around the baggage area.

"Last Thursday. He called from Mom's. That was

the ninth. I think. They'd been out camping and ski-ing on Holston the sixth."

"What did he say?"

"He said that they'd found . . ." she began, then gave a powerful shiver. She quaked in Troy's arms.

He stopped to hold her. "Are you all right?"

"Didn't you feel that cold breeze? Hey, where are you going?"

Troy felt a bit confused. "To rent a car. I don't see Denny anywhere, so he probably hasn't gotten the message I left on his answering machine. I couldn't reach anyone else. Besides, I'm going to need trans-portation if I'm going to search for your brother." He paused, then added, "What cold breeze?" In spite of the air conditioning, he was roasting.

"Let me take you to dinner," Silke offered. "I'll be your chauffeur."

"I'm probably going to be here for several days."

"I'll drive you around all week. I'm on vacation. Besides, I might be able to help you find Dillon, and I can't think of a better way to spend the week than with you."

"Okay, I'm convinced. I know I can't get a better offer. Let's go."

"Luggage?"

"In hand."

"This way," she said and slipped from under his arm. Silke grabbed his hand and quickly led him out of the airport.

"In a hurry?" Troy asked.

She gave him a quick glance, then all but pulled him across the street. Silke stopped at a topless tan Landrover, opened the door, and waved Troy inside. She walked around and slid behind the wheel. She immediately started the engine before Troy settled in.

"Silke, why the rush?" Troy asked.

"I'd like to get back before dark." She shifted into gear and they were off.

"Back where?" They rapidly passed two cars.

"Bluff City."

"What's in Bluff City?" Troy asked. Pulling onto the highway, Silke stepped on the gas. They sped off down the road. The wind whipped through Troy's jet black hair. He hung onto the roll bar.

"My Aunt Jada's house."

"I thought we were going out for dinner."

"We are . . . at my Aunt Jada's. She's a fabulous cook."

Troy was quiet for a time and just watched Silke. Wisps of dark hair danced around her as the anxiety left her eyes. The muscles in her strong chin relaxed and her cheekbones became less pronounced. Her grip eased on the wheel and her shoulders grew less stiff, but she didn't slow down.

"Dillon's disappearance has you tense and worried too?" Troy asked her, already knowing the answer. He tried not to stare at her. He'd nearly forgotten how beautiful she was.

"It's that obvious?"

"Yes," Troy told her.

"Mom's worried too, and she doesn't even feel the sense of foreboding in the air."

"What are you talking about?"

"When I spoke with Dillon, he was investigating John Traylor's murder."

"How is that foreboding? Dillon works on unusual stories all the time. It's his specialty. It's what he lives for."

"I'm thinking of the open graves they found on Cemetery Ridge and all the scattered coffins. There

61

aren't supposed to be any graves on the hill."

"Cemetery Ridge is really exposed? Your mom mentioned that, but I thought maybe she was confused. It's usually thirty or so feet under water." They passed a highway patrol car. Silke didn't give it a second glance.

"It's the drought. Maybe that's why this area feels so drained . . . and dead. I felt it as soon as I arrived, and I've been worried since I spoke with Dillon last week." She looked at him with gratitude. "Troy, I'm so glad you're here."

"I wish we could get together under better circumstances. Anyway, what do you know? I feel kinda in the dark." Troy leaned back and listened carefully. He hadn't realized how much he'd missed the Smokies. There was something in mountain air that rejuvenated him. He felt better already.

"Dillon and the gang were waterskiing on South Holston Lake on Monday night—"

"Your mom was serious. They were skiing at night?" Troy shook his head in mild amazement. He thought they would've mellowed.

"Sure, it's not much different than the time y'all went snowskiing down Beech Mountain at night. Anyway, Marader was skiing when they saw trash floating in the water. They dodged it, but Marader crashed into something. It was John Traylor's corpse, broken neck and all. Dillon also told me something the papers didn't report. Traylor's neck had been ripped open as if an animal had attacked him. And the trash in the water wasn't the usual debris, it was empty coffins exhumed from the island."

"The coffins were in the water, not on the island?" Troy asked, puzzled.

"Yes, at least six. It's caused a huge flap."

"I'm sure," Troy said. "I thought by law that the TVA would have relocated all the coffins in the graveyard before flooding the valley."

"They're supposed to. They must have missed a few . . . an official explanation has yet to be released. Just lots of accusations. All they have said so far is that a series of accidents put them behind schedule, then caused several workers to quit, leaving some things to fall between the cracks. The rest is speculation."

"What did Dillon say about this?"

"I spoke with him before the police had really begun their investigation. The guys had only found the body the previous night."

"I'm sorry I'm asking so many questions," Troy apologized. "Dillon calls it reporter mode."

"It's okay, there's so much to tell. For one thing there were no signs of digging equipment on Cemetery Ridge, only scuba and skiing equipment."

"Doesn't sound like Traylor was excavating for buried treasure, possibly diving for it, though."

"That's what Dillon thought. The Ridge is real close to Wreythville. Dillon said that the dry season had allowed the water to clear and that the visibility was excellent."

"Had Dillon been diving?"

"He didn't say."

Troy had a feeling that some diving of his own was in order. He wondered if Knives or J-Man might be interested.

"Dillon figured Traylor probably explored the submerged town, but he wouldn't do it alone. There were two sets of tanks, but no signs of anyone else . . . and the boat was still there. Troy, how could the murderer leave the island, unless they had another boat? Maybe two people killed Traylor. It's all very strange."

"Any suspects?"

"Only one, his girlfriend. Her name is Terry Bray. She's a pharmacist, but she was ill at the time and has three witnesses to prove it. Someone had seen Traylor with a blond, but it couldn't have been Terry. Traylor was known to date several women at once. Terry was just one of a stable of beautiful ladies. I'm sure Dillon is looking forward to interviewing as many as possible."

"I wonder if one of them—"

"I don't think so," Silke said quickly.

"Why not?"

"Well, Dillon said they found a few hair-raising things."

"Like?"

"Traylor's body was basically drained of blood from the gash marks in his neck. As I mentioned earlier, it looked like an animal bite, but Traylor shouldn't have lost that much blood."

"How did he know Traylor was drained?"

"Dr. Knives. Another thing bothered him; the earth around the graves appears to have scratch marks on it."

"Come on! You're not serious, are you?" Troy asked.

Silke nodded.

"Sounds like I need to talk to Denny and the guys. Have you spoken to them?"

"No, I wasn't able to reach them by phone and I just arrived myself. I promised Aunt Jada I'd come see her this evening."

"Why this evening?" They slowed down and exited off the highway. Dillon was amazed by the color of the foliage along the side of the road—it was flat green, almost brown. He'd never seen it like this.

"Aunt Jada was excited, claiming that she had something important to tell me." Silke laughed, then added, "She also told me that you were arriving from Charlotte."

"I thought you said you guessed."

She smiled sweetly, "I lied a little."

"How did your Aunt Jada know I was coming?"

"She's psychic."

"I don't believe in that," Troy said. "What else did she tell you?"

"That we'd make good companions for each other." Silke gave him a big smile. "But we already knew that."

Troy had always been extremely skeptical of psychics. It seemed like an easy way to make money off people who wanted to believe in the paranormal. "Isn't that a difficult judgment to make about someone she's never met?"

"My aunt's amazing. She's very intuitive. She reads tarot cards and does horoscopes. Of course her neighbors think she's a kook. They call her 'The babbler.' I know the local children make fun of her . . . or avoid her. They claim the place is haunted. Of course, when you meet Aunt Jada's maid, nurse, and living companion, Sister Elva, you might agree."

"How's that?"

"She's creepy. The woman is so pale, she looks like she rose from the dead. I guess I'm not surprised, though. Sister Elva has lived in seclusion with my aunt for over forty years."

"You mean your aunt is hiding from the world?"

"Sort of. In the early forties, her husband and sons disappeared under strange circumstances. My aunt tried to tell people that there was evil afoot, but no one believed her. Still, no one could prove any differently. Instead they shunned her and she withdrew from the world. Personally, I think she's a wonderful lady."

"You're related," he quipped. She gave him a rueful grin. "By the way, I thought you were a doctor. I'm surprised to find you're interested in the occult."

"It's not the occult. And I'm not much different than you. I've read your book, *The Will to Win*. We are both interested in the mental, emotional, and spiritual side of the body as well as the physical. You study it in sports because the intangibles, like desire and gut feelings often make the difference between winning and losing. I study the mind. At the pain clinic, I've seen several people make themselves sick, as well as healthy. Those events keep my mind open to psychic abilities. My aunt seems to have them."

"Which is why we are going to see her, I guess. Right?" Silke nodded. Troy took a long breath. He felt like he was wasting time, and he was tired. "Silke, I truly enjoy your company and I appreciate your help, but why am I going to meet a lady who believes she can predict the future, when I should be talking to the guys? I want to find Dillon. I don't want to waste time."

"We aren't. I'm worried too. I've been concerned from the moment Dillon and I first discussed this. I swear I knew the instant he got into trouble. It was Friday morning and I was with a patient. All of a sudden a cold chill struck me and Dillon came to mind. I knew he was near water and there was something . . . a timelessness nearby. I know that sounds weird. I called Mother. She called our friends. No one knew where he was. As you know, Dillon and I

66

have always been very close. You're like family to us both, maybe you too sensed he was in trouble?"

"Could be," Troy replied.

"Dillon has always claimed that he had hunches about news; don't sports reporters?"

"Yes."

"Isn't it sort of a gut feeling as well as a heightening of the imagination and senses?"

"Sometimes. Often it's a nagging thought or two — almost like a whispering in your mental ear."

"My Aunt Jada works the same way, only more refined. She uses tools, like star charts, numerology, her cards, and crystals."

"Silke, first you tell me a story about a floating corpse, animal attacks, and open graves, and now you're taking me to a psychic who's probably a very nice woman, but no doubt a few cards short of a full deck. I'm sorry, if that sounds mean, but what am I supposed to think?"

"I always thought you were open minded."

Troy frowned. "Oh well. You did say she is a fantastic cook."

"Besides," she continued, "I want to spend some time with you before you get lost with the guys."

"Lost with the guys?"

"That's what I used to tell Dillon. All you guys get together, and no one else sees y'all for weeks. You're off hiking or skiing or hunting, or God knows what else. All these strong personalities, so distinct and intense, yet somehow you guys always got along."

"We got along most of the time." Troy noticed that the road had narrowed and there was no shoulder. The edge immediately dropped off into a steep forested grade. He hadn't seen a house for a while.

"You're still mad at Tom?"

"Yes."

"Want to talk about it?"

"No. How long until we get to your crazy aunt's house?" Troy teased. The trees formed a long canopy over the road. They sped through the shadows.

"Not long, and Troy, please, you'll behave?"

"I will. Now for the second most important question after 'where the hell is Dillon Urich?' How have you been? I haven't spoken to you since you graduated from Stanford. What's going on?"

"I'm an intern at a pain clinic just outside San Francisco. We explore anything that might help a patient cope with pain. As you might suspect, pain is often more than just physical. When drugs, surgery, or physical therapy don't work, we finally look at alternative methods of easing the suffering; tenser units, biofeedback, yoga, relaxation, and creative visualization. I've even seen laugh and scream therapy work. Just recently we've begun to study Non-Contact Therapeutic Touch. One of the doctors is investigating healing by laying on of hands."

"California sounds like the perfect place to study all of that."

"It is, but it takes me a long way away from the Smoky Mountains. The Sierras are beautiful, but I miss the Blue Ridge Mountains, just like I miss a lot of things about home. Ah, we're here." She took a left into a driveway that was nearly hidden by foliage. They stopped in a circular driveway in front of white double doors. The house was snuggled back among a thick array of huge trees.

"This place looks old and big."

"It's both. It was built in the late thirties. It even has a maid's quarters over the three-car garage. There were some truly spectacular gardens out back.

That's what keeps Aunt Jada busy. There used to be a stable too."

"I wonder why Dillon never mentioned this place. It looks like a great place to romp as a kid."

"I did, all the time. Dillon preferred to stay away. Aunt Jada scared him. Are you hungry?"

"Starved."

"Let's go in. I know Aunt Jada is looking forward to meeting you." They climbed out of the jeep and Silke led him up the steps.

She knocked on the door as Troy wrapped his arms around her. He hugged her tightly, then kissed top of her head. "Silke, I'll do whatever is necessary to help —"

The door was yanked open and they found themselves staring at a wild-eyed woman in a bright green blouse.

She reminded Troy of an overweight and elderly Lucille Ball. With a life of its own, her blazing red hair moved in all directions at once. Sparkling jewelry hung from her ears and around her neck. Her lips moved, but no sound escaped.

"Aunt Jada, are you all right?" Silke asked.

The smell of sandalwood incense struck Troy, making him dizzy for a moment. He watched the shaking woman attempt to gather her wits. As if to communicate by sign language, her hands fluttered in front of her, causing her bracelets to rattle. Finally, Aunt Jada calmed down enough to say, "Oh Silke, I'm so glad you're here! I saw a dead man in town today!!"

Chapter Three
Exhumed History

"What?" Silke asked in astonishment. "Aunt Jada, did you say you saw a dead man in town?"

"You don't believe me, do you child?" A sad smile came to Aunt Jada's face. "And I was so looking forward to your visit. No one else would believe me, especially Sister Elva, but I was so sure you would. I always felt that we were kindred souls. And now you too think I'm a crazy old fool."

"No, I don't," Silke said. "It's just that I . . ." She didn't know what to say next. There was an uneasy silence between the two women. With downcast eyes, Aunt Jada began to slowly close the door.

"Please wait," Troy began. "Won't you tell us more, give us some information to evaluate? Give us a chance to believe you. I . . . I mean, if someone told you that they saw a man fly without wings, wouldn't you want to know more before making a judgment?"

Aunt Jada stared Troy down for a moment. Her crystal earrings flashed in the setting sun. "Depends on who told me they saw the flying man. But the older one gets, the more one's credibility is questioned. It's not something I deal with well, not well at all."

"Sometimes we doubt the senses, not the mind or honesty of the person. People make mistakes," Troy told her.

"You must be Troy Bane." Troy nodded. "Silke has spoken of you. Welcome to my home." She stepped back and motioned them within.

Troy let go of Silke but not before she turned and quickly kissed him on the cheek. Suddenly, he didn't want to let her go.

Inside, the two women hugged each other and Troy felt that the crisis had momentarily passed, but in gauging Aunt Jada, he wondered if wild mood swings were commonplace.

Besides the smell of sandalwood, Troy thought he smelled something else? Garlic? Maybe it was dinner he smelled. No. Wrapped around a cross posted over the doorway was garlic and something else . . . Belladonna? Troy wondered. Was the old woman afraid of vampires? There was also a bowl of salt on the floor near the door.

"Would you two like some tea? Dinner will be ready in a few minutes. Sister Elva's cooking a roast."

"Yes, ma'am," Silke responded.

"Then follow me." Aunt Jada turned and led the way.

71

Troy felt as if he were entering another world; time had stopped within the house decades ago. Everything was an antique and had the musty smell of age despite the thick incense.

A mirror etched with a unicorn and a waterfall hung on the wall opposite the door. Candles burned on each side while a statuette of the Virgin Mary sat on the table below. Troy followed the two women down the short, heavily carpeted hall. Even the pictures were yellowed.

As they entered the living room, Troy's senses were assaulted by a myriad of sights, lights, colors, and smells. All the drapes and curtains were pulled shut, cutting the room off from the orange twilight. Several lights illuminated the room, shining through crystals which cast dazzling beams of light. Bright colors seemed to dance about the room. Troy felt like he had walked into a rock garden. There were amethysts, rose quartz, and various stones of green hues. Every tabletop, every surface, housed a crystal. An ivory statue of Buddha sat in the far corner. Plants hung from the ceiling and vines crawled along the walls. Several more bowls of salt were scattered about. He'd never seen anything like it.

"I shall return with the tea in just a moment," Aunt Jada told them. She left the room.

"I can see why Dillon might have been a little bit spooked by this place. It's not typical," Troy told Silke. His eyes continued to roam. Numerous candles and tapers burned throughout the room, giving it a golden glow.

"But you're not?" Silke said, as she took his arm

and led him to the couch.

"I feel like I've stepped into 'The Twilight Zone.'" The furniture looked stiff, elegant, and uncomfortable. Sitting confirmed it. Antiques weren't designed to be comfortable, he thought.

"Silke, this place looks like something out of an occult film."

She laughed and hugged his arm, breaking the spell of the room. "Forty years ago, people thought my aunt was a witch. Fortunately, burning people at the stake was illegal. Instead they ostracized her. She was socially dead."

"And still is, but only because she desires it," came a gruff voice.

Troy started. The thin woman in the doorway was one of the harshest-looking people he'd ever seen. Her peppered hair was pulled back tightly, revealing a high forehead and black beady eyes. Deep lines etched her face and her sharp nose twitched as if smelling something foul. She was dressed entirely in black and white.

"Troy Bane, Sister Elva, my aunt's nurse and maid."

"Hello," Troy managed.

Sister's Elva's eyes dismissed him as she concentrated on Silke. "Silke, I hope your visit will be a short one. Fantasies are running rampant in Jada's mind. Her heart can't take the strain. She's had enough excitement for one day. Don't fan the flames. You wouldn't want to be responsible for anything, would you?" Her eyes burned like coals.

Troy felt Silke stiffen. "Of course not."

"Good. Dinner will be ready shortly." Sister Elva

turned abruptly and left.

"Whoa, now that's what I classify as a witch," Troy muttered.

Silke laughed. "Oh, she means well. Elva's been with Aunt Jada for a long time. They both lost family about the same time. Sister Elva lost her husband and sons when a church burned down out along Highway One-twenty-one. Ever since then, they've been very protective of each other."

"Well I guess everyone has a weird relative or two in their closet."

Aunt Jada entered the room. "I like to think of myself as unique, Troy, not weird." She set the silver tea set on the table before them. There were two teapots.

"Poor choice of words, ma'am. No offense intended."

"None taken, young man. I've been called far worse." Aunt Jada laughed, easing Troy's mind a bit. She toyed with a pendant, a rose-colored orb with a silver snake wrapped around it. "There are two types of tea, traditional English brew and herbal on the left."

Silke poured herself a cup of herbal tea. When she looked at Troy, he nodded. "Dinner is almost ready, you may have to pardon me if I check with Sister Elva every now and then to see if she needs help."

"We understand," Silke replied.

"Oh, Silke, I'm so glad you're here and that you've brought a friend. We will need all the friends we can find," she said cryptically. Then her tone abruptly changed and she asked, "How was

74

your flight from San Francisco dear?" Troy couldn't believe that just minutes ago this was the same woman who'd gone on about seeing a dead man.

"Long but fine," Silke replied. "Getting up so early just made it seem that much longer. I was in a hurry to get here and find out what I could about Dillon. I'm worried about him."

The old woman turned to Troy. "You, Silke, and Dillon go back a long way, don't you?" Aunt Jade asked.

"Yes, ma'am."

"You and Dillon are blood brothers along with the others, are you not?" she asked.

Troy was surprised. Very few people knew about that and he doubted that Silke would have mentioned it. He shrugged. "Yes."

"Sometimes friendship is thicker, more powerful, than blood. You can choose your friends, you don't choose your kin—at least consciously," she said with a smile. "Did you two spend a lot of time together?"

Troy recovered and said, "Yes. We grew up together, went to the same schools, enjoyed the same sports—"

"Ah yes, you were a superb basketball player, were you not?" Aunt Jada picked up an oversized deck from the table and began shuffling through them. Unlike normal cards, they were brightly colored and had pictures on them. Troy recognized them as tarot cards.

"Yes, until I severely damaged a knee."

"So you had to give up basketball?" She stopped

shuffling and looked at one of the cards. She smiled and put it back in the deck.

"Yes, I followed Dillon to North Texas State. I also had a sister in Dallas. There were . . . there were some things I needed to leave behind." Aunt Jada gave him a sympathetic look. "I studied journalism, and that's why I'm doing what I'm doing today, sports reporting. Reporting the events is the next best thing to participating in them."

"Destiny leads us along many strange paths and fate has many designs on us, does it not?" Aunt Jada asked. Troy shrugged. "You are an author, too, are you not?"

"Yes." Troy sipped his tea. He noticed that their hostess had grown more relaxed. Still, her hands riffled through the cards as if it were a nervous habit.

"I have read it. It applies some interesting concepts to sports. Those ideas can also—should be— used in life." Her eyes glazed over a bit, as if she were miles away. Suddenly her voice changed, sounding strange. Detached. "You shall need them. There is a dark woman, an intimate relation from the past. Beware her kiss, her touch. She means you harm, beware of her. She is poison to your blood."

Troy was taken aback. He suddenly felt like leaving. Silke stepped in and redirected the conversation. "Aunt Jada," she said tactfully, "you told us that you saw a dead man in town today. Did you mean you saw someone die?"

Aunt Jada's green eyes became focused once more. "No, dear. I saw Tom Aldridge. At first I

76

wasn't sure, you know your eyesight goes when you're in your seventies, so I moved a bit closer. Besides looking very pale, he didn't look any older than when he died in nineteen-forty-two. When he saw me, he waved. I was so shocked, I couldn't wave back. He just gave me a huge, smirking grin and walked away. I . . . I was so flabbergasted that I immediately left and rushed home." She paused to collect her thoughts. "Something is terribly wrong. The devil is loose. Troy, do you believe in insidious evil? Evil handed down through the centuries? Evil as old as time itself?" Aunt Jada began shaking.

Silke reached over and touched her. It seemed to calm the nearly hysterical woman. "We are here to listen. Tell us."

"How did Tom Aldridge die?" Troy asked.

The old woman took several deep breaths, then replied, "He fell off a platform in the spillway area while working at the Holston Dam project."

"Are you sure it was Aldridge? A lot of time has passed since then."

"Tom Aldridge and I dated for nearly two years and stayed friends even after I married David. I wouldn't mistake Tom for anyone."

"Aunt Jada, what is this evil, this darkness that has broken loose? What does it have to do with Dillon?" A hint of desperation crept into Silke's voice.

"The horror, the evil, has been around for centuries . . . countless centuries, preying upon mankind. I thought it was gone, I thought it was buried . . . and it was for decades. But now . . .

77

now it has returned. Now darkness walks in the light and we can't tell the difference any more. *The horror walks among us. I saw it today in Tom Aldridge.*" Aunt Jada began to shake again. "And it's going to get me," she whispered, "I know it."

Footsteps came rushing down the hallway. Sister Elva was on her way.

"Aunt Jada, please, tell me, what does this have to do with Dillon. Please tell me."

"Child, he is in danger, mortal danger. He has discovered the darkness. He knows that they can walk in the light, and it will cost him his immortal soul. Soon . . . oh, lord, very soon, he will embrace the darkness and *be lost forever!*"

"Do you see him? Do you see Dillon anywhere?"

Aunt Jada closed her eyes. "It is damp all around him. There is water . . . water has poured in. Red lights, like burning eyes, dance around him. He is surrounded by earth. Above, there are thousands of trees. Trees upon trees and rocks piled upon rocks. A towering wall of rocks—"

"That is quite enough!" Sister Elva commanded. Silke, I'm disappointed in you. You know your aunt is old. Her heart isn't what it used to be. Yet, you still support her fantasies and help her work herself into a frenzy," Sister Elva scowled, moving to the old woman's side.

"Oh God, help us," Aunt Jada muttered. "The evil is all about. They are outside watching us. Oh Silke, please be careful. Dillon doesn't have much time . . . and neither do we."

"Go now!" Sister Elva commanded, then her voice softened. "Go and wait outside. I will pack a dinner for you. I don't want you to leave hungry. But now, please . . . go!"

"Wait, Silke, take this." Aunt Jada reached inside her green blouse. "Take this, it will protect you." Silke took the crystal cross from her aunt and kissed it, then put it around her neck. She hugged her sobbing aunt. Under Sister Elva's burning glare, they left.

They sat quietly in the Landrover, watching the shadows shift as the sun worked its way toward the horizon. A slight breeze rustled through the trees, giving life to the silent forest around them.

Silke's eyes were closed. Troy could tell that she was holding back tears. He reached over and took her hand. "Troy, I'm so worried about Dillon. I'm so scared."

"It's Sister Elva that scares me," Troy replied.

"Oh," Silke said, tears rolling down her face, "she really does mean well. I know you don't believe my aunt, but she isn't deranged or senile. I believe her, even when nobody else does. My mother won't admit it, but she believes too. Aunt Jada has been right about too many things for me to dismiss it."

"Silke, you're a doctor. I don't totally discount the possibility that humans might have some untapped psychic potential, but dead people walking around? It sounds like *Night of the Living Dead*".

"You don't find it odd that Traylor's neck was ripped open, that they found coffins floating in South Holston Lake, or that there were graves in a cemetery that should have been empty?"

"Silke, I don't know what to think. I'm tired and

I just got here. Reporters, good ones anyway, are supposed to investigate and base their judgments on fact, not heresay and psychics. I don't work for the *Inquirer.*"

She smiled. "No, you don't work for the *Inquirer.* Be skeptical, that's okay. I need a skeptic around to keep me grounded. But please, let's keep Aunt Jada's warning in mind."

"I plan to be careful. If Dillon has truly disappeared, then there is good reason to be cautious."

"Here you are, children," stated Sister Elva. Troy almost jumped from his seat. She had moved so quietly that he had no idea she was there.

Silke took the picnic basket. "How is Aunt Jada?"

"She is resting comfortably. Why don't you call her tomorrow after lunch?"

"I will."

"Good-bye."

Watching Sister Elva walk off, Troy shivered. "I'm ready to leave. I need to call one of the guys and find a place to stay."

"Nonsense. You can stay with us. We have plenty of room," she told him. Before he could open his mouth, she said, "No argument."

They drove along in silence for a few minutes. The air had cooled and the shadows had deepened. Suddenly Silke said, "Why don't we stop for a drink."

"I thought you wanted to get home by dark. I think we only have an hour or so left before it sets," Troy reminded her.

"Spoilsport."

"Besides, there's 'evil all around us,' " he said melodramatically.

Silke laughed. "I just wanted to spend more time with you before Mother ties you up for the rest of the evening with questions."

"Tell you what, I can feign tiredness . . . heck, I won't even need to feign it, and you can sneak into my room," Troy told her in half seriousness.

Her eyes growing bright, Silke turned to him and said, "Now that sounds like a good idea."

"Silke, look out!" Troy cried.

At the last second, Silke saw the baby doe collapse in the middle of the road. Silke slammed on the brakes and the front of the jeep bore down. Tires squealed. Troy put his hands on the dash as his body strained against the safety straps.

The Landrover slid, beginning to twist sideways. The doe didn't move. Beseechingly, it stared at them.

Silke spun the wheel and released the brake. The Landrover leaped forward, swerving to the right. It straightened for a moment, then skidded along the shoulder of the road. They shot around the deer and came to an abrupt halt a foot away from a tree.

"Wow!" Troy told her. "That will wake up your passengers."

Silke glanced sideways, then gave him a crooked smile. "Practice driving in Bay-area traffic."

Troy lightly pulled her forward and kissed her. Silke's arms wrapped around his neck and held him tightly. His hands stroked her hair.

Silke sighed. "I've wanted to do that for ten

years."

"I'm sorry it took so long, but it was worth the wait," Troy told her.

"We won't wait so long the next time, I hope."

"No, we won't."

"Shall we check out that doe?"

"I thought I was a better kisser than that," Troy teased.

Silke laughed as she climbed out of the Jeep. Troy followed.

The baby doe's eyes were glazed over and it was twitching. Silke reached out and touched it. The tiny deer tried to rise but couldn't.

Troy noticed the trail of blood leaving the forest. "It's been attacked by something. Look." He pointed to the deer's rear legs. Both had been chewed nearly to the bone. "It's a miracle it made it this far."

"I wonder what attacked it?" Silke mused as she examined the bite marks. She walked to the Landrover, unfolded a heavy carpet, and spread it across the back. "Come on, I know a vet that might be able to save it."

"It might not live that long."

"It's not far."

The two lifted the doe and carried her to the Landrover. As gently as possible, they hefted it into the back. The doe tried to get free, but Silke wrapped the carpet around it. It was too weak to leap out.

"Interesting things happen to you," Troy commented wryly.

"You too. I just hope we have time to reach the

vet."

Hopping behind the wheel, Silke fired up the engine. Troy barely climbed aboard before she took off. Tires squealed.

"It's lucky you didn't run it over."

"God's grace," Silke replied. She slowed to steer through a series of S-curves.

"I wonder wh—" There was a heavy thud in the rear of the jeep. Suddenly, a snarling sound came from behind them. Teeth snapped in Troy's face as he turned. He raised his hand. The wolf attacked again, snagging his sleeve. It tore free and the wolf staggered back. A second wolf leaped from the hillside, sailed through the air, and landed awkwardly in the rear. It collided with the first beast, momentarily distracting it.

Troy tried to fight down panic. The two wolves were huge, their red eyes burned like coals. Without thinking, he reached under the seat for something to use as a weapon. All he could find were a fire extinguisher and a screwdriver. Recovered, the wolves attacked together.

Loping out of the woods, more wolves swarmed around the Landrover. Some ran alongside the Jeep while several waited in the road as it approached. One leaped forward, bouncing off the front windshield. Silke screamed. Blood and saliva spattered the cracked glass.

The Landrover rocked violently as it ran over several of the beasts. Their howls of pain echoed through the woods. The wheel jerked out of Silke's hands. They veered toward the drop at the side of the road. Silke grabbed the wheel and stomped on the accelerator, wrestling the Jeep back onto the blacktop.

Before she could speed up, a third beast ran alongside, then sprang. It barely reached the Landrover. For a moment it hung from the door, half in and half out of the racing vehicle, then it scrambled into the back. Sharp, jagged teeth shot forward, snagging Silke's hair. "Troy!! HELP ME!"

Troy swung the fire extinguisher, striking the nearest wolf across the muzzle. Bleeding from its mouth it moved back. The second one lunged. Troy jammed the screwdriver into its side. Yelping, it pulled back, ripping the tool from Troy's hand. The first sat back and watched. Intelligence shown in its eyes.

"Troy!!" Silke screamed again. The wolf was on her back now.

Howling surrounded the jeep as they sped along out of control. The pack pursued them. In full stride, one leaped and slammed against Troy's door. He reached over and pushed the wolf attacking Silke from the Landrover.

"Oh God!" Silke yelled as she grabbed the wheel.

Another beast leaped, scrambled over the door, and partly into the front seat. It snapped at Silke and her hands slipped off the wheel. The Landrover swerved toward the trees.

Snarling, the wolf tried to crawl into the car. Troy smashed it over the head with the extinguisher. Yelping, the wolf let go and tumbled into the road. The one wolf in back continued to *just* watch. The other attacked again.

84

The unpiloted Landrover headed for a second pack of waiting wolves. Defiantly, they stood in its way as it ran over them. Bucking like a bronco as it crushed them, the Landrover reversed directions and headed for the incline. Silke grabbed the wheel and slammed on the brake, but it was too late.

The Landrover shot off the road. For a moment they were airborne; then they crashed through bushes and small saplings. Trees seemed to fly toward them. Troy hung on for dear life as the wolf tried to maul him.

He screamed as a wolf bit his left arm. Pain shot up it and through his shoulder. He tried to shake the animal off. Teeth snapped in his ear. He squeezed the handle on the extinguisher. Dry chemical shot from the nozzle, covering the wolf. It let go of his arm. Both wolves jumped from the Landrover.

The Rover sped down the steep incline. It careened wildly over rocks and fallen limbs. Silke screamed. Troy heard a terrible screech of metal—then nothing. He lost consciousness as he was thrown forward over the windshield, past the tree that had stopped them.

Chapter Four
Friendly Faces

Darkness . . . Yes, it was all around him. Fangs and claws drew closer, attacking, biting, slashing for his . . . soul?

Horror? Evil? Troy's mind wasn't quite connected to his body. It ran independently, his subconscious taking over. Had the horror finished attacking them? Wild eyes . . . red claws. The howling and growling tore at his memory. Troy listened and found it quiet. The growling and ripping had ceased.

His consciousness still wobbled unevenly, dazed by the impact. Troy tried to find his body, but couldn't. It didn't respond.

Oh God, he thought, his mind beginning to focus. The wolves . . . those ripping sounds . . . were they flesh? *Silke!* How long had he been out?! *Silke!*

Pain overwhelmed him even as his body was stimulated by adrenaline, driven by the thought of Silke in danger. Sharp needles cut through his right shoulder and arm. His head pounded. There was a raw feeling around his right eye as if the flesh had been ripped. He remembered being bit in the left arm, but couldn't feel it.

Troy attempted a deep breath, but his lungs protested. All he could do was gasp. Trying again, Troy inhaled dirt. Coughing and wheezing, he instinctively rolled onto his back. Fire ripped through his body, protesting the movement. He tasted blood in his mouth.

Opening his eyes, he found it was not yet dark. He couldn't have been out too long, Troy thought. He tried to sit up, but his head throbbed. His vision seemed to expand as the woods enlarged, then shrank back. He was going to have to wait a moment. If he couldn't sit, he couldn't stand.

Troy wiped the dirt from his face and gingerly touched the area around his right eye. He felt a gash along the side of his face. Blood trickled down into his mouth.

Wait, he'd been in the Landrover with his seat buckled, yet he'd still been thrown free. Wait, he hadn't had time to buckle up after loading the deer. The wolves had attacked so quickly, then they'd flown off the road and down the hill.

Silke . . .

Rolling over, Troy managed to kneel. His legs seemed to be okay, although his back was stiff. His right shoulder alternately screamed and throbbed, but he was still able to move his arm. As he straightened, his vision flashed red, then cleared. Troy checked his left arm and found that the wolf's bite had only scraped it. He had to check on Silke.

Leaning against a tree, Troy stood. The woods whirled around him for a moment, then halted. Looking up the hill, he spotted the Landrover.

A tree had stopped their wild ride. The tree trunk had been driven deeply into the front end, nearly reaching the warped and shattered windshield. The hood had buckled like an accordion; the motor had rammed its way free, and was now sticking out from underneath the Landrover.

As Troy staggered up the hill, sometimes crawling, other times hanging onto saplings, he prayed for Silke. Ahead, he heard running water . . . or did he smell gasoline? He stepped over a dislodged headlight and around the Landrover's battery.

Troy worked his way around to the driver's side. Blood was spattered on the windshield and had run down the side of the Jeep. Peering in, he saw Silke bent forward. She was drenched in blood. Her dark hair was matted with gore, and hung over the steering wheel, which was cracked in half. Troy's heart sank. Angrily, he yanked on the door, and it slowly gave way with a screech of metal.

Inside, blood was sprayed everywhere. Not only was the windshield painted, but the upholstery nearly dripped crimson. He looked closely at Silke and noticed that her clothing wasn't ripped or shredded. Gingerly, Troy placed a hand on her shoulder and pulled her back. Despite all the blood, Silke appeared to be unharmed except for where her forehead had hit the wheel.

Then Troy noticed that small pieces of flesh and brown fur were clinging to the interior. He carefully let her rest on the wheel, then looked into the back seat and gagged. He found the source of the tearing sounds — the wolves had mauled, then devoured the deer. Little besides bone remained. Troy stepped away for a moment, breathing the mountain air until he had recovered.

He turned his attention to Silke. With care, Troy leaned her head back. "Silke?" he pleaded, brushing the hair from her face. A large lump protruded from her forehead. The black-and-blue flesh around her left eye was also swollen. She bled from the mouth.

"Silke?" he asked again, lightly shaking her. There was no response. Troy searched for a pulse in her neck and found it. He breathed a sigh of relief. Next, he found a mirror shard and checked her breathing. It fogged as he held it before her nose. She appeared to be doing fine considering the circumstances. After fearing what the wolves could have done to her, Troy was happy to find her alive and in one piece.

Troy gently lifted her from the Landrover and laid her on the ground. Looking for his travel bag, Troy found it several yards away in a bush. He removed a jacket and sweatshirt, then returned to Silke. Troy propped her head up and wrapped her in the jacket. Her bleeding seemed to be slow, nothing to immediately worry about. She probably had a concussion. Instead of carrying her up the steep hill, he decided to climb to the road and flag down help.

Troy looked around and finally found the flashlight lodged under the gas pedal. He pulled it free and began his climb. His breath quickly grew harsh and ragged. His vision wavered and blurred. With each step, his legs grew more leaden.

Despite his dizziness, Troy wondered what had become of the wolves. His flashlight beam didn't spot any carcasses. There should have been several. Surely they couldn't have crawled away, he thought, through the haze in his head. He would check the road when—

if—he reached it.

Time stretched and he wondered if he would make it to the top before passing out. Fearing that he wasn't making progress, he refused to look up. His knees ached. Each time he pulled himself up by a tree with his right arm, his shoulder felt as if it would come free.

Suddenly, Troy reached the top. He thanked God and gulped down air. He waited for a moment to gain his bearings. He surveyed his surroundings. They'd done a good amount of damage as they'd left the road. He walked past the bent trees and flattened brush toward the road. He didn't see any dead wolves.

Troy stumbled and collapsed to his knees. The woods spun about in a whirlwind of muted lights and shadows. He momentarily blacked out, then recovered.

Doggedly, he climbed to his feet. He lifted the flashlight and scanned . . . a graveyard. Troy's mouth dropped open. It was the same cemetery he'd dreamed about earlier today. He didn't understand and the pounding in his head didn't help.

Once again the hill stretched before him. Hazy sunlight streamed down upon the headstones through the fading mist. The same small town stood in the background. Again, there was the sound of machinery in the air.

Looking down, Troy discovered he was standing on a grave plot. Immediately, he backed away.

The grave exploded and the earth shook. Troy wanted to run, but couldn't gain his balance. His legs felt rubbery. Where was the road? Was he still lying unconscious on the ground or in the jeep? Was Silke really dead? Frustrated, he tried to cry out, but his voice had deserted him.

Dirt and stone rained down. Rock pummeled him and Troy choked on the dust. The crater grew larger and longer as the grave vomited earth. A sheet of wood was blown from the pit and a shadow rose from the grave. A darkly cloaked figure stepped forward.

Troy was paraylzed by the sight. Standing before him, the entity reached out a pale hand and touched his face. Again, Troy tried to run, but his legs refused to respond. The creature's fingers slowly worked their way over his facial wound.

The figure pulled back its blood-covered finger and licked it. "Yum, yum. Poor boy, you look like you've been in an accident. But it doesn't look serious. May I be of help?"

It swatted Troy with a backhand. The blow opened his lip and sent him reeling. Troy stumbled and fell, his breath coming in ragged gasps. His eyes watered from the pain.

Troy looked up and began to speak, but stopped, eyes wide as the figure pulled back its cowl. The flesh on its face was translucent, clearly revealing its skull. Stringy and matted hair like something off a voodoo doll hung down across its forehead. Its dry flesh was torn. One of its ears had fallen off and fluid ran down its neck.

The dead man smiled. His teeth elongated, becoming fangs. He gnashed them together.

Bewildered, Troy looked about. The mist was gone and the sun was shining brightly. It warmed Troy, and he found his voice, "You're dead . . . and it's daytime."

"Yes, I wondered if you'd noticed. Maybe so are you. It's a wonderful state of being."

"No, no, NO!" Troy screamed. He looked directly

into the sun.

Hands touched him and the sunlight was transformed into headlights. Troy heard the hum of a car engine. A voice said, "I'm here to help."

Troy looked at the hands on him. They were fully fleshed and hairy. He tried to look up, but his neck was too stiff. "You're going to be fine, just relax. My wife has already called an ambulance and the sheriff on our radio. Help is on the way."

Troy relaxed and blacked out, welcoming dreamless oblivion.

He awoke slowly from the darkness. He heard voices all around him. They sounded familiar, although he couldn't put a name to them. He flexed his fingers, then tried to stretch. The movement sent dull pain rippling through him. Troy groaned. He didn't know where he was or what was happening. Troy barely recalled his own name. What day was it? What time was it? As if to answer, Troy heard someone ask for another shot.

Opening his eyes to grayness, Troy tried to focus on the voice. Slowly, color came to his blurry vision and he saw distorted faces hovering above him. "He's awake," the blond and bespectacled man said. His brown eyes were concerned. Troy thought he knew who he was, but his mind wouldn't function. The man's jaw seemed massive and out of proportion. It reminded Troy of Dudley Doright. As he spoke, his words and lips were out of sync.

"He looks confused. I'd say he's not quite with us yet," a thin-faced man added. He appeared to be growing a goatee and had a bandana around his head. His dark brown eyes bored into Troy's own. His front teeth were abnormally long and Troy was reminded of his dreams. He closed his eyes for a moment.

An older woman reached out and touched him. "Troy, it's okay. You're in Bristol Memorial Hospital. You and Silke were in a car accident. She's fine and resting in the room next door. You're going to be just fine too." Troy tried to speak, but his tongue was thick. She appeared to anticipate his questions. "Don't try and speak; you're medicated. It's late at night — the same night as the accident. Rest and we'll speak more in the morning." She gave him a motherly pat.

As Troy closed his eyes, he knew the names which matched the faces: Denny Rentzel, Spider Adder, and Mrs. Urich. He tried to call out to them, but it was too late. They were gone. His voice carried across a grassy knoll covered with tombstones. Troy had returned to the graveyard.

The sun beat down upon him unmercifully and Troy wiped the sweat from his brow. He put on his sunglasses and surveyed the area. The mist was long gone. All around the hill were mountains, still shrouded in cloud cover. The wind seemed to slowly push through the valley and the trees swayed in slow motion.

Not far away, Troy could clearly see a small town. It appeared to be an old one. The buildings were short and mostly built of wood. They appeared weathered; most of their paint peeling away. He was surprised by the number of porches, shutters, and awnings. The construction seemed simple and basically early American. The tallest of the dozen structures was a church with a bell tower.

Troy wondered why he was here again. His dreams rarely repeated, let alone advanced in sequence. This didn't seem to be a coincidence. It might have something to do with Dillon, he mused. He might as well look around and see what he could learn.

At Troy's feet was a black cloak. He remembered the undead that had struck him last time and shivered. A few feet away lay the empty grave. The gray headstone had fallen inside the coffin.

The slight breeze carried two sounds. The first was digging. It came from the other side of the hill. As if bidden by a supernatural curiosity, Troy followed it. The second was a grinding noise, accompanied by a clashing of metal. Troy thought of construction.

As Troy rounded the hill, the digging stopped. He saw movement off to the right. Partly obscured by a tall, cross-topped monument, a crouched figure opened the coffin lid and helped a corpse climb from a grave.

To get a better look, Troy crept closer. He hid behind a tall headstone. Before his eyes, the corpse regenerated. The ugly red warts and bags faded away as the dry skin became supple. The rotted flesh grew firm. Greasy, matted hair glowed with natural highlights. Sagging muscles grew strong and lean. Suddenly, the hag was stunningly beautiful with long, jet-black hair and finely chiseled features. Sunlight glinted from her smile and her laughter carried to Troy. She whirled around in a lacy white dress which swept the ground. Suddenly she stopped, and the couple turned to stare at Troy. They waved to him, calling for him to join them.

The distance between them shrank, the landscape blurring as he neared. Troy was only a few feet away. As his stare met the woman's deep emerald eyes, he felt a sudden, impulsive attraction. He wanted to be in her

94

arms—feel her caress. Without thinking, Troy began to move forward.

His attention focused solely on the beautiful woman, Troy never saw the open grave. He stepped into space, then awkwardly fell forward. He crashed into the far edge, but he felt no pain. Crumpling, Troy tumbled to the bottom of the pit. He landed hard, knocking the wind from him. Troy sucked in a breath and breathed earth. He tasted dirt and gagged. Spitting and coughing, he cleared his nose and throat. As he turned over, he felt squeezed. Tremendous force pressed on him and it was difficult to breath. The walls closed on him.

Pebbles rolled down the sides of the grave. They slowly piled up. Dirt trickled in, then increased in speed. Troy looked down and saw himself buried to his waist. He tried to pull himself free, but was stuck fast. The dirt fell faster and faster. Soon, he couldn't free a hand. Looking up, Troy cried out for help, but earth filled his mouth. He began to grow hot as he suffocated. Sparks danced in the darkness before his eyes. For a moment, it cleared and a man suddenly stood overhead. His blocky features looked familiar. There was a scar along his left cheek.

"Troy, what kind of trouble are you in this time?" the man asked.

"Denny?" Troy asked, finding himself staring at his friend. "Am I awake?" Troy looked around and found himself inside a hospital room. The sun streamed in through the miniblinds, creating picketed shadows on the walls.

"Yeah, you're awake. I have a better question. How do you feel?" Denny scrutinized Troy through horn-rimmed glasses.

"Beside strange dreams, I feel pretty good." He gingerly touched the stitches along his cheek, then stretched his right arm. It was stiff, but barely protested.

"Well, I'm damn glad to see you're all right. I was afraid I'd lost a blood brother. We can't have that, can we?" Denny said. Troy shook his head. Denny continued, "You received several stitches in your left arm where it looks like you were bit. Did something bite you?"

"Yeah, a wolf. We were attacked by wolves," Troy stated with a bit of hesitancy as if Denny wouldn't believe him.

"Why would a pack of wolves attack a Landrover?"

Troy thought for a moment, shaking the cobwebs from his head. "Hungry, I guess. Silke and I found an injured baby doe. We were taking it to a vet when about a dozen ambushed us."

"Ambushed you?"

"That's what it seemed like. They came at us from all angles. Several jumped in the Landrover while we were moving. That's why we wrecked."

"Oh, that explains everything," Denny told him.

"Eat shit," Troy responded. Denny laughed. "How's Silke?"

"She's been awake for a while and has been asking about you. She's sustained some pretty good injuries though. The doctor said that she got the worst of it. You seem to have been lucky."

"Especially since I was thrown from the car." Troy caressed his bruised forehead. "My head feels pretty good. I don't think I have a concussion."

"If I recall, you've had several of those," Denny said. "Let me get a nurse, so she can call the doctor. He probably wants to ask some questions, as does the sheriff. I'll be back in a minute." Denny started to leave.

"Uh, Denny, wasn't Spider with you?" Denny nodded. "Good. I thought I was dreaming things again. Hey, do you have a morning paper?"

Denny cocked his head. "You feel like reading?"

"Yes. It's my livelihood, you know."

Walking over to a chair, Denny picked up the paper. "You want just the sports?"

"No, the whole thing, please."

Denny gave him the thin stack. "Such fine reading, the *Bristol News*. If you get a headache, stop."

"Thanks, Dad," Troy said. Denny smiled and left the room.

Troy snapped the front page open. The headline read, "King College Graves Robbed, Attendant Slain." Strange stories predominated the news. There were stories about the Traylor investigation, a second disappearance at Camp Sequoia, a follow-up on the Beecham chemical break-in, and a tobacco farmer slain by wolves. Above the headline, next to the weather and the thought for the day, they advertised a special report on missing street people, and an interview with a hit-and-tell driver with no victim. Troy shook his head, understanding what Mrs. Urich had told him over the phone.

He skimmed the articles, wondering how it all was connected to Dillon's disappearance. As Troy read, he thought the city seemed to have gone crazy. According to the paper, the past week had been chaotic in Bristol.

King College Cemetery had been looted last night sometime after midnight when the late-night attendant, Mr. Tim Barton began working. He had been slain without a mark on his body, although the article hinted at some sort of cover-up. They had a photograph of the rough-looking man. He wore his hair in a flattop and he had a long scar along the side of his face. Troy thought he wouldn't have wanted to meet the man in a dark alley. In total, six plots had been raided. The names were listed and of course an investigation was underway. The police had no suspects.

The Traylor article told him very little. The police had cleared Ms. Terry Bray, Traylor's most current girlfriend. The testimony of three brothers gave her a firm alibi. A dusting of the boat for prints revealed nothing. Bray's prints were discovered, but that was no surprise. The authorities suspected that a second person had been on the boat because all four dive tanks were near empty and there were two sets of diving equipment. Divers explored the area but came up empty. The operation was currently suspended due to a lack of manpower. Police bemoaned the fact that a full autopsy hadn't been performed since the body had been stolen from the police morgue five days ago. A broken neck was still listed as the cause of death.

Troy's head started to throb a bit, but he continued reading anyway. He was afraid a doctor might come in and take his paper. There was something about the news that made his reporter's instincts tingle, if he could only put his finger on it.

Another disappearance had occurred at Camp Sequoia, an all-girl camp. This was only one of several disappearances around Holston, most attributed to drownings. The woman who was missing was the girlfriend of a young male counselor who had disappeared a week earlier. Foul play was not suspected— romance was reasoned.

The attack on the tobacco farmer was the second in his family in less than a week. His daughter had been injured earlier, so the farmer had been waiting in an ambush for the beast when he was killed. It reminded Troy of his own episode with the wolves.

He started another article when the doctor entered. Behind him was a burly sheriff, Denny, and his lanky friend, Spider Adder. "Good morning, Mr. Bane, I'm Dr. Robinson." They shook hands. "How are you feeling?"

"Very good, considering. I feel lucky."

"From what Sheriff McDaniels tells me, you are. We've taken x-rays and found no broken bones or serious injuries. Despite the blow to your head, I don't find any indication of a concussion, just a mild contusion. I would advise avoiding any strenuous activity or exercise for several days."

"I will," Troy responded. He saw both Denny and Spider smile.

"Your shoulder was slightly dislocated and will probably be tender for several days. I surmise that you landed on it after being thrown from the vehicle."

"It felt like it."

"Ms. Urich states you were attacked by wolves. Is that correct?" the doctor asked. Troy nodded. "You were bit in the left arm by a wolf?" Troy nodded again. "We have no idea if the beasts were rabid, but from Ms. Urich's description, we don't think so. Rabid beasts rarely travel in packs. The only precaution we've taken is a tetanus shot. The treatment for rabies is painful and complicated so we only administer it if absolutely necessary."

"I appreciate that."

"Any questions?"

"When will I be able to leave?"

"We've taken you off all medication, except Percocet—a minor painkiller. I see no reason to keep you here any longer. I don't think observation is necessary, but I would like to see you in three or four days."

"Okay."

"Have a good day and get plenty of rest, Mr. Bane. I'll send a nurse in with a wheelchair." He turned to leave.

"Uh, Dr. Robinson, are you treating Silke Urich?" The man nodded. "What's her condition?"

"She's stable. She sustained a concussion. There is a minor fracture in her left wrist, but she won't be in a cast. She also has multiple contusions and minor whiplash. I suspect she'll spend some time in physical therapy."

"How long do you think she'll be hospitalized?"

"Two or three days at the most."

"Thanks."

"I'll see you later this week. Remember, take it easy." Dr. Robinson said. "Good day."

The stout sheriff moved next to the bed. He had a handlebar moustache and thinning blond hair. The officer held out his meaty hand. "Mornin' Mistah Bane, mah name's Kermit McDaniel. Ah'm a deputy sheriff. Ah just spoke ta Ms. Urich earlier this morning and took her statement, and if you don't mind, Ah'd like ta ask you a few questions."

"Sure."

"This is jus' preliminary, a formal statement will have ta be made at the Tennessee police station."

"I'll do that this afternoon or tomorrow. Do you know if Detective Glazier's working this week."

"Damn straight he is. With all the shenanigans goin'

100

on, both sheriff departments and city police forces are working overtime. Damnest thing Ah've ever seen. Anyway, are ya the same Troy Bane that played basketball for Tennessee High?"

Troy looked over the sheriff's shoulder at Denny and Spider who shrugged. "Yes," he replied.

"Hot damn, Ah thought ya were. Ah used ta watch you all the time. Boy, could you scorch the nets. Damn shame you screwed up your knee."

"I appreciate that," Troy replied. Both his friends were stifling laughter.

"Ah tell mah boy 'bout you all the time. He wants ta be a good ball player. Ah'm sorry. Ah'm gettin' off track. Let me get official. Who was drivin' when the accident occurred?"

"Silke."

"What was your speed?"

"I don't know, maybe twenty-five to thirty miles per hour."

"In your opinion, what caused the accident?"

"About a dozen wolves."

"Ah was afraid you'd say that."

"Why?"

"There's been more attacks in the last week then in the last twenty years, though game wardens claim the population is actually down this year." The deputy shook his head. "Why d'you think you was attacked?"

"I can only guess that the smell of the blood from the injured doe we were transporting to the vet whipped them into a frenzy."

"Purty strange. Well, Ah don't have any more questions, but Ah appreciate your time. Ah hope the rest of your stay is peaceful. Good day, Mistah Bane." He put on his hat and left.

"Welcome home," Denny said.

"Yes, welcome back," Spider said. He reached out and they clenched hands.

"I wish I could say I was glad to be home. Things seem to have gotten more exciting than the last time I was here."

"Well, you know Bristol, something exciting happens once every twenty years or so. I'm sorry we missed you at the airport. We were running late—all the traffic, you know," Denny said with a wide smile. Troy laughed.

"Troy, what are you doing in town? We expected you here last week for the reunion," Spider said.

"Well, I'm looking for Dillon. He seems to have disappeared and that's worrying several people, including me. He hasn't called into work and no one's heard from him since last Thursday. How about you guys?"

"Not since Wednesday," Denny replied. Spider squinted, then nodded. "We didn't know he was missing until Mrs. U called us. Everything's been crazy since we discovered Traylor's body. You know how annoying newsmen can be," Denny said with a huge, toothy smile.

Troy ignored the statement and said, "I'm sorry I wasn't here for the reunion. I had to substitute for a colleague in—"

"Sure you did—we heard your Marader tolerance was low," Denny interjected.

Troy smiled, but his eyes hardened. "Isn't it always. Can you guys give me the inside scoop on what happened the night you found the corpse and coffins?"

"Better than that, we can show you," Denny said with a wide grin.

"You can show me?"

"Sure. We videotaped the whole evening. Of course, I dubbed a copy before turning it over to the police. Dillon liked the idea. Tonight is barbecue and poker at Marader's boat dock. We can show the viddy then, and you can ask questions. The whole gang will be there. Maybe one of the guys will know something Spider or I don't. I know everyone will be glad to see you, even Marader."

"Who's going to be there?"

"The whole gang."

"Hey, could one of you guys drive me to a rental car place? Silke was going to be my chauffeur, but we seem to have totaled her Landrover."

"I'm not working today. I'll drive you," Spider offered. "If you're worried about Dillon, then so am I."

"Thanks, I appreciate it. I'll take all the help I can get . . . and you're better company than Marader."

"Maybe I should rescind my offer," Spider said.

"But not better company than Silke, right?" Denny winked. "She sure has blossomed." Troy smiled and nodded. "She looks good, even after the accident."

"You've seen her?"

"Yes, you ought to before you leave. Mrs. U and Aunt Jada are administering holistic healing." He rolled his eyes. "She claims she'll be out in a day or so. Speaking of which, I have a lunch meeting in an hour. I'll see you guys tonight at Marader's dock of sin." Denny walked to the door. "You know, for someone who reports the news, you sure miss the obvious sometimes." Without another word, Denny exited.

Troy looked questioningly at Spider who shrugged. "I'll pull the car around and meet you in the lobby. If you get there before I do, I'm in a blue VW Rabbit."

"Okay, I'll see you in a few. I want to stop and see

103

Silke before I leave," Troy said as he climbed out of bed. Spider nodded and left humming a tune by Pink Floyd.

"I wonder where they hid my clothes?" Troy said to himself. He stretched, then crossed the room to the closet. Inside, he found his soiled clothing, briefcase, and travel bag. Deciding to change into clean clothes, he searched his bag. Pulling out a pair of pants, underwear, and shirt, he set them on the floor.

Curious of the time, he dug into his pants on the hanger. Troy removed the watch and was checking the time when he felt feminine hands on his shoulders. Instead of whirling around, he froze. Troy knew her touch . . . knew her presence. Soft lips danced down his neck, then she bit him.

Interlude One
The Prisoner

The pain returned as Dillon awoke to darkness. It had been a hard rest, one brought on by mental exhaustion. He tried to return to sleep, but the burning in his wrists, ankles, and waist wouldn't allow him. He wondered if his hands and feet were turning blue beneath the bindings, ready to rot and fall off. He couldn't tell in the darkness.

A drop of water spattered on Dillon's cheek, bringing him to full awareness. That was unfortunate. His inquisitors left him alone when he passed out. Only then was there peace and quiet — no more questions and no more burning red eyes. Every time they appeared, the fiery eyes speared through him and clawed into his brain.

Just thinking about it caused sweat to break out on his brow. Each time the glowing eyes focused on Dillon, he could feel his will ebb and his strength weaken. He'd lost count of how many times they'd silently badgered him with their hypnotic stares.

Lord, how long have I been here? Dillon asked. How

long had it been since he'd seen the sun? How long since they'd pulled him from his boat? Although Dillon suspected his capture hadn't been long ago, it seemed like forever; yet, the event was still clear in his mind as he thought back on it. . . .

While the sun set, Dillon had piled all his dive equipment in the front of the boat. Ready to go home, he toweled off and turned on the boat's lights. In the twilight, he heard the soft putter of another craft approaching. At first Dillon figured it might be the game warden, but it wasn't. He wasn't even slightly suspicious when the old couple surrounded by fishing gear waved at him. The man yelled something as they got closer, but Dillon didn't understand.

"We're a mite confused, young man," the old gentleman said. "Can you direct us to Observation Knob Park?"

Dillon smiled, knowing that Ob Knob was near Marader's dock. "I'm heading in that direction. Just follow me."

"Thank you, we sure appreciate it," the man said with a smile. He was missing his front teeth.

"Could I trouble you for something to drink?" the elderly woman asked. Her pink cap was askew. Her eyes were a bit glazed, and she looked thirsty. "We ran out a while ago."

Smiling, Dillon said, "Sure, but all I have is water."

"Wonderful," she'd said and the boats softly bumped together.

Her smile was broad, thankful, and innocent. Dillon was stunned when she grabbed his wrist instead of the water jug. With incredible strength, she yanked him into their boat. His head spinning, Dillon tried to rise from the deck. Then all went black and silent as

106

something crashed into his skull.

Since then, everything had stayed black and silent except for the questions, an occasional wisp of movement, and the two pairs of searing eyes that glowed in the darkness.

A sound . . . first a flutter, or was that just a breeze? then a soft footfall. More footsteps and Dillon shuddered. They had returned. Dillon prayed for Troy, Spider — anyone — to save him, but he knew better. He was as good as dead . . . or maybe worse. Dillon wondered if he should be praying for a quick death instead of rescue.

Interlude Two
The Inquisition

Glowing malevolently in the dark, crimson eyes hovered before Dillon. They didn't float, sway, or blink; the burning orbs were perfectly still. The tiny black pupils at their center didn't flicker, but seemed to bore into him with steady determination.

The stare was mesmerizing. Dillon tried to turn his head away, but couldn't. He bit his lip, drawing blood in hopes that the pain would free his attention, but it didn't. Dillon blinked quickly. It was all he could do — that, and sweat.

His eyes were hypnotically magnetized to the seemingly disembodied orbs. They held his entire body captive. Dillon couldn't shudder, shiver, or stretch. His muscles were dead. If he hadn't been so stubborn, he might have given up struggling.

Each time the eyes appeared, the ache at his wrists, ankles, and waist dulled as if he were being pulled from his physical form. The eyes were trying to steal his soul! Dillon fought to stay in contact with his flesh.

A second set of eyes appeared. They were smaller and a little more oval than the first, but they still blazed like hot coals. "Hoyt, is he finally awake?" asked a feminine voice.

"Yes, Elsa. It is time to begin again," Hoyt responded in a deep voice. "He is incredibly strong-willed."

"Stubborn."

"He would have been ours by now, otherwise. Our time is running short. We haven't been able to find Von Damme and I can feel him growing in power. Our other agents have failed, but Mr. Urich has a special quality about him."

"He is also very familiar with the lake."

"True, but I fear that if Mr. Urich isn't ours soon, it will be too late," Hoyt finished.

Dillon shifted slightly under the penetrating gaze. He wanted to scream questions, but couldn't. Who were they? What agents? Who was Von Damme and how was he growing in power? Why were they doing this to him?

"Tell us what you know about the strange events around Bristol and the lake," the female purred, but it struck like a command.

Dillon tried to hold the words back, but they seemed to burst free of their own volition. "Some horror, some abomination, was released from Wreythville by John Traylor. How I don't know. I believe he found something in a jewelry box. Releasing it killed him.

"Whatever has been freed is freeing others from their graves. Now the abominations are stealing people and their ranks are growing. Darkness is spreading through the Appalachians like some ancient evil."

"See," Hoyt began, "he knows very little. He doesn't

know about the amulet or Von Damme's curse."

"True, but he knows enough to be a problem."

Hoyt laughed. "He will be ours soon. Dillon Urich will find Von Damme and there will be a reckoning again, just like there was nearly a half-century ago."

Hoyt's deep voice continued, but began silkily cajoling. "You want to help us, don't you, Dillon?" Dillon shook his head. "You want to be one of us, don't you?"

It was difficult, but Dillon managed to shake his head no. "Don't you? Can't you feel the power, the wonder, the vitality, the chance at immortality? It's here, waiting to touch you, to take you to places you've only imagined."

"In nightmares," Dillon managed to croak, but he couldn't pull his eyes away.

"He is incredibly strong-willed," Elsa said. "It is too bad we can't just make him one of us."

"He must walk in the light. But don't fear, my dear Elsa, we will win in the end. We always do." Its eyes enlarged and grew brighter. Then they moved closer.

Dillon felt Hoyt's power grow. He felt his walls of resistance crumble as a force reached into him and grabbed his spirit. There was a wrenching feeling inside, as if he just realized he'd committed some heinous crime the night before while dead drunk.

Unseen hands covered with filth seemed to lovingly caress him. The dark force pulled him forward . . . and, oh Lord, he wanted to follow!

Dillon's thoughts were desperate. His soul wanted to scream, but there was no outlet, no release. He fought against himself—fought against the piercing gaze. If only he could escape the crimson eyes!

Unable to break free, unable to pull his eyes away,

Dillon sidestepped. He let his vision lose focus. Sight blurring, Dillon no longer saw the eyes. He visualized being elsewhere. Dillon's mind drifted, and he slipped away.

As Dillon appeared in the forest with Denny, J-Man, and Troy at his side, Dillon felt his soul breathe a sigh of relief. It returned to him, still his spirit.

"I thought I winged it," Dillon claimed. He pulled his hunting cap down tightly on his head and shifted his rifle into his left hand.

"You never were the world's greatest shot," Denny said with a broad smile. His brown eyes danced with amusement. As he approached, Denny put his rifle on his shoulder. He was perfectly decked out in hunting gear, boots, camouflage fatigues, and a backpack. Denny had even dirtied his face, claiming that deer ran at the sight of pink flesh.

"Not all of us have laser scopes," J-Man said, coming to Dillon's defense. He was dressed in all brown. His hat was on backwards. Jay hadn't shaved in several days.

"Guys," Troy said, "if Dillon significantly winged the buck, it still might be around." His friend pointed between the two hills and into the leaf-covered clearing. A brief whirlwind spun the brightly colored leaves around in a circle.

"He's right guys," J-Man said. "Let's sweep the area."

"We don't have very long. The days are getting awfully short," Dillon said. He popped a piece of gum in his mouth.

"You in a hurry? Got a date?" Denny asked. "You might kill something bigger than a squirrel yet."

"Let's sweep," J-Man repeated. Rentzel gave him a

dirty look, but he saw that Troy had already moved off to the right and was climbing the hill. He followed, but veered to the left, heading more toward the clearing. The wind had died and the birds were quiet, just leaving their footsteps to make noise.

J-Man and Dillon moved up the closest hill. The smell of the woods filled Dillon with wonder, overshadowing the thrill of the hunt. Squirrels rambled through the branches overhead. The trees seemed to shuffle and something shifted with each step Dillon took. Leaves crunched under foot despite his careful efforts to move quietly.

As Dillon crested the hill, he moved to the left. He sensed something ahead. Beck waved and drifted right, more toward the clearing.

Dillon moved more quickly. He saw a flash of brown. Something broke through the woods, staggering along and lurching drunkenly. A rack of antlers blended in with the tree branches.

Steadying his rifle, Dillon fired. *Crrrackk!!* The rifle jumped in his grasp. The blast exploded through the woods. The buck fell after running a few feet. It collided with a tree and slumped to the ground.

As he moved toward the fallen deer, Dillon heard his friends call out. "I got it!" Dillon yelled. After three years of hunting, at age fifteen, Dillon finally got his first buck. His father would be proud. Mom and Silke would be disgusted. Now his friends couldn't call him the Blankseye.

Dillon pushed through the underbrush. Branches swiped at him, but soon enough he reached his kill. It laid there, rolled on its side. Blood ran from its mouth. Its empty black eyes stared at him.

Crashing sounds came from the woods to the right

of Dillon. Beck arrived first. "All right!" J-Man yelled.

Denny ran up next, almost out of breath. "Did you get him?" he asked with eyes wide. He looked to J-Man, then Dillon, who was kneeling and examining his kill. "Yee-haw. We have a newly crowned game hunter. Good-bye squirrels, rabbits, and doves!"

"Next we'll have to go to Africa and go big-game hunting!" J-Man laughed. He moved to stand over Dillon. "Looks good, boy-o. How many points?"

"Eight."

"Not bad at all!"

A stinging slap brought Dillon back to the darkness filled only by the crimson eyes. They were angry. Dillon almost managed a smile. Sweat stung his eyes. He was so tired, he could hardly stay awake and that was just fine with him.

"This is taking too long," Elsa told her compatriot.

"Yes, maybe we should try another method."

Mercifully, Dillon passed out before Hoyt could continue.

Chapter Five
Lay of the Land

Troy whirled around and the teeth slipped away from his neck. He clamped a hand to his throat. He stared into luminous, jade green eyes. His voice faltered. She was as entrancing as she'd always been, Troy thought.

"Troy, Ah used t' bite you all the time and you loved it," the darkly tressed beauty drawled. First a pout, then a crooked smile graced her striking features. The sun cast reddish highlights through her wavy hair as it flowed over her bare shoulders. Curious at his silence, her full eyebrows arched over eyes that danced with amusement. "No words for an ole friend? Cat got your tongue?" Strong fingers caressed his face.

Troy didn't know what to say to his high school love. At one time he couldn't breathe without thinking about Racquel Sterling. Unbidden, Troy was surprised to find his intense feelings return. He thought he'd purged her from his heart, but then he confessed that Racquel's natural beauty, forged by the winds and sun of outdoor life, would probably always stir him. "You claimed you only bit me in the midst of passion," Troy responded.

"That's true," Racquel said with a devilish smile.

Troy ignored the insinuation. Racquel was clad in worn jeans, sneakers, and an emerald halter top that left little to his imagination. She'd added lean muscles to her already curvaceous build. Keeping his eyes off her figure and on her face, Troy said, "To what do I owe the honor of your visit?"

Racquel frowned, "Ah heard you were in an accident and came t' wish you well. Is there anythin' wrong with coming to see an ole friend?"

"Racquel, we haven't seen each other in eight years, and I gathered you wanted it that way."

"You were rather bitter last time we spoke."

"With justification."

"Ah'd hoped that time would've healed old wounds. So Ah was young and stupid—are you goin' to hold that against me forever?" Her eyes burned hotly, but pleaded at the same time.

Troy tried not to wilt. "I don't know. Everything works out in its own time. I've found that forcing things to happen rarely yields favorable results."

"Then let's take some time. How long are you in Bristol?"

"I don't know, at least a week."

"Have dinnah with me tomorrow night."

"I'm not sure I'll have the time."

"Babysittin' Silke Urich?" she asked cattily.

"No, looking for Dillon Urich. He's missing. I think he was investigating John Traylor's murder and something happened to him. He's my friend . . . and I don't let friends down."

Racquel was slightly taken aback and looked pained. "No, no you don't . . . but you have to eat sometime."

She looked determined. "Say yes."

"How about I'll call you tomorrow morning. I'm spending the evening with the guys. Dillon was with them when they discovered Traylor's corpse."

"Ah read about it. If you get involved with those guys, Ah might never see you."

"I promise I'll call."

"Good enough for me. Here's mah card." It read *Sterling Sporting Goods*.

"Yours?"

"Yes, Ah opened 'bout a year ago. My home number is on the back. Ah'll tell you all about it tomorrow over dinnah. Ta ta," she said with a smile. Racquel quickly kissed him on the cheek, whirled around with a laugh, and walked to the door. Before she left, she looked at his bare legs visible below his medical smock. "You still have great legs." Hair flying behind her, she breezed out the door, leaving Troy confused.

He shook his head and began dressing. That's all I need right now, Troy thought. Well, he could always just refuse the date—how hard could that be? Troy laughed at himself. It's not like he hadn't forced himself to forget her on several occasions—like for years.

Clothed, Troy went next door to visit Silke. On his way out, he left a note on the door for the nurse, telling her he was next door. Troy was ready to be released. He was hot to begin his search for Dillon. Things seemed to keep getting in his way . . . and he couldn't help but feel that time was running short.

Troy lightly tapped on the door, then entered. "Good morning," he told Silke. She was sitting up in bed. Bandages were around her head. With her hands resting on Silke's head, Aunt Jada stood next to her.

The old woman coolly appraised him. "You have

seen your bane, Mr. Bane." Troy was speechless. "It is all right; you have grown strong," Aunt Jada told him. He wasn't sure he could handle Aunt Jada's idiosyncrasies again.

"About time you got up and around," Silke said with a cheery voice and smile. "You look good. The doctor told me you'd been released. I'm jealous, but I hope I'll be out tomorrow to help you look for Dillon."

Troy was amazed by Silke's state. The memory of her covered in blood and unconscious against the steering wheel flashed through his mind. Before she had been pale, now a glow of health surrounded her.

"Don't be in too much of a hurry," Troy responded. "I want you in good condition before we traipse through the forest and mountains. Truthfully, I'm just thankful that you're alive. When I first saw you after the accident, I was afraid. I can't believe we were attacked by wolves."

"The sheriff indicated you were just one of several," Aunt Jada interjected. "The darkness grows, spreading its evil influence. It won't be long before it's too late for many. Many an immortal soul will be lost."

Troy gave Silke a bit of an exasperated look. "Aunt Jada's resilient," Silke interjected. "She's helping me heal. Mom's downstairs having breakfast and making phone calls." Troy's expression was blank. "Aunt Jada's channeling healing energy." Troy shook his head. "I'm feeling better already. Soon I'll be your personal chauffeur . . ."

"And stunt driver," Troy added.

". . . again," Silke said with a smile. "Mom has already called the insurance company and they'll provide us with an off-road vehicle, probably a Jeep or Bronco, until all the claims are completed. The Rover is

117

totaled."

"It looked like it. With your wrist, maybe I should drive. I'll still need company."

"Nonsense, Troy. I'm going to be fine. You'll see. Have a little faith. Are you going to look for Dillon today?"

Troy nodded.

"Where?"

"Spider's my driver for today. First we're going to just look around Bristol. I haven't been here for a while."

"Nothing's changed, except several more companies have either folded, merged, or moved. It's still just a small town of fifty thousand."

"Maybe they've fixed the light bulbs in the 'Bristol, a Good Place to Live' sign," he told her. Silke laughed. "Then we're off to the police station to file a report and snoop around. Maybe Bill Glazier can provide some clues. Tonight I'm meeting with the crew at Marader's. Denny videotaped the whole episode. Maybe that will help."

"Only Denny would videotape someone trying to ski at night, then continue to tape the entire gruesome evening. I'll bet Dillon encouraged him." Silke changed the subject and asked, "Are you sure you can get along with Tom?"

"For a while, then I'll hit him when I can't take it anymore. I'll call you tonight to see how you're feeling and let you know where I'm staying."

Silke pouted. "Another missed opportunity, and I've waited ten years."

Troy smiled, then leaned over to lightly kiss her. "When you're not so fragile, we'll continue where we left off."

"Sounds good to me. Troy, before you leave," Silke said as she reached behind her neck, "promise me you'll wear this." She handed him the crystal and silver cross Aunt Jada had given her.

"It has been blessed by a priest," the elderly lady said, nodding in approval.

"I will," Troy said as he slipped it around his neck. "Tell you what. I'll come by tomorrow, probably in the evening."

"Good, I hate being a patient. Something about lying in a hospital bed gives me bad dreams."

"Oh?" Troy said, her words sparking his interest. "Like what?"

"I dreamt I was in a graveyard."

"Was the sun shining?"

An odd look of concentration crossed Silke's face. "Oddly enough, yes. Why?"

"Was—"

The door opened and a nurse walked in. "Ah, there you are Mr. Bane. Your wheelchair has arrived."

"Silke, we'll continue this discussion later. It sounds similar to a recurring dream I'm having. Get healthy." He leaned over and kissed her again.

This time Silke wrapped an arm around him, holding the kiss. "I feel better already," she said as they parted. "Troy, I just found you again. Please be careful. Some very strange things are going on around here . . . and I worry about you. In many ways, you and Dillon are a lot alike—curious, sometimes reckless, and stubborn."

"I'll try and be good until you can keep an eye on me. Bye." He joined the nurse in the hall. In a few moments, he was being wheeled down the hall.

There was the usual delay with paperwork, then they headed for the lobby. Spider was studying the paintings on the wall when Troy arrived. He walked over to lend a hand. Spider took his bag and briefcase. "You can let me off here," Troy told her.

"I'm sorry Mr. Bane, but we have to wheel you to the door," she told him.

"That's so you don't slip, fall, and sue them," Spider said. Troy laughed and the nurse frowned. "It's not a limo," Spider said, pointing to his car which was slightly battered with fading blue paint, "but it's better than walking."

"I'll take it. It looks better than the last one I rode in," Troy laughed as he stood. He bid the nurse good day, then they climbed into the Rabbit.

"I called Jambo at Wild Bill's. He says it's slow and he can take the afternoon off. He said he'd be ready whenever we arrived," Spider told him.

"Good, the more the merrier." Leaving the red-brick hospital behind, they drove down the winding hill towards Bluff City Highway.

"Where to?"

"How about a sightseeing tour to see what's new and different?"

Spider smiled. "That should take about five minutes. They're adding a store or two to the mall. I think I read they're doing some repairs on the Bristol Tiger's baseball stadium. Uh, we have a new Arby's." They stopped at the light. K-mart was across the way. To the left and right fast-food places predominated "The Strip."

"How's the Loaf at the Barn?"

"The place you and Dillon once worked?" Spider asked. Troy nodded. "It closed down. I think it was bought out."

"Ah, the hustle and bustle of the big city."

"I like it here," Spider told him.

"I did too. I miss it; the area and people, not the town."

"They've just remodeled the old train station," Spider said. "There's a bunch of small shops and restaurants inside. We can pick up Jambo then go eat. You hungry?"

"No, how about we go to the police station first? I'd like to see Bill Glazier before he heads out for lunch."

The light changed to green. "We're off." They turned left, heading toward downtown Bristol. Troy marveled at the lack of cityscape. There weren't any high or even medium-rise structures — none of the gleaming glass or metal of the Metroplex. Many of the buildings were made of brick and few were over three or four stories high. Spider turned right on State Street which ran along the state lines and passed the donut house they had frequented as high school students. Denny, Tom, and Bill had powerful sweet tooths.

"Hey, they've closed down the Giant grocery store."

"That happened years ago. That's small news. Sperry, Univex, Beecham, and Bristol Meyers have all left Bristol. Rumor is that Burlington is next. The only place that's a solid employer is the phone company."

They passed numerous used car lots and several mom-and-pop stores. There were a good number of pedestrians and several bicyclists along the road. Despite the lack of traffic, cars crawled as if no one were in a hurry. "I can't believe the number of car-repair shops. There's more here than in the towns surrounding Dallas," Troy said.

"They've redone the main stretch. I believe it was a funded project. It only took about three years." The easy pace of the town made Troy feel as if he'd stepped into a time warp. All the open space felt comfortable.

Houses could be seen lining the hills on each side of State Street.

There were more lights along the main road than he remembered, but then besides Volunteer Parkway, State Street, Bluff City Highway, and Edgemount, traffic lights were nearly nonexistent.

"They needed to redesign downtown. I never knew if I were in a turn lane or not. They seemed to change them all the time."

Spider smiled. "I'll never forget the time you helped Knives move, you guys violated more traffic laws."

"Hey, it was raining and you couldn't see the lines on the streets."

Without signaling, Spider whipped around a corner past a gas station and small yellow bank. They were immediately in a residential housing area. The houses were old, but still well tended. Most of the homes had covered front porches and many had swings. The trees were tall, but had less foliage than usual.

"A lot of brown grass." Troy watched a litter of puppies romp in someone's front yard under the watchful eyes of two young girls.

"It's the drought. We've had several fires just because people pitched cigarettes out the window."

"Is it that bad?"

"Wait until you see Holston. There's islands I never knew existed." They halted at a stop sign and waited for a lady walking her baby to cross. An Irish Setter followed her. When they had passed, Spider hit the accelerator. They raced down the hill and leaned through a sharp curve. "I love driving these back roads. It brings back the spirit of adventure."

"Speaking of adventure, that night-skiing trick must have been quite a trip."

"It was. One minute we were cruising along, Jay's rigged halogens lighting the way, jamming to the stereo, and the next we were dodging coffins. Marader was asking us to go faster just before he crashed." Spider shook his head, then said, "He was knocked so silly that he thought the corpse was alive and attacking him. Now, it's funny. The look on his face was truly priceless, but then you'll see for yourself this evening." They zipped through a green light on Volunteer and flew past The Wooden Nickel Restaurant.

"Did you find anything strange on the island?" Troy caught a brief glimpse of the white steeple of the Volunteer Baptist Church to his right. Before Spider could respond, Troy said, "Don't they have radar in this town anymore?"

Spider briefly smiled, then said, "Besides open graves and a blood-spattered boat, no. There was lots of diving equipment, but no digging utensils. We found a bloody knife, but no wounds on Traylor, except for his hand. The place was spooky though and I'm not supersti—wait, I remember Knives finding a jewelry box. It had been pried open, probably with the knife or maybe a screwdriver. There was blood on it, but it wasn't corroded as if it had been under water. The silver wasn't oxidized."

"What did the police think of it?"

"They didn't see it." Spider made a rolling stop at a sign, then swung left.

"What?"

"Dillon wanted to examine it. I think he took pictures and was going to check at some shops. He thought it might be a antique. Marader's keeping it for him at the dock."

"You guys kept evidence?"

123

"Yeah, I guess. There was just something strange about it . . . almost like an attraction. Denny and Marader fought over it for a while. They wanted to keep it. Dillon agreed that they could while he researched it. Marader said he could claim that he found it later if he needed."

"Well, that's not the first time he did something illegal."

"And probably not the last." He studied Troy. "I can't believe you're still angry over that joy-riding incident."

"Not only did he lie to me, he made me part of a criminal act. He stole that car just to go cruising."

"That was almost a dozen years ago."

"So I don't forgive easily. He also put the moves on Racquel when we were an item. The man's an egotist with a genital complex," Troy told Spider who abruptly laughed, slapping his knee. They passed the track and playing fields of Tennessee High, then came to an oversized building next to the entrance of the school. "What is that?"

"The new gymnasium — Viking Hall. They built it several years ago. I thought you knew about it."

"No," Troy said. They left the castlelike structure behind.

"You're out of touch."

"I guess so. What is everyone up to these days?"

"I'll let you ask them tonight. That way you can get it straight from the horses' mouths. Besides, we're here." They pulled into a large parking lot full of new cars. Spider parked in front of the showroom.

The front door opened. Jambo stepped out and then turned around to say something to someone inside. Troy climbed out of the car and waited. He was amazed by the change in his friend Jamie "Jambo" McGillis.

Jambo was easily six four and once weighed over two hundred and fifty pounds from rigorous weight training. Since Troy had seen him last, though, the large, soft-spoken young man had slimmed down to around two hundred or so. Without his shoulder-length hair and earring, it almost didn't look like the same man. Married life had changed him.

Jambo gave Troy a slow but wide grin. As he approached, he stuck out a massive hand. "Good to see ya, Troy!" Jambo said excitedly, then hugged Troy. Jambo began to pick Troy up, then thought better of it. "Sorry about the accident. Spider told me about it."

"Thanks, climb in. We're going to see an old friend," Troy told him.

Jambo squeezed into the back seat and folded his knees. They nearly touched his ears. "Who?" he asked.

"Detective Bill Glazier." Troy moved the seat up and put his knees against the dash.

"How come?"

"To see what he knows about the Traylor murder and if he's spoken to Dillon recently."

Spider pulled out of the lot and headed down Main. Jambo groaned. "You're not going to investigate the case too, are you?"

"You mean you knew Dillon was investigating the murder?"

"He didn't tell me, but it didn't take a genius to figure it out," Jambo said.

"You're right."

"How's Silke?"

"Doing well. She's in good spirits."

"Have you kissed her yet?" Jambo asked.

"What kind of a question is that?"

"A straightforward one. That lady has been crazy

about you for ages," Jambo told him.

"It's been full-speed emotional turmoil since I got here. First, Silke meets me at the airport and it's instant magic. Then she takes me to see her weird aunt who's into the paranormal, then we're attacked by wolves and trash the car, ending up in Bristol Memorial. Finally, while I'm gathering my wits and getting dressed, Racquel shows up and asks me out to dinner."

Jambo groaned. "Don't get started with her, Troy. She broke your heart once. Don't let her do it a second time."

"We're here," Spider interrupted.

Dillon looked into the parking lot. The station was a small, one-story building. Next door was city hall. They were across from the train station. Stretching across the tracks was an arched sign which proclaimed "BRISTOL, A VA-TN GOOD PLACE TO LIVE."

"Want company?" Jambo asked.

"Sure." They parked the car and walked to the entrance.

The day had grown hotter and the mountain mist had already burned away. "Strange weather," Troy stated. There was less morning fog than usual.

"Very little humidity. Just heat. An editorial in the paper claims that it's the heat that's making people see or do all these strange things," Spider recounted.

"That's possible, I guess. In Houston they shoot each other on the highways when the weather gets too hot. Of course, all the road construction would drive any sane person crazy."

Troy stopped at the receptionist and told her what he wanted. She called ahead, then directed him to Sergeant Powers's office. They found the sergeant next to the coffee pot. After offering them a cup, he directed them into the office.

Sergeant Powers gave Troy several forms to complete along with a few instructions. Before the officer could leave, Troy asked if Detective Glazier was in. When the sergeant nodded, Troy requested that he tell Glazier that a Mr. Bane was here to see him. Powers said he would.

Nearly thirty minutes later, Spider said, "I don't think he's coming."

Troy signed the accident report and said, "Maybe he knows it takes a while to complete this complicated form and doesn't want to disturb—"

"Good mornin', gentlemen, are y'all under arrest?" said Bill Glazier. A smile flickered across his face below a handlebar moustache. He ran a hand through thinning jet black hair.

"Is that department issue?" Troy asked, pointing to his face.

Bill looked confused, then touched his moustache. "Oh," he laughed, "you must have met Deputy McDaniels." He walked in and they shook hands, then briefly hugged. Bob smiled at Spider who nodded.

"In the hospital," Troy responded.

"Yes, a crazy thing. I heard about your accident. Not a very nice welcome home, was it?"

"It started out all right. Silke met me at the airport."

"She's here too? A fine-looking lady if I ever saw one. I was always surprised you didn't stake a claim to her."

"Maybe I will." Troy glanced sideways at Jambo, who grinned. "How's Martha and the kids?"

"Gone."

"Gone?"

"Yessir, we got divorced about ten months ago. It

127

was peaceful, neither of us wanted our pound of flesh. She couldn't take all the late hours," he patted his stomach, "and pastries I was consumin'."

"You're not a lean machine anymore."

"Comes from bein' married for a dozen or so years. But you didn't drop by to check on my weight. What can I do for you? God, it's good to see you. How long's it been?"

"When did we last go hunting with Denny and Dillon?" Troy asked.

"Must have been nineteen-hundred-eighty-five, I think. I'm a better shot now. I think I could beat Dillon or even Denny now," Bill said, his brown eyes clouded as they wandered down past roads.

"We think Dillon's missing."

"You do? Why? I just saw him last week."

"No one's heard from him since Thursday morning. He was supposed to be at work yesterday and wasn't. He didn't call in, either."

"I'd love to help if I could, but we're swamped with all the missin' people and the two murders in the last two weeks. I just don't have the time. Even if you file a missin' person's report, we may not get to it for a while. We need double the manpower we've got."

Troy stared him down, but didn't say anything. Bill wiped his forehead, then sighed. "You're goin' to search for him?"

"Yes. I feel in my gut that something is wrong."

"You two were always real close."

"We all were."

"How can I help?"

"I think he was investigating John Traylor's murder," Troy explained.

"That sounds right. We discussed it last Wednesday

when he was here filin' a report. Damn! It didn't occur to me that he'd take off on his own and pursue it. He's not a detective."

"Come on, wake up, Bill. He's an investigative reporter. That makes him part writer, detective, salesman, and even part con man."

"And he always did enjoy lookin' for trouble," Bill said with a wan smile. "Some things never change."

"Tell me what you know about Traylor's death."

"I'm not workin' that case anymore. I'm on the King College Cemetery murder and grave robbery."

"Sounds like an interesting job," Spider said.

"You always did have a different opinion of interestin'," Bill retorted.

"Can you run some scenarios by me?" Troy asked.

"You're not writin' a story?"

"Damn it, Bill. I'm looking for a friend of ours. If he's alive, I'll let him write the story. How about it?"

Bill looked at his watch. "I'm headin' over to the morgue for the coroner's report on last night's victim, Tim Barton, the evening shift cemetery keeper. Would you guys like to join me? They promised me a report by lunch time. We can discuss things on the way."

"We're with you."

"Where is the city morgue?" Jambo asked. Wind ruffled his curly hair.

"It's just a few blocks up the street, behind the bank," Bill told them. Troy squinted as his eyes searched the buildings ahead. He thought he spotted it beyond the fountains next to the bank. Troy donned his sunglasses. It had grown noticeably hotter. "It's just a short walk. I like to get out into the sunshine every now and then. It keeps me healthy. Y'all don't mind do ya?"

"Not at all. I need to stretch my legs," Troy responded.

"Spending too much time sittin' down?"

"Sitting in airplanes and lying in hospital beds."

"Usually, I'd tell you that a pack of wolves attackin' a car is really strange," Bill scratched his double chin, "but with all that's been goin' on around here, it's not."

"What's been going on? I really haven't taken the time to do more than skim the front page of the newspaper," Troy said. Once again he found himself marveling at the mountains. They were almost part of the city itself; yet, he was disturbed by the lack of green.

"Well, y'all know this is a quiet place," Bill began. "Though we do have an occasional murder, few are quite as bafflin' as John Traylor's. We can't find a motive or a clue. Anyway, it's not just a body floatin' in a lake that has the city uneasy, it's all the other crimes and disappearances."

"Such as?"

"Well, first we've had two large robberies, both involvin' chemicals. Beecham was hit first, then Kodak in Kingsport."

"I thought Beecham had closed down."

"They still store some chemicals here. They're waitin' to be shipped. In both places all the security systems were workin' just fine. Kodak even has heat sensors, but they didn't pick up anythin'."

"Were they bypassed?"

"No, they weren't touched."

"Guards on duty?"

"Just at Kodak."

"They didn't see anything?"

"Funny thing. They all fell asleep around the same time. All four guys, can you believe it? Thieves steal several hundred pounds of chemicals, not a whole lot

130

mind you, but the guards don't wake up. That's some sound sleeping." Bill pulled out a cigar and lit up.

"It sure is."

"Y'all know what's the strangest thing of all?" They waited expectantly as Bill puffed on his stogie. "Both places had surveillance cameras set up. In both cases, the cameras weren't tampered with. What's odd is the fact that neither system caught any of the thieves on tape. The tapes do show movement, like boxes and barrels bein' moved around and opened, but there's nobody in sight. When I watched the tapes, my hair stood up. It's as if ghosts robbed Beecham and Kodak."

"No finger prints?"

"Nope."

"That is odd."

"I don't remember reading that in the paper," Jambo stated. "All it mentioned is that you had no clues."

"That's right. We have nothin' to go on. These guys were good."

"Why no mention of the unusual scenes on the tapes?" Troy asked.

"It was done at the request of both companies and the papers complied." A whistle blew in the distance. It was followed by a clanging as a nearby gate closed off a road.

"You mentioned disappearances?" Troy prompted.

"Yeah. We usually have a few around the lake—booze-related drownings, usually, but there's been over a dozen missin' persons around Holston in the last two weeks. We've found four empty boats just floatin' along."

"That include the disappearances at Camp Sequoia?" Troy asked. He heard the train's approach.

"Naw, that's just young love. They'll show up."

"Are the disappearances at Holston in any way related to the recent number of vanishing winos?" Spider asked. Troy gave him a surprised glance. "Hey, I read the paper . . . every now and then."

Troy remembered this morning's edition had a special on the topic. "Well?" he asked.

"We don't know for sure, but I don't think so. It's no big deal. Street people disappear more often than you think. Some move to different locales, a few find places to live or an organization to take them in, while others crawl off to die like cats."

"You're real sympathetic," Jambo snorted.

"Fact of life. Most of them beg money, then drink it away. It's a problem here but not a serious one like say," his eyes gleamed, "in Dallas. You know those reporters," Bill said with a smile as he continued to tease Troy, "they're just looking for a story. To answer your questions, Spider, I don't think they're related."

"The deputy sheriff mentioned that there'd been several animal attacks."

"Several is right. It seems like an epidemic, except none of the animals are rabid and there's usually more than one. I'd say there's been at least a half-dozen or so."

"Seriously?" Spider asked. Looking introspective, he rubbed his stubble. His left eye was squinted.

"Yeah, enough that they don't all make the papers, only the serious ones. See if I can remember 'em all. Near Holston, there's been one at Observation Knob Park, one near the 421 bridge, and two near the dam. Only the one near the dam, actually closer to the overflow, was truly serious. Two of the three people who were attacked died."

"Lots of activity near Holston. Coincidence that

132

Traylor was found there?"

"There's been attacks in other places too. One near Bristol Caverns, that one wasn't serious. Hmm, there was that tobacco farmer yesterday towards Abingdon, y'all near Bluff City, and even one near Sullin's College. The one near Sullin's was the only one near a well-populated area. Happened near a church—the assistant minister of the State Church was out for a walk and was harassed. I don't think he was even bit, just frightened."

"I wonder if any of this is related to Traylor's murder?" Troy mused aloud. Ignoring the "Don't Walk" sign, they crossed another street.

"I don't see how."

"Silke said that's what Dillon told her over the phone."

"There's nothin' to connect them besides the wounds on Traylor's neck which gave the indication that he'd been attacked by a wolf or something, but there was blood all over the boat and no tracks," Bill said.

"The coroner isn't sure if he bled to death or if his neck was broken. Most of his blood was smeared all over the boat, though some was on shore. I wish I could tell y'all more about the cause of death, but his body was stolen from the city morgue the next day."

An elderly man left the paint shop on the corner. "Morning, Detective Glazier."

"Mornin', Mr. Peterson."

"I thought this was a short walk." Jambo said.

"I lied, we're just past the workout gym, near the martial arts school," Bill told them.

"Who would want a dead body?" Troy asked.

"Only someone who thought we'd find something to connect them with the murder."

"Any sign of a second boat?"

"Not besides Rentzel's Baja. They might have anchored off shore though," Bill replied.

"There had to be someone else," Spider stated. "There were two sets of diving equipment and four empty tanks. Nobody dives alone."

"Y'all really scoped out the place before calling us, didn't you?" Bill accused. Spider showed no reaction.

"I wasn't there," Jambo said quickly.

"No suspects?"

"Not any good ones. Our best suspect has three witnesses. In fact, every woman Traylor's been seen with or any potentially jealous boyfriends or husbands are all accounted for. An employee at Slagle's Dock remembers seeing a foxy woman with Traylor, but he was so interested in her figure that he can't remember anything else about her—like hair color or height. But from his description, the woman with Traylor couldn't have broken his neck. We're at a loss."

"Then it's a good thing that you were switched over to an easy case of grave robbing," Troy teased.

Bill laughed. "I can tell you've already spent too much time around Spider. You're developing his sense of humor. Ah, we're here." They halted before a frosted door with black painted words reading "City Coroner" across it. "This shouldn't take long," he said, reaching for the knob, "then we'll have lunch, my treat. It's been too damn long since I've seen—" Bill stopped and stared at the door. He tried the knob a second time. Again, it didn't turn. "That's odd. They shouldn't be out to lunch yet. Besides, they always leave a note."

Bill knocked, then waited patiently for a minute. He glared at them as he chomped on his cigar. "Something's wrong." He pounded on the door. It was still silent.

"Any sign of a second boat?"

Reaching inside his pocket, Bill brought forth a large ring covered with keys. "I'm surprised you can stand up with that in your pants pocket," Troy said. Bill slid a key in the lock.

Troy's eyes swept the room. Nothing seemed to be out of the ordinary except for a few papers scattered on the floor. There wasn't any sign of a struggle. Soft music carried to them through a door which led to a hallway.

"Dr. Pete!" Bill yelled. "Stanley! Hey, is anybody home?" Silence greeted his welcome.

"Y'all wait here," Bill said and headed down the hallway. Spider and Troy followed. Bill glanced over his shoulder, but didn't say anything to his friends. Bill opened several doors but didn't find anyone.

"Maybe they're downstairs," Bill told them. He walked to the doorway which led to the stairway. "Hello, anyone awake down there!" he yelled over the music. "Odd, the lights are off." Bill flicked the wall switch and nothing happened. He put out his cigar. "I don't like this."

"Any windows in the basement?" Troy asked.

"No."

"That means it's real dark," Troy said.

"What's kept down there?" Jambo asked.

"The vaults. It's where they keep the bodies." Bill drew his revolver.

"We need a flashlight," Troy said.

"*I* need a flashlight," the detective corrected. "I think I saw a small one in the last examinin' room. Wait here." He turned around and headed up the hallway.

"I have a small one on my key chain," Spider said. He held up a pencil-thin flashlight.

"Maybe a torch would be more appropriate," Troy

135

tried to joke.

"Not funny. I have the same feeling I had when I was on Cemetery Ridge." Spider shuddered. "Did you hear that?"

"No," Troy responded.

"All right," Bill said as walked toward them. "I found one. Y'all wait here." Snapping on the flashlight, Bill slowly descended the concrete steps.

A cool breeze blew by Troy. He smelled blood and formaldehyde. His nose stung and his eyes watered. The odor was more powerful than he would have expected.

"Well?" Troy said. Spider turned on his flashlight. Jambo shrugged, then waved toward the steps.

Spider whispered, "Jambo's the tank, he should go in front."

"You're quicker than I am," Jambo retorted. Troy looked over his shoulder and found his friend smiling.

They followed Detective Glazier down the steps. Troy kept his hand on Spider's shoulder. His friend was shaking. Troy understood the feeling. The last day had him a bit spooked, too.

They could see Bill's beam sweep along the walls and the steps. Spider's beam reached Bill's backside and barely outlined him. The detective advanced in a crouch.

The darkness seemed heavier than usual to Troy — or was it his imagination? He wanted to ask Spider, but his throat was dry. His heart pounded loudly and Troy felt a twinge of fear. Their lights were pale flickers in the darkness. The walls of the stairs seemed to stretch high above them. It reminded Troy of a tomb — then he reminded himself that it was. He touched the cross Silke had given him. As they neared the bottom, the scuffling of their footsteps created a ghostly echo. Troy heard the faint sound of dripping water.

Having reached the bottom, Bill stopped. He waved his flashlight about. "Oh God!" he gasped, then staggered back as if struck. Hunched over he coughed and gagged. Bill stumbled back against the steps and collapsed.

Chapter Six
Unexpected Visits

The tension was palpable. The darkness along the stairs to the morgue's vault seemed to thicken. Spider's light barely reached Bill, who lay shaking on the steps. Troy barely found his voice as he asked, "Bill, are you all right?"

"Y'all stay back," he coughed.

Spider looked back and Troy nodded. They stubbornly continued onward. Suddenly, Spider slipped and started to fall. Rays from his light flashed wildly about. Troy grabbed him under the shoulders and held him upright until Spider recovered.

Spider pointed the light at his feet. The steps were smeared with blood. "I don't like this," Spider whispered.

"We shouldn't be here," Jambo agreed.

"Give me the light," Troy told Spider. "You can head upstairs."

Without speaking, Spider continued down the steps. As they reached Bill, the detective slowly stood. Sadly shaking his head, he mumbled, "What a mess. What a fuckin' mess!"

Between the two lights, Troy saw more than he wanted

of the gruesome carnage. The atmosphere was so thick with fumes that they distorted vision. The room appeared out of focus, but both death and devastation were still obvious. "It looks more like a slaughterhouse," Troy gasped.

His light sweeping the room, Spider took a few steps, then turned around to gag. "Lord, what happened here?!" Troy placed a hand over his mouth to quell his nausea. Jambo vomited. Glazier held his light steady as it worked across the room.

Cabinet doors had been flung wide open, their contents smashed on the floor. Broken glass was everywhere, glinting with reflections of light. Trash cans were knocked over, leaving stained towels and autopsy remains scattered about the floor.

In the center of the room, the examining table was overturned. Tools and papers were strewn about in pools of crimson. Collapsed on the top of a metal tray, a man laid dead. His clothing was ripped and shredded. Several scalpels protruded from his back.

Troy took Spider's flashlight from limp fingers and took a few steps forward. The beam touched the corpse, then Troy quickly pulled it away from the headless form. He tried to focus his attention on the rest of the room, but it was just as bad.

The walls were sprayed with blood. To his left, Troy noticed that one of the vault doors was ajar. It hung from one hinge. Bent outward in a convex shape, the door appeared to have been blown open from the inside out. "Another robbery," Troy stated quietly. He wiped the tears from his burning eyes. Spider continued coughing. The disinfectants were overwhelming.

"Murder," Bill said, then let out a string of curses. He moved forward in his search and kicked something. It flopped across the floor like a rag. "Oh Lord," Bill said, staring at a severed hand. "I wonder where Stanley is?"

Bill stepped around the appendage and walked across the room to a central lamp which hung over the examination table. When he pulled the cord, the room was illuminated in fluorescent light. Troy almost wished he'd left it off. The harsh glow only highlighted the tragedy.

To his right, Troy spotted shoes stretched out in the doorway just beyond a set of file cabinets. "I think he's over there," Troy said as he pointed. Bill's eyes followed his lead, then he moved in that direction.

"This . . . this is horrible," Jambo stammered. He wiped his lips.

"Go get some air," Troy suggested. He wanted to leave also, but he was looking for clues. Jambo left. "You too, Spider." His friend looked numb for a moment, then straightened. A look of determination set his features.

Troy nodded and walked over to the damaged vault door. Spider followed. Hesitantly, Troy began to pull it open.

Troy felt a bit of pressure — something pushed against the door from inside. He backed away as the missing head fell out. In shock, Troy watched. His light glinted off its spectacles. Sounding like a wet sponge, it hit the floor. Blood splashed onto Troy's pants.

He jerked his eyes away and bit his lips. His nails dug into his palms as he clenched his fist. His stomach churned, and he had to lean forward against the vault. One of the doors shifted under his weight. Troy heard Spider leave.

Clearing his mind the best he could and controlling his emotions, Troy continued his search. He peered into the empty vault from which the head had fallen. In the dim light, something caught his attention. The walls appeared scored. He turned his light on it. Yes, there were grooves along the walls and ceilings as if a trapped animal had clawed its way out. Troy's dreams came back and he winced. He started to feel suffocated. He wiped the sweat from his brow and continued his examination. On the back side of the door there was a footprint. Troy read the name tag on the outside of the door.

Bill walked over to Troy. Anger and sadness mixed in his expression. "Stan's dead too. He doesn't have a throat and his heart's been cut out." He saw the severed head at Troy's feet. His eyes hardened. "You better leave. You're not supposed to be here."

"Bill, I need help." Troy leaned on his friend, placing an arm over his shoulder. Bill all but carried him to the stairs.

"Troy, my friend, if Dillon is mixed up in this I fear for him. Keep in touch. Don't repeat his mistakes."

Troy nodded. "Bill," he asked, "wasn't T.M. Barton the King College Cemetery nightwatch?"

"Yes."

As Detective Glazier returned to the gruesome scene, the trio staggered out of the building. Weak-kneed, they leaned against the wall. A few minutes later, they wordlessly stumbled back to Spider's car.

Numbly, they sat on the car. "I can't believe it," Spider said in a whisper.

"I'll never forget it," Jambo said, his eyes still closed.

"I need to forget," Spider said. "How about a drink or fifty?"

"Sounds good. Someplace out in the sunshine if we could," Troy suggested.

"We could just grab a case," Jambo suggested, "and go to the park."

"I have a better idea," Spider suggested. He stood up

141

and headed across the street towards the Train Station Mall.

Two hours later, they were feeling better. It was amazing what fresh air and a few beers could do. Troy leaned back against the seat as they pulled out of the Train Station parking lot. The wind striking his face helped his condition. It blew the remaining tension away. Troy had seen enough blood and guts in the last twenty-four hours to last a lifetime.

They decided to arrive early at Marader's boat dock. The mood had lightened enough for a few attempts at levity. "I think the best way to cope with Marader is either absence or a buzz," Troy told his friends. Jambo laughed, and Spider gave Troy a brief, tight-lipped smile. He turned on the radio and found a jazz station among all the country broadcasts.

"Jeez, Spider, don't you have any decent tapes?" Jambo said from the back seat. Spider glanced over his shoulder and shrugged.

They drove under the Bristol sign and over the railroad tracks. They passed a church on the left and a small grocery on the right. "I still see plenty of street people," Troy mentioned.

"Yeah, too many," Jambo said. "They always seem to be there. Have been at least since I was little." They zipped through a light, passed an ice-cream parlor and suddenly they were outside the city. To their left, rows upon rows of headstones stood along a series of rolling hills, King College Cemetery. A green light loomed ahead at the bottom of the hill. Spider sped up.

As they neared the light, Troy made a decision. "Let's make a quick stop at the graveyard."

"Troy, for God's sake, why get more morbid?" Jambo groaned. His blue eyes rolled to the heavens.

The tires squealed as they screamed left under the light. They cruised through the gates marked "KC" and entered the graveyard.

As they drove along a narrow road through the sea of resting places, Troy scanned the scene. He looked for some sign of familiarity—something that would connect it with the dreams he'd been having, but he found nothing.

Spider scrutinized Troy, then asked, "What are we looking for?"

"Somebody tending the place. I want to ask some questions." They passed by a row of neatly manicured bushes. Several tents were set up, but none were attended.

"Don't you want to talk with someone who works nights?" Jambo asked.

"I need to find out what time he comes on. Besides, you never know when a clue might pop up. You need to just keep asking questions, keep jiggling the pieces of the puzzle."

"What does this have to do with Dillon?" Spider asked. The road curved and headed down a hill. To their left sat a small fountain with a woman holding doves in her hands.

"I don't know, but Dillon claimed all these strange things were related to Traylor's murder. Maybe working backwards we can discover something. You have any better ideas?"

"No. No need to get testy," Spider rebuked.

"Sorry, seen too much blood recently and I haven't slept well."

"You're forgiven," Jambo said graciously.

The road came to an end. "I'm out of pavement," Spider said.

"Let's walk."

Spider parked and turned off the engine. He gave Troy a long look. "How about you and Jamie walk, I'll stay with the car?"

Troy turned around and looked at Jambo. "Why not? I often spice up my day with a walk through a cemetery," Jambo replied and grinned.

Troy was still amazed at how easygoing and resilient Jambo was even in uncomfortable situations. "Okay, we'll try not to be long."

"If you're not back in an hour should I come looking for you guys?"

"No, send in the marines," Troy said with a wan smile. He opened the door and climbed out. Jambo squeezed out of the rear and followed him onto the lawn. The breeze carried the smell of lilies, and Troy stood for a moment just enjoying the idyllic surroundings.

"Ya know, it's too bad people wait until they die to find such a peaceful place," Jambo said.

"Yeah, it is." Troy continued on. The caretakers had kept the lawns well watered and brilliant green leaped out at Troy. Grass never looked this healthy in Texas, he thought.

"Let's head for the highest point and see what we can see," Troy told his companion. The largest knoll was just a hill away. From that vantage point, Troy figured he might find the caretaker. He'd hoped to discover him mowing the lawn, but the cemetery was silent except for the sound of an occasional passing car.

They walked in silence, both deep in thought. None of this made any sense, Troy told himself. Bristol was a peaceful, slumbering town. People didn't shoot each other on the highways, the city wasn't high in divorce, rape, murder, or crime. What the hell was going on? Was there a full moon? Why was there an outbreak of atrocities—of wickedness?

Was Dillon really missing or was he just undercover or out of pocket? Who murdered John Traylor and why? He gingerly touched his left arm where the bite wounds softly throbbed. Why all the wolf attacks? What had stirred them up? He thanked the Lord that Silke was okay. He'd never really contemplated it, but she enchanted him in a way he had been blind to before now.

His mind continued racing. Stolen bodies—who was stealing corpses from the morgue and the cemetery and leaving a bloody trail? And all the missing people—was there a connection or were they fragments of different stories. In his gut he felt there was some connection, but what?

Dammit Dillon, Troy cursed, why didn't you call me before you disappeared?

"We're here," Jambo's deep voice seemed to rumble from a distance.

Troy nodded and suddenly found himself staring at a cross-topped headstone. For a moment it triggered the dream sequence while he was awake. Beyond the cross, he saw the beautiful, dark-haired woman. She turned to stare. Her green eyes pierced him.

Troy felt himself being drawn in when Aunt Jada's words came to him—something about a dark-haired woman. Racquel was a dark redhead—did that count? No, this woman looked nothing like her. The woman before him had fine features and her skin was as white as if she'd been carved from marble. Her emerald eyes continued to draw him in. She was shapely but her muscles were lean, not sculptured like Racquel's. The woman was young and her lips were fuller. . . .

The vision smiled, revealing large incisors. They glistened in the sunlight. She licked her lips as she said, "Come, Troy, come join me. Live in the light, thrive in the darkness. I'll be all yours. Come join me. Join Dillon . . ."

"Iz one of you Mistah McMillian?" said a thickly accented voice, snapping Troy from his waking nightmare.

"No," was all Jambo said. He wanted Troy to do the talking.

Troy shook his head to clear it. He turned to the man who'd spoken. The balding gent was covered in grass-stained overalls. His skin was deeply tanned and wrinkled from the sun. He looked to be in his fifties. "No, neither of us is Mr. McMillian. My name's Troy Bane and this is Jamie McGillis."

Jambo nodded.

"Ya all right, young fella? Ya don't look too good," the man drawled. He squinted at Troy, then wiped his head with a rag and replaced his cap.

"Just a long day. I'll be find. Are you the caretaker?"

"Yup."

"Can I ask you a few questions about the night of the grave robbing?" The man didn't respond. He slowly removed a pouch of chewing tobacco and placed a plug in his mouth. "I'm a reporter from out of town. I used to live here."

The man's sleepy eyes brightened. "Bane, Bane . . . did ya play ball?" Troy nodded. "Wish Ah could tell ya somethin', but Ah cain't. Ah don't no nuthin' 'bout it. Ya need to talk to Phillip Barton, he wuz workin' with his brother that night. Now Ah reckon he might know a thang or two."

"What time does he start?"

"He works graveyard shift," the old man chuckled, "if'n ya know what Ah mean." Troy gave him a blank

146

look. "What Ah mean is he comes on at eleven tonight and works until seven in the mornin'. But there's one problem." Troy waited patiently. "He don't like reporters. Think's they're nosy good fur nuthin' gossipers. He probably won't tell ya nuthin' — won't even see ya."

"Does he like cash?"

The old man's eyebrows raised. "Well, he ain't a damn fool."

"If you tell him I'll make it worth his while, will he meet me? I promise not to take up much of his time." Troy handed him a twenty-dollar bill. The caretaker continued to scratch his head. Troy gave him a second one.

"Well, Ah cain't promise nuthin', but I reckon' he will. Tell ya what, youngster, he's got a lot to do tonight. Several funerals tomorrow — busy, ya know. Come tomorrow night at the beginnin' of his shift, that's eleven P.M. The gates is usually locked tight, so if'n they be open, ya know he'll see ya."

"Thanks, I appreciate it." Troy gave him another bill. The man smiled.

Troy turned to leave. "Now, don't ya fergit. He won't wait on ya. If'n ya's late, ya missed yer chance."

"We'll be here." They began to walk off.

"One more thing, young fella."

"Yes?"

"Ya wuz a damn fine ball player. Sorry 'bout what happened to ya."

"Fate could have been worse," Troy replied.

"I reckon."

"Have a fine day, Mister. . . ?"

"Browning, Ernest Browning."

"Mr. Browning." Troy waved and they headed back to Spider's car. On his way back, Troy noticed numerous flowers, some real and some plastic, that he didn't see on his way in. The grass was slightly damp and springy underfoot. I must have really been out of it, Troy told himself. He gingerly touched his head and pressed on the bandages. His wound was very tender.

Troy was beginning to worry. First he had nightmares, which were in some sense common enough, but now he was seeing things while awake. Was he losing his mind? Why were all the dreams and visions connected? Were there supernatural forces involved? Troy silently laughed at himself for even considering it.

"Troy, I hate to sound chicken, but I really don't want to come here at night. The scene at the morgue is still running around in my head," Jambo said. "Jane would think it was—"

"Jambo. It's okay."

They found Spider lying on the hood and basking in the sun. "That didn't take long, did it?" Troy asked.

Spider didn't move. "I've decided I want to be cremated."

"What?" Jambo exclaimed.

"I've decided I'd rather be cremated than buried."

"What brought that up?" Troy asked.

"Today, but I think about it often." Spider sat up and slid off the front of the Rabbit.

As they got in the car, Jambo leaned over the front seat and asked, "Why cremated instead of buried?"

"Nothing to dig up, nothing to rob. I'll donate what I can and they can fry the rest." Spider started the car.

"Can we change the subject?" Troy asked.

"Sure. What would you rather talk about?" They backed up and turned around.

"I don't know."

"Would you like to make a friendly wager?" Jambo asked.

"On what?"

"On whether Marader's either gouging a customer or making some young babe when we arrive," Jambo proposed.

Spider's expression didn't change, but Troy couldn't help but laugh. "Ah, my friend, that is a hard choice. A very hard choice. I believe I will place my money on the young babe." Spider put the car in gear and they left the cemetery.

They got back on King College Road and headed past the pool and golf course. Soon they passed the brick buildings of King College. At the stop sign they took a left. Spider sped up. "Want to stop and tell Denny about what's going on?" he asked.

"No, we'll see him tonight. I'd like to go out on the lake before it gets dark, if that's possible," Troy suggested.

"It probably is. The days are long. Besides, I think Marader's got a new boat he's itching to show off," Jambo said.

"Things must be going all right for him."

"Yup," Spider responded. They passed several convenience stores, a small apartment complex, and Holston View Elementary School.

"Ah, the good ole days, much simpler times," Troy said wistfully.

"You mean playin' ultimate frisbee?" Spider asked. His eyes showed that the thought had crossed his mind too.

"And skiing all summer," Troy added. He ran a hand through his dark hair and sighed.

They raced by several residential entrances: Redstone, Willow Brook, Kingsbridge. The houses were on good-sized lots and the trees were tall. Troy breathed deeply of the mountain air. Off to his left he saw the small dam of

149

Middlebrook Lake. Troy pointed and said, "Jambo, you still live there?"

"Yeah, just down from my parents' place. We changed houses because we found an excellent fixer-upper and got a good price on our old home. We're closer to the pool now. We ought to go out for a canoe ride while you're here. We bought one last month."

"I'd like that," Troy said.

They cruised by another golf course. Spider changed the radio station to some rock-and-roll. He began humming, then said, "What did you guys find out at the cemetery?"

They hung a left at the stop sign, then passed Bristol Country Club. The tennis courts were empty. "Not much. I'm going to meet the late-shift caretaker, Phillip Barton, at eleven p.m. tomorrow. He's the victim's brother."

"And a good time will be had by all," Spider commented. "Count me out."

"Hey, I already appreciate your help. Jambo doesn't want to go either. Maybe I can con J-Man or Denny into going with me." They cruised through Goosepimple Junction, population ninety-seven. They were surrounded by farmland. The road became rougher and there were more curves. Spider didn't slow down.

Spider appeared deep in thought. "Sounds like something Jay would like to do."

"I'd advise taking Bill St. Martin along if I were you," Jambo suggested.

"Our soon-to-be minister?"

"The same."

"That would be a bit more comforting," Troy mused. They wound their way over larger and larger hills. Guardrails appeared. Several bait shops came and went.

Soon the lake was in sight. Majestic mountains and forest surrounded it. The base of the Appalachian Mountain ridge stretched left and right.

"We're almost there." Spider turned left and then quickly took a right down a gravel road.

"He's added gravel," Troy noticed.

"It's a classy establishment now," Spider told him. Bumping along, they drove down the incline. Through the trees, Troy once more spotted the lake. He was amazed at the water level. It looked very low. As usual, the wind had died and the surface was perfectly smooth.

Spider drove toward a walkway which lead to a large floating structure. A sign read "Marader's Dock". The combination gas station/store was two stories high and constructed of wood. It was painted brown and beige. A balcony surrounded the second floor.

There were only two cars in the parking lot. Troy didn't see any boats out front and no one was in sight. "I don't see any customers," Troy said.

"Looks like I'm gonna lose my bet," Jambo said.

"It looks renovated since I was here. This place was refuse on an oil slick," Troy said as he left the car. He held the seatbelt for Jambo who struggled to get his massive frame out of the back seat.

Spider nodded and led the way to the gangplank. "Denny, Jay, Jambo, and I helped him renovate—actually rebuild it—a couple of years ago in the springtime."

"I'm impressed," Troy said. He followed Spider down the swaying bridge. Jambo walked on down the shore as if searching for something.

Spider and Troy headed for the front, passing bait tanks as they went. Troy took it all in. The paint looked fresh and the pumps and vending machines were new. Green indoor/outdoor carpet had been laid down across the dock. A few greasy trash barrels were in sight and the water was almost clean. Waiting for a handout, ducks paddled around the dock.

They moved along the side of the building. Music could be heard coming from an upstairs window. "Should we knock?" Spider asked.

They heard moans and grunts mingling with the music. "No," Troy said with a smile. "Let's surprise him." They walked by the empty boat slips and peered into the store. It was deserted. "Nice place," Troy stated. "Well stocked for fishing, camping, or water sports."

"We could rob him."

"Nah, too subtle," Troy replied. "It would take him a while to get upset. We want him to be his normal, excitable self. I have an idea that'll have an immediate impact." Looking for the right spot, he walked around to the front of the dock and almost fell over a sunbather. To maintain his balance, Troy grabbed the side of the lounger. The sudden jarring awoke the young woman who had been sleeping.

The attractive brunette didn't seem perturbed. "Can I help you?" she asked. She peaked out from under her sunglasses. Her turquoise eyes matched her bikini and sparkled like gems. She smiled at him, then closed her eyes and stretched like a lioness. The movement accentuated every curve of her gleaming body.

It took Troy a moment to find his breath. He wondered why he'd ever moved to Texas. She didn't look like the type Marader usually coerced, although she was probably young enough. Spider rounded the corner and asked, "Are you the attendant?"

"Yes. Do you need something . . . or are you looking for Tom?" A squeal from upstairs was followed by a devious laugh.

"We're friends of Tom's," Troy told her.

"Are you here to beat him up?"

Troy began chuckling and had to stifle full-blown laughter. Spider remained serious and looked annoyed, "No, we've arrived early for tonight's poker game."

The young woman eyed them, then stood up. She wobbled and Troy caught her. "Thanks." She remained uncomfortably close to him, but spoke to Spider. "Are you Spider Adder?" she asked.

"Yes. How'd you know?"

"I saw you last week when all the guys were here, and there's a framed photo of y'all on the wall." She placed a finger on her lips and gave Troy the once over. "You weren't here last week. I would have remembered you. Without the bandages you look a lot like Dillon only bigger." She spread her hands. "Ah, you must be Troy Band."

"Bane, but you're close. And you are?"

"I'm Elle Richards. I work the summers when I'm not attending V.I. I'm an equestrian major. I like to ride." She looked boldly at Troy. "Since you're friends of Tom's, you know he'll be busy for a while." Elle jerked a thumb up toward the balcony. The grunting grew louder. Maybe he misjudged her, Troy thought. As if reading his mind she said, "I just work here, I don't get involved with the boss like some of the gals."

Troy smiled. "Do you mind if we play a little practical joke on Mr. Marader?"

"Not at all, he deserves it. Can I be of help?"

"I want to set afire a can of oil rags along the front planks, but away from the balcony so the smoke will roll into the upstairs."

"I love it," Elle said with a wicked smile. "He'll freak out." She pointed to the far side of the platform.

153

"There's a trash barrel around the corner. I think it has oil rags in it and a little bit of paper." She headed for the store. "Let me get a fire extinguisher and some matches."

Spider and Troy lifted the barrel and carried it out to the edge of the platform. "Look for something to fan the smoke," Troy said. Spider found a large piece of cardboard. "Perfect."

Elle returned and gave Troy the matches and Spider the extinguisher. Jamie rounded the corner as Troy struck a match. "What are you guys doing?"

"We're torchin' the place," Troy told him. He dropped the match into the barrel. The rags immediately caught. Fire leaped to the edge, then died down as black smoke twisted upward.

"He's going to be really pissed. Troy, why do you bait him?" Jambo asked. "It'll only make things worse between you two."

Troy watched the dark cloud thicken and crawl over the lip of the balcony. "It's a hate/love sort of relationship," he responded. He watched his handiwork. "All we have to do is wait."

"I hope I don't get fired for this," Elle commented. She stood back next to Jambo.

"Oh hell. Don't worry. Tom won't fire you, you're too attractive. He never fires good-looking help, especially if he thinks he can bed them, and he always thinks that," Jambo reassured her.

The balcony was almost obscured by the oily cloud. It seemed to cling to the place. Troy fanned the cloud to send it upward. "He should be out in a minute."

Chapter Seven
Into the Deep

It took less than a minute. The balcony stopped shaking and the moans halted. Troy heard Marader ask, "Do you smell something?" Two voices responded no. Spider, Troy, and Jambo immediately met eyes. Jambo smiled.

"Hey Elle!" Marader yelled from upstairs. Troy shook his head at Elle. She gave him a sweet smile. "Hey Elle! ELLE!! Oh shit! Something's on fire."

There was scrambling upstairs. Heavy footsteps ran across the ceiling, then thundered down the stairs. Nude, Marader burst from the store. He carried a fire extinguisher.

Tom Marader stopped immediately when he saw his friends standing casually on the dock. The look of intense concern faded from his flushed face. He relaxed, then tossed the extinguisher onto a bench. "You shitheads!" Then he broke into a huge smile and laughed. "I should have guessed I had visiting pyromaniacs. Troy, damn good to see you again."

"We knew only something serious could interrupt you," Troy said.

"I love it! I love it! I thought I had another meeting with my insurance company, but hey, put it out and come on in for a beer. Elle, would you get these guys a brew while I put on some clothes?"

"Sure. Anything to speed up that process."

Marader looked at Troy. "I don't know what's wrong with that girl. She could have me . . . ME in a heartbeat." He tried to comb his thin blond hair into place. "I don't know why I even keep her around. I'm good to her and she won't go to bed with me." He waved his hands about. "Troy, you'd probably like her." Still ranting, he went back inside.

Elle wasn't fazed. "What kind of beer do you want?"

"What do you have?" Troy asked. Spider sprayed down the fire. The chemicals immediately smothered the flames. The smoke slowly faded away.

"You name it."

"Molsons," Jambo suggested. Troy looked at him. "I'm a regular."

Spider set the extinguisher on a table, pulled a chair away from the wall, and then sat. His brow was furrowed and he frowned. He looked like he planned to stay for a while.

"So guys, what's up? You're early." Marader walked out with a woman under each arm. They appeared to be in their late teens. Both were scantily clad and well-endowed.

"We came for the fabled Marader boat tour of South Holston Lake," Troy told him. Elle slid past Tom and brought them their beers. She sat next to Troy on the bench. Jambo leaned against the wall.

Marader smiled broadly, took his arms from around the ladies, and walked over to Troy. "Ya know, I've really missed you, Troy." He stuck out a hand. "That barrel fire was cute." They shook hands. "What happened to your head?"

"Car accident?"

"How bad?"

"Totaled the jeep. Silke's still in the hospital with a concussion and a broken wrist. I'm just sort of banged up."

"Ah Silke, I've always wanted to do her. Was it a drunk driver?"

"No, we were attacked by wolves," Troy stated. Elle gasped.

"You're pulling my leg again, aren't you?"

"No."

"Strange things are afoot," Spider said cryptically. He placed his chin in his long hands.

The redhead nudged Tom. "Oh, sorry, I'm being my usual rude self. Troy Bane and Spider Adder, this is Heidi." He motioned to the flame-haired young woman on his left. "And this," he said as he hugged the blond, "is Sandy. You've all met Jambo before. The ladies are full-time help in the summer and work weekends in the spring and fall. They go to Virginia Intermount College."

"Jambo, do I win my bet?"

"I'm not sure, Troy. You only said one." Tom looked confused. "Call it a draw?"

"You knew this, didn't you?" Troy accused.

"No. Honest. Last time I was here he was overcharging a guy for toilet paper," Jambo said innocently.

"You're kidding?" Troy looked at Marader.

"Hey, his wife looked desperate." Marader gave him a shit-eating grin.

"That's disgusting. It's a draw, Jambo."

"What are you guys talking about? Troy, why are you here? You're a week late. We missed you. You're the only one who didn't show. It was pretty exciting."

"I wish I had," Troy began, "but then I might not be here now." He took a sip of his beer.

"I don't understand," Tom said. He pulled up a chair and sat down. "Sandy, bring me a beer . . . please." The blond disappeared. Heidi sat in his lap. "Well?" he asked, spreading his arms.

"When was the last time you saw Dillon?" Troy asked.

"Thursday around noon. He borrowed a boat."

"Then you're the last person to see him, at least as far as we know."

"What'd you mean?"

"He's missing. No one's heard from him since Thursday."

"I just figured he went back to Dallas."

"What was he doing Thursday?"

"Claimed he was just cruisin' the lake. I think he was scopin' out the area where Traylor was killed. He also borrowed some diving equipment," Tom said. He took a swig of beer and wiped his chin.

"Any reason you didn't go?"

"I couldn't. I had a meeting with several vendors in Kingsport that afternoon."

"Did he return the boat and equipment?" Troy continued probing.

"Of course."

"What time?"

"I don't know. I wasn't here, in fact nobody was. The jerk left the keys in the boat. Someone could have stolen it. When Elle and Sandy closed up, he still hadn't returned."

"What time was that?" Troy asked.

"He docked after sundown," Elle said, "which is when we close up. I'd guess about eight-thirty." Her eyes grew luminous as she stared at him. "Why?"

Troy shifted uncomfortably. Something about the young woman unnerved him beyond her boldness. "No reason. I'm just looking for clues." Troy leaned back and stretched, then rubbed his eyes.

"Want another beer?" Marader asked. Troy shook his head. "Another picture-perfect day on South Holston

Lake — clear blue skies, mountains, fresh air, smooth water, and no people." He kissed Heidi on the cheek. "Everything we need except for some evening or early morning rains. Can you believe how low it is?"

Troy scanned the unusually rocky shoreline. Large red boulders were all over. At this time of year, the water was often near the tree line, giving skiers access to long winding coves and channels to cruise. "No. I've never seen it this low, even when they're doing dam repairs. Even the coloring of the trees looks wrong."

"There are new islands and warning buoys all over the place. You should see Cliff Island. It's over one hundred feet tall. In fact, if it weren't for this drought, Cemetery Ridge would have never been above the surface and we would never have had this problem."

"What makes you think that?" Troy asked. He leaned back and casually appraised his sometime friend and blood brother.

"Traylor was diving around the island and the remains of the city of Wreythville. He probably found something valuable and his diving buddy killed him for it," Marader speculated. He drained his beer and motioned for another.

"That's an interesting hypothesis. Why do you say that?"

Marader shifted uncomfortably under Troy's gaze. "Interested in going for a ride? I've got a new Renken Classic II I'm dyin' to show off. You'll like it." He looked at the group with raised eyebrows. "It's a beautiful day and, Troy, my good man, you won't believe how different it all looks. We can cruise by Cemetery Ridge. The gals will watch the place. It's dead during the week and crazy on weekends."

"I'm game. I'd like to go for a cruise." Troy noticed that Spider was intently watching Marader.

"I'll just stick around here," Jambo said. "I didn't

bring a suit and I'd like to take a quick nap. I need to catch up on my sleep, and I suspect it'll be a late night."

"You're always sleeping," Marader accused.

"Jane doesn't let me do it very much," Jambo said with a wolfish grin.

Marader shook his head and turned back to Troy. "Would you like to ski?"

"Ah, a tempting offer, but neither my head nor my left arm is up to it. I almost dislocated a shoulder. If it weren't for the painkiller and beer they'd probably hurt like hell. I'll take a rain check, though. I may be in Bristol for a while."

"Good! We can party like old times."

"No, not like old times," Troy cautioned.

"Are you still pissed about the joyride?"

"And Racquel."

"Hey, I said I was sorry, didn't I?"

"Just saying your sorry doesn't mean much, you have to—"

"Marader," Spider interrupted, "did Dillon ask to see the jewelry box?" Marader tried to act like he didn't know what Spider meant. "The box with silver clasps that we found," Spider continued. "I emphasize *we*."

"Yeah. He did. It's fine," Marader answered a bit quickly. Troy thought he looked nervous.

"Can I see it?" Troy asked.

Marader's lips worked as if to say no, then he took a deep breath and said, "Sure. Up, Heidi." Marader climbed out of the chair and disappeared.

"He's pretty possessive about that case," Elle told them. "He keeps it locked up, not that I blame him. It appears valuable. Yet, it's almost a federal case to look at it."

"That doesn't sound like Tom," Troy said. They heard a car arrive. It slid to a stop on the gravel. A single door slammed shut. "I wonder who?" Troy looked at his watch. It was almost three o'clock.

"Hey guys, the fun can start now. The life of the party is here," Denny said. He carried a cooler and a basket. "I've got beer and steaks." He was dressed in brightly colored jams, a white tank top, and sneakers.

"Denny, you need a hand?" Jambo asked.

"Naw, I've got it." Denny flipped up the shades on his glasses. "Troy, you look better than when I saw you this morning."

"Thanks, but I don't see how."

"Well, you look more relaxed. Did something happen?"

"Don't worry, Denny, I'll explain later, but not too close to dinner," Troy said.

"Hi, Elle. Where's Marader?"

"Upstairs," Elle told him.

"Heidi, Sandy, would you put these in the cooler?" Denny asked. They nodded and took the load into the store. He stretched, then punched Jamie in the shoulder. "Good news," he said as he sat down. "I got in touch with Dr. Curran and Mr. Beck. They will both be here. Beck will pick up Knives and fly back to his house, then cruise on down. They should be here by seven at the latest. And Bob, Pete, and Aaron, and the gang will all be here."

"Except for Dillon," Spider noted. There was a heavy silence.

Troy broke it. "Didn't J-Man just move?" Troy asked. Denny nodded. "Where's he living?"

"He's just up the lake a ways, you know where all the houses are on the northern Virginia edge, near the river inlet?"

"He's there?" Troy was surprised. Denny nodded in response. "He's high rent now."

"He's got a good place to land his chopper," Denny explained.

"Denny, you're early. Let's party!" Marader came out

161

carrying something wrapped in white silk. He removed the cloth and gave the box to Troy. "Want a beer?"

"Of course," Denny replied. Marader gave Troy a long look as he handled the case. Tom hesitated, then went for the beer.

Troy rolled the ornate wooden case over and over in his hands. It was in perfect condition, not a scratch on it. He couldn't place it, but the jewelry box had a strange feel—like it was ancient. He hefted it, finding it was extremely light. Troy examined it more closely and noticed strange black markings grooved into the surface. Suddenly, as if he were looking through a zoom lens, the whole thing seemed to grow larger in his grasp.

The silver at the corner reminded him abstractly of claws, and the clasp reminded him of teeth. Troy undid the bite between the clasp's incisors and opened it. The lid swung open easily. Troy didn't understand why Marader thought this was found underwater. It wasn't tarnished and showed no sign of decay. The inside was empty except for some dark stains . . . maybe blood?

Troy watched, his eyes widening as the case began to slowly fill up with blood. Suddenly the pool belched and the crimson flowed more quickly. It reached the brim and ran over the edge. Blood dripped onto Troy's hands. It burned, but Troy couldn't let go of the box. He closed his eyes, but he still felt the warm liquid running down his forearms.

Elle shook him. "Troy, I said are you all right?"

"Sure, sure, just absorbed," Troy said. He put on a stone-faced expression and slowly rewrapped the case. Something was very strange about the case, Troy thought. Either the medication and contusion were causing hallucinations or . . . Troy shook his head—he didn't believe in the supernatural. Everything that had happened had a good explanation.

Elle touched him again. By the look in her turquoise

eyes, Troy could tell she didn't believe him. Troy handed the box to Marader who tucked it under his arm.

Spider's eyes changed to obsidian. He didn't believe Troy either. "Strange little jewelry case, isn't it?"

"Very. You found it on Cemetery Ridge?"

"Knives did, next to two broken wine glasses, an empty bottle of wine, a bag made out of netting, and a knife. Both the knife and case were covered with blood. Marader took a fancy to it and they haven't parted company since."

"I wonder how the blood got in it," Troy mused.

"Funny, I don't remember there being any blood in it." Denny said.

"Neither do I," Spider stated. "Marader, let me see that." Tom handed it to Spider who opened it. "Nothing, clean as a whistle." He showed it to Troy. It was spotless.

"I think I've been drinking too much."

"No, it's probably that you've seen too much red since you arrived yesterday," Spider said. Denny gave them both a questioning look.

"Marader, do you have enough equipment ready if I wanted to do a quick dive this afternoon?" Troy said suddenly. He knew he shouldn't dive in his condition, but felt compelled to do so.

"Sure, I'm set up for several people, why?"

"I'd like to make a short dive off Cemetery Ridge," Troy told him.

Jambo groaned, "Are you sure that's wise?" He pointed to Troy's head. "You might be pushing it."

"Let him do what he wants. He's a big boy," Spider said.

"Why? There's nothing to see," Marader told him.

"How would you know?"

"I dove there just the other day . . . and earlier in the year I dove the remains of Wreythville. It's kind of neat, swimming through old houses, but nothing mysterious

163

and nothing valuable. I looked."

"The visibility is that good?" Troy questioned. He sat forward. Since handling the jewelry case, he'd felt energized, restless.

"Yeah, due to the drought nothing's stirred up. It's a bit cool, but if it's a shallow dive, you won't need a wet suit. Since I know the area I'll be glad to guide. Come to think of it, I actually wouldn't mind going back to either place."

"Good, Wreythville might be later in the week. But between the beer and my head injury, I don't want to dive to any great depth, I don't think I could take it. In fact, the doctor would probably scream and holler."

"As would Knives. It's a good thing Dr. Curran isn't here yet," Denny interjected.

"I should be okay for a few minutes at twenty or thirty feet." All but Spider looked at him like he was crazy. "Do you folks have a serious problem with it?" Marader shrugged and Jambo held his tongue.

Denny said, "It's your life. I'd like to go, but I have an ear infection."

"I'll stay and start up the grill," Jambo offered.

"Sure," Denny began, "just like the time you were supposed to watch camp and fell asleep in the rain letting everything get soaked."

"Speaking of diseases, how are you going to protect your open wounds?" Spider asked.

"Tom probably has some first aid cream," Troy replied. Marader nodded. "That and a plastic bandage should keep them protected for the short while I'm in the water. This isn't going to be a long dive. I promise."

"Diving's good for hangovers," Marader told them. "Puts extra oxygen into your blood. You'll feel like a new man."

"It also makes you feel like you've had more to drink than you have," Jambo mentioned. "Troy, be careful."

164

"I want to go too," Spider said. Troy gave him a long look, but his friend's stoic expression showed nothing. Troy knew Spider wasn't a diving fanatic.

"We should dive in even numbers. With buddies," Marader told him. Spider set his jaw. An argument was forthcoming.

"I'll go," Elle offered. "I'm certified. Denny can watch the boat while we're below."

Troy looked at Marader, who shrugged. "Okay. The boat's out back. Jambo, before you fall asleep, will you help me load the tanks?"

"Uh huh."

"Great. I'll prepare the boat. Either of you have swimsuits?" he asked Troy and Spider. "I have spares if you don't."

"In Spider's car," Troy said.

"Ditto," Spider said.

"Great. After you change, meet y'all around back." Marader and Denny went inside. It only took minutes for them to load all the equipment into the boat.

"Jambo, if we're not back by six, please start the charcoal," Marader told him. "Heidi, Sandy, wake him up about five forty-five." They smiled sweetly.

Marader adjusted the throttle lever, taking the engine out of idle and asked, "Is everybody set?" Silence was his reply. He put the boat in reverse. Water gurgled about the Inboard/Outboard's prop. Spider and Denny guarded the edges of the boat as they slid out of the slip.

"Nice boat," Troy said. He gave it the once-over. There was a good-sized sundeck up front through the split windshield — enough for Denny to stretch out all his six-foot frame. The driver and copilot, Marader and Spider, sat in bucket seats. Troy and Elle occupied the U-shaped bench lining the rear of the compartment. The sun platform behind them was cushioned in gradations of gray, as was the rest of the boat.

Tom turned on the radio as they cruised to the buoys. As soon as they passed the markers he gave the engine full throttle. The bow rose and the engine emitted a mighty roar, then the boat leaped forward. Suddenly they smoothly planed out and sped across the calm water. The engine grew quiet and began to purr. Marader began driving with his feet as he applied suntan lotion to his burnished flesh.

"The lake really does look different," Troy stated as they passed Observation Knob Park on the right. All along the shore were large rocks. The treeline was over one hundred feet above the water level. A lot of the shrubbery was brown. Troy noticed that Marader stayed in the center of the lake.

"Anyone want a beer?" No one did. "Troy, are you sure you don't want to ski out? Look how smooth, how inviting, that water is. It's calling your name—Troy, Troy, Troy," Marader said with a smile. "We have everything we need," he continued. No one took him up on his offer. "Well, I want to. Denny, the rope and handle are under the right front cushion. Can you throw it back here?"

Denny handed it to Spider. As he gave instructions, Marader slowed down. "Just latch it onto the ski ring." Spider gave it to Elle who performed the tasks. "Thanks, babe."

Soon the rope trailed behind them. The handle skipped and bounced along the surface. "You want to drive?" Marader asked Troy. The boat slowed as Tom put it in neutral.

"Sure." They traded places.

"I need my gloves, my magic gloves," Marader said in a loud voice. He reached over and turned up the stereo. "I'm gonna jam—jam on skis. PARTY!" Spider got them from the glove box. Grinning, Marader slipped into his vest, then pulled on the gloves. "All I need is my

SKI! and a beer." Elle gave him both.

Marader tucked the can of beer in his vest, then grabbed the ski. "Oh boy," he exclaimed as he dove into the water. He came up sputtering and holding his sunglasses. "Damn, I almost did it again." He tossed the shades to Spider, then swam to the rope.

Troy engaged the throttle. This is what he needed, some boating and relaxation. He felt a little guilty, but he wasn't sure where to proceed next in his search for Dillon. His friend's last known whereabouts were on this lake. Maybe it would give him a clue.

Troy shifted and kicked something. He looked down and found the wrapped jewelry case. "Spider," Troy called to his friend. Spider looked at the case Troy held in his hands. "Don't you find this a little strange?" he asked. Spider nodded.

"I'm ready! Go for it!"

Troy set the case back under the dash and gave it full throttle. There was a momentary strain, then the boat shot forward. "Whoa!" Denny cried, almost falling onto the floor. That brought a smile to Troy's face.

"He's up," Elle said. The Renken steadied and they glided along. They cruised through a long, snakelike channel and headed for the bridge. The majestic mountains seemed to watch as they sped by them. Troy looked at the gauges and saw they were doing thirty-five.

Elle's touch surprised him. She leaned over, pressing against him. "How does it handle?"

"Just fine. How's Marader doing?"

Spider spoke up. "He's got his beer open. Ah yes, he's chugging it. I don't think he spilled a drop."

Marader finished his beer, then replaced the can under his vest. "At least he's not a litterbug," Denny pointed out."

"Ah, he's got one good trait," Troy retorted.

The bridge loomed before them. They had plenty of

clearance. Screaming as he went, Marader skied under it. He waved at the sunbathers on one of the many houseboats lining the right bank. A fisherman to his left flipped him the bird. Marader returned the favor.

Soon, they rounded a point and headed for the center of the lake. The towering island of rock, Cliff Island, was dead ahead. "Take a right into the bay," Spider told him. "Do you see Cemetery Ridge?"

"I see it," Troy responded. The rounded knoll stood at the rear of the deserted bay. It seemed to jut up from the water. It was barren, except for mud and rock, unlike most of the other islands which were rarely submerged. Troy slowed the boat. Marader swung around to the side and let go. He pointed underneath him as he slipped into the water.

"What a ham," Denny commented. Troy cruised over to meet Marader.

"Go ahead and turn off the engine," Marader told him. He handed his ski to Denny, then climbed aboard. Elle handed him a towel, then leaned against the back of Troy's seat.

"This is a good spot. It's between the town and the graveyard," Marader told them as he shook the water from his hair. "How'd it handle?"

"Wonderful," Troy told him.

"Ready to dive?"

"Let's do it," Troy said. "Do you have a dive watch I can borrow?"

"I put one in the bag for you."

"Thanks. And the first aid gel?"

Elle was at his shoulder with the bottle. "I've got it. Let me." Troy gave her a long look, then unwrapped the bandage around his head. She frowned, then gently applied the gel. When she was finished, Elle placed a bandage on it. Troy stared at her. Elle had removed her T-shirt and wore a green one-piece. She'd also removed

168

her glasses. Her eyes were now green.

"Your arm, please?" She examined his wound, then asked, "What bit you?"

"A wolf. Your eyes are green." Troy couldn't stop a growing, irrational fear. He didn't know why he couldn't get the words of Silke's crazy aunt out of his mind.

"They're sort of like chameleons often matching what I wear, but they're naturally this color. You like?" She finished tending to his arm and applied the bandage.

"A woman once told me to beware of women with green eyes," Troy said as he stood.

Her eyes grew large and she gave him a devilish smile, "Troy, you have nothing to fear from me. You'll see."

"If you two are through," Marader said. He and Spider had the tanks ready, the regulators connected. Fins and masks were set on the sun platform. They began donning their tanks. "I'm taking a noteboard down so we can communicate. Troy, what exactly do you hope to accomplish?"

"I'd like to circle the island and see if I can spot anything interesting. Dillon came back out here for a reason and dove. Traylor was killed and he'd been diving. It seems to me that if one dives here, one might disappear."

"Divers have been all though this area," Marader said as he buckled his belt. He pressed on the regulator and it hissed compressed air.

"They were looking for weapons or other bodies, I suspect. Sometimes you don't know what you're looking for until you find it. Know what I mean?"

Marader nodded. He strapped on a knife and stuck a grease pen in his belt. "I like to be prepared," Tom said, answering Troy's quizzical glance. "You'll also find exploring sticks with straps in the sack."

"Great." Troy removed his shirt and climbed onto the deck. The sunlight flashed off his crystal cross. Elle flinched as it glinted and said. "Are you sure you want to wear that in the water."

"Yes," Troy said. He pulled his tank over his head and slipped into the straps. Spider helped Elle.

"Since you two seem buddy-buddy," Marader began, "Spider and I will pair up. See you below. You have twenty-five-hundred psi." Before Troy could protest, Marader was gone. Stepping off backwards, Spider followed. He waved as he hit the water.

"Don't worry. I'm experienced and very good," Elle told him with a secretive smile. She tied her hair into a ponytail.

"I think you're in good hands," Denny said with a huge smile. He tossed Troy a foot-long stick.

Troy grimaced as he caught it. Ignoring Denny's clowning, he tightened the straps around his waist. He put on six pounds of lead weights, then sat to put on his fins. Elle joined him. Putting the regulator in his mouth, Troy blew out, checking and clearing it at the same time. Then he breathed in. His air flowed easily. He slipped his mask into place, then turned to Elle. "Ready?" he asked. She nodded.

Leaning forward and covering his face, Troy fell into the water. A small splash kicked up, then the lake swallowed him. He let himself sink slowly so he could get adjusted. He immediately started to equalize the pressure in his ears. Just moving his jaw didn't work, so he grabbed his nose and blew. He felt the pressure lessen. Sparkling in the streaming light, Troy's cross floated up before his eyes as he sank. Several fish darted toward it and Troy smiled.

A splash above let Troy know Elle had entered the water. Moving with the ease of a dolphin, she fluidly swam toward him. Elle gave him the okay sign, and he returned it.

Troy checked his watch. They passed fifteen feet. Bubbles floated by him, heading for the surface. He watched them rise lazily to the surface, amazed by the clarity of the water. It was almost an emerald green near the top. It grew a bit more olive and opaque as they descended.

The only sound Troy heard was his heart fluttering with excitement and the hollow sound of air released by his regulator. For some reason, he felt he was going to discover something. He could feel it in his bones. Troy glanced at Elle. She was tightening the belt around her slim waist. The water and her high cut suit made her long legs look even longer.

Troy continued to equalize. He spread his legs to slow his descent. Spinning around in a circle, Troy took in the view. The island was to his right. Everything else merged into a muted darkness. Troy reminded himself he wasn't here to have fun, but he was enjoying himself.

A feeling of relaxed freedom came to him. Troy relished the multiple dimensions of diving. He wasn't only confined to moving left or right, forward or back; he could also swim up or down. It seemed like he hadn't been diving in ages.

Troy found the path of rising silver bubbles and glanced down. Waiting just below him were Marader and Spider. They sat on the slope which dropped away from Cemetery Ridge. Tom was drawing something on his board.

Troy floated to a soft landing next to them. Water was seeping in his mask. He tilted his head back, mask pointing towards the surface, and blew air through his nose. Bubbles exploded from under his mask and it cleared. For a brief moment Troy felt dizzy, then he was fine, although a bit light-headed.

He focused on the sensation and had a feeling he'd been here before. Troy shook his head, thinking that was crazy. He checked his watch. They were thirty feet down and the water was still warm. He thought they might have hit some type of thermocline by now, but they hadn't.

Elle tapped Troy on the shoulder, pulling him from his thoughts. They swam next to Spider and Marader. Tom had sketched out a crude map. At the bottom were some boxes labeled "Wreythville" and at the top was a hill with little tombstones sticking out of it. Marader tapped the squares and then pointed over Troy's shoulder. Then he repeated the motions with the hill and pointed up the incline.

Marader pointed at himself and Spider, then drew a line circling left around the island. He indicated that Elle and Troy were to go right. Troy nodded. They swam off in separate directions.

As Troy slowly kicked his way along the bottom, he prodded and poked it with his stick. Mostly he kicked up mud and rock, but once he surprised a large carp. He noticed that the water was warming and he looked at his watch. He was surprised to find his vision a bit blurred, so he shook his head. It cleared. They were at twenty feet.

There was a large ridge ahead where the gradual slope ended in a four to five-foot wall before continuing. Elle swam up and over it. Troy paused, his stick ever questing. It hit something hard which gave off a metallic ring. He continued digging. An iron spike appeared. Troy pulled on it, but it wouldn't budge. He dug away more dirt to find that it was part of a fence or railing.

When Troy looked up to point it out to Elle, he found her gone. He spun around and still didn't see her. Peeking over the edge of the ridge, he continued searching for her. She didn't seem to be anywhere in sight. Finally, he spotted her in the shadows of a large boulder. She seemed to be intent on something. Laboring a bit, Troy swam to her.

Troy saw that Elle had chipped away at something in the shadows. As he reached her, she turned. Elle smiled around her mouthpiece and pointed. Her green eyes were bright through the mask. Troy looked down.

The shadows swirled. Suddenly a bony hand shot out, reaching for Troy. Surprised, he couldn't evade its long fingers. They wrapped around his neck. Troy thrashed about and kicked up silt. He futilely struggled against the powerful grip. It tightened its grasp, and he couldn't breathe. Troy gurgled in his regulator.

He struck at the arm but to no avail. As if he struck stone, his blows only rebounded. He began to panic. His heart thundered in his chest and in his ears. He was slowly being drawn into the shadowy pit. Troy saw the wooden edges of the coffin. A growing cloud surrounded him.

With wide eyes, Troy sent a pleading glance to Elle. With deliberate slowness, she swam closer. Her smile seemed fixed and her eyes glowed like fiery gems. She reached out for his necklace.

Troy pushed her hands away. Undaunted, Elle came at him again. With a powerful grip, she grabbed his arm. Troy kicked her away. His foot dislodged her mask and regulator. Her fingernails raked his flesh, drawing blood as he gained partial freedom.

His thoughts collided with each other and he grew hot. The water closed in, leaking around his mask. His chest heaved. Finding strength in desperation, Troy pushed off the ground and threw himself back. He jerked the skeleton from its grave.

Its jaw dropped and it laughed, teeth chattering loudly in the water. Dark pits for eyes mocked him. Troy continued struggling. Slowly, he dragged the clawing skeleton along the bottom of the lake. It tried to grab him with its other hand, but Troy knocked it away. Elle pursued them.

Again, it reached for Troy. It groped for his cross but the hand was snatched away as if it had touched fire.

Nearing unconsciousness, Troy changed directions and launched himself forward. His pendant struck the undead across the skull.

Its mouth dropped open in a soundless scream and its grip lessened. Troy gulped in a short breath, then jammed his stick between its ribs. He wrenched it upward and broke a rib. Troy jiggled it around. The skeleton shuddered, but wouldn't let go.

Troy stuck his stick between the bones in its forearm and twisted. They snapped cleanly. The hand remained. Troy surged backward and frantically loosened the lifeless hand from his throat. It sank to the bottom.

Troy fled. With a few desperate kicks he began to outdistance the creature. It stood, picked up its hand, paused to reattach it, and then staggered along after him. Elle still chased him.

Troy kicked with all his might. He had to get away. He had to be free. Troy still felt the skeleton's grip around his throat.

His heart threatened to explode and his vision wavered. He looked over his shoulder to see the skeleton stalking him. Gulping down air, Troy headed away from Cemetery Ridge and toward the bottom.

Time stretched as he swam with a fury. His shoulder began to ache, then throb with pain. He tried to ignore it as fear drove him deeper. For a while his desperation unfailingly pushed him on. The darkness seemed to melt away as he swam down the ridge. Structures loomed in the distance.

Suddenly, Troy felt very heavy. With each kick, he began to tire. His breathing grew labored. He glanced at his watch and it read seventy feet. He continued swimming, then he had to stop—he had to catch his breath and give his aching limbs a rest. His shoulder felt as if it were ready to fall off.

Troy floated limply in the water. He was so tired he almost couldn't move. A warning signal sounded in Troy's head and he checked his gauge. He had six hundred pounds of air left.

Troy searched for signs of pursuit but found none. Again, the feeling of having been in this place tingled his senses. He turned around to stare at the structures. They looked familiar. He floated closer.

The short buildings were lined up as if along a narrow street. They appeared to be made of rotting wood. The closest of them was a church with a bell tower. Troy swore he'd seen it somewhere before.

He spun around again and looked back toward Cemetery Ridge. In his mind's eye he saw the land as it was before the lake had arrived. A wrought-iron fence surrounded the grassy hill.

Suddenly it came to Troy. He turned again to the buildings. In his imagination, he added several short structures. The street became paved. Troy shivered. His mind cleared, leaving him fully lucid for the first time in the last several minutes. Troy knew where he stood. He'd been here already . . . in his dreams.

Chapter Eight
Gathering

As Troy stared at the town, powerful, unseen hands suddenly gripped him. One pair grabbed his left arm and wrapped around his waist. The second set held his right arm and looped around his neck.

Troy kicked and struggled, but their weight was too much. He bit into his lip and drew blood. Every muscle wanted to explode but couldn't. Water poured into his mask.

Troy couldn't move, let alone get free. Elle appeared before him. Her jaw was set and her face reflected determination. Troy paled; he saw his death coming. He read her eyes and didn't see a killer; and yet . . .

Elle reached around behind Troy and grabbed something. With her other hand she ripped Troy's regulator from him. Air exploded from his mouth. A froth of bubbles headed for the surface.

Troy watched the last of his air float away. Panic seized him. He could feel his lungs already longing for another breath. Troy knew he couldn't reach the surface even if he got free. He prepared to fight until he was dead, then Elle shoved a second regulator between his teeth. In heaving gulps, he sucked down air. His attackers' grip didn't lessen, but neither did they threaten him with harm.

Elle stood patiently and watched. She smiled at him, then waved in a dainty way. Then Elle pointed up. Turbulence surrounded Troy and his captors kicked their way toward the surface. They pulled him along towards the lighter water. The visibility increased.

A mask followed by long, flowing hair came around from his right. Troy's vision began to clear and he recognized Spider. Their eyes locked and Spider let his arm drop from around Troy's neck. He gave Troy the okay signal. Troy nodded and Spider let go of his arm.

Turning, Troy saw Marader. His friend cocked his head, then made a decision. He let go of Troy's arm but kept his arm around Troy's waist as they ascended. Troy placed a hand on his regulator. He was buddy-breathing off the octopus on Marader's tank. The second regulator was feeding him air.

Troy rapidly ascended. Looking up, he saw they neared the surface. Less than ten feet below the surface, Marader pressed a button on his BC and it inflated. Troy followed suit. With a hiss, his BC was automatically filled from his tank. They broke the surface and burst into the air.

Leaning back, Troy removed Marader's regulator from his mouth. He floated on his back, enjoying the warmth of the sun on his face. Troy let it bake him. What a wild, almost deadly experience he thought. Was it a dream . . . or was it real? It seemed that the two were rapidly merging. In his mind, it was getting difficult to explain everything as either a hallucination or a dream. Could Silke be right? Did the paranormal or supernatural exist . . . and was he involved in it?

Spider popped to the surface followed by Elle. The boat was several hundred feet away. Marader yelled, then waved at Denny. He started the engine, reeled in the dive markers, and then headed in their direction. "What the hell happened?" Marader asked.

"You wouldn't believe me if I told you," Troy said.

"You must have been narked. It can happen at thirty feet, especially under the conditions you dove. Man, you fought like a madman," Tom said anxiously.

"I rarely get narked. I tell you—"

"Hey, your lips are blue! Damn! Let me see your fingertips," Marader demanded. Troy raised them. The tips were tinged with blue. "Damn! Damn! Damn! I'm sorry, Troy, you got a bad tank of air. Shit!"

Troy stared at his hands, then knew that Marader was right; yet, part of him knew he hadn't imagined everything. He was unsure of the skeleton and even Elle's attack, but Troy was positive he'd been there before . . . in his dreams. The nightmares had taken him to Cemetery Ridge and the town of Wreythville prior to the building of South Holston Lake Dam. What did it all mean?

Elle swam close and asked, "Troy, are you all right?"

"I'm fine now. Did I strike you?" he asked. The boat slowly approached. Denny circled them.

As Elle spoke, Troy noticed a bruise on her right cheek. "Yeah, but it's all right. You were acting real strange and I reached out to touch you and wham! But seriously, it's all right. I'll let you make it up to me." She smiled wide as if anticipating what it would take to make amends, then stuck her tongue out at him. Troy shook his head.

Denny eased the Renken to a halt nearby and cut the motor. They converged on the boat. Spider tossed his tank onto the back and it landed with a heavy thunk. His mask followed, then he crawled onto the ski platform. Denny helped him up. "You guys were down there a long time. I thought this was going to be a short dive. I almost finished all the beer," he said with a smile.

Marader helped Elle remove her scuba tank and then

178

helped her board. She turned and gave him a searing look that said to keep his hands to himself. Marader shrugged and said, "Troy had a bad tank of air which caused some problems." Denny looked concerned.

"Been one helluva day," Spider said. He reached for a towel, then spat over the edge. Elle flipped on the radio and then began drying off. Soon she was combing her hair as she watched Troy.

Troy undid his weights, then slipped out of his BC. Hanging onto the edge, he was the last to undress. "How do you feel?" Denny asked.

"Like I could just hang out for a while." Troy handed Marader his gear. Tom strapped down the final tank, then inspected them before climbing inside the boat. He headed for the cooler.

Troy dragged himself onto the platform and just laid there for a moment. "Did you find what you were looking for?" Denny asked.

Troy sat up and removed his fins. "Yeah, sort of. Actually, I'm not sure." He even sounded confused to himself. "I have to think about what happened. Something really strange is going on around here, and I swear I'm gonna find out what it is." Troy slammed his fins into the bag. "I'm gettin' pissed off." He rubbed his eyes. Troy felt as if he'd been dragged by wild horses.

"Pissed off about what?" Denny asked innocently.

Troy hefted the sack and shoved it into the boat. It landed heavily on the floor. "Late flights, weird aunts, bitchy nursemaids, wild wolves, old flames, disappearing bodies, and goddamned dreams," he said all in one breath. Nobody said anything as he collapsed on the back bench. All his muscles ached and the injuries throbbed with the rhythm of a bass drum.

Spider tossed him a towel. "We're glad you're here," he said without changing expression.

"Dillon was right," Troy muttered. Everyone stared at

him, but he didn't say anything else.

"Want something to drink?" Elle asked. She looked concerned.

"How about a soda?"

"Grape?"

"That'll do." She tossed it to him. He popped the top, put on his sunglasses, and leaned back.

Marader moved into the driver's seat and started the engine. "Ready to head back?"

"Fine by me. I'd prefer to go cruising another time," Troy said. Judging by the sky, Troy guessed they only had a couple of hours of sunlight left. "The guys might be arriving soon. I'm ready to see Denny's videotape."

"Oh shoot, I forgot," Denny said.

"You didn't," Troy responded venomously.

"You're right," Denny said with a smile. "I didn't forget. It's in the car. Honest. You had a sense of humor once." Denny wiped his forehead as if he had just escaped a beating.

"It either got knocked out of me in a car crash, grotesqued out in a morgue, or scared out of me at the bottom of the lake," Troy said in a monotone. He wished he were in the comfort of the sportswriters' box at Arlington Stadium. Nothing seemed to be headed in a straight direction and the clues were wild, sometimes mind-staggering.

"I warn you, the tape is not a positive, upbeat experience," Denny said. Spider nodded. "In fact it can be rather gruesome at times, and I'm not talking about Marader's skiing." He took off his glasses, examined them, then began to wipe them clean. Denny's expression was somber.

Marader put the throttle in gear and they slowly headed off. "If you like a little gore and pale, bloated bodies, you'll love it," Tom tried to joke, but his voice was flat. Troy noticed for the first time that the experience had scared them. He would have never known from Spider's stoic mask, but he could read it on Marader and Rentzel. Elle moved back and sat next to Troy. "Let me see your head," she told him. He started to say no, but one look at her made him change his mind. She was truly beautiful, he thought, then wondered if she might be as deadly.

Troy flinched. "I really don't need a babysitter."

"I know you don't, but you do need someone to keep you out of trouble." She gingerly touched his wound, then wiped it with a towel. He winced. "Sorry." Elle dabbed more gel on it. "Clean it with hydrogen peroxide when we get back."

"Thanks." Troy noticed how quiet everyone was. Troy felt a wrongness in the air and wondered if anyone else did. How could they not?

Troy surveyed the magnificent surroundings of God's Country. The Appalachians stretched out like an earthen wall built by giants. The white sun had begun to take on color as it started to slip towards the horizon where later it would appear to set behind Holston Dam. Several fluffy clouds lazed in the sky.

Troy shook his head as he contemplated the last two days. All around him the lake was placid, looking like a seamless pane of glass. Not a breath of breeze stirred. All was at peace. No wonder one could get lulled into a feeling of centered serenity. Nothing *appeared* wrong. His friends couldn't feel the wrongness because their eyes overrode their senses . . . except maybe Spider. He had always danced to the beat of a different drummer. Still, Spider and the others hadn't experienced his dreams — his nightmares. Troy slammed a hand onto the seat.

"Want to talk about it?" Elle asked.

"Not really. It wouldn't make sense." Suddenly, he wanted to talk with Silke. She would understand. Troy closed his eyes and saw her face. Silke's amber eyes were warm and her smile touched him deeply, bringing a rejuvenation he didn't think was possible. In his mind, Troy found himself running his hands through her long hair, then kissing her. Yes, he would call her when they reached the dock.

They passed under the 421 bridge with a hollow roar. Clacking like stuttered metallic steps, cars drove by overhead. Then they were in the open air once more. Usually, Troy thought, the wind blew his cares away, but not this time.

Dillon had disappeared because he had discovered something . . . something sinister. First, they found Traylor's body dumped in the lake and nearly drained of blood. Then they found coffins, albeit empty ones. All this happened on Cemetery Ridge, the place where all of Troy's nightmares began and often ended. Somehow it all had to be connected with the town that was buried under a couple of hundred feet of water over forty years ago. That seemed to be obvious. It was the links that were invisible.

How was it all connected? Why didn't the TVA find the coffins and move them like they were supposed to? Wait, didn't Aunt Jada see a dead friend alive in Bristol — a friend and former lover who had died working on the Holston Dam project? Was that his next lead? Should he check out the TVA project and see what was involved in the construction and what happened to Wreythville? The TVA's library was in Knoxville just a couple of hours away. He wondered if there were any inhabitants left alive.

Troy had a feeling there was more, much more. People were disappearing in the city and on the lake. Damn, people were being removed from morgues and graveyards . . . just like on Cemetery Ridge. Every time a body was stolen someone had died. Had Dillon made the connection?

Then there was the jewelry box that Marader hoarded as if it were made of gold and diamonds. What other pieces of the puzzle were missing? Troy hoped Dillon would be able to tell him when—not if—he found him. In his heart, he still felt Dillon was alive.

"Yo, boys and girls, we are here," Marader said, pulling Troy from his thoughts. "We have a crew awaiting our arrival. I see Doc Curran, Beck the J-Man, Aaron and Peter Ackles. I don't see Jambo—he's probably still dozing. Hey, the preacher man is here." He stopped as if dumbfounded for a moment, "There's smoke rising. They actually started the grill. I don't believe it. J-Man must have done it. Hey, I see three women—Heidi, Sandy, and who's that with her arm in a sling?"

Troy sat up and peered into the sun. He immediately recognized the slim young woman who waved at him. "I don't believe it. It's Silke."

"One tough lady," Spider said. "She's supposed to be in the hospital."

"She's one fine-looking female," Marader said as he slowed the boat. They could hear music from the dock. "Yeah, she belongs in a bed, but not a hospital bed."

"Marader, you're disgusting," Denny told him. Tom gave him a wide smile.

They eased into the slip. J-Man and Knives slowed the boat and helped guide them in. Denny tossed Peter a rope. "Troy, my man, let's party!" said the tall, stout man holding beers in each of his hairy fists. His orange cap was on backwards. Jay "J-Man" Beck's shirt read "CO ME DE" while arrows pointed out from the words in every direction. He grabbed both bottle necks in one hand and shook Troy's hand with the other. As he did so, J-Man helped Troy out of the boat. His shoulder complained.

"Dr. Knives, you've grown a moustache," Troy said

with surprise to the second man. Knives was tall and lean with dirty blond hair, a thin angular face, and blue eyes. Marader climbed out of the boat and past Troy. Tom carried the bundled jewelry box. He went inside.

Knives laughed. "I needed something to make me look older. I think some of my patients were a bit concerned because I looked so young. Troy, it's good to see you again." Dr. Stephen "Knives" Curran patted him on the back.

"I'm glad you could make it," Troy said. He reached out an open arm to Silke and she slid into it. Her gentle hug felt like a warm and comfortable blanket. Troy squeezed back and kissed her. "Wonderful to see you," he whispered. Elle watched the action and stiffened. She followed Marader inside.

Knives's smile all but danced as he watched the two hug. "Well, I wouldn't have wanted to miss such a gathering. I don't have surgery until tomorrow afternoon and I can't turn down a free flight in the J-copter. Hey, you two make a fine couple, but you both look like you need some medical attention."

"I wanted to make an impression on Troy so I totaled my mother's Landrover," Silke said with a laugh that wiped away most of Troy's worries. "How was the dive?"

Spider answered first. "A rough one, first Troy had too much carbon monoxide in his tank, then he got narked."

Silke eyes flashed to met Troy's. "Oh no!"

Knives's face showed concern. "How do you feel?"

"Fine."

"Don't drink any alcohol."

"I don't plan to."

"The steaks smell good," Denny said as he and Spider finished unloading the boat. They stacked the tanks up along the wall. The towels were hung along several hooks.

Pete Ackles, looking a bit distanced, snuffed his cigarette and stuck out his hand. "Long time no see, stranger." Pete seemed to talk with a catch in his voice as if he weren't sure of what he was going to say. He wore a white shirt with a dragon riding a surfboard.

"How's the custom T-shirt business?"

"It pays the bills, and I can work for myself." Pete smiled shyly.

"The party is moving upstairs to the balcony," called a deep voice. Troy would have recognized Bob St. Martin's baritone anywhere, anyplace.

"Yeah, y'all come up," Jambo said, leaning over the railing. He held a pool cue.

Most of the crowd headed upstairs. "I'll be up in a minute. I've got to get the videotape," Denny said. He walked out toward his car.

"If you girls want, you can take off now," Marader called from the store. Moments later, Sandy and Elle departed. Elle gave Troy a long look over her shoulder as she left. Her eyes seemed to burn holes through him.

"She's very attractive," Silke said, "and attracted to you. I wish I could have been that brazen."

"You probably were and I just didn't notice it because you were my best friend's sister," Troy said, then he kissed her. He was careful not to hold her too tightly, but her lips parted and she intensified the kiss. With her good arm, she squeezed him. Troy broke it off before he began breathing too hard.

"Yeah, I'm glad to see you too," Troy told her. "How'd you get released from the hospital so soon?"

"I felt the hot breath of another woman on your neck," she replied with a smile.

"Seriously."

"I heal quickly. The doctor was amazed. It almost made him a believer in holistic healing. My aunt has such a marvelous touch. I almost feel normal, although I don't look it."

"And your concussion?" He gingerly touched her head.

"Oh, my vision's still a little blurry. I got Bob to pick me up. He's such a sweetheart." She smiled slightly then said, "He talked my ear off."

Troy kissed her again. After all that had happened to him today, he needed her touch. With Silke in his arm, Troy could pretend everything was all right . . . for the moment.

"You at least ought to step around the corner," Denny said as he passed.

"Are these free kisses?" Marader asked as he stepped out of the store. Silke shook her head. "Oh well." He plugged in several bug zappers. Their lights were almost invisible in the sunlight. "See y'all upstairs."

"Hey Troy!" Spider called. "When you get a change of clothes, will you get mine from the front seat?"

"Sure," Troy responded. He quickly kissed Silke on the forehead and said, "Looks like we'll have to finish this discussion later."

She pouted. "And I wanted to hear how your day went."

"You will. It hasn't been pleasant, but it has been exciting." He kissed her lightly then headed out to the car. As Troy walked along the bridge, he heard the music grow louder. Despite his joy at seeing Silke again, there was too much on his mind to be festive—too much had happened. He could almost feel the emerald eyes of his dream wraith touch him. Troy shook it off.

He opened the door and reached inside. Gathering up his clothes as well as Spider's, he crawled out of the car. As he turned, she was in his arms. Her dark, fragrant hair flew across his face. Green eyes sparkled, then she passionately kissed him. Troy was too surprised to move. For a moment, he once again confused Elle with his vision.

She stuffed a piece of paper into the pocket of the pants he held. "I haven't given up on you. My number is on it. Who knows, I may be able to tell you something about Dillon that might be of help." Before Troy could respond, she slipped from his arms. With a saucy smile that spoke of the many delights she could inflict, she sashayed up the road to where her car awaited. Troy couldn't shake the feeling that he'd just held a succubus in his arms.

Regaining his composure, Troy shut the door and headed inside. He quickly changed clothes in the downstairs bathroom, then walked up the outside steps. He heard the tapping of billiard balls as he ascended.

Troy almost bumped into Bob St. Martin as he topped the stairway. Bob nearly burned him with a candle. "Playing the acolyte?" Troy asked him.

Bob's high-pitched laugh was rapid and almost wheezing. His laughter shook his whole body like Santa Claus. His dark-rimmed glasses slipped down to the end of his wide nose. "Nay, nay, I say nay. Marader says these candles help keep away the mosquitoes. I claim that the smoke Jay puts out when he cooks will keep them away." J-Man waved a spatula at them.

The only other person on the deck was Jambo. He was swinging in a hammock. It hung just inches above the floor. Several empty bottles were lined up in a row. Bob followed Troy's gaze. "Selling cars must be an exhausting occupation," Bob said, almost tittering. He set the candles along the railing.

"How are the studies?" Troy asked.

"I'm through. All I need to complete is my internship and an initiation," Bob replied.

"From computer wiz to spiritual guru," Troy joked.

"Troy, please, this is serious stuff."

"I know, I'm sorry. I guess I was nervous about asking

187

you this next question."

"That doesn't sound like you," Bob said, his dark eyes curious.

"You haven't heard the question." Troy drew a breath and said, "Would the seminary have any information pertaining to the undead, evil spirits, Satan worshippers, or the like?"

Bob's mouth almost hit the floor. "Wh-wh-why? For heaven's sake, why, Troy? What do you need that for?" He removed his glasses and wiped them clean. His hands were flighty and looking for something to do.

"I'm not sure. An ounce of prevention, I guess. Something strange is happening in this area and it app—" He almost choked on the next few words. "Appears to involve the supernatural."

"I think the strain of the day has strained your brain," Jambo's deep voice rumbled.

Troy ignored him. "Would it bother you to look?"

"Well, I don't know. I'll have to think about it. We'll talk more later," Bob said, walking off and shaking his head.

"That blew his mind," J-Man said. His meaty hands danced over the grill as he turned over the steaks. The flames jumped high and singed his hairy paws. Dancing back, he doused the flames with water from a spray bottle. Jay Beck wore a grin. He wiped the sweat from his brow, leaving a black greasy spot across his forehead. His pale skin was pink from the heat.

"Why the question?" J-Man asked.

"Missing bodies, floating coffins . . . I'll try and explain after I've seen the videotape of last week's Cemetery Ridge visit."

"Fair enough."

"What's wrong with Bob?" Silke asked as she walked onto the balcony.

Troy was amazed at how beautiful she still was despite

the bruises from yesterday's accident. He shook his head—no, he was astounded she was even on her feet.

Silke touched his arm. "You okay? You looked at me like you saw a ghost."

"I'm sorry. I was telling myself how amazing it is that you're even here. When I remember the state you were in when I found you in the jeep just yesterday, I—"

"Hush," Silke told him, then kissed him on the cheek. "Jay, can you and Jamie handle the steaks by yourself?"

"No problem."

"I'm taking Troy inside."

"You'd be better off taking him down to the docks where y'all can be alone."

"That's for dessert, when the moon's out." Silke grabbed him by the arm and led him inside.

Troy stopped at the door. Almost all the gang was here, except for Bill Glazier who'd gotten married young, then joined the police force. Of course, Dillon was missing too. Troy cursed under his breath damning the absence of their two best investigators. With all that was going on, he could sure use their keen minds.

He tried to shrug it off. Marader who had a pool cue in one arm and Heidi in the other had teamed with Denny to play the Ackles brothers. The pool table sat near the center of the room with a stained-glass lamp hanging above. To the right of the table was a couch and end table where Bob and Spider sat. The two appeared to be having a heated discussion. Beyond them was a door which exited to the balcony.

To the left was Marader's bed, television, and chest of drawers. Knives was fumbling through a stack of CDs on the queen-sized mattress. He finally found what he was looking for, stood up, and moved over to the stereo which sat on top of the dresser beyond the chest of drawers. Speakers were in all four corners. On the far side of the table, opposite Troy, was a cabinet filled with rifles and guns. Several knives hung on the wall. Left of it was the entrance to the bathroom and a closet.

"What are we having for dinner besides steaks?" Pete asked.

"Potatoes are in the oven and we'll nuke some peas," Denny replied. He sunk the five ball in the corner pocket.

Pete and Aaron Ackles nodded simultaneously. The two weren't twins, but looked a lot alike. Pete was taller and leaner with shaggy blond hair. He had a long nose and a pointed chin which looked as if it had grown from too much stroking during deep thought. Pete missed an easy shot and Aaron lightly smacked him on the back. As usual, Aaron was demonstrative and Pete's expression rarely changed.

Aaron looked up, gave Troy a smile, and said, "You play the winner?" Troy thought that Aaron and Pete had gone in opposite directions. Aaron was shorter, stockier, and had cropped brown hair that didn't even touch his ears. Pete ran a T-shirt shop in the mall while Aaron was an accountant. That had never made sense to him.

"No, thanks," Troy finally said. "I've had enough excitement for one day." Marader belched in agreement. Heidi gave him a dirty look.

"Nice place Tom has here," Silke said. "Pool table in the bedroom, upstairs/downstairs bathrooms, a kitchen and store downstairs, and water and mountains all around. I'm jealous." She smiled, then pulled Troy into a chair immediately to the left of the balcony exit. "I'll bet it's peaceful when the music's off."

Troy didn't say anything. She gently touched his face. "What are you thinking about?"

"What an unusual group of characters are here. I mean, look: Knives is a surgeon, Marader runs a boat dock, Denny owns a construction company, Aaron's an accountant — which makes absolutely no sense to me, at least the other guys fit their professions." Silke laughed.

He continued. "Pete runs a make-your-own T-shirt shop, Spider's a part-time architect, full-time social worker, Bill's going to be a minister, Jambo sells cars, and J-Man flies a helicopter for coal company executives. Then Dillon and I are journalists. Or, at least, he is, I'm a sports writer. We're all the best of friends, in many ways brothers — Hey, you're the psychologist, please explain all of this to me."

"Well, to start with, you all have very strong personalities. Still, you've found a way to blend. Probably because you're all comfortable with who you are and don't care what others think. Even when you guys were young, if somebody didn't want to do something, that was fine. There was no peer pressure between y'all when you were kids, that's why I enjoyed being around you, as well as being attracted to you.

"Everyone could be who they wanted to be, not who someone else expected them to be," she continued. "If they fit in, fine; if they didn't, that person didn't stick around. A great amount of loyalty was founded a long time ago as well as genuine interests in each other. And you do share several interest, love of the outdoors and several sports as well as gaming and needling each other. You complement each other." Troy leaned back as if to examine her. "Well, that's what Dillon always said and I think he was right," she added. "Did you discover anything today?"

"You know those dreams?" Troy began. Silke nodded.

"So how's the return visit to Bristol going?" Knives interrupted. His blue eyes showed a trace of inebriation.

"Do you really want to know?"

"Of course. Jambo told me you're looking for Dillon, thinking that something underhanded has happened to him. So what's up?"

"Well," Troy hesitated. "Silke picked me up at the airport and dragged me off to meet her crazy Aunt Jada—"

"Oh yeah, Dillon introduced me to her once." He rolled his eyes.

Troy laughed. "She claims that some evil, a darkness, is terrorizing Bristol. She told us she saw a man who'd been dead for forty years walking the streets of Bristol." Knives gave a quick laugh. Troy heard Bill guffaw. The game of billiards had stopped.

"Upon leaving her house, we were attacked by wolves and wrecked the jeep. From what Bill Glazier and a sheriff have said, there's been lots of wolf attacks lately."

"There have been," Denny confirmed. "One of my watchmen on a worksite was attacked not far from here."

"The next morning, today, I awoke in a hospital. I was released and Spider and Jambo gave me a tour of the city. We stopped at the police station to see Bill who took us to the morgue. He's investigating the grave robbery at King College Cemetery." His voice grew grave. "Both the doctor and his assistant had been slaughtered, torn apart. The place was a bloodbath." Several mouths opened at once, but no one spoke. A grim silence gripped them before Troy continued.

"Someone had stolen the caretaker's body, the guy who'd been killed the previous night. Traylor's body was also stolen from there. The odd thing is that it looked like the caretaker clawed his way out of his drawer in the body vault." Troy turned and saw Jambo standing in the doorway.

Jambo spoke up, "It was horrible, Stephen. We stopped for a few beers to try and forget the scene. Then, we stopped at the cemetery. Troy has set up an appointment with the night watchman tomorrow. What fun."

"A lot of missing bodies, aren't there?" Knives said to no one in particular.

"Yes, and it seems to have started about the time the coffins were found floating around Cemetery Ridge. Dillon thought so too. That's why I want to see the tape. It might have some clues. I think the island is the key."

"No one's heard from Dillon?"

"Marader was the last, and that was nearly five days ago."

Wreck popped his head in through the door. "The steaks are done, let's eat."

Almost everyone headed for the balcony. Denny went downstairs along with Heidi. Knives waited, sensing more. "Go on. There's something else isn't there?" Troy hesitated. "Hey, I'm your family doctor, if you can't tell me, who can you tell?"

Troy nodded. Spider stopped to listen. "I've been having strange dreams, both while awake and asleep."

"Could be stress."

Troy gave him an exasperated look. "I saw Cemetery Ridge the way it was before it was covered in water. I kept hearing machinery in the background."

Silke gasped. "Keep going," she said.

"Did the machinery sound like construction equipment?" Spider asked.

Troy nodded. Knives gave them odd looks all around. Troy continued. "In all of my dreams it's been daytime. The first time, something rose from the dead in broad daylight. Then it exhumed a body which grew younger. She was beautiful; she looked a lot like Elle. And this was before I'd ever met her. The lady in the vision kept calling me, telling me to join Dillon. I found myself in a grave with dirt piling up."

"Could it be the accident?" Knives asked.

"I've had similar dreams," Silke said.

"When I was underwater, when Marader said I was narked, I found part of the railing around the graveyard. Next to it, I think I found a coffin. Then it all gets questionable. I thought a skeleton reached out and tried to drag me in. That's when I went crazy."

"That explains it," Spider said simply. He didn't express any shock or disbelief.

"Sounds like we need to dive in the area again, maybe visit Wreythville," Knives said.

"You believe me?" Troy said incredulously.

"I didn't say that. I'd like to help you find Dillon . . . and to tell the truth, I've seen several things in the hospital and the operating room that I can't explain. Let's say I'm open-minded."

"One other thing," Troy said. "Watch Marader and that jewelry box you found. Ask to see it, then tell him you want to borrow it for a few days. See what happens." Spider nodded in agreement.

"I'll do it."

"Folks, the steaks are either gonna burn or get cold. Come and get it," J-Man called out.

They all looked at each other. No one really felt like eating, but they joined the party on the balcony anyway.

Chapter Nine
Replay

"Now that was a good meal," J-Man said as he rubbed his stomach. He leaned back in his chair as if to survey everyone. A breeze coasted over them and the coals still flared, like embers in a blacksmith's kiln.

"Yes, it was," Silke agreed. She leaned against Troy who sat next to her on the bench.

Troy had been quiet for a while, listening to his friends chatter and watching the day come to an end. The shadows arrived first, stretching out over the lake, then the brilliance of the day dimmed and the color of the sky changed. Coolness was only a whisper in the air. Troy thought that much had changed in his friends' lives, but they still seemed to be the same people that he'd always known.

"A toast!" Troy proclaimed. Everyone looked at him. He raised his glass. "To the best friends anyone could ever ask for."

"Here, here!" several of them cried.

"To brothers!" J-Man said. They drank again.

"To finding Dillon," Knives said more quietly. The enthusiasm died, but they all still took a swig of beer.

"When do we get to see the videotape?" Silke said, breaking the uncomfortable silence. She stared into Troy's eyes and wondered what he was thinking.

"You may not want to see it, Silke. It gets pretty gory when we find the body. I got sick and Jay had to tape."

195

Denny said.

"Thanks for the warning, but Dillon's on that tape and there may be a clue," Silke told him.

"Tape? What tape?" Aaron asked. He was finishing off a second helping of potatoes and peas.

"Troy wants to see the video we made last week when we found Traylor," Denny told him.

"Oh, I haven't seen it. Pete told me about it. Gruesome stuff."

"I don't particularly want to see it again. Once was enough," Jambo said as he lit his pipe. He puffed a few times and smoke curled away.

"I'll go set up the VCR," Denny said. He got up, dropped his plate and scraps in the trash, and then went inside.

"Well, Mr. Beck." Troy began, "business must be going well for you to move out onto the lake."

"I must confess I told these guys a small lie. Actually, I didn't lie, I just told them I was moving out here. I'm housesitting," J-Man finally said. "I help keep the place up and perform security functions."

"Sounds like a nice setup," Troy said.

"You and Silke should come visit before y'all go home," he offered.

"I think we can arrange it," Silke said, glancing at Troy, "when we're not wandering through graveyards above or below water."

"Troy, would you like to dive Wreythville tomorrow?" Marader asked.

Rolling his head back as he answered, Troy said, "I don't really know what I want to do. I'm tired. I'll decide tomorrow."

"How come no wives are present?" Silke asked.

"They don't approve of gambling," Aaron responded.

"They don't approve of some of my friends," Bob said. "The old oil and water routine." He shrugged.

"We invited Karen, but she said since Denny's out with the boys, she's taking the night to go out with the girls," Pete told them. "Truthfully, she just doesn't get along with Marader.

"Don't you feel honored?" Knives asked Silke.

"Not really, this is sort of old hat for me. Remember, I grew up with it."

"Hey, Marader," Knives called, "Can I take a look at that jewelry box I found?"

Marader's nostrils flared and he said a bit harshly, "I just locked it up. It hasn't changed."

Knives was taken aback. He looked over to Troy who nodded. Knives decided to press the issue. "Now Tom, I found it and Dillon left it with you for safe keeping, not—"

"VCR is ready," Denny called.

"Maybe later," Marader said. "Now, we'll need to take some of these chairs inside."

"Now Tom. I'll check it out during the video," Knives said sternly. Marader began to say something, then went inside.

"Cattle time," J-Man told them. Knives and Troy exchanged worried glances. Spider nodded.

They all cleaned up, then ambled inside. The pool table had been moved to the far side of the room. On it sat the television set and the VCR. They all gathered around it. Marader dumped the jewelry box in Knives's lap, then sat down. As he sulked, his eyes never left Knives or the jewelry box.

Heidi turned off the overhead light, then climbed onto the bed with Tom. He didn't seem to notice her. In the dim light, Tom still watched Knives handle the box. Some light came in through the window from the candles flickering outside, and the bug zappers.

Denny punched a button on the remote and the television came on. He repeated the motion and the VCR kicked in. Music came over the speakers mixed with the roar of the wind and the whine of the motor. A picture came on the screen. The camera panned the lake, following the streaks of light that raced across the water and scoured the surface. Pinpoints sparkled, then the picture shifted to the dark mountains. "This is the place," Denny's voice began, straining to be heard over the music and motor, "South Holston Lake and the time is ripe for another adventure with the Immortals of Skiing. Today's fool is Tom Marader."

The camera moved to Marader who had a silly grin on his face. One couldn't tell if he were awake or asleep behind the dark sunglasses. He flipped them a bird.

"Can we fast-forward?" J-Man asked. "Troy wants to see us find Traylor's corpse and search the island, not watch Marader ham it up."

"Yeah, I've seen Marader ski enough times already," Bob chimed.

"But guys, you're missing history in the making," Marader defended himself.

"Go ahead Denny. Forward to just before you see the coffins," Troy suggested. The screen raced through the images. The water foamed, then Marader rose from the water. He tugged on his shorts, then began zigzagging back and forth, then he tried to dip his elbow in the water. The camera panned across the water and part of the dusty red shoreline. The fast-forwarding stopped and Denny's voice faded. ". . . make a great addition to the video . . . Marader skis graveyard." Troy recognized the shoreline where they'd been today.

There was superfluous bantering as the camera stayed on Marader, then the camera was suddenly jerked from watching Marader and panned across the sky. "Where?" Denny's voice asked. The camera zipped by the rising moon, then flashed back to the red orb. It hovered just above the mountains and highlighted the island. Specks of moonlight sputtered across the surface as if fire wavered on the water.

Suddenly much of the light disappeared and something rose from the island. A dark shape seemed to blink several times, then was gone.

"Hold it," Troy asked. The picture froze.

"We didn't know what it was," Denny said.

"It looked like a huge bat to me, maybe several huge bats," J-Man recalled.

"Can we see it again?" Troy asked. Denny reversed it and they saw it again. It was hard to tell, but there was more than one thing leaving the island.

"They would have to have been prehistoric bats. Those were large shadows," Silke said. She shivered.

"Maybe it was Batman," Jambo stated ominously. Spider gave him a dirty look.

"Maybe something just flew by instead of leaving the island," Pete suggested.

"No, it was flying up, I swear," J-Man told them.

"I wonder what the police thought?" Knives asked aloud.

"Not that shadows killed John Traylor, that's for sure," Bob said. "They probably didn't notice it. I didn't when I watched this. Seriously folks, I don't understand why Dillon and Troy are looking for some fantastic story. It was probably a plain and simple murder. There were probably just two boats."

"Bob, I'm just trying to find Dillon. I don't know what's going on, but I'm trying to be open-minded. Please try the same. Maybe your beliefs don't cover everything thing that's possible," Troy told him.

Bob opened his mouth to retort when Spider spoke, "Bob, let him be. It's been a strange day, okay?" Bob nodded.

Denny let the tape continue to roll. The boat and the camera began to weave. A confused look appeared on

Marader's face. Suddenly, the camera view went wild and they could hear bumping and cursing. The screen went dark, then the camera was picked up. "Jay!!" Denny's voice admonished. The lights flickered, then the music died.

"We're dodging coffins, there were six," J-Man told Troy.

"Another one ahead," Dillon said on tape.

"What is this, a minefield?" Jay's voice asked. The viewer could make out a couple of dark shapes in the water. Marader flipped them off again. For a moment, it seemed he didn't notice, then he began an evasive maneuver. His eyes widened, then narrowed.

"Marader's flipping you off," Denny's voice said.

"Shit! There's a third one," Jay's voice screamed and the picture bounced all over.

"This is great stuff," Denny's voice told the viewers.

On screen, several of the guys mused over what the objects were. Speaking over the tape, Denny said to the quiet audience, "This is my favorite part."

"Me too," Knives added.

On the screen, Marader motioned that he wanted to go faster. Suddenly, his eyes widened and he seemed to launch. He somersaulted as water flew about. The ski stopped immediately as if stuck in something. Marader buried a shoulder and went underwater. Several in the room applauded. "I've got it on viddy," the narrator told the boat crew. "I hope he's all right." The view stayed on Marader's floating body, then it zoomed in.

"See the flash of flesh next to him?" Knives pointed out. "Dillon noticed it first. I couldn't believe it." The screen went blank. Denny put it on hold.

"Is that it?" Troy sounded disappointed.

"No, there's more," Denny promised. "Everyone's dinner settled?"

"I think I'll step out," Heidi said as she climbed off the

bed.

"I'll join you. I could use a smoke break and have seen enough gore for one day," Jambo said.

"I could use a smoke too," Pete agreed and the trio departed.

"This is where it gets interesting," Knives said. "Tom, here." Knives tossed him the jewelry box. Marader's jaw dropped open as it sailed through the air. He caught it like an egg, wrapped it in a sheet, and then slipped it under the bed.

"At least we see something besides Marader's ham shots," Aaron joined in.

"It wasn't all that interesting," Spider said in a grave voice that was hardly more than a whisper, "more like morbidly fascinating."

"Denny, please continue," Troy requested.

The blackness disappeared and the scene moved from the edge of the boat to the pallid mass of flesh which floated in the water. To Troy, it looked like something that had lived in the depths of the ocean where the sun's light never shone.

"Tom hit that?" Spider's voice was incredulous.

"I've never heard of anyone hitting a corpse while skiing. Another first for Marader," J-Man's voice strained for joviality, but failed, his comment falling flat. There was silence. Troy could tell just by watching that his friends were shaken by the incident.

Bob turned to J-Man and said, "You're a heartless man, Jay Beck."

"Hey, excuse me for living. I was just trying to loosen everyone up so no one would be hysterical," J-Man responded. His expression defied Bob to say anything else.

The picture moved to Marader. Hunched over, he sat in the back seat with a towel in his lap. He appeared to be shaking. "Shouldn't we pull this guy out and see if he's alive?" Denny asked. His voice cracked. Troy looked

201

over at Denny — his face had grown somber as if he were remembering how he felt.

Bob spoke over Knives's reply. "I'm sorry, Jay. I wasn't there and I didn't intend for you to take it that seriously. Mea culpa."

J-Man smiled. "It's okay."

On the screen, Marader held his face in his hands, "Oh man, I thought the Creature from the Black Lagoon or something had me. Jay, what in the hell were you doing?"

"I was dodging debris, tree limbs, crates, or something," the boat driver replied. "They were all over the place. I'm sorry. God, I hope I didn't run over any bodies!"

"You could have slowed down, *dammit!*" Marader accused. He looked wildly about. "Oh God!" Standing up, he was white and shaking. "I hit a dead man. I can't —"

Knives struck him solidly across the face. "Sit," he commanded.

Marader called over to Knives who had a smile on his face. "You enjoyed that, didn't you?" Knives nodded. "Bastard."

On the tape, Knives was being Dr. Stephen Curran. "How're your legs?"

"Stiff," Marader replied. Knives began poking, prodding, and twisting. "My muscles and joints are fine."

"Back?"

"Same."

Dillon's voice was in the background. "Spider, you okay? You need a shot of whiskey? You look pale."

"I'll be okay."

Knives continued probing. "Head?"

"Fine. Why?"

"Vision?"

"Clear. I hit so hard it knocked the buzz out of me."

"Stephen, of course he's fine," J-Man interrupted.

"Marader landed on his head, the hardest part of his body."

"I need a beer," Marader told Knives. "Shit," he said, then collapsed on the back of the boat.

"We should take him back to camp," Knives suggested.

"I'll be fine," Marader moaned.

Denny interrupted the audio and said to everyone, "See, he is a tough guy." The forced smile didn't touch his eyes. Troy was watching everyone's reaction. He hadn't thought about how the evening had touched them because he hadn't been there. The film obviously disturbed Denny and possibly Marader. He couldn't tell with Spider. After seeing the morgue, Troy understood their feelings — he wouldn't have wanted to replay the grizzly scene. He wondered if he was doing the right thing.

"Next time," Marader told J-Man who had slumped in his chair, I'll drive." Jay spread his hands wide in a "that's fine" gesture.

"Guys," Troy said, "if you don't want to watch this . . . and it doesn't appear pleasant, I can watch it by myself."

"Doesn't bother me," Knives said. J-Man agreed. Spider was expressionless, but didn't look at Troy.

"I'll survive," Denny told Troy.

"Let's check out the corpse," Dillon said on the tape as it continued.

"Always the investigative newshound." Denny laughed tersely as the camera turned from Marader onto Dillon who was scanning the water with binoculars. "We're here on South Holston Lake investigating a report that corpses are grabbing unwary waterskiers." Troy felt Silke begin to shake then she sniffed. He held her tightly. "Mr. Urich, what do you have to say about this?"

"They're not crates, they're coffins," Dillon replied. The camera wavered, then recovered, zooming in on a geometric shape. The edge of the box protruded from the water.

"Excuse me, can we find my ski before we go fishing for corpses?" Marader suggested. "That baby cost me over four hundred dollars."

"Boy, Marader," Bob said, "you recovered quick."

"A man has to know his priorities," Marader told his friend. The sound of the engine starting came over the speakers.

They recovered the ski and Marader hugged it. "My baby."

J-Man's voice could barely be heard over the engine as it moved slowly forward. "You look like a buzzard."

The camera swung again from Marader to Dillon who was leaning out over the front of the boat. "More like a news hawk," Denny corrected.

Dillon didn't respond and didn't move. Finally he said. "Shut off the engines and grab a paddle." There were flashes of light as he began snapping photos.

"I can't believe I hit a body," Marader's voice said in the background. "I still don't believe it!" Marader yelled as he watched the TV, his voice incredibly loud in the small room.

Troy began to say something, but the tape did it for him. "It's all right. Let it go," Knives said. "He was already dead. You didn't kill him."

"It's a male," Dillon said. Spider handed him a paddle. There was a clunking noise and Dillon, still leaning over the edge, worked his way along the side of the boat and to the back. The camera followed him. Troy guessed he was directing the body towards the rear.

Dillon and Knives climbed onto the ski platform. The camera followed them, then rose, looking down on them and over their shoulders. The two grunted as they heaved

204

the body onto the platform. There was a flash of distorted limbs twisted like pretzels and bluish white flesh. The eyes were stuck open and as wide as saucers. "Oh gawd!" Denny's voice blared in the camera. The screen wobbled, then dropped to the bottom of the boat. The picture sat there for a while.

Troy looked at Denny who was staring out the window.

The voices continued. Knives said, "I'd guess that he's been dead a few hours at most. You can tell by the puffiness of the skin and the fact there's no stiffness in the limbs. See? No rigor mortis." There was a pause. "I wonder why he's so pale."

The camera seemed to be dropped on a seat and someone, Denny, threw up in the background. "Den, I'll take over," J-Man offered. Denny whispered a thanks.

"He hasn't been dead that long. See how the flesh responds to touch?" Knives pointed out by pressing his finger onto the corpse's chest.

"The expression on his face, check out his expression," J-Man said as the camera was moved. "It's shock and surprise."

Once again there was a scene on the tape. The face of the man appeared. The muscles were locked tight. His eyes were wide as if he saw death, scythe in hand, riding towards him on a pale stallion. The mouth was open, still gasping for air. Troy felt like he'd been slammed in the gut; it hardly looked like John Traylor.

"Is his neck broken?" Dillon asked.

"The head wound is the ski—" The corpse's head lolled over and exposed a massive wound on the right side of the neck. The camera shook. Both Dillon and Knives visibly blanched, and so did everyone in the room. Denny coughed and Spider shifted. Aaron whispered something unintelligible. Silke buried her head on Troy's chest. Bob looked away.

Troy didn't. He looked at Spider and they remembered. If Jambo had been present, he might have mentioned the morgue. Neither of them did.

The rip in the corpse's throat looked similar to the attack on the medical examiners. On tape, the torn flesh glistened with dark blood clots that filled the wound. The flesh was mangled, almost appearing to have been chewed. Blood slightly oozed from the rent.

"It looks like an animal attacked him," Dillon said. The camera had grown steady once more. Dillon's face could have been cut from stone it was so rigid.

"Small bite radius," Knives said clinically. Denny could be heard retching once more. No one could understand what Spider was saying to him. Marader had been silent. With the body on its back, Knives supported the head and slowly turned it to the left, meeting no resistance as the head turned a full 180 degrees until it was lying face down on the ski platform. "His neck is broken," Knives stated. "Despite the neck wound, I'd still say someone broke his neck. Someone very, very strong. Look at the bruises under the arms." Knives held them up and they could see the bluish black spots. "And on the back of his neck."

"This place gives me the creeps," J-Man could be heard to say. "I mean, we're near an old graveyard, there're coffins all over, and we find a dead body that looks like it was mauled by a wild beast."

"More like gnawed," Knives corrected.

"Still, this sounds like the beginning to one of those horror flicks," J-Man continued.

Troy mumbled to himself, "You may have been prophetic, my dear friend." His eyes were glued to the screen. He couldn't get the morgue out of his mind. The similarity was as striking as it was ghastly.

"Pardon me, I'm going for air," Bob said.

"How much longer do we have to do this," Marader's

voice came from behind the camera.

"Everyone dies sooner or later," Spider said. "Won't you want your justly deserved attention when you go?"

There was silence. The screen went blank. Then it re-appeared and they were approaching Cemetery Ridge. The moon had risen and now appeared to have been carved from gleaming ivory.

"Hey, wait. What happened after you guys recognized the body?" Troy asked. The frame froze.

"I wanted to call the police," Spider said. "J-Man and Dillon convinced me to keep looking for a while longer. I was so out of it, I'm not sure I knew which way was up."

"Dillon noticed that Traylor wore a sheath on his leg and that the knife was missing," J-Man told him. The replay of the events appeared to have very little effect on him.

"There were fresh cuts below a bandage on his hand," Knives added. Troy gathered that in many senses, it was just another cadaver to Knives — he had to look at things that way to handle his profession.

"We concluded that he had been diving, so we searched for signs of a boat," J-Man continued. "Despite wrapping the body in towels, Denny wouldn't let us carry Traylor in the boat. You know how superstitious Den is. So we tied him to the ski platform."

"Dillon convinced us to check out a coffin or two," Denny reminded them. "That's what's coming up. I wanted to leave. Marader claimed we could make big bucks by airing the tape on 'Geraldo' or 'A Current Affair.' I gave in, but not for that reason. I don't know, I felt we needed to look into it."

Knives tried to lighten things a bit. "Marader's resiliency is amazing, isn't it? If we could just study him and find out what is. . . ."

"The female of the species wouldn't allow that," Silke said. "Can you imagine a test going awry and thousands of Marader clones escaping to terrorize the country side?"

"Now that sounds like a horror flick," J-Man laughed.

"Hey, this isn't fair, it's ten against one," Marader complained. The tension left the room for a while and Troy watched several of his friends smile.

"All you gore lovers, the rest is pretty tame," Knives told the crowd.

"Thank God," Silke muttered.

"Roll tape," Aaron said.

The boat glided alongside one of the floating objects. Except for the section jutting from the water, the coffin was dark. To Troy, it looked more like a crate. There were extra supports on the outside that one didn't find on a coffin. About two-thirds of it was underwater.

An oar poked at it and the coffin shifted almost all the way over before it rolled back. "It's not very water-logged," Spider informed them.

"Is it sealed?" Dillon asked.

The camera was steady on the coffin. "Not too hard," Denny said.

"I don't believe in evil spirits," Spider said. The oar slipped underneath the box and rolled it over. The oblong crate shifted and spun. The dark, open maw spewed water.

From the tape, Troy couldn't tell if it was empty or not. He remembered the skeleton that had grabbed him while under water and shuddered. Silke placed a hand on his cheek but Troy didn't speak.

"I can't tell if it is empty either," Dillon said. "Let's adjust the boat lights and I'll snap a photo with my flash this time." The suggestion was greeted by silence, then the lighting shifted. Again the oar was shoved under the coffin. It didn't roll over.

"Mr. Muscles Marader, give me a hand," Spider

asked. A second oar joined the first. With grunting, the coffin was spun to face them. There was a flash of light. It was empty.

"Nothing moved," Denny said breathlessly.

"Nothing leaped out and grabbed us," J-Man said with a tinge of humor.

"No *Night of the Living Dead,* either," Spider laughed. The whole boat rocked for a moment. The camera jiggled.

"Denny," Troy asked. "Please replay the part where the flash lights the opening."

"Sure." The screen blurred, stopped, then the dueling oars rolled it over. The picture stopped.

Troy stared. Yes, he thought he'd noticed it. Along the edges there were what looked to be fresh grooves and scratches as if something had ripped it open. It hadn't been opened with a shovel, Troy told himself. For a brief moment, his mind flashed back to a dream. The undead leaned over a coffin, there was a tearing sound as if wood were being ripped apart. The woman rose—

"Troy, are you all right?" Silke asked. He nodded. "Are you sure?"

Troy nodded again. "Go ahead." Spider met his eye. Spider hadn't seen the inside of the vault. Desperation had marked the coffins just as it did the drawer.

The play repeated itself until, "Hey, is that a boat I see on shore?" Knives asked. No one answered. "See, just around the right side of the mound." Still no one said anything. Knives sounded exasperated. "Beyond that set of rocks." The camera moved from the water to the island once more. The moon was beginning to take on a silver quality like a newly minted coin caught by the sun's rays.

"I don't see anything," Marader muttered.

"I say we find out," J-Man said and the boat moved forward. The camera stayed on the island as they grew closer, and it loomed larger. It was mostly in shadow. There weren't any trees, just rock.

The picture died and the screen flashed white. The speakers hissed. "End of tape," Denny said. "There's some on the second. It'll be ready in just a minute."

J-Man stood up and walked to the door. "Hey folks, the second reel is beginning. Anybody interested?" Heidi and Bob said they'd return.

"Silke," Troy said, "I'm going to stretch my legs. I'll be right back. Give me a yell." She moved off his lap and he walked outside. Bob and Heidi passed him.

As Troy stepped through the door, the ambiance of evening on the lake kissed him like a long-lost lover. The clouds were bloated, flying castles of color — a mixture of pink, red, and orange. The sky was lavender. All around, echoing across the lake, was the deep-throated burping of bullfrogs. It combined with the chirping of the crickets to create a lazy symphony of nature.

Troy's eyes moved past his friend as he looked at the lake, muted colors from the clouds stretched wide until they reached the shadows of the surrounding mountains. A slight breeze carried the scent of the woods, but it was dry and reminded Troy of past autumns. He also thought the air hinted of skunk. The zap of a bug light brought him back to reality.

Jambo had been watching Troy. Their eyes met and Jambo took a long, slow pull on his pipe. After a moment, he blew smoke rings and said, "Do you really think something sinister is going on?" Troy nodded. "I'm scared. I can't get the scene of the morgue out of my mind. That's why I didn't want to see the tape, it reminds me of the morgue."

"Me too."

"I'm not sure I can sleep tonight," Jambo said. Pete just watched them, absently drawing on a cigarette. Finally, Jambo said, "You're going to find out, aren't you?"

"Going to try, but I don't know what I'm doing. I cover sports, not murders and missing persons. I've only been here a day and a half and I'm sort of at wit's end."

"You're just tired," Jambo said.

"You look dead on your feet," Pete told Troy.

Both Jambo and Troy looked at their friend. Troy said, "Don't say that."

"We're ready," J-Man called to Troy. He went back inside.

The screen showed the island. Dillon was talking. "Has anyone ever been here before?"

"Tom, Spider and I have," Knives said. The island slowly grew larger. The distant boat was becoming more distinct as the moon grew brighter, clearly outlining shadows.

"I have? When? Was I sober?" Marader's voice sounded confused.

"You were life-guarding at Camp Sequoia when the water got real low. We rested here while waterskiing this cove." Marader was silent. "Racquel was with us. It was senior year." Troy felt his gut tighten. This would have been shortly before they broke up.

"Oh yeah, I remember now, but only about a fifth of this was visible. I don't remember it being this rocky. All I really remember was Racquel finding that sapphire ring. That was a piece of work — blazing blue and silver." The cinch grew tighter in Troy's gut. His news sense was working overtime, but would tell him nothing.

They were almost on shore. "We're here," Dillon said. Lights rolled across the water, then crawled over the boat. The shore was illuminated. It looked washed-out, like part of a desert. The camera moved to the boat.

Pulled ashore was a twenty-two-foot craft painted in gradual shades of blue, dark on the bottom and light at the top. The camera did a slow pan back and forth. It moved closer as J-Man guided them nearer. They could see diving gear strewn about the compartment. Towels hung over the windshield. A few clung to the boat and hung in the water. "Nice boat. Bayliners aren't cheap." Knives's whistle carried from the speakers.

"Finder's keepers," J-Man said.

"Slow down," Dillon said. The camera moved to watch him as he climbed on the bow. He landed on shore, spun around, and slowed their landing. Flashlight and camera in hand, Dillon headed toward the other boat.

"Any tracks?" J-Man asked. Dillon shook his head. "Wait up." Jay came into view.

"You know," J-Man interrupted, "just watching this tape reminds me of how eerie that place felt. I could hardly keep my knees from shaking. Dillon was sure cool, though."

Marader climbed out of the boat carrying a rifle. "Hey," he said, "after getting the shit beat out of me a couple of times, I decided to keep one of these babies around just in case." He caught up with Dillon and J-Man. They approached the Bayliner.

The camera jiggled, then moved dramatically and Denny jumped onto shore. A flashlight shone from behind the camera. Knives walked by. "Diggings," he said. The video followed his light as it danced over oblong pits.

"Looks like graves." Marader could barely be heard. His voice cracked.

"About the right size and shape," J-Man's voice carried to Denny. He was once again approaching the boat, keeping the camera focused on the trio.

"That would explain where the coffins came from. Now how and why?" Dillon said.

"Maybe someone pitched a fit and threw them in," Marader said. No one answered.

"I found a small wet suit, pink and turquoise," Knives yelled to them.

Dillon's light flashed over the boat. Silver, black, and red colors jumped forward — blood was spattered over equipment as if someone had tossed a bucketful. Crimson painted the air tanks, weights, mask, fins, and towels. "Not pretty. I wonder if he died here or if he was just gutted here." Pause. "Two sets of dive gear."

"Guys, guess what I found?" Knives yelled.

"More blood," Dillon said. He climbed into the boat.

"Yes, and what else?"

"A knife?"

"Okay." Knives sounded surprised. Dillon was carefully examining the equipment, especially the tanks. "What else?"

"A knife."

"Okay," Knives sounded surprised. "What else?"

"Wine glasses and a bottle." Dillon pointed to the tanks, "They're spent, all four of 'em. Somebody's been diving."

"Last chance," Knives said. "Anything else."

"I have no idea," Dillon said. "A breadbox?" Knives gasped.

J-Man moved from the boat. The camera followed him. Knives held the jewelry box in his hand. "Scary," J-Man offered. "You were close." The wood gleamed and the silver danced as his flashlight inspected it. It was the object of Marader's current obsession.

His light dropped to the ground. "Blood and a knife," Knives said. "Probably Traylor's." He reached down and held up a clump of netting. "A bag?"

"I think so," Dillon said. Marader reached for the knife. "Don't, that's evidence."

Marader looked at the box in Knives's hand. His eyes were wide open and his jaw grew slack. Then his face suddenly grew intense and he grabbed the box from

Knives's grasp. "Let me see that." He rolled it over and over again in his hands. Troy's eyes met Knives's and they nodded. They weren't sure why, but this was important.

"I'm going to check out the graves," Dillon told them. "Anyone join me?"

"I will," J-Man offered. He followed. J-Man spoke over the tape. "We found six pits, they almost looked like they'd been dug by hands, sharp hands, maybe clawed." Troy felt the hair rise on his neck. "None of this nice clean digging stuff—there weren't any shovel marks."

"Six is the number of Satan," Spider said dryly. His voice echoed in the room. Bob nodded.

"I'll stay with the boats," Marader's voice said. The screen was still focused on him. He set down the gun and spun the box over and over in his hands. Lights moved off behind him.

Knives interrupted the audio, "Kind of fond of that box, aren't you, Marader?"

Troy was watching when Marader turned his attention to Knives. Marader's eyes were cold. "Yeah, it has a good feel to it."

Troy heard a scratching noise over the audio. It sounded as if a dog were moving around downstairs. He listened closely and heard the scrape again. He was sure it came from downstairs. A cold chill washed over Troy. Jambo muttered something unintelligible outside.

Troy stood. "Bob, will you close those doors. I'm getting a bit cool."

Bob gave him a long look, then moved to the door. He shut the downstairs one first. As he readied to close the second, he said, "Hey, what was that?" He started to stick his head out.

"Aaron, close the door!" Troy commanded. He reached for the doorknob next to him. "Jambo, Pete . . ." There was a low, guttural growl. Then several vicious snarls. "Guys, get—" Troy heard the scratching approach. "Aaron!" Jambo whirled around and faced Troy. His eyes widened. Pete flicked a butt off the balcony.

Aaron yanked on Bob and closed the door. "Hey," Bob complained, "I saw a flash of gray."

There was a loud crash of glass and metal downstairs. "What the hell?!" Marader said, jumping off the bed. Denny stopped the video.

The building shook. The next few seconds were interminable. As Troy started to slam the door, the balcony was flooded with wolves. He froze in horror as the beasts tore into Pete, dragging him down in a killing frenzy amid screams of agony. The rending and tearing of flesh assaulted Troy's ears. The noise made him sick. It was too late for Pete. Maybe Jambo . . .

A huge, hairy gray blur shot through the air. White teeth snapping and snarling, it struck Jambo in the chest. He staggered back. The jaws bit his shoulder, missing his throat. Jambo grabbed it, trying to hold it off. Another one knocked him over the balcony. There was a sick thud from below.

Troy started forward but change his mind as a large wolf dove for the partially closed door. Troy threw his weight against the door, trapping the animals between the door and jamb. Troy held the door tight as the wolf struggled to get inside. Its teeth gnashed and spittle dripped on the floor. It was strong and began to force its way in. Silke smashed a lamp base over its head. The beast withdrew and Troy slammed the door shut.

Outside, the rending and tearing continued. Claws raked the three doors and the snarling grew louder. Suddenly, they were jumping against the windows. Glass shattered and one tried to crawl through. Others tried to follow.

Interlude Three
Blood Brothers

"Damn the sun, we're losing him again," the one known as Hoyt said.

As Dillon passed out from the strain of keeping his soul free, Hoyt's cursing grew softer, as if moving farther away. The struggle of wills had worn him out. Dillon couldn't close his eyes, but he could shut his mind down, and for whatever reason, they needed him conscious to work their black magic—to steal his spirit and capture his soul.

Dillon didn't understand what was going on. One minute he was investigating a murder that wove a complex and possibly supernatural web. The next, darkness surrounded him, populated by eyes that glowed like fiery oil lamps and voices as subversive as a siren's song.

Dillon barely heard the female, Elsa. Her voice was like a hushed whisper, but what she said made him shiver. "We must be patient. After all, we are immortal. We are making progress. We will win. He is weakening. Darkness always returns to blot out the light."

With that last word, Dillon traveled in the land of dreams. On this excursion, he didn't journey through an unpredictable dreamscape. Instead, he recalled a memory.

Dillon and friends were sitting around a roaring campfire. The night was cool, but the friendly flames that danced with autumn's vivid colors kept them warm. The world beyond was dark and hazy as if nothing existed besides the seven friends.

His eyes wandered over their faces. As often was the case, Troy's gaze was turned within. He appeared lost in thought, or lost in the night. The flames didn't seem to touch his blue eyes, leaving them cool. His dark hair looked burnished in the fire's light.

To Troy's left, Jay Beck was laughing at something Tom Marader had said. His normally curly locks were matted down from a day's worth of sweat. Even at the tender age of sixteen, complete with baby fat in cheeks and chin, Jay needed a shave. He leaned back and chugged a beer. White foam dribbled out of the corners of his mouth.

Marader poked J-Man in the shoulder with a comb, then ran it through his greenish-blond hair. He paused to swig from a bottle of wine. He said something else and Jay almost choked. Marader grinned like a cat that just ate Tweety Bird.

Across from Dillon was Spider. He sat hunched over the fire, occasionally poking it with a stick. His eyes were in shadow and his expression was brooding. Dillon gathered that his friend pondered the philosophies of life in the small inferno. Was God in the fire?

What an unusual collection of personalities, Dillon thought. Not a one of them was the same. Each had a different nature. Each was a close friend. Dillon shook his head, not really understanding what glue held them together. His eyes continued moving across their faces. Denny spat on his glasses, then rubbed them on his dirty gray T-shirt. His brown eyes were out of focus. He

217

looked overly relaxed, a bit sleepy. A huge yawn stretched his square jaw wide and long. The beer was taking effect.

Knives had taken off his left hiking boot and was searching for a rock within. It looked like his quest for a pebble was the most important thing in the world. They all were tired but looked content from a full day of hunting and roaming through the woods. All of them were drunk. Several of them were roaring drunk.

"It doesn't get much better than this," Dillon pronounced as he held up his can of beer. It foamed and ran over, dripping to the ground. "Being outdoors in a beautiful place, good food, a blazing fire, beer . . ." He belched. "And fan . . . I say, fantastic friends."

"Ah, the birthday boy speaks the truth," Troy said without looking up. "Better friends I'll never find," Troy stated, then finished his beer. He crushed the can. "Calling number seven," he said. Marader opened the red and white cooler and threw him a beer. It left a glittering trail of water.

"Twu . . . truer words were never spok'n," J-Man said. He held his golden can aloft.

"A toass, I profoze a toass," Knives called out. Every one turned to him.

"Do you mean to say, propose a toast?" Spider asked with a penetrating stare.

" 'Xactly," Stephen said unfazed. "Ta za bess of friends. May we all ssstay that way." Everyone vigorously raised a can or bottle, slinging alcohol every which way. It rained down upon them.

"Till death do us part," Spider added just before they began drinking.

"Yes," Dillon agreed, "till death do us part." They drank heavily.

There were several belches and sighs before Spider spoke again. He had a wild look in his eyes. "I say we do more than toast our friendship."

"Like what?" J-Man asked. He scratched himself.

Spider dug through his olive backpack, then removed a knife. The blade was the color of bronze. The edges glinted in the flickering light. He took it and lightly ran it across his wrist. A thin line of blood appeared. His face was serious when he said. "We should be blood brothers. Should confirm our friendship like the Indians once did."

Spider passed the knife to J-Man. Without hesitation, he cut his wrist. "Ouch."

J-Man handed it to Troy who gave him a dubious look. Finally, Troy placed the blade against his wrist and gritted his teeth. "I'm going to need a chaser after this."

"Be a man!" Marader said.

Troy passed the knife to Marader who followed and then gave it to Knives. Knives cut himself and handed it to Denny.

Finally, Dillon touched the sharp edge to his left wrist. He caught his breath as the warm blade bit. Crimson seeped from the wound.

"Now what?" Knives warbled.

"Each one of us walk around and touch wrists," Spider said firmly.

On their knees and one by one, they silently walked around the interior of the circle. The blood of friends blended as they touched wrist to wrist. Soon everyone had made the trek.

"To a long life," Denny proposed. They lifted their drinks. Smeared blood marked their raised wrists and then tricked down their arms.

"Till death do us part," Dillon reminded them.

Chapter Ten
Rending and Burning

His heart jamming in his throat, Troy was stunned by disbelief. In a split second, he relived a bad memory. The wolves were attacking again — just like they'd swarmed over the Landrover. The noises outside the door, the snapping, gnashing, growling . . . the tearing of cloth and flesh brought back Troy's horror. It overwhelmed and paralyzed him. Unable to cope, Troy leaned limply against the buckling door.

Just twenty-four hours ago, he had been through the same trial. Troy recalled it with vivid clarity: hot breath, the heaviness of death in the air, thrashing. Yesterday evening had been bad, now could be worse. He and his friends were surrounded by savage wolves, trapped in the loft at Marader's dock.

The smashing of glass jarred Troy from sluggishness.

"Oh God!" Denny yelled. Heidi screamed.

A ball of savage fury, a mottled black and gray wolf exploded through the window. Shards flew like sprayed water. The beast bounded off the couch. J-Man swung a pool cue, striking the wolf. It broke over the creature's back. As it jumped toward Heidi, the slavering beast knocked Denny aside. Denny's head hit the pool table, and he slumped to the floor.

The hellish creature hit Heidi, driving her backwards. She slammed into the gun rack. The door buckled and glass exploded. Snapping jaws caught her arm. She screamed. The wolf began to twist, its claws burying in her stomach.

"Spider! Axe in the closet!" Marader yelled. He reached for a dresser drawer.

Next to Troy, the front window spewed sharp, crystalline hail as another wolf breached the loft. Silke ducked. Like a steel trap, the beast's jaws snapped closed and barely missed her. The red-eyed wolf sailed over Silke and struck Aaron, sending him sprawling. Shocked and winded, he leaned against the pool table. The wolf pounced again. Aaron waved his arms, trying to protect himself. It landed on his chest and struck at his throat. It missed, tearing off an ear.

"Shut the shades!" Knives screamed. Troy moved instantly, knowing what had to be done. They had to close Marader's interior shutters, his "thief guards," before others attacked. There was no good alternative: they were going to lock themselves in with two killing machines.

"Bob, the blankets! Help me!" Denny yelled.

Kablammm! One gunshot. Two. Three. "Oh God! It's not dying!!" Marader yelled. *Kablamm!* Four. Five. Six. Marader screamed.

Troy jumped up and grabbed the edge of the large board. He yanked on the shutter. It didn't budge, held by strong hooks. Silke leaped up and hung on. Troy joined her. They hung suspended for a moment, then the hooks began to slowly bend.

Aaron's screams lessened to gurgling as his life was draining away. There was a tearing of fabric along with grunting, pleading, and cursing.

The wood groaned. Turning toward the window, Troy

watched as another wolf leaped toward him.

Behind them, the other panel slammed against the wall.

The hooks broke. All of Troy and Silke's weight pulled the shutter down. The wolf's head entered the window. The board slammed down, crushing its head and driving the beast backwards. Blood and teeth sprayed the chair below the window.

"Lock it!" Troy told Silke who laid sprawled on the floor. She scrambled to her knees to batten down the panel. Troy pushed the bolts into place with a click of metal. Now they were locked in.

"Help me! *God help me!*" Marader screamed, followed by two more gun shots. Chopping sounds like a butcher at work echoed in the room.

A brief look over his shoulder told Troy things were bad. Draped on the edge of the pool table and barely conscious, Aaron was bleeding profusely from the neck. His eyes rolled back as his hand feebly tried to staunch the flow.

Denny and Bob had thrown blankets over the wolf and pulled it to the floor. "Hold 'em! Hold 'em!" Bob screamed. Tossed about, they tried to contain the frenzied beast while Knives beat on it.

"Die, die, dammit!" Knives hammered at it with a pool cue. His eyes were wide and his face was contorted.

Sharp claws and fangs began to tear through the blanket. Unaffected by the blows, it slowly wormed its way free. A wild bite caught Bob's hand and his grip loosened. The beast almost escaped. It was a matter of seconds before the demon beast would be loose again.

Behind Troy, Marader danced with death. Covered in crimson and pinned to the bed, he grappled with the wolf. Like a bird of prey, the ravaged beast stood atop his chest. Holding the axe handle across its neck and pulling backward, Spider attempted to restrain it.

As it raged, the beast's long teeth snapped air just inches away from Marader's face. The wolf had been shot several times. Blood and gore dripped from its eye, jaw, and throat. Spasmodically, Marader's finger continued working the trigger of the empty gun.

Astride the animal, Spider strained. His face was scarlet. Spider leaned back, pulling all his weight against the axe handle which dug into the wolf's throat. Hunks of flesh hung from where the axe had bit deeply.

"Troy, do something!" Silke screamed, jolting him.

Troy ran for the gun rack. His mind whirled — Marader's bullets had done nothing. He desperately searched for a weapon. Inside the storage chest he found nothing — no bats, sticks, or ropes — only a space heater . . . *Kerosene!* He'd burn the damned beasts. Looking for fuel, Troy pawed through everything. There wasn't any!

In the bathroom, Troy ripped open the closet and found a half-empty can. "Silke! Set something on fire, anything you can throw!" Troy yelled.

He ran to where Denny, Bob, and Knives were still struggling. The blanketed beast was nearly free. Desperation was in his friends' faces. The moment of truth — death — was seconds away. Bob's and Knives's arms were wounded, their clothing torn and bloodied. "Ah yes!" Denny grinned in triumph as Troy poured the kerosene over the struggling creature.

Silke dropped a match. Troy staggered back. As the blanket caught fire, a ball of flame engulfed them. The wolf howled.

Tearing free, the burning beast snapped at itself. Knives and Denny tipped over the pool table and slammed it down on top of the wailing fireball. They jumped on top, crushing the beast. The table bucked beneath the duo, but the wolf was held fast. As it fried, the stench of cooking hair and flesh filled the air.

Troy turned to Marader, J-Man, and Spider. Spider

was weakening. The creature's fangs brushed Marader's throat. Troy realized the same trick wouldn't work. He set down the can. "Bob! Anybody! We have to help Spider!"

Troy grabbed one side of the axe handle while Bob grabbed the other. With all their strength, they pulled. The beast was incredibly powerful, but they crushed its windpipe. It began to gag and wheeze, weakening slowly. They peeled the wolf back. Marader rolled out from underneath it.

Troy darted a look at Spider as they fought to hold back the hellish creature. Their strength was fading. The wounded wolf thrashed wildly, spraying spittle and blood. As its black eyes bored into Troy's, they glowed red and spoke volumes of hatred. He swore he saw intelligence. Troy's arms grew numb. Each time the beast jerked, he grew weaker.

Marader returned. He cocked the shotgun and placed it next to the wolf's head. *Kaa-Boomm!!*

The concussion knocked them away from the beast. Its head exploded. There was a wet slapping sound as if a car had hit a puddle. The four laid on the floor with heaving chests, gasping for air.

"Guys," Denny said calmly from atop the overturned pool table. "I think this one is finally dead." All was silent except for the howling outside. "Guys," Denny continued, his voice beginning to quiver, "we need to put out this fire."

Troy struggled to rise as did Jay. Knives was already next to Denny. Bob and Spider were too exhausted to move. Bob kept muttering, "My hands, my hands, oh lord, my hands."

Marader, shotgun in hand, still stood over the carcass of the beast.

Troy grabbed the axe from Spider's hands. J-Man ran for the bathroom. Silke followed, as did Bob who, groaning, finally rose.

Troy hacked at the edge of the smoldering table, knocking off chunks of burning wood and felt. It didn't help. Smoke still curled from underneath the table. The smell was rancid. It burned his eyes and nose.

The trio returned with dripping wet towels. They draped them along the edges, but the table continued to grow hotter. "We need to turn it over," Knives told them.

Denny climbed off. Troy and Knives grabbed sides and they lifted the table. A smoldering black blur shot out. The burning wolf leaped toward Silke who was too stunned to move.

Kaa-booomm!! The shotgun blast rattled the loft. The wolf seemed to disintegrate, then showered the far wall. Everyone was drenched in gore. Bob and Silke fainted. Denny and Troy tried to throw up. Denny succeeded.

With cold eyes, Marader stood with smoking gun in hand. "That finished the bastard," he said.

Knives and J-Man threw the towels on the burning table. It hissed and sizzled. The flames were smothered, but table continued to smolder.

Now that the immediate danger was over, everyone was quiet, listening to the howling and scratching of the pack outside. Death wanted in. Heavy bodies banged against the doors that shuddered but held. How long would they hold? Could the creatures feel the deaths of their brothers? Troy wondered. He remembered the intelligence and the hate in the wolf's eyes, just like in the Landrover. Again, he dry heaved. He tasted bile, then spat and shook his head, attempting to clear it.

"What now?" J-Man asked. No one answered. Troy crawled over to Silke. He took her in his arms and caressed her pale face. Troy found her pulse and sighed. She looked at peace, no terror contorting her beautiful features.

Knives moved over to Aaron, whose eyes were partly open, but unseeing. "He's dead," Knives said, shaking his head. He ran a bloody hand through his hair, leaving dark streaks among the blond. His blue eyes were sad. "Half his neck is missing. Either the shock or loss of blood killed him."

"That makes three. I . . . I don't believe this is happening," J-Man said. Troy couldn't believe it either, but it was happening. He looked at J-Man. His jaw quivered, then firmed. "How's Heidi?"

Returning from far away, Marader's eyes focused. Finally, he lowered his shotgun and walked over to her. He knelt and checked her pulse. "Bleeding and unconscious, but still alive, thank God. I think she's in shock."

"Aren't we all," muttered Spider. "Lord! Jamie, Pete, and now Aaron — gone. Who's next?" His face was haggard. Dark circles surrounded his eyes.

Still holding Silke in his arms, Troy leaned against a chair. The wall shook behind him. At his feet were black legs and a little of the burned wolf's carcass. Was the supernatural at work in Bristol? Troy couldn't believe it, until he looked around. Then he began to reconsider his views. Troy promised himself that he would think it out more fully if he survived long enough.

Denny rolled onto his side, then tried to sit up. He put a scorched hand down, then quickly raised it up. He twisted up and sat back against the dresser. He tried to straighten out his spectacles and an ear piece broke. Denny cursed. Exhaustion, pain, and frustration chiseled his expression. He wiped the blood from his face and closed his eyes. "I think I have second-degree burns." Spider crawled to take a look.

Across the smoldering table and at the other end of the room, Marader held Heidi. His eyes were vacant, but a small snarl twisted his lips. Knives returned from the bathroom and began bandaging her wounds.

J-Man sat down on the shredded and sullied couch. The shotgun blast had taken away most of the right end. They all stared at each other in silence. Troy thought both J-Man and Stephen were the most composed. No one said anything, then Bob groaned from the floor.

"Might as well wake him up," Marader said. "Don't want him to miss all the excitement." Spider laughed hollowly, then coughed.

"What next? I think I need a doctor. Any ideas?" Denny asked. He licked his lips.

"We call for help. Dial nine-one-one," Troy suggested.

J-Man moved over to the phone, picked it up, listened, then slammed it down in frustration. "Dead?" Denny asked. Anger showing in his eyes, Jay Beck nodded.

"I should have bought cellular," Marader said.

"Don't you have a CB radio?" Wreck asked.

Marader closed his eyes. "Downstairs."

"I don't like this at all. I've hunted enough to smell a trap," Denny said.

"I agree," J-Man said.

"I guess we wait until morning," Knives suggested. "Heidi should survive the night if we keep her warm. Will everybody else?" No one said anything to the contrary.

"So we sit it out?" Bob groaned, finally awakening. "I'm not sure my hands can take it." He fumbled around for his glasses, then finally found them. One lens was cracked.

"We can reinforce the doors with furniture," J-Man suggested. "Put the chairs, couch, dresser, pool table, and the rest against the openings to make sure the wolves can't break in."

"Damn tough suckers," Marader mumbled. "I shot that one eight fucking times and it didn't seem to be bothered at all."

"We should have saved somebody: Pete, Jambo, Aaron—somebody!" Spider said.

"Maybe they're werewolves," Knives commented. No one laughed. Troy had momentarily thought the same thing, then dismissed it as if that train of thought were forbidden.

"Denny," J-Man said, "can you give me a hand with this couch?"

"I can try." Denny slowly rose and moved to help him. They set it before the door.

"I hit it with the axe several times," Spider told Marader. "It wouldn't die, just like some beast from hell." His brown eyes were glazed over. He shuffled over to help Denny and J-Man push the pool table over against the door to the store. They changed their minds and leaned it long ways.

"I don't know if Knives is right or not, but they aren't regular wolves," J-Man said, cocking his head. The howling outside seemed to grow even more intense. Several times, the upper parts of the door would seem to buckle, then regain shape. "I can't believe that one we set on fire still attacked Silke. Troy, how is she?" J-Man asked as he approached.

Troy stroked her hair and caressed her face. "I think she's coming around. She hasn't regained her strength from yesterday's accident and now this happens." Troy had the nagging feeling that he had forgotten something important, but he couldn't remember.

Silke groaned. Lids fluttering, her amber eyes opened then closed again. Troy moved so his friends could slide the chair over before the balcony door. This seemed to infuriate the beasts outside. The onslaught heightened as did the angry howling.

In a short time, they had moved the dresser, gun rack and small table against all the openings. They leaned the box spring against one wood panel, and the mattress against the shutter. "I think we're about set," J-Man told them. "Unless they can walk through walls, that is."

"What about Jambo and Pete?" Bob asked, his voice hoarse.

"They're dead," Troy said flatly. "We have to be concerned with us, the living. We'll mourn them and Aaron when the time is right. It isn't now."

The fortifications continued. As they set another chair against the balcony door facing the lake, Spider sniffed, then said, "Do you guys smell something?" Troy remembered what he'd forgotten.

"No," J-Man said, breathing deeply.

Denny cocked his head. "I hear something . . . a crackling like — the dock's on fire!"

"I think I saw the wolves knock over the grill," Troy said quietly.

"Yes, that's what I smell," Spider confirmed with grim finality.

"Fuck!" Marader yelled. "We either get eaten or blown up!" He waved his arms. "If the gas tanks go, we'll ride the crest of the explosion to Kingdom Come."

"You're going to hell anyway," Knives corrected.

"I think now's a good time to pray," Bob suggested. He gingerly folded his hands. There were tears in his eyes.

Silke stirred in Troy's arms. Her eyes fluttered then opened. "Troy? What's happening?"

"We're in trouble," Troy told her. "The phone is dead and the dock is on fire."

"On fire?" She abruptly sat up, then grabbed her forehead. "Oh."

"Troy," J-Man said, "you have such a gentle way with women."

"Guys, come on! What are we gonna do!?" Bob asked. "I don't want to die!" His face was alight with growing fear. He'd wrapped strips of his shirt around his arms to staunch the blood flow.

Outside, the wolves began to howl in concert as if they were singing at the moon. The noise was deafening, cutting deeply into everyone's soul. The loft seemed to quake under the vocal onslaught. Troy wondered if the wolves could smell their fear.

"Shut up, *goddammit!*" Marader yelled as he banged the butt of the shotgun against the door.

"The fire doesn't seem to be bothering them!" Denny said. Knives was bandaging his forearms.

"Marader," J-Man said, "isn't there a trapdoor, a trash dump of some type, in the downstairs storeroom?"

"Yes." Marader fought to remain calm.

"Jay, in case you haven't been paying attention," Denny said, "there are wolves in the stairwell."

"True, but probably fewer than on the balcony. Marader's shotgun worked once already."

"Tom," Troy asked, "do you have any more shells?"

Marader pulled open the drawer of the gun cabinet. "Sure do. In fact, I have another shotgun in the closet." Troy kissed Silke and leaned her against the chair. He started toward the closet. "It's in a black case."

Troy came out with a shiny new double-barreled shotgun in hand. It had a clip. "Shells?" Marader handed him a box. Troy loaded the clip, then began stuffing his pockets. He didn't have a good feeling about this, but he couldn't think of any alternatives.

"What do you guys plan to do?" Knives asked. He was now working on Bob's arms.

"We're going to blow our way clear down the steps and into the storeroom," J-Man explained. "Then, we'll slam the door shut to the store. We can escape through the trap door and swim to shore."

"I have a bad feeling about this," Silke muttered, echoing Troy's thoughts.

"Jay, if we swim to shore, they'll catch us before we can

230

reach our cars," Troy stated. J-Man thought about this and nodded.

"Maybe we should stay in the water," Spider suggested.

"How long can you tread water?" Bob asked.

"Hey, we could swim to the boats anchored offshore!" Denny thought aloud.

"Yeah, yeah!" Marader said. He smiled. "I have an idea, if only . . ." He moved to his dresser and pulled open another drawer. There was silence as he began digging through clothing.

"I smell smoke all the way over here," Knives said. He finished taping Bob's arms. Bob carefully touched them and grimaced.

"It's getting worse," Spider said.

Troy walked over to the front door. He touched the wall, then the floor. "They're hot."

"I still hear the wolves," Denny said. "How can they stand the flames?"

"Aha!" Marader said. "It's still here." He held a key. "To my old boat. I can swim out first, fire up the boat, and then move closer if needed."

"You have to clear the stairwell first," Spider said gravely. His face showed he wasn't hopeful.

There was a dry crack and pop toward the front like logs in a fireplace. "Time's wasting and the tanks are up front below the balcony," J-Man said.

"Let's go splatter some wolves," Marader said. He turned to Knives. "Watch Heidi." Stephen nodded.

Silke nearly clung to Troy as he tried to move way. "Be careful," she said with wide eyes. Troy gave her a tight smile and joined Marader.

J-Man picked up the axe and moved to the door. Spider followed.

Denny was at the gun cabinet, loading a rifle. "Every little bit helps," he said.

Together, they moved the pool table aside. "Jay, yank the door open, I'll begin firing," Marader suggested. Raking sounds struck the door like a hard rain.

"Just shoot through the damn door to clear some space," Denny suggested.

Marader gave him an evil grin. "I like that idea." He looked at Jay, then Troy. "One shot, then open it and get the hell out of the way."

J-Man nodded. Troy cocked his shotgun. J-Man unlocked the door. It shuddered and shook like a creature in death throes. J-Man pressed against the wall.

Marader pressed the nose of the shotgun against the door and pulled the trigger. *Ka-Boomm!!* The concussion knocked him back as wooden shrapnel flew. Troy closed his eyes. Splinters lodged in his cheek. The blast echoed in the room like a giant's roar.

Nearly unable to see due to the sawdust in the air, J-Man groped for the handle. He yanked the door open.

"Shit!" Marader yelled. Without part of its left shoulder and head, the wolf was still standing there. It grinned with dagger-like teeth, then attacked, nipping Marader's leg and snagging his jeans. He screamed and placed the shotgun's barrel on the wolf's back. He pulled the trigger, then staggered back as the wolf let go. Undaunted, with its head dragging on the steps, it crawled forward, still snarling. Troy kicked it.

A second beast leaped over the first. Troy fought his fear and held his ground. He pulled both triggers. The blast forced him to stagger back where Spider held him upright.

The double blast caught the red-eyed and slavering beast full in the chest. As fur and flesh flew, the wolf was flung back. It tumbled down the steps. Another wolf took its place. Troy pumped the gun and fired again. *Ka-Boomm!!* The beast fell back. Using Spider for support, Troy unleashed everything in rapid-fire sequence. His actions were devastating, but not deadly.

Blood and flesh painted the walls. He fired, pumped, fired, pumped. The shells tore into the wolves, downing them. One fell, but two took its place. The smell of gunpowder stung Troy's eyes and nose. The gun grew warm.

Ka-bah-booomm!! Troy let go with both barrels, wreaking havoc. His head throbbed and his vision grew blurry. His right arm threatened to fall off.

As Marader reloaded, Denny stepped into place and started firing. Bullets tore at an oncoming beast. Others followed it. The number of wolves swelled in the stairway. They crawled over each other in an attempt to reach their victims.

The ones Troy had blasted began to rise. He cursed.

"We aren't killing them! The shotguns don't work!" screamed Denny.

"Get out of the way!" Spider yelled. Bob pulled Denny from the door. Troy dove out of the way. J-Man slammed the door and Marader locked it. A snout jammed through the hole in the door. Teeth snarled and saliva dripped down its chin.

Quickly, they replaced the pool table against the throbbing door. Breathing heavily, Troy studied his friends. Sweat shone on their faces. Each barely contained his desperation and frustration. No one knew what to do now. The certainty of death was in their eyes. The howling of the wolves mocked them. The sound was almost ear-shattering, making it hard to think.

It was growing warmer. The smoke was beginning to choke them. Troy looked up. A thin haze clung to the ceiling. They were running out of time.

"That wasn't such a hot idea," Bob yelled over the noise.

"Tom," Denny asked, "what were you using in the shotgun the first time?"

"Dimes."

"Dimes?"

"Yeah, I saw the movie *Pat Garrett and Billy the Kid* on television. One guy had his shotgun loaded with ten thin dimes. I thought it sounded neat, so I did. As you can see it works well and makes a big mess."

"And we're glad you did," Knives said, "otherwise we would either be dead or still fighting two wolves."

"Guys, we may be dead in a minute anyway if that fire hits the tanks," Marader reminded them.

"Silver. Dimes contain some silver," Troy said. "We need silver to kill these things." He shuddered. He couldn't believe what he was thinking. Were they really fighting werewolves? Silke moved to Troy. He tried to put his arm around her, but couldn't.

"Troy, you're talking crazy!" Bob said.

"Bob, the whole thing is crazy!" Denny told him.

"But you're talking about Evil incarnate. *Werewolves* . . ."

Another series of loud, crackling pops assaulted their ears and diverted their attention. They all turned to the front of the loft. The walls had started to blacken and smoke poured around the door and windows. Like a ghost, it coalesced, then stretched across the ceiling.

"I can feel the heat," Silke said.

"Anyone have any ideas?" J-Man asked. The smoke was growing increasingly thicker. Soon it would be hard to breathe. Black, smoldering streaks climbed up the walls and touched the ceiling. Suddenly, the lights flickered. There was a hissing, an electrified pop, and then the lights went out, plunging them into darkness. The smell of burnt wiring filled the room.

Chapter Eleven
Last Gasp

Pitch black surrounded them. It was as if death's dark shroud had dropped over them, Troy thought. It added to their desperate plight as the wolves howled and the fire crackled, edging its way towards the gasoline tanks, and the smoke poisoned the air.

Troy felt all hope depart. Stay calm, he told himself. He put to use everything he'd learned from competitive sports to keep his mind clear. Stay calm and channel your emotions, Troy told himself, but hopelessness reared its ugly head. He pulled Silke close to him and wondered if he'd ever see the sun, the water, the mountains, Dillon, or if he'd ever hold Silke without fear again. Troy tried to summon the image of escaping.

"Shit!" Denny exclaimed.

"I can't take it anymore!" Bob yelled. He tried to stand, then fell over something.

"Just when you thought things had gotten their worse—" J-Man began.

"Beck, will you shut up!" Bob yelled.

"Yes, please!" Silke agreed.

For long moments they all sat quietly in the cavernous dark. The wolves sang for their flesh. Their scratching and clawing combined with the angry crackle of the fire created a symphony of death. The flames slowly devoured the front walls, snapping like a bonfire. Flashes of orange and yellow light sprang up the wall. Someone coughed. The smoke grew thicker.

Silke stifled a sob that could be felt by everyone in the room, then she said, "I don't want to die. Please God, I don't want to die."

"Let us pray," Bob suggested.

"Dammit, Bob, God only helps those who help themselves," Marader said bitingly.

Troy's mind raced. Maybe their previous plan wasn't so bad after all. Maybe they had just gone about it wrong. "Tom, you have the key to the boat, don't you?"

"Yeah," he said, coughing. "A fat lot of good it will do me."

"We can try to make a run for it," Bob suggested. "Fling open the front door and try to jump over the railing. At least a few of us would make it. It's better than dying in here."

"We might suffocate before the place explodes," Knives said.

"Thank you for that consoling fact," Spider said.

"I think it's time to pray for a miracle," Bob suggested again.

Light flared as Silke lit a match. "We don't need to die in the dark. Candles?" Marader stood and walked into the closet. He came back with several tapers.

At least they had light, Troy thought. Then he felt a wave of heat swell through the room. He turned to see the wall burst into flames. Blue and yellow ran up and down along the surface like fingers dancing across a guitar.

"The only reason we haven't gone ka-boom already is that the heat and flames are working their way up instead of down," J-Man said.

"Jay, please put your mind to use in figuring a way out of here?" Spider quietly suggested.

"Why don't we create our own door?" Troy asked.

"Yeah, why don't we create our own door?" Denny echoed.

"How?" Marader asked.

"An axe and a few shotgun blasts ought to do the trick," Troy explained.

"Out the roof!" Bob agreed.

"Better yet, the closet wall or this one," Troy said, pointing to where the chest of drawers had been. "It faces the boats. We could just dive out and swim for it."

"I like it," J-Man said. Spider nodded.

"Let's hurry," Knives said. "I don't think we have much oxygen left."

"Let's do it!" Marader yelled. He crawled over to the far wall. "If we do this right we may not even need the axe!"

"Knives," Troy said, "toss me a box of shells."

He did. The two loaded their guns.

Flame and sound exploded from both barrels and tore into the wall. Troy turned his head, but he would always remember Marader's leering face. Wood and dry wall flew, filling the air with more debris. The shot created a hole about two feet wide. Marader reloaded.

Troy pulled both triggers. *Ka-booomm!!* Another crashing explosion ripped the air. A whirlwind of fragments sailed around them. Troy coughed and closed his eyes. He fired again. The blast rocked him. His separated shoulder was aflame with pain.

He opened his eyes. The hole had widened on the left and in the center. They could see outside.

Marader fired, the concussion pushing him back. Immediately, Troy let loose with both barrels again. Troy's ears rang, nearly drowning out the howling of the wolves. The sound of guns excited the beasts.

Bob was choking; he curled up in a ball. Tears ran down their blackened faces. Troy felt like he was trapped in a sulfur mine. He could barely see a few feet in front of him. The smoke was mixed with the acrid fumes of gunpowder.

"Guys, hurry, please!" Knives called. Then no one could speak and no one could breathe. Twisted shadows danced through the smoke-filled room as the fire began to spread across the ceiling and along the floor. It was crawling toward them.

Like machines, Troy and Marader fired and reloaded, fired and reloaded. The thunderous roaring came again and again. Now the group was deaf as well as nearly blinded. The air became unbreathable.

The explosions went on for a minute, seemingly continuous, then stopped. Fresh air wafted through the room. "Spider!" Marader coughed—he was covered in dust—"bring the axe."

Spider snaked across the floor. As he neared his friends, he could feel a hint of coolness. Suddenly, he sucked in a breath of fresh air.

Spider started to stand, then was almost knocked down by the heat. He staggered forward and fell to his knees next to the gap in the wall. It was a jagged tear nearly three feet wide and over four feet tall. Fragments still hung in the way, cluttering the opening. With a few swipes of the axe, Spider easily cleared them away.

"Let's get out of here!" Troy yelled. "Go Marader!"

"In a minute. Where's the jewelry box?" he yelled.

"I've got it," Spider replied. "I found it safe and sound under the bed. Now get the hell out of here and get the boat started!"

Marader hesitated and Troy pushed him forward. Tom dove out through the gap. He cleanly carved the water.

"Next best swimmer!" Troy yelled. Denny moved past them and out the breach. He landed awkwardly with a loud splash.

"Quick, before the wolves get wise!" Troy yelled.

Bob moved to the gap. "What about Aaron's body?"

"If those things are werewolves of some type, we'd be better to let him burn," Troy said harshly. Bob's eyes widened.

"We don't have time for dead weight," J-Man said.

"He'll get a viking funeral," Spider said. He pushed his friend out the hole. Bob landed on his back, but quickly recovered. Silke kissed Troy, then leaped out after Bob. They could see Denny swimming furiously after Marader. Tom slashed through the water, rapidly nearing his boat.

"See you on the boat," Spider said. His shirtfront bulged. "I've got the box." He cocked his head. "It may be what they want. J-Man, you go first. Troy can cover and help Knives with Heidi."

Without questioning, J-Man yanked off his shoes and threw himself out the gap in the wall.

As J-Man began stroking for the boats, he heard a splash behind him. He paused for a second and saw Spider's head pop to the surface. Over his shoulder, he saw the wolves mass on the edge of the dock, ready to follow. Jay Beck struck out with everything he had left. Gun blasts carried to him from behind. J-Man didn't turn.

Troy watched as the beasts turned from the building to the water. They moved to the edge, ready to pursue his friends. He wondered if Spider were correct; they'd seemed oblivious to their departure until Spider hit the water. Coincidence? he wondered. Troy unleashed both barrels as two wolves jumped off the dock. They spun in the air and dropped like stones.

Troy knew he couldn't kill them, but he could slow them down. Even as he reloaded, Troy watched them shake off the blast and begin to swim after Spider and J-Man.

"It's just you and me," Troy told Knives.

"Just like old times," Knives said, forcing a smile.

Troy unleashed another round. The swimming wolves rolled over, stunned for a moment. Troy thought he saw Marader and Bob reach the boat.

"Hey Troy, give me hand, will ya?" Knives said just before a coughing fit set in. The air was almost unbreathable. When away from the opening, they had to hug the floor.

Feeling the heat scorch his back, Troy crawled along the floor. It seemed to take forever to travel a few feet. He finally reached Knives and helped him drag Heidi to the hole in the wall. Even with both of them pulling, they only seemed to progress an inch at a time. Troy's eyes and nose watered so badly he couldn't see. Finally, they reached the breach.

Knives's face was black and streaked with tears. His blond hair was stained gray. "I hope they hurry and bring the boat. Time's running out."

"Yeah," Troy coughed. He stuck his head out the gap, and breathed in the fresh mountain air. "This place could blow any minute."

"You go on. No reason for you to wait," Knives said.

"You might need help. Two people can drag better than one." Troy squinted into the darkness. He thought he saw the tarp pulled back from the boat. "Besides, I can hold my breath longer than you."

"No shit. I thought you were going to drown while trying to learn to barefoot. I swear we" — he coughed — "dragged you for two minutes."

Troy laughed harshly and hacked. "More like three."

"God, it's getting hot," Knives said. His eyes were out of focus and Troy pushed him closer to the gap. Both were drenched in sweat. Black clouds rolled past them and out into the night. They huddled around the only source of clean air and coolness.

Only minutes ago they could see the fire clawing its way along the ceiling, floors, and walls. Now because of the oily black cloud that filled the loft, they could only hear its cackling laugh as it slowly ate its way toward them. Massed on the dock below, several more wolves leaped into the water and joined the pursuit.

* * *

Arms pounding like paddle wheels, Marader raced for the boat. He swam as if death chased him, and it did. Stroke, stroke, stroke, breath. His legs pushed him forward. Churning water washed the sweat away. Stroke, stroke, stroke, breath. Again. *Don't stop*.

Marader expected his dock to explode at any moment. His life's work, his dream, his sweat and blood would be blown to smithereens. Marader forced those thoughts from his mind and drove himself onward. Stroke, stroke, stroke, breath. Again. Cool water calmed his desperation. *No . . . don't stop*. He hadn't tried to swim this fast since he'd raced in college. Now, so much depended on it.

His imagination teased him. It told him that, at any moment, another corpse would reach up and drag him under. *Ignore it*. Stroke, stroke, stroke, breath. Again. Legs fired like overheating pistons.

Tom heard splashing behind him, but refused to turn around. Surely, he thought — he hoped — it was one of his friends. Close now, he could see the boat. It was within reach. *Stroke harder, faster*.

Marader reached the boat and hung onto the ladder. Quickly, his hands danced along the bindings which held the cover in place. Suddenly, heavy hands dropped onto his shoulder.

Expecting death, Marader whirled. "Ya need help?" Jambo said.

"Jambo, damn, am I glad to see you! I thought you were dead!" Marader cried. He hugged his friend.

"I landed on top of the wolf. Stunned it, I guess. When I hit water, I swam underwater for as long as I could. I thought my lungs were gonna explode. I've been here ever since. I was worried about y'all."

The splashing behind them stopped. "Jambo! Hey, it's good to see you! Thank the Lord!" Bob said, his face smiling.

"Marader, get it in gear," Denny sputtered as he reached them. "The place might explode any minute. Holy shit, Jambo! You look like shit!"

Jamie touched his bloodied scalp, "Yeah, but I'm alive."

"Let's save the reunion for later," Bob suggested. "We have some rescuing to do."

Galvanized into action, Marader and Jambo unfastened the cover. Marader burrowed underneath and crawled to the ignition. He prayed it would start. He hadn't run it since he'd bought his new boat a month ago. His hands clumsily felt their way across the gauges.

Jambo and Denny rolled the tarp back. Bob and Silke climbed into the boat. Marader slid the key in and pulled out on the choke. He turned the key and the dashboard lit up.

"I'm firin' up!" Marader yelled. "Watch the motor!" he warned as he turned the key farther right. The engine gurgled, then died. He tried again. *Gurgle, click* . . . died. "Damn!" Marader adjusted the choke. Jambo unhooked them from the anchored float.

"Hurry!" Silke pleaded. "Troy's still in there."

"The place is going up in flames and those damn things are just dancing and prancing in the fire like they were bathing in it," Denny said breathlessly. His eyes locked onto the dock. The entire balcony was a gigantic bonfire. The roof as well as the front of the second story were rippling from the heat and flames. As if some charnel pit had opened, great gusts of black clouds billowed upward.

Whirr, gurgle, click, whirl, gurgle . . . silence. "Goddammit," Marader screamed. He tried again. Same sound.

The flames didn't bother the wolves. They seemed to revel in the destruction. Their howling pierced the night. Denny felt Bob shudder. "I . . . I don't believe this," Bob stammered. He, too, watched the grizzly scene. Some of the beasts still scratched at the burning walls. Their fur smoldered, but they were unharmed.

Whirr, whirr . . .Water churned. *Buzz, click*. Marader jammed the choke forward all the way. His left hand pounded on the dash. "Start, damn you!"

"Look!" Silke cried. She pointed to J-Man and Spider. The sound of the shotgun blasting rolled across the water. All but Marader turned to see the leaping wolves twist just before hitting water. "The wolves are chasing them! Come on, guys, swim faster! Swim faster!"

The wolves recovered and another blast struck them in the water. J-Man and Spider closed in. Spider labored as he tried to hold onto the jewelry box. The demon beasts sputtered, howled, then followed. They swam faster than Silke thought possible. They were gaining!

Whirr, whirr, gurgle . . . Water churned. *VAAROOOOM!!* "Yahoo!" Marader cried as the engine caught. He eased back on the choke, but not too much. He didn't want it to die. Marader was itching to click it into gear, but he knew he had to wait, he simply had to let it warm up a little.

"Swim faster!" FASTER!" Silke yelled.

Silke's screams reached Spider over the water splashing around his ears. His head was reeling and he was dizzy. Like lead weights, his legs threatened to sink to the bottom. He heard splashing behind him.

Spider's throat and chest burned. His breath came in heavy rasps. He sucked down water. Coughing, he drove himself forward. The box slowed him down, but he wouldn't let it go. Exhaustion hung about him like a mourner's shroud.

Jambo grabbed Marader's shoulder and said, "Look over there! Do you see him?" Jambo pointed into the woods beyond the lit area of the parking lot.

Marader squinted. He didn't see anything—then he

saw it. A figure stood in the woods, just watching. Anger burned hot within Marader. He gave a quick glance at J-Man and Spider. They wouldn't reach the boat for a few more seconds . . . and the boat had to warm up a little longer.

Moving quickly, he went down to the locker in search of a rifle. He always left one in the boat — he got into too much trouble to ever be unarmed. He found the leather case and unzipped it.

He pulled the old Weatherbee out. Yes! it was loaded. Anger drove him on. He glanced into the water. J-Man and Spider were going to make it. Marader had time. He undid the safety.

Carefully, Marader sighted down the barrel. He was going to blow that sucker away. He slowly began to squeeze the trigger, then stopped. Somehow, his focus changed. As if looking through a scope, he met his victim's burning red eyes. They glowed in the dark! It smiled and a row of gleaming white teeth snarled at him. Marader's hand shook. He tried to pull the trigger, but couldn't. There was something in that smile, something in those eyes that stopped him. Tom willed himself to pull the trigger, but his finger wouldn't move.

"Give me your hand!" Denny yelled. Jambo and Denny yanked J-Man into the boat. Sputtering, he collapsed onto the floor.

"Faster! Come on, Spider. Move it!" Denny screamed. The wolves were less than fifteen feet behind Spider. He was ten feet from the boat.

"Get ready!" Jambo said and grabbed a paddle. He looked at Marader who stood paralyzed, staring into the woods. Jambo whacked him lightly with the paddle. Marader's mouth dropped open and his eyes came back into focus. "Get ready!"

Marader immediately clicked on the safety and sat down. He put his hand on the throttle.

"Lord, they're close," Bob said. He uttered a quick prayer. The wolves were less than five feet behind Spider. Closer, ever closer, the trio drew. Spider's face was white and his strokes were weak. Closer . . .

Denny and Bob reached out and hauled Spider up. As they pulled him from the water, one of the wolves snapped at him. It snagged a pant leg, then ripped free. They all tumbled into the boat. Spider still clutched the jewelry box.

"Let's go!" Jambo yelled. A wolf tried to scramble up the back. Jamie McGillis put all his weight into a blow and slammed the oar on top of the beast. As the oar shattered, the wolf howled, then fell back into the water. Marader jammed the throttle forward into gear. Red-colored foam churned behind the boat.

"Just swing by," Denny told Marader. "They can jump."

Marader whipped the boat around toward the inferno. On the shore, wolves still danced in the flames. The fire had finally caught hold on the lower level of the building. It seemed to slowly advance on the gas pumps. Glass exploded. The trash cans caught fire.

"Wolves! Swimming toward us!" Bob grabbed Marader.

Tom smiled. There were hollow thuds as he ran them over. He sped up and shot in directly under the hole. Marader could see dirt-streaked faces peeking out of the burning building.

"Give them room," J-Man said. He helped Spider to his feet.

Using every ounce of skill he'd learned from years of piloting boats, Marader whipped the boat into a spin. The bow reversed and the stern swung around in a 180-degree turn. The stern settled just to the right of the gap in the second floor. The wolves began to regroup. They slowly moved to surround the boat.

Knives jumped with Heidi. Jambo and Denny caught them. They tumbled into a heap. A wolf scratched the side, then struggled to climb in. "We've got to leave!" Denny shouted.

"But —," Bob started.

"Throw the ski rope out! Troy can barefoot!" Marader commanded. As Denny did, Marader jammed the throttle into forward. He ran over the closing wolves, leaving them thrashing and gagging in the wake.

Troy's eyes widened. Before they'd even slowed, they were leaving! He prepared to leap.

To his left, the front wall caved in. Troy turned. Through the smoke he saw the burning wolves charge him. He dropped the shotgun and jumped.

His shirt caught on a jagged edge, leaving him dangling half in, half out. His fingers fumbled. Troy yanked on it, but couldn't get free. Below, the boat was out of reach. Behind, snarling jaws lunged for him.

It was death to stay. Troy pushed off with his feet and tore free. Teeth snapped at thin air.

Troy spun head over heels. He screamed as he saw only wolves below. Circling like sharks, they waited for him.

Just before Troy hit, he spotted the ski rope. The handle bobbed just below him. The rope was uncoiling, straightening, then started to slide away. He reached for it.

As Troy crashed into the water, his right hand grasped the handle. Breath left him as he struck the water flat, ribs exposed. Choking, Troy reached for the handle with his other hand. He tried to pull it to him. It had been years since he'd barefooted.

The wolves closed in. Their red eyes skimmed across the surface.

The rope grew taut, then jerked. Troy's right shoulder burned, then went numb. His left hand grasped the handle. Troy hung on for life as his arms were nearly pulled from their sockets. His arms screamed for him to let go.

Water hammered at him, trying to dislodge him. It surged, churned, thrashed, and choked him.

Troy rolled onto his back and skimmed across the top of the water. He shot by the gaping jaws of the wolves. Clear, he tried to spin around and stand. For a moment, he thought he was going to make it, but with a hammering impact, Troy slammed face first into the water. Barely conscious, he managed to hang on. That's all he wanted to do: hang on.

The boat raced out into the center of the lake, leaving the inferno and the horror behind. Seconds later, they stopped to pull Troy into the boat. He was limp and crying, his hands cramped and clutching the handle. He passed out in Silke's arms.

As they started off again, the dock exploded. Geysers of flames shot into the night. The war had just started.

Chapter Twelve
Recovering

Late that night, they finally arrived at Jay Beck's house on the lake. They docked, J-Man disarmed the alarm, and they headed inside. Like zombies, they trudged up the walkway. Marader carried Heidi in his arms. No one said a word. For the first time since the attack, the weight of the evening came crashing down around them. They'd lost two friends.

Troy could hardly move. He'd inhaled too much smoke. While riding in the boat, Knives had popped his arm back into its socket. Now he leaned on Silke and Denny. Troy's thoughts were hazy, and he kept imagining that something lurched at him from the darkness. He started several times. Only Silke's soothing voice in his ear kept him calm.

Inside, there was a brief argument. Stripped and covered in blankets on the couch, Troy was only dimly aware of what it was all about. Denny, Jambo, and Bob wanted to drive immediately to the hospital. Spider and Knives suggested they wait until morning. Knives had checked all their wounds and pronounced they'd all live at least until then. Marader told them to act like men and tough it out.

He called the police and his insurance company. Troy mumbled that he should call Bill Glazier, then despite

248

his wracking cough, he fell into a hard, dreamless sleep. He didn't even wake when the ambulances or police arrived.

The next morning, Troy felt as if he'd spent days being stretched on a rack. At breakfast, Knives fed him a muscle relaxer that he claimed wouldn't make him too drowsy. Troy still hurt, but at least he could move around. Silke gave him a massage, then he tried to stretch out. Each move was torture. His body had endured a tremendous amount of abuse.

Only Troy, Silke, Knives, and Spider were at the house, having returned from the hospital where they'd received medical attention that morning. Knives was bright and businesslike while Spider was depressed. The death of the Ackles brothers was hitting him hard. He'd been very close to them.

Denny, Bob and Jambo were still at the hospital. Knives said their wives were taking care of them. Denny and Bob were released as outpatients while the doctor wanted to observe Jambo for a day or two.

Marader and J-Man had gone with the police to the dock.

About an hour and a half behind the duo, Knives, Troy, Spider, and Silke had driven J-Man's Blazer to the site of last night's horror. It was another hot, cloudless day. They arrived around eleven.

The parking lot and street leading to the dock were jammed with police cars, marked and unmarked, a couple of vehicles from the fire department, and a Nova with State Farm Insurance decals on it. "Probably the most crowded his parking lot has ever been," Knives commented as he stopped the Blazer.

They walked down the road and through the parking lot. Along with men in uniforms, there were several tel-

249

evision crews and a few reporters. Marader had a crowd around him. He wore a big smile and a bandage on his left cheek. J-Man stood behind him. "Marader's eating it up," Knives commented. Spider grunted.

"Probably thinks of it as advertising," Troy said. He studied the grounds. In the beauty of the day, it was hard to believe that last night happened at all, except for the wounds his friends had.

Troy's gaze moved behind Marader to where the dock once stood. There was no semblance left of the structure. An island of flotsam spread for several hundred feet. A lone boat with several divers scoured the area. They were probably looking for the remains of the Ackles brothers. Troy looked at Spider whose face was gaunt. Right now, Troy felt too tired to mourn.

Last night proved that something terribly wrong was happening in Bristol. He didn't want to believe in the supernatural, but it had stuck its nose in his face. Troy forced himself to open his mind. He promised himself he would no longer brush away or rationalize the unusual. His eyes moved back to the police boat and divers. Troy wondered if they'd find any wolf skeletons during their search.

Through the crowd, Troy spotted Elle as she walked toward them. She coolly appraised Troy who still leaned slightly against Silke. "You look the worse for wear." She inclined her head toward Knives. "Good thing y'all have your own personal doctor around."

"Hi, Elle," Troy said. He felt Silke stiffen. "Any word on Heidi?"

"She's doing fine. She'll be hospitalized for a few days." She smiled and said, "I warned her about hanging out with y'all, that you were heavy partiers, but even I didn't suspect that your bbq would turn into a house-burning party. Wow!" No one responded as she glanced at their faces. "I guess y'all aren't exactly ready for

250

humor yet."

"We're just glad to be alive," Knives told her. "Not all of us made it."

Elle sobered up. "Tom didn't mention that."

"I'm not surprised," Spider said bitterly, glancing over toward the media mob around Marader.

"Seems like you'll be unemployed for a while," Troy said. Over Elle's shoulder he saw Detective Glazier approaching.

"Not for long," she said, throwing her hair back. "The insurance folks have already visited and a temporary dock will start construction tomorrow. I should be working again by the weekend." She paused before speaking, then asked, "Were y'all really attacked by a pack of wolves?"

"That, young lady, is my question. If you'll excuse me," Bill Glazier said in an official tone as he flashed a badge, "I'm Detective Glazier. I'd like to ask these folks some questions. In private, if you don't mind."

"Sure." Then with a wink, she said, "Later, Troy." She sashayed off as if going to a party.

"I think I'll rip her hair out," Silke muttered. Troy gave her a squeeze.

Bill Glazier put his hands on his hips and gave them a slow once-over. He shook his head. "Troy, you seem to be around a lot of trouble."

"So do you," Troy replied.

Bill laughed heartily. "Yeah, but it's my job. I'm not a sportswriter, I'm a law-enforcement officer." He wiped his eyes then asked, "Are you all right?"

"Better than Heidi, not to mention Pete or Aaron Ackles," Troy replied bitterly.

"That's not what I asked."

"So far, it's been a helluva two-day visit to my hometown."

"You don't look too steady."

"Is this official concern, or personal?" Troy asked.

"Well, you are just a ray of sunshine this morning, aren't you?"

"He dislocated a shoulder and inhaled lots of smoke last night," Knives stated.

"You don't look too well either. Have you seen a doctor?" Glazier asked.

"I'm fine. I inhaled a good amount of smoke too. And I *am* a doctor," Knives said with emphasis.

Bill grinned. "It's sometimes hard to remember that, considering I knew what you were like when you were young."

"It's hard to believe you're a detective," Silke said with a small smile.

Bill laughed again and pulled out a cigar. "Nice to know someone still has their sense of humor intact." He lit his stogie, then asked, "Troy, do you get the feeling something or someone wants you dead?"

Troy paused for a moment, thinking about all that happened, then said, "Not exactly. Feels more like being in the wrong place at the wrong time."

"Huh, I don't understand. You've been attacked by wolves twice in less than twenty-four hours if I can believe the statements from you and your friends."

"But we have no proof, right?"

"You guys don't have it on videotape this time?" he asked.

"We were a bit busy," Knives said, "trying to stay alive. Maybe next time."

"Another testy one," Bill said. He blew a smoke ring, then said, "There is some evidence to support y'all's story." He let the pregnant pause linger, puffed a few times, then said, "We dredged Pete's body from the lake." Bob grimaced. "He was chewed up pretty bad." Troy felt sick. Spider looked the same.

"No sign of Aaron, I expect," Knives said.

252

"Not even fillings."

"No wolf skeletons?" Troy asked.

"Not a one. Can you think of any reason you'd be at the wrong place at the wrong time, twice?"

"No."

Marader's interview seemed to be over and the reporters were beginning to disperse. Several of them paused by the fivesome, but Detective Glazier waved them on. "You can hassle 'em later, by God. Why don't you go interview Jamie McGillis, if the medical staff at Bristol Memorial will let you!" Several of them ran for their cars.

"I appreciate that," Troy said. "I already have a pain in the neck."

"I figured you'd like reporters," Bill said with a smile. "Anyway, I'm pretty sure the hospital won't allow interviews for a while. Now, back to business. You're not holding out on me, are you?"

"Nothing you'd believe. It's all speculation and some of it's supernatural," Troy told him.

Bill snorted, almost disappearing in a cloud of smoke. "Shit. You still looking for Dillon?"

"Yeah."

"Any luck?"

"Not yet. We're heading down to Knoxville this afternoon to do some research."

"Where?"

"TVA library."

"Why?"

"I agree with Dillon. I think everything is tied to Traylor's death, but maybe even more specifically to Cemetery Ridge."

"Do you want to expound on this theory?"

"Not until I learn more," Troy said. Bob started to protest and Troy interrupted him by saying, "I promise we'll sit down and talk when I have something concrete.

I promise." He raised his hand.

"Okay, but I still feel you're holding out on me." Troy smiled. "Hot damn, I got a smile by claiming that I don't trust you. You're getting weird in your old age, my friend."

"Don't I know it," Troy laughed, then coughed. "At this rate I won't get much older, so I have to be strange while I can. Have to be to survive in this world."

"You got that right," Bill agreed. He looked Troy directly in the eye and said, "If I don't hear from you by Friday morning, I'm gonna put a warrant out for your arrest."

Troy rolled his eyes. "Fair enough."

"Well, I guess that's enough grilling for the day. I feel like I've done my duty. I will need a statement from all of you before the weekend arrives."

"Yes, officer," Silke said.

Bill pointed at Troy and said, "Troy, I've always liked Silke. You take care of her and yourself. I don't want to have to bury any more friends." Heavily puffing on his cigar, he left in a cloud of smoke. Bill waved to an older man and got into his car.

A mousy-looking man smoking a cigarette approached the foursome. J-Man was just behind him. Jay was waving his arms. Troy had the balding man pegged as a reporter.

"Hi, I'm Morton Simpson with the *Bristol News*. Mind if I ask you folks some questions?" he asked. He was met with stony silence. "Uh, you folks look familiar. Any of you happen to be here last night?"

Spider walked off and headed toward J-Man.

"You didn't get enough of a story from Tom Marader?" Knives asked pointedly.

"I'm looking for a different angle. Say, I know who you look like," Morton said, his eyes widening. "You remind me of a guy who played basketball at Tennessee

High about a dozen years ago. Your name, uh, Tom Bane?"

"No," Troy said.

"Why do I smell a story here?" he asked.

"Too much coffee can throw off a reporter's instinct," Troy said.

"Well, you folks have a nice day." He looked up at the sky. "I don't think we have to worry about rain." Morton reached inside his jacket. "Tell you what, if you have something to say, give me a call. Here's my card." He held out his card.

Troy didn't take it. Silke did. She gave him a sunny smile. "If we think it's worth printing, we'll call."

"Thanks, ma'am. I recommend you take your friends to a comedy. They look like their best friend died."

Troy barely contained a snarl. "Why don't you go find some missing people, do some investigating like good reporters are supposed to do, instead of preying on people," Troy said coldly.

The reporter gave him a long look, then turned and left. "I see you don't like reporters," Knives said. "I figured there was professional kinship or something."

"There are good doctors and bad doctors, aren't there?"

"Sure."

"I rest my case."

J-Man and Spider walked up to them. Troy looked beyond them and saw Marader talking to a willowy blond. Her skin was the color of alabaster, making her red lips and nails stand out at a distance. She was very attractive and Marader seemed drawn to her like a magnet. His smile nearly outshone the sun.

"Well," Jay said, "you folks don't look any the worse for wear."

"Who's that woman?" Troy asked, nodding over J-

Man's shoulder. Something about the woman made Troy feel uneasy.

"Oh, the blond?" J-Man asked. Troy nodded. "She's an insurance investigator, a Ms. Samantha White. Marader's on the prowl again. Just like him, his latest squeeze is in the hospital and he's hitting on another woman." J-Man rolled his eyes. "So are you ready to fly to Knoxville via J-copter Express?"

"All of us?" Troy asked. "I thought Knives had surgery."

"It was canceled," Knives said. "She came down with the flu. Tomorrow's operations are elective, so I postponed them. I want to see this through if I can."

"Welcome aboard, my friend."

"We still need to dive Wreythville," Knives said.

Troy gave him a weak smile. "Maybe tomorrow. I don't feel up to it today."

"Let's go then," J-Man said. They started to leave.

"Hey, where are you going?" Marader yelled.

Troy gave the insurance investigator a quick glance. Her eyes were darker than a moonless night. "Jay's going to give us a tour of the mountains via copter," Troy said, twisting the truth. For some reason he didn't want to say anything in front of the blond-haired woman. "I've never ridden with him before."

"Take a parachute!" Marader laughed at his own joke. "Hey, according to Ms. White," he pointed to the blond woman, "they'll start work on a temporary dock tomorrow and I might be back in business by Saturday. Great, isn't it?"

"Wonderful," Silke agreed.

"What're you up to after your ride? Any ideas about Dillon?"

"None on Dillon and I don't know about this afternoon. We should probably stop by and see Aaron's widow, maybe see Mr. and Mrs. Ackles. See if any arrangements have been made," Troy told him.

"Oh yeah," Marader said, seeming to brush it off. He turned to Spider. "Spy, my man, Ms. White was asking me about valuables. What happened to the box," he said, finishing in a whisper.

"It fell out of my shirt when I was swimming for the boat," Spider said with a straight face.

What! Goddamn you!" Marader flew into a rage. His face flushed to bright red. "You promised you'd take care of it! I ought to —"

J-Man grabbed Marader's arm. "Marader, get a grip. We've been through a lot."

Very evenly, Spider said, "I had wolves chewing on my socks. I'm sorry. We can dive for it later," he said coolly.

"Yeah! Sure! You can count on it." Marader nodded. "Maybe in the morning." Spider nodded.

Troy had been watching Ms. White's reaction as Marader spoke. Her interest had heightened when Tom asked Spider about the jewelry box. A small smile appeared on her face when Spider claimed to have lost it.

"Let's go folks; I'd prefer to fly in daylight on the return trip," J-Man told them.

"We'll see you this evenings at Jay's," Knives told Marader.

"Yeah, we'll throw back a few brews in memory of Aaron and Pete," Marader told them.

"Bye," J-Man said and headed for the Blazer.

Troy handed him the keys. As they neared the truck, he spoke to Spider. "You didn't lose the box, I remember seeing it last night."

Spider smiled. "I know. I hid it. It's under the sink in the guest bathroom," Troy laughed.

Troy was almost asleep in Silke's arms before they'd

257

left the ground. The rhythmic whipping of the copter's blades put him out. His body needed down time to heal. His mind wasn't going to get it.

Troy awoke with a start. It was dark. He wasn't in the helicopter. He was alone and in the graveyard. It was night on Cemetery Ridge.

Troy was amazed at how clearly he saw in the dark, then remembered he was dreaming. He decided to roll with it. Listening carefully, Troy discovered that the machine sounds were missing — they probably didn't work at night — or maybe now that he'd identified the sound, it wasn't important any longer.

Remembering that he'd fallen into a grave last time he was here, Troy carefully scanned the area. He'd "awakened" in a grove of some type at the bottom of the hill. Small trees were all around him. Behind him was the entrance to the yard. In the distance, he could see the hazy patches of light in the growing fog. The mist rose from the valley floor and slowly approached the cemetery. Troy gathered that the lights were from Wreythville.

At Troy's feet were long concrete slabs that covered three graves. He began to study the intricate carving when the sound of chanting reached his ears. It had an unearthly cadence to it, but its rhythm reminded him of a distorted funeral march.

Looking through the trees and up the hill, he discovered a series of flickering lights, like sputtering will-o'-the-wisps. Long shadows crawled down the hill, over the tombstones, and danced along the trees that surrounded Troy. He thought that the voices came from the lit area.

Shaking off the chills that rippled along his flesh, Troy left the grove and climbed the hill. Like a hunter, he moved in bursts, then waited, hiding behind tombstones and trees. A cool breeze wafted by him, pulling in the fog. The wind seemed to whisper to him to join the dead that were rising. Troy rubbed his ears, then continued.

His imagination toyed with him and his progress slowed. He kept looking down to make sure that something didn't reach up from below and grab him. Now the breeze through the trees sounded like a dry, mocking laugh. Despite the cool night air, Troy wiped the sweat from his brow. The chanting grew louder.

Troy stole closer to the lights and the voices grew clearer. He still couldn't understand the droning. Troy topped the hill and kneeled behind a blocky headstone. It was cool to his touch.

Troy's eyes widened as he watched the scene. A crowd of darkly clad figures stood in a circle, torches raised above their heads. They appeared motionless, like statues, except that the light breeze ruffled their cloaks. Troy heard a splashing sound as if someone had jumped into water. There was a flash of movement inside the circle.

Suddenly there was a triumphant cry that rattled Troy down to his toes. He didn't know what it was, but he couldn't stop shaking. It sounded as if some demon had just been brought to earth. Within the circle, hands were raised in a sign of victory.

Despite his fears, he was compelled by curiosity. He quietly moved up the hill to get a better view. He slipped off his shoes and crawled from stone to stone. An occasional bush or shrub gave him extra cover. A soft wind through the leaves claimed that he was dead, dead, dead. Troy clamped down on his imagination.

Now he could see within the circle of shadowy figures. Inside, there appeared to be some type of pool. It shimmered and smoke rose from it. A cloaked figure with two sets of red eyes — he had one set in his chest! — led a pale and scrawny woman to the edge of the pool.

259

Slowly, the crone walked into the liquid. She kept moving until she was submerged. The waters bubbled and hissed. The chanting grew louder.

Suddenly, one of the torchbearers turned. His burning eyes locked on Troy. He screamed out, and they all turned to look at Troy. Troy stood, then tried to run, but he seemed rooted to the spot, paralyzed by their gaze. The one with the two sets of eyes tipped his brand toward Troy.

Fire erupted from the torch and arced across the yard. Like a comet it shot toward Troy. Screaming at himself to dive out of the way, Troy stood, watching it rocket to him.

He was blinded as it struck the headstone to his right. The heat scorched him and set his clothes and hair on fire. The stone melted into slag. Molten rock burned his feet. Troy screamed as he tried to beat out the flames consuming his body.

The figures started up the slopes. "We're coming for you, Troy. We're coming for you, Troy!" They laughed and aimed another torch at him.

"Troy, Troy! Wake up!" Silke shook him back to reality.

He woke up with a start, his hands still patting his body and trying to put out the flames. His wild eyes caught Silke's worried ones. "Oh Lord."

"Another nightmare?" she asked. Troy nodded. "A visit to the graveyard?"

"Yes, another trip to Cemetery Ridge, this time at night."

"Tell me about it." He did and she listened intently, as did Knives. After Troy had finished his tale, Silke said, "As usual, it doesn't make sense. This one seems much different than the others we've had."

"Yes. They were always during the day. They all seem to have something to do with a rebirth of some type.

And the man with two pairs of eyes . . ." Troy shivered. He could still feel the eyes of the dark ones upon him . . . and the flames.

Silke stroked his cheek. "You still need rest. Too much has happened to you in the last couple of days. Jay," she called to the front over the whirring of the blades, "how long until we reach Knoxville?"

J-Man looked over his shoulder, pulled the headphones from his ears, and asked Silke to repeat her question. "Oh, about thirty minutes or so," he answered. "I've already talked with Brit Cottage, and he's going to let us borrow his car. The library isn't far from the field."

"Good," Silke said. "Troy, go back to sleep now and have pleasant dreams this time." She hugged him.

Troy began fading into sleep in no time. He briefly thought of his phone call to Racquel to cancel dinner. She'd been coldly furious, he could tell. He'd promised lunch the next day. Troy laughed, thinking he felt safer in daylight.

Just before hanging up, Troy had asked about Cemetery Ridge and a sapphire ring. Racquel was surprised. Yes, she still had it. In fact, she was wearing it right now. She'd only found it last week.

With that disturbing thought, Troy finally fell into undisturbed sleep.

The afternoon had been boring and seemed to stretch on forever. The library had been deserted and they roamed about at will. Troy thought that doing research always made time drag. He'd discovered this altered Theory of Relativity in college. The longer one did research, the more time slowed.

Troy removed his sunglasses and rubbed his eyes as he waited for Knives to climb into the helicopter. The blades whipped up a wind that pulled at his hair and stung his eyes. He was already tired. He must have skimmed over twenty books. Troy looked at his friends. They looked tired too.

As he helped Silke climb inside, Spider said, "I hope we didn't waste an afternoon."

Troy had to yell a bit to be heard. "Only time will tell how valuable it really was. If some of those people are alive, they might provide some extra insight." Spider nodded and crawled into the front seat.

"Y'all ready?" J-Man asked. Everyone nodded affirmative. Jay's fingers danced across the dashboard, flipping switches and adjusting a dial. "We'll be home in a little over an hour."

The copter slowly and smoothly rose like a giant dragon fly. It hovered for a moment, then tilted a bit before heading for Bristol.

"What do you think?" Knives asked Troy.

"It all seems to fit," Troy said. "According to the records, the building of the dam set a record for the number of deaths during construction."

"Not all during construction, actually," Silke corrected him.

"That's true. Related to construction of the dam, I mean. There seemed to be problems everywhere. There were accidents in relocating Wreythville's population, in surveying the area, in transporting the materials, as well as the actual construction; in fact, there were problems and slowdowns in every conceivable phase of the operation."

"As if something were trying to prevent the completion of the lake," Knives concluded.

"Sure seems like that." Troy looked down at the list of names they'd scribbled on the sheet of paper he held in his hands. "I hope some of these workers are still alive and living in the Bristol area. They might be able to tell us something that the records couldn't."

"How do you find that out?" Knives asked.

"Well, we can either take the list to Bill G. or . . ." Troy said, stopping to think.

"Or?"

"We can use a phone book and look up the names. I don't want to bother Bill at this point. Maybe after we interview a former TVA employee, we'll have something to pass on besides speculation."

"Only time will tell," Knives said.

"Yeah. I just hope that Dillon's time hasn't run out." Troy hugged Silke. The return home passed quietly and quickly.

Chapter Thirteen
A Witness From the Past

The sun was about an hour away from setting when Spider turned into a narrow driveway on a back country road. Troy glanced at the mailbox and the name J. Corning confirmed that they were at the right place. The car eased through the gate and headed up the bumpy gravel road.

Troy felt fortunate that they'd found what they were looking for: a former TVA employee who lived nearby. Over the past couple of hours, the five had inhaled dinner and flipped through phone books. They'd only found four possibilities.

Troy's stomach felt a little queasy. The food, stress, and medication were not complementing each other. His arms and head were still throbbing.

"I hope we don't get shot," Spider said.

"We should have called first," Silke added.

"I wanted to surprise him, and it probably would have taken as long to call as it did to get here."

Spider turned left and slowly drove up the hill. The forest was thick on each side, then it suddenly opened onto fields. Troy recognized tobacco plants. Several dilapidated barns and sheds surrounded the field. It was currently being irrigated.

Beyond the plane of leafy green foliage was a small

house. It was one story, mostly composed of red stone on the bottom and wood on the top. The stain had faded and the boards seemed to be warped. Draped in shadow, a covered porch stretched along the front. Both front windows were illuminated, shedding some light on the stoop. A solitary figure sat in a rocker. A hint of red, like an ember being stoked, flashed, then dimmed.

As Troy climbed out of the Rabbit, he marveled at how typical it all seemed. He breathed deeply, noticing the all-too-potent smell of fertilizer. A woodpecker pounded on a tree near the house. Troy smiled tightly. It was almost too tranquil—too normal. Troy shook his head. He was beginning to see danger everywhere.

Silke and Spider followed him up the walkway. The figure hadn't stirred.

Troy stopped just before the steps and asked, "Are you Jeremiah Corning?"

The cigarette tip grew bright red then dimmed. A cloud of smoke drifted from the porch. Troy tried to see the man's face, but he wore a hat. Troy could tell that he was old, as Troy expected Jeremiah to be, and was dressed in overalls and boots. "Depends on who's askin'," the man replied in a thick drawl.

"My name's Troy Bane. I'm a reporter. I'm sorry to bother you, but I'd like to ask you some questions about your employment with the TVA on the South Holston Dam Project."

The man leaned forward and squinted as he adjusted his glasses. Again, he took a long draw on his cigarette before speaking. "Ah was wonderin' when one ah your kind was gonna visit, askin' all sorta questions. Funny stuff goin' on again." He turned to the window and yelled, "Martha, we got comp'ny."

The man rubbed his chin. "Name Bane rings a bell. Some reason Ah'd know it?"

"I don't think so. Uh, are you Jeremiah Corning?"

"Sure as shit am," Corning said as he stood. He wobbled for a moment as he gained his balance, then walked across the porch. He stopped and called again, "Martha! We's got comp'ny." He shuffled down the steps.

Troy got his first good view of Jeremiah Corning as the old man descended the steps. His hat was made of straw and filthy. Stringy gray hair hung from under it, framing a badly sunburned and wrinkled face. His nose was flat and round over blackened lips. Corning's eyes were barely visible, deeply set, and surrounded by folds of skin, but they seemed to twinkle when he set his eyes on Silke. As he held out his hand, the old man asked, "Who's with ya?"

"This is Todd Adder and Silke Urich."

"You're a purdy thang," Jeremiah said, smiling. He stroked his chin. "Urich. Damnation, mah mem'ry ain't as good as it usta be. Mar—"

The door banged open. "Hold ya horses, Jer," the elderly woman said. She wiped her hands on a towel, then moved toward them. "Ah was cannin' 'n had ta clean up a bit," Martha said with a smile. She had a gentle face with soft blue eyes. Her hair was short and black, peppered with gray. Her cheeks were flushed. She patted her hair into place.

"This here's Troy Bane, a reporter wantin' to ask me some questions about TVA," Jeremiah told her. She nodded. "The honeh is Silky Urich 'n the lean one iz Todd Adder. Where do Ah know the name Urich?"

Martha ushered them up onto the porch saying, "Welcome, 'ave a seat, 'ave a seat. Rest yourselves a while." She looked at Jeremiah and shook her head, "Your gettin' old when ya cain't remember Lawrence Urich."

Troy saw Silke's eyes widen. Martha noticed too. "Iz

that'n your grandpa, dah'lin'?"

"Yes, ma'am. You knew my grandfather Lawrence?"

Martha laughed. "Mah sister dated 'im fur a while. We usta go on picnics in 'Ginya, 'specially when the leaves was changin'. Come 'n sit, child. It's sucha small world, ain't it?" Jeremiah Corning was nodding.

Silke and Troy sat on the porch swing. Spider stood, leaning against a post. "Would y'all like somethin' ta drink? Beer or soda. We got Coca-cola or rut beer," Jeremiah said. Troy saw that Corning had relaxed. He had forgotten that in a small town somebody almost always seemed to know a relative or a friend of yours.

Everyone agreed on soda and Martha disappeared into the house.

"Now what can Ah do fur ya?" Jeremiah asked. He leaned back in his rocker and puffed on his cigarette. His eyes had lost their hard edge, and Troy thought that Martha remembering Grandpa Urich was the first true bit of good luck he'd had since arriving at the Tri-Cities Airport.

Somehow, surviving the car accident or the attack at the dock seemed too desperate to be considered luck. Besides, two of his friends had died. Troy shook his head and tried to put it in the back of his mind. He had to concentrate on finding Dillon — only the Lord knew if he were alive or not.

"You all right, son?"

"Yes, sir, just trying to sort out pieces to a puzzle. Maybe you can help."

"Ah'll try. Ah reckon Ah mite."

"You worked on the building of the dam, didn't you?"

"Yup."

"Were you involved with any of the relocation of Wreythville?"

"Nope," Corning replied. Troy's shoulders sagged.

267

"But Ah knew purt many fellers that did."

"Anything particularly unusual or troublesome about the process?"

"Damn nar everythin'," Jeremiah said in a grumpy tone. His eyes had hardened once more. "Every day somethin' new and diff'rent went bad. Whole thang was bad. Ah quit 'fore the thang was finished."

"Why?"

" 'Fraid Ah was gonna turn up missin' or gone. Martha talked me inta quittin'." He smiled. "Smartest thing Ah've ever done."

"What do you mean by 'gone'?"

"Missin', dis'peared." He waved his hand abstractly. "Folks dis'peared on nightwatch like they nevah was. Walk behind a pile a rocks or dirt and nevah come back. That's what folks were say'n anyhow.

"Nevah worked nights myself, ya see. But Ah remembah at sunset one day watchin' a friend of mine ease inta the woods ta pee and he nevah returned. Ah waited and waited, an' Terence nevah showed. They nevah did find 'im. 'Appened ta several workers."

Martha returned and passed out refreshments. As quiet as a church mouse, she folded into the chair next to Jeremiah.

Troy didn't remember reading about disappearances; accidents yes, missing persons, no. "Was that kept quiet?"

"Not really. Juz sorta blended in with all the accidents."

"Unusual accidents or typical ones?"

"Both. Folks fallin' in pits 'n breakin' their fool neck. Loads droppin' on 'em, cables snappin'. Rock slides an' the like. Strange ones was eerie, sorta like tales ya tell round a fire when yur campin'.

"A truckload a dynamite slipped a brake, rolled ovah a couple a folks, then boom." He waves his hands.

"Killed plenty that time." He shook his head. " 'Nother truck accident 'appened when they was movin' the coffins from the town cem'tary. Driver 'ad a heart attack an' keeled ovah. Plowed inta a tree. Fella ridin' shotgun slipped inta a coma. Just 'fore he did, he babbled on 'bout a dark woman with red lips. Scared a bunch, that's for sure."

"Why?"

"Wasn't the furst time that the dark lady 'ad been mentioned. She was credited with lurin' most of the missin' fellers away.

"Fact, poor Thomas Hillwood got 'imself stinkin' drunk one night and claimed that the dark lady came from Wreythville. Convinced one a the night watchmen that bulldozin' the town was the right thang ta do and set 'bout doin' it. He hit a powah line that was supposed ta be dead. It made Thomas dead. Lit up like a Christmas tree they say.

"Afta that, no one went near the town or the cem'tary. Nope, not a soul, no mattah how much they pay'n."

"So were all the coffins moved?"

"Yup, all loaded on the truck that crashed. Shouldn't a been a one left. Story in the papah and on the TV confuses me. Strange thangs happenin' round here again. Reminds me of the old days."

Troy nodded. "Was there anyplace where more strange things happened than others during the project?"

"Don't rightly know." Corning scratched his chin. "Lotsa strange thangs 'appened where Ah worked as well as the cem'tary and Wreythville."

"Where did you work?" Troy asked.

"Ovahflow spillway. Helped pour ceement. Lotsa caves ovah thar. Smelled strange too."

"Anyone ever attacked by wolves?" Spider asked.

"Yup, several times, always at night. Fellas that lived were kinda crazy afta that, claimed the beasts came from hell, with red eyes burnin' like coals and breathin' fire," Jeremiah responded.

Troy felt his skin crawl. His mouth was dry. He wasn't sure what else he wanted to ask. Silke took over for him.

"Do you know of anyone else who's still alive and lives near Bristol?"

"Yup, thar's a few. Lemme see." He rubbed his squared jaw as he thought. "Thar's Lester Pickard that lives in Bluff City, 'n Joey Leonard who lives near State Street Methodist Church. Pop Homgreen lives out toward Abingdon—"

"Dear, don't ya remembah? Pop moved ta Richmond ta be near his grandkids."

"Oh yeah, bad 'nuff gettin' old, gettin' senile too," Jeremiah said, but smiled as he said it. "Tom Smith still lives near the dam, Ah think." His eyes widened. "Almost forgot the Barton brothers. They work at King College Cem'tary." Martha tapped him. "Oh, that's right. Tim just died the othah day. He usta joke all the time 'bout visitin' with his friends every day. Now thar's just Phillip."

Suddenly, Troy wondered if the names of the missing graves would match some of the names on his list. He could ask Phillip Barton when he saw him tonight at eleven at King College Cemetery.

As Silke answered questions about her grandfather and family, Troy's mind was far away. He didn't realized that a grimness had stolen over him. Dillon, where are you? Lord, I wish you'd come back so I could drop all of this, Troy thought. It has gotten so out of hand. He was starting to believe in the supernatural. Everything seemed to point in that direction. Absently, he played with his crystal cross.

Finally, they thanked the Cornings for their hospital-

270

ity and the information. The old couple suggested they come back anytime. Troy briefly wondered if anyone connected with the building of South Holston was going to be alive for very long. He had powerful feelings of dread as Spider pulled out onto Highway 421.

The three of them were resting at J-Man's place—now Troy's temporary home. He felt he needed to stay close to Holston. It was somehow all connected to this area.

Trying to piece together parts of the puzzle, Troy was reclining on the beige sofa in the middle of the great room. Silke was in the kitchen fixing a salad. Spider was on the phone.

"I'm going for a walk," Spider said as he hung up the phone. His face was drawn. Despite trying not to show it, the past two days were telling on Spider.

"What did the Ackleses say?" Troy asked without opening his eyes. There were almost too many emotions and thoughts to juggle and stay sane, he thought. First Dillon, then Pete and Aaron—who would be next?

"No arrangements yet. I promised to drop by tomorrow. They should know something by then." He ran his hand through his hair, leaving it wild. The corners of his mouth drooped. Troy saw tears in his eyes. "I need some air. I'll be back soon. Maybe Jay and Stephen will be back by then."

"Are you sure you want to accompany us to the cemetery tonight?" Troy asked.

"Yes," Spider said. "I want to see this through." He opened the door to the back porch. The calm waters called to him, and he stepped outside.

"Be careful," Silke said from the kitchen. "It will be dark soon."

"I will." He closed the door and headed for the lake.

Silke finished what she was doing, then came over and sat next to Troy on the couch. Her amber eyes looked at him with love. Silke brushed her hair back, then laid down with her head on Troy's lap. He put his arms around her, hugging her. After a moment of silence, Silke asked, "What are you thinking?"

"That we need to call in some super psychic detective . . . or the Ghostbusters," Troy said quietly. Silke chuckled softly.

"Last night," he said, "Jambo and Marader talked about seeing a figure in the woods. It was just watching things happen. Tom thought it was directing the attack. Jambo sort of agreed."

Troy let out a long sigh, then continued. "Marader said he was going to shoot it. He readied his rifle but couldn't pull the trigger. Tom remembered seeing blazing red eyes as clear as if he were standing a few feet away.

"Jambo said that Marader appeared dazed, sort of paralyzed. Said he had to hit him to bring him back to reality. Then y'all raced over and rescued Heidi, Knives, and me."

"Burning eyes, that's familiar. Oh yes, like in the dreams." She stroked his arm.

"Exactly. Have you seen them in your cemetery nightmares?"

"Yes. Sometimes, even during the day, I feel like they're staring at me, watching me," Silke said softly and shuddered. "Can't we get the police involved, maybe Bill Glazier? He is our friend, and I'd feel better if he went to the cemetery with you tonight."

"Silke, he's a policeman first and foremost, that's what happens when they don a badge. And he wouldn't believe what I have to tell him. He'd probably try and keep me from the cemetery. Besides, I'll talk to him tomorrow as promised." Then he added with a smile. "I don't need the police looking for me." He kissed the top of her head.

"I'm not comfortable with you going to the cemetery." Silke hadn't liked the idea from the start. Troy saw her lovely jaw tighten.

"Knives, Spider, and Jay are going to be with me. We'll be armed. Jay is picking up some hunting equipment from Denny's arsenal today."

"With silver bullets?"

"He mentioned he was having some made."

"Will he have them blessed?"

Troy laughed. "Somehow I can't see our Bob St. Martin blessing bullets."

Silke laughed too. "I guess you're right."

"We could wear garlic," Troy suggested. Silke laughed even harder, then began to cry.

As she sniffled, her fingers dug underneath his shirt and found his crystal cross. "Don't take this off."

"I won't." Troy remembered how it had saved him in his dreams.

"Troy, I'm worried. I'm not sure we'll ever see Dillon again." Tears rolled down her cheeks.

Troy hugged her. "I think we will. I keep getting the strange feeling that he's close."

"Even if we do, I have the feeling he won't be the same person," Silke said quietly.

Troy was caught by her beauty even in grief. He wasn't sure what to say. "None of us is going to be the same after this is finished—whatever the finish might be."

"Will I see you after this? After you leave Bristol?" she asked, her golden eyes beseeching.

"Definitely. I'd like to spend some time alone with you when all hell isn't breaking loose."

"We're alone now and all hell isn't breaking loose."

"Maybe it should be," Troy said, pulling her closer.

His hands kneaded her back.

She smiled, but her eyes were still watery. "Can we be selfish and forget about everything other than us for a while?" Her hands began to roam his body, caressing him.

Troy kissed her. The contact started lightly, then grew in intensity. Silke's fear was replaced by a growing desire.

Troy kissed her cheeks, her eyes, her neck. She moaned. His passion grew and his hands ran down her back and over her tight buttocks. "What do you have in mind?" he asked in a hoarse whisper.

"Take me upstairs and I'll show you," Silke responded. Her hands slid into his jeans.

"With wings," Troy replied. He began to scoop her up in his arms, but his shoulder was still too tender. "I can't carry you," he said with a sad smile.

"That's quite all right," she laughed. "I would have felt like a wench working in a bordello."

Troy laughed, then led her up the spiral staircase. "We may not have a lot of time to ourselves."

On the way up the stairs, Troy had a strange sensation. There was a sharp pain in his neck, followed by a bout of dizziness. Then suddenly he was fine. For some reason, Marader came to mind. Then Silke kissed him again, and he thought about nothing else.

They didn't have much time before the others arrived, but they made the most of it. Troy hoped their first time together wouldn't be their last.

Interlude Four
Lust Bites

"Oh, baby!" Samantha White cried in passion, "I love what you're . . . you're doing to me." She groaned and reached down between her legs to caress Marader's blond head. Then she lurched and pulled his hair. "I want you . . . *now!*"

Tom Marader smiled to himself as he kissed his way up her inner thigh; he still hadn't lost his touch. He'd only known Samantha since this morning and already he was banging her in the back seat of her Nova. Nothing made him forget the problems of a day better than a good lay.

He nibbled along up to her knee and said, "I just can't get enough. You taste sooo incredible."

"Fuck me!" she whispered. It was more than Tom could stand.

Marader slid his hands under her knees and pushed her legs way back. Then he steadied himself, placing his hands on each side of her buttocks. Tom centered himself between her thighs.

"Hurry, oh please hurry!!" She groaned.

Tom smiled to himself again, kissed her quickly, then said, "Guide me in, baby."

She did. Hard and erect, Marader pushed until he'd penetrated her deeply. Samantha let out a gasp and bit him lightly on the neck. Tom laughed and straightened up. Her high heels dangled over his shoulders. He licked her ankle.

They ground against each other, heightening the contact. Then, Marader began to move his hips. Slowly at first, he slid back and forth. Samantha began to moan.

He watched her eyes close and her red lips parted slightly. Samantha pushed back. Her hands wrapped around his neck.

The tempo of passion demanded a faster pace. Tom sped up. His breathing grew ragged, almost in gasps.

She tightened herself. The increased friction made him groan. Grunting, Marader began to pump even faster. She was driving him crazy — to the edge. A fine sheen of sweat covered them both.

Suddenly, Samantha spread her legs even wider. Her ankles slipped off his shoulders and down along his arms. Tom didn't slow down.

With incredible strength, she crossed her ankles behind his back and squeezed. Marader's arms buckled and he fell forward. "Huh!? What?"

Her legs clamped around him like a steel vise and he couldn't move. Her head snapped up and her lips parted. Gleaming teeth gnashed and she growled.

Samantha bit his neck, drawing blood. Marader thrashed about and tried to pull away, but couldn't. Her legs held him fast. Tom tried to jerk his head away, but her mouth followed, still adhered to his throat.

Then he came in spasms.

Weakened, his head lolled forward. Her incisors burrowed farther into his flesh and ruptured his jugular. She tasted blood and purred. Marader tried to scream, but only managed a gurgle.

Blood ran down his neck, but most went into her mouth as she began to suck him dry. She paused only once, her eyes alight with amusement and fulfillment, to say, "You're going to tell me everything you know about an ornate wood and silver jewelry box you found at the lake."

Too weak to move, his eyes barely flickered. "Isn't this how you pictured us together, lover?" she asked, then laughed. With a smile, she finished feeding.

Interlude Five
Break Down

When Dillon opened his eyes, the fiery orbs were waiting for him. "This can't go on much longer," he heard the soft feminine voice say. "Von Damme is growing more powerful, amassing followers, and destroying our way of existence. We have to find him!!"

"I know. I don't believe Mr. Urich can hold out much longer, can you, my friend?" For the first time, Dillon saw something other than their neon orbs. The thing had smiled. It was hideous. His teeth gleamed a luminescent green. The incisors were extra long, like that of a canine beast. Dillon thought he smelled a faint odor, one usually associated with something long buried.

Face it, Dillon told himself. His inquisitors, the one called Hoyt, was right. Their brainwashing was taking hold. When he passed out, his dreams had become bloody nightmares. In one, he was four-footed and hunted prey with slavering jaws. Dillon shuddered. In another, he was able to see in the dark and swoop down on his victims from above. He drank blood in both and reveled in it.

Again, the crimson orbs held his attention. Dillon wasn't sure how much longer he could last. He was growing weaker each time the eyes focused on him.

The hypnotic stare began to draw his soul. He felt detached. Dillon's spirit screamed, desecrated by the touch of whatever stood before him. It had an air of ancient evil, of something living in darkness. Its presence sullied him and made him want to vomit. Suddenly, Dillon couldn't breathe.

There was the sensation of separation. And then he realized what was happening. He was being pulled from his flesh. With a force as physical as strong hands, it tugged on his soul.

Before it was too late, Dillon sidestepped into his imaginary world once more—his world of dreams and memory. He tried to find a peaceful place, visualize any place other than where he was right now.

Once again, Dillon found himself in the woods with his friends. It seemed his fondest memories were either in the forest or on the lake.

He climbed a hill, hoping that the wounded buck he'd just shot was still near. Dillon turned and looked for Jay. He didn't see J-Man anywhere. He must have already rounded the top of the ridge, Dillon thought.

He turned and found Denny moving into the valley. He suddenly blended into the trees and was gone. Troy was nowhere in sight.

Dillon suddenly felt all alone. A cloud passed by the sun dimming the fading light. The woods darkened. It was silent except for Dillon's breathing. Not a creature stirred. The birds hadn't sung since before his last shot.

Dillon slid the bolt and put another bullet in the firing chamber. He felt that his prey was just ahead. The thought excited him. He'd never successfully hunted anything larger than a fat rabbit. Before this moment, he hadn't really enjoyed hunting all that much. Dillon had liked the companionship of his friends and being in touch with nature. Now he understood. The wind kicked up, whistling through the woods, and the leaves rustled the language of fall. Soon winter would arrive, bringing rain, and then snow. But for now nature had painted its playground in brown, yellow, and orange. Soon Dillon would add red.

The air smelled of dampness, moss, and hardwoods. The aroma made him smile. There was a pounding sound, a woodpecker in the distance, Dillon thought. He moved and the woods suddenly grew silent once more, pregnant, expecting something. Was it another death? Part of the cycle of life—of survival?

Dillon thought he could feel the presence of another living creature. It seemed to call out to him and direct him. His eyes scanned the forest. The buck was near, very near, Dillon thought.

He readied his rifle. Stalking without rhythm, Dillon quietly moved from tree to tree. He was amazed at how quiet he'd become. He smiled as he thought he moved like a specter of death. He was finally learning the tricks of the hunt.

There was a flash of brown. With astounding speed, Dillon reacted. He sighted and fired. *Karrrack!!* The rifle bucked in his grasp and the smell of gunpowder caressed his face.

As the sharp crack of the gun danced between the trees and rode the winds through the woods, Dillon thought he heard the beast cry out. His prey crumpled and he heard it crash among the leaves.

Dillon lowered his rifle and approached. He thought it strange that the deer's cry had sounded almost human.

He arrived at his prey and stared. Jay Beck, J-Man, his friend, lay sprawled on the ground. His face was upturned to the sky, eyes open in disbelief. Blood ran from his mouth. Most of his neck and part of his shoulder was missing. It had been one helluva shot—dead on. There was a moment of grief, of horror over what he'd done, then Dillon smiled a ghoulish grin and his mouth watered.

The wind blew by him and Dillon thought he heard it

whisper, "The first one is the most difficult. It gets easier. It's survival of the fittest." Dillon looked to see if J-Man's lips moved. He didn't think so, but he wasn't sure. The breeze carried away any grief, any regret.

The hunt was on. He'd tasted blood.

"Hey!" Denny yelled, breathlessly running through the woods toward Dillon. "Hey," he puffed, drawing closer, "did you get it?"

"Yeah, I got him." Dillon ejected the shell and cocked the bolt, readying another shell. Metal clicked. He held the rifle casually.

"Got him?" Denny asked. He stopped a few feet away. Denny's eyes widened as he looked down. His mouth fell open in shock. "Oh God, you shot Jay!" Wildness painted his expression. He looked up at Dillon.

Denny did a double take, blanched and stumbled back, "No, Dillon! What—"

Karrrack! A huge hole exploded open in Denny's chest, soiling his clothes with lifeblood. Clutching himself, Denny stared down at his hands, watching crimson run through his fingers. Then his eyes rolled back and he collapsed.

The ghoulish grin returned to Dillon's face. His eyes were alight with excitement. A thrill flashed across his flesh and he licked his lips. It did get easier, Dillon thought. That one took very little time and almost no thought. It was almost instinctive, second nature.

Dillon looked around. He wondered where Troy was hiding. Troy would be difficult to kill. Troy was very much like himself—it was almost like they were brothers. Wait, they were brothers? Would be brothers? Had been brothers?

That didn't matter, Dillon thought, it got easier. And he laughed. Two other voices joined him.

Chapter Fourteen
Death Calling

In need of rest, Silke laid down on the couch. She hadn't noticed her aches and pains during her lovemaking with Troy — passion and pleasure had drowned them out. Now, the past twenty-four hours — the wreck, the fire, the travel — had caught up with her.

Her head throbbed and her wrist alternated between a dull ache and sharp, jangling pain. She swallowed her prescription medication, an anti-inflammatory and a weak painkiller. Closing her eyes and laying her hands on her stomach, Silke concentrated on healing herself — on feeling well again.

But Silke's mind wandered to things other than her own health. Only a few minutes ago, the guys had grown tired of waiting on Marader and had departed for Troy's interview at King College Cemetery. Impending doom thick in the evening air, Silke had felt torn between staying and going. She wondered where Tom Marader was right now. She shook her head. Hadn't enough people disappeared already?

Silke had wanted — still wanted — to accompany Troy to the graveyard. For some reason, she felt she could protect him. Troy had refused to let her come. He could sense that she was wearing down and needed rest. Silke didn't understand what kept Troy going — he should be dead on his feet, but something drove him on.

Troy had suggested she stay at J-Man's place while Knives, Spider, and Jay joined him on the excursion. Silke had reluctantly agreed. She was torn: she felt that something terrible was going to happen at King College Cemetery; yet, she also felt she needed to stay at J-Man's for some unknown reason. They both needed to be in the right place at the right time.

Silke sighed heavily. She was beginning to love Troy more deeply than she would have ever dreamed—and she had dreamed a lot. Ever since she was a teenager, Silke had felt something profound and different for Troy. He was like a refreshing ray of sunshine to her, even in dark times like now. Silke didn't understand it, she just followed her heart. She couldn't bear it if anything bad happened to Troy. Finally, with tears of both joy and sorrow running down her cheeks, Silke fell asleep.

Brrring . . . Brrring . . . Brrring . . . The incessant jangling of the phone awakened her. For a moment, her dream lingered. All she could remember was the night watchman transforming into a vampire. Silke shivered, trying to push away the nightmare.

Brrring . . . Brrring . . . She picked up the receiver. "Hello?"

"Silke? I'm so glad I found you!"

"Aunt Jada?"

"Yes, dear!"

"How did you find me, I mean—"

"I just let my fingers walk across the buttons and they found you!"

"Oh." Silke was still sleepy, her mind moving at a slow pace. The medication made her feel thick and sluggish.

"Silke dear, I have to warn you!" Aunt Jada's voice grew louder and higher. "Dillon is free; yet, he isn't free.

283

Beware his return. He's coming back, but he's changed. He's a creature of the dark now!"

Aunt Jada's voice verged on the hysterical. "They have won. He no longer lives in the light but *embraces darkness! Darkness!*"

"I don't understand," Silke began. She put a hand to her forehead as if pressure would help her mind function.

Aunt Jada wasn't listening. She was babbling. "And another thing. More darkness. Watch out. Your friends, they too are being touched by the immortal shadows!"

Silke tried to interrupt, but had no luck. Aunt Jada continued. "And the man you love, Troy, don't let him visit the burial grounds. *Death awaits him,* no, worse, *damnation awaits him!*" She sobbed a bit, then said, "It could be tonight, it could be tomor—"

There was a sharp intake of breath, then a thudding sound as if something heavy had hit the floor. The phone tap-danced across the floor, then rested, leaving only silence.

Silke immediately became more awake. "Aunt Jada? Aunt Jada!" Her knuckles white, her hand tightly gripped the phone. Aunt Jada, is everything all right?!" The phone grew hot and slippery. "ANSWER ME! Please."

Aunt Jada didn't reply. The only answer was silence. That was enough for Silke. She knew Aunt Jada was dead.

Silke hung up the phone. She had to rush to the graveyard and warn Troy. Something deadly waited for him!

She stood up and the world reeled about her. Feeling faint, she quickly sat back down. What to do? she wondered.

Her mind raced. She wanted to rush to Aunt Jada's

house; she wanted to rush to Troy's side.

She would call Detective Glazier. Yes, that was it! She would get Bill Glazier to go to King College Cemetery with a warning for Troy. He might even take some help with him! That would take care of Troy and leave her free to race over to Aunt Jada's.

Silke picked up the phone. There was no dial tone. Dead air mocked her. She cursed. Aunt Jada had called her. Silke couldn't dial out until her aunt's phone was hung up.

Suddenly, she remembered that Jay had said there were two phones in the house. Jambo had used the second line, a business line, in the upstairs office.

Gingerly Silke stood. She found her equilibrium and crossed the room. Silke touched any piece of furniture she could use for support. She reached the stairs and hauled herself up them.

Grabbing the beige touch-tone phone, she put it to her ear. The dial tone was music to her ears. She punched the buttons and called information. Seconds later, Silke breathed a sigh of relief. William Glazier was listed.

She punched his number and waited. To Silke, the phone seemed to ring a million times. Finally, someone answered. "Hello, this is Bill Glazier."

The foursome waited in the driveway in front of King College Cemetery. J-Man paced back and forth across the entrance while Spider and Knives sat on the hood of the Blazer. Troy zipped up his windbreaker, surprised at the coolness of the summer evening, then scanned the darkness.

The sun had set nearly two hours ago, leaving the mountains shrouded in indigo skies and dark purple clouds. The moon had already risen. Nearly full, it played hide-and-seek with the clouds, beaming its cold, pale light upon the graveyard. A chilly breeze came from the north, tousling his hair and cutting across the back of his neck like a knife. Troy shivered. It felt more like fall than summer. Even the rustling of the leaves had a dry quality to it. They sounded more like bones rattling, Troy mused. He laughed at himself. His imagination was really getting out of hand.

He grew serious when he fondled the .38 revolver in his pocket. Troy hadn't used a handgun in a long time. It was cool to his touch. Jay had given it to him. It was loaded with silver bullets with hollow tips.

Troy's eyes searched every shadow, every nook and cranny, expecting something to jump out and attack them. This time, they were ready for werewolves. The silver bullets would open gaping holes in the beasts. He checked himself: did he really believe in werewolves? Well, he wasn't sure, but he felt better taking precautions.

"Maybe he's not coming," J-Man said, walking by the gate for the hundredth time. He had pulled the hood up on his sweatshirt, giving him an unearthly appearance.

"We're early. Let's wait a while longer," Troy suggested. He checked his watch. It was half past ten.

"We seem to be visiting lots of graveyards nowadays," Knives said. He was on his back, speaking into the sky.

"And will be visiting more, very soon," Spider said quietly. His head was bowed, so Troy couldn't see the agony in his friend's face. Spider was still thinking of the Ackles brothers.

"What time did you say the funeral was this Friday?" Knives asked.

"Starts at one o'clock at Brightway's Mortuary."

"Thank God Jamie survived," Troy said. "Two deaths is enough to bear. Did he get out of the hospital

286

today?" Knives nodded. "Good. Things are going bad enough without another fatality."

J-Man shook his head, then said, "Dillon missing, a lot of us injured by wolves, Marader's dock burns to cinder, the Ackleses killed, Jambo mauled . . . where will it end?"

"It could end now. We could go stick our heads in the sand like ostrichs," Troy suggested. He watched the moon slip behind a cloud once more.

"I think not," J-Man said. "Better to come prepared, than to give up." He pulled his pistol from his pocket, as well as a couple of auto flares he'd tucked under his jacket. Then he displayed a silver cross. "I also have a surprise in store," he said with a smile.

"Did you bring stakes and hammer?" Knives grinned.

"Nary a sign of a vampire, only werewolves so far," J-Man said. His smile was tight-lipped.

"We're not sure they're werewolves," Spider spoke softly. "We haven't seen any transformations. The ones we killed stayed wolves. Besides, we haven't reached a full moon yet and already the wolves are out in force."

"Maybe the legends are inaccurate," Knives suggested. "Legends quite often are only based on half-truths, not what really happened." Spider remained silent. "Are we still diving Wreythville tomorrow?" Knives asked as he sat up.

"I'm feeling up to it," Troy lied. He still suffered from dizzy spells. "Let's plan on it. Jay, can you join us?"

"If we do it in the afternoon."

"Done," Troy confirmed. He wasn't sure his body could take it, but then he didn't have a whole lot of choice. Troy felt time running out.

"Good," Knives said. "I'm not sure how much longer I can stay in Bristol. I have patients depending on me."

"I appreciate you being here," Troy told him and put

a hand on Knives's shoulder.

"Hey, we blood brothers have to stick together. Even if I have to leave for a short while, I'll be back as soon as I can."

"All for one and one for all?" Troy asked with a smile. Knives nodded.

They both looked at Spider who still stared at the ground. "Spider, are you sure you want to be here?"

"Yes," he responded dully.

"I wonder where Marader is?" Jay wondered aloud.

"Last time I saw him," Knives said, "he looked as if he were trying to get beneath Ms. White's skirt."

"Knowing Marader," J-Man continued, "he succeeded."

"The man is fickle," Troy said.

"Yeah, Heidi's still in the hospital," Knives said. "That's the Marader we know and love, that's our boy."

"He's only fickle to women and strangers," J-Man defended. "He wouldn't screw any of us over." Troy gave him a dirty look. "Well, not seriously anyway. He's a blood brother."

"He's ruled by his passions and lusts. He lives for the moment," Troy said.

"It would take a serious offer," Knives added, "like, say, a good lay before he'd give you the shaft."

"Just from what I observed," Spider said quietly, "he's as obsessed with Ms. White as he is with that jewelry box."

Troy agreed.

A jangling of metal reached Troy's ears. Troy turned around and looked at the gate. A shadowy figure moved behind it.

The clouds passed the moon, and its cool rays illuminated the yard. The man wore a dark, long-sleeved shirt rolled up to his elbows. His baseball cap hid most of his face, but Troy thought the man looked in his late fifties.

As he turned to slip the key in the lock, more light struck his face. Troy spotted a short scar along his right cheek.

As the night watchman turned the key, the lock shrieked. The hinges were silent as he pulled the door open a few feet.

His right hand resting on the gun in his pocket, Troy approached.

"Are you Phillip Barton?" Troy asked. The man nodded and motioned him inside. Troy took a step, then stopped. "Are you willing to discuss your brother's death?" Troy asked and the man nodded again. "And the time you worked for the TVA?" Barton hesitated, then nodded.

Barton looked straight at Troy, who couldn't help but flinch. The man's eyes gleamed with the coldness of black ice. His skin was pale, almost pasty white. Dark circles were cut deeply around his eyes. The scar was short and jagged, more like the healing of a rip than a cut. When he saw that Troy was hesitating, he said. "It'd be easier to explain what happened if y'all come to the caretaker's building." He waved his arm across his body and welcomed them in.

Troy walked by the man and entered. As he did, Troy shuddered. There was something about the man that gave Troy the creeps.

J-Man, Spider and Knives followed Troy inside. Barton closed the gate behind them with an echoing clang.

Troy waited for Barton to lead. The old man glided by him with an ease that astonished Troy. As he followed, staring at Barton's back, Troy didn't notice any limp or hitch in his step. There was no sign of age. The man moved fluidly, belying his years.

They walked up the driveway and headed into the graveyard. As they progressed, a thin ground fog rose. The moon was still clear of any clouds, touching the yard with a silvery radiance. It ignited the fog, transforming it into glowing tendrils.

Hills rose on all sides, obscuring the sight of anything outside the cemetery although they were near Bristol and the residences surrounded them. It was as if they were cut off from the real world, having entered the realm of the dead.

For as far as the eye could see, Troy spotted only tombstones and grave markers. The moonlight seemed to magnify the stones, making them looming, foreboding. The shadows were as dark as an unlit cave. Even the vegetation, the bushes and trees, appeared more gnarled, almost bony. As the wind blew through the leaves, the sound was dry and worn.

"This place gives me the creeps," J-Man whispered.

"Me too, and you don't need to whisper," Troy told him. "We aren't going to wake anyone."

"Are you sure?" J-Man asked without raising his voice. Before Troy could respond, Barton laughed. It was a dry, hollow sound, more like a cough.

"Mr. Barton, mind if I ask you a few questions on the way?" Troy said.

"Nope. Ask 'way." Barton didn't ask for cash upfront like many people did.

"How long did you work for the TVA on the dam project?"

There was a pause, as if it had happened long ago, in another lifetime. "Mah brother and Ah worked part time for 'bout six months purt near the end of the project. A lot of men were quittin' 'n they paid well. We needed jobs."

"Why were a lot of men quitting?" Troy quickened his pace in order to walk shoulder to shoulder with Barton. The man's head never turned.

"Heh, heh, heh," Barton laughed. "A lot of them were dyin', sort of inspired me to take up this job after it was all over. There's a certain security tied to workin' with death; people always dyin', ya know."

Troy looked over his shoulder at Jay, who shrugged. "Any reason so many were dying?"

" 'Pends on what you wanna believe."

"What did you believe?"

"Not what Ah believe now."

"What did you believe back then?"

"That a lot of freak accidents were goin' on. A lot of men whispered tales of the Dark Lady who'd ensorcered men's souls 'n drove them to dyin', but Ah didn't believe none of it. Ah've worked construction many a time, and sometimes certain projects just 'ave bad luck, almost like they're cursed. Ah figured South Holston was like that. Ah dinna believe any of the rumors. It was just a lot of superstitious mishmash." Barton shook his head.

They entered a small courtyard with a fountain in the middle. A statue of a blindfolded woman stood in the center of the pool. The water was turned off so nothing poured from her jug. Circling all around them were tall headstones, some reaching nearly four feet in height. The ones in shadow reminded Troy of monoliths. Plastic and silk flowers still decorated the graves.

"What do you believe now?" Troy asked. Darkness descended as the clouds buried the moon.

"That all the rumors was based on the truth. The project was more than cursed. It was damned. The Dark Lady and others exist. They've been round for centuries. They stole men's souls and drove others crazy. Accidents was planned. The immortals didn't want the dam to be built."

Troy wondered why the Dark Lady and her cohorts didn't want the dam to be built. Was it the dam . . . or the lake?

They left the courtyard. Troy noticed his friends had

been extremely quiet. Something about the cemetery demanded somberness. Troy looked to the sky. Stars peaked through the patches of clouds.

"What made you change your mind?" Troy asked.

"The past several days, startin' with Tim's murder."

They were approaching a small building with a door and several windows. No lights were on. The door was ajar.

"What happened?"

"The immortals came for a visit. They came to revive a few friends." Barton laughed. He reached inside the door and flipped on a dim light. Troy briefly shielded his eyes. "After sunset, the mist rolled 'cross the ground, hidin' the yard in fog. Then three of 'em came, lords and ladies of the night. One of 'em kissed Tim and he passed on."

Troy stopped moving. The tone of Barton's voice had grown colder, warning Troy.

Barton took a step inside. "Yes," he almost hissed, "she was a purdy thang, downright magnificent. Dark eyes like a midnight sky, skin as pale as white linens, and full, blood red lips. Hair, long 'n black like coal, flowed down her back."

Troy broke out in a cold sweat. Without thinking, he began to draw his revolver. Knives and Spider looked surprised. J-Man pulled out his .38. "She kissed Tim Barton, givin' im a new life," Barton continued. "Freed 'im from worry, from time, from the limitations of weak flesh. Now he has time to enjoy life's passions.

" 'N Ah passed this legacy onto mah brother, Phillip Barton," the man said. "Just finished buryin' 'im in fact. Soon he will be one of us. You," he said, eyes boring down on Troy, "are just gonna die." He smiled widely, revealing canine-length incisors.

His gaze struck Troy like a hammer, knocking him backwards. As Troy staggered, his finger froze on the trigger. The gun grew heavy and his arm dropped.

"Goddamn vampires, you killed my friends!!" The blasting of Spider's revolver wrenched Troy from his paralysis. Screaming bullets sailed past Troy's ear and ripped into Tim Barton.

The undead watchman was driven back by the impact of the shells. Holes in his chest and shoulders bloodlessly erupted. Barton staggered, then hung onto the doorjamb.

J-Man followed suit, opening fire. His revolver bucked in his hand.

The silver bullets tore at the vampire, but he held his ground as the slugs tore at him. His grin grew broader and he laughed.

Troy pointed and fired. Four of his bullets blew holes in the creature of the dark. Two ripped into Barton's forehead and he still laughed. Troy kept pulling the trigger, even after the chamber was empty.

"Are you through with your noisy toys?" it hissed, then straightened. Suddenly, all the holes disappeared and its flesh appeared whole. Its tongue flicked over its teeth. "Time to die," it said.

Laughing, it leaped forward.

Chapter Fifteen
The Cold Reach of Darkness

In front of Aunt Jada's home, Silke's rental Bronco screeched to a halt in the driveway. Silke noticed that only a light in the living room shone through the front blinds. The rest of the house was swallowed in darkness.

She ran up the steps to the door. Silke didn't ring the doorbell or knock, she just turned the knob. Somehow she knew she would find it unlocked.

Her heart pounding, Silke stepped into the house. A soft light emanated from her left and dimly lit the entranceway.

A dark shape appeared before her. It grew larger. Silke caught her breath and stopped. The shape halted.

Silke reached out to touch the mirror. Scared of my own shadow, she thought.

Following the hallway, Silke headed for the living room. A lamp on the far end table of the couch dimly illuminated the room. Aunt Jada lay on the floor, next to the handset of the telephone.

Silke placed her hand over her mouth, silencing her own scream. She rushed to her fallen aunt. Aunt Jada was lying face down on the carpet. The coffee table had been overturned and magazines, dried flowers, and crystals were scattered everywhere, as if a tiny whirlwind had struck.

Silke rolled the body over to find her aunt's eyes closed. No look of terror was on her face, just an expression of peace. Her skin had taken on a bluish hue. Silke checked for a pulse and found none.

Silke began to weep. She couldn't believe her aunt was truly dead. On her drive over, Silke had pushed the idea from her mind, hoping against what she felt must be true.

Through her tears, she noticed sparkling bits of glass around Jada's body. Silke touched them. They weren't glass, but quartz crystals.

Dangling from Aunt Jada's ears were silver wires. Silke checked her necklace. All the stones were gone. It was as if they'd exploded. Silke found tiny crystalline shards everywhere.

What had happened? Did she have a stroke? Or had the darkness she feared reached out and touched her? And where was Sister Elva?

Silke wiped away the tears from her cheeks, but more kept coming. Sobs escaped her.

Something shuffled behind her. There was a thud.

Before she could turn, a hand dropped on her shoulder. Screaming, Silke stared into the wide eyes of Sister Elva.

The sharp-faced woman grabbed Silke by both shoulders and turned her around. Sister Elva shook her. "Silke! Silke! What has happened?"

Silke looked at her aunt's nurse and the scream died in her throat. A look of anguish was painted on Sister Elva's face. Silke couldn't speak.

"What has happened? Tell me!" Sister Elva voice grew shrill. Then she recovered. "Have you called an ambulance?"

Silke nodded her head. "Yes," she whispered.

* * *

Teeth flashing, Barton attacked Troy. The vampire reached out to grab him when a searing light exploded before Troy's face. Clutching his eyes, the undead staggered back.

"Troy, run like hell," J-Man said from behind him. He pulled the flare from in front of Troy and threw it at the undead. "Run for the car, come on!" J-Man urged.

Almost blind, Troy ran. He could hardly make out J-Man's back as they sprinted across the lawn. Muffled footsteps came from ahead of him as Spider and Knives raced for the car.

"There's a hammer in the Blazer," Jay breathed loudly. "We . . . we can make a stake. God willing we have time, that is!"

Troy staggered along, his breath exploding from his lungs. The stare of the vampire had taken something out of him. *Run faster,* he yelled at himself. He stumbled but stayed on his feet as the grass turned to concrete and they raced through the courtyard.

A loud, chilling laugh carried on the wind. Suddenly, heavy wings flapped and passed overhead.

"It's landing in front of us!" Knives yelled. He skidded to a stop. Spider almost ran into him. Knives fired his gun as the bat enlarged, exchanging wings for arms. Barton blocked their path. His teeth shone brightly in the moonlight.

J-Man stopped and pulled a thin tube from his jacket pocket. There was a flash of light and then a spark. Troy heard a sizzling. "Denny gave me a couple sticks of dynamite!" He tossed it toward Barton. *"Run, guys!"*

J-Man went left. Troy went right. The stick landed at Barton's feet. Spider and Knives dove away.

Run, run, run . . . faster, Troy thought. *Faster!* Troy stumbled through some bushes. They tore at his legs, slowing him.

Boooommmm! It echoed through the yard and across the mountains.

The explosion rang in Troy's ears. Now he was half deaf as well as blind. He staggered along through an open stretch of lawn. Troy shook his head. His vision began to clear. *Run!*

The ground disappeared beneath his feet. Arms waving wildly, Troy fell forward. His chest struck the far side of the grave, ripping away his breath. Gagging, Troy slipped into the pit. His grasping hands raked dirt along with him as he fell. Earth rained down upon him.

Troy collapsed on the bottom, giving up. He waited to be buried, just waited. Seconds passed. The last few pebbles bounced down, then all was still. Nothing happened. He wasn't buried like in his dream. A light wind blew over the grave and a leaf tumbled inside. All was silent.

Slowly Troy recovered his breath. He stifled a moan. His ribs ached and his shoulder was pounding. He gradually opened his eyes.

He looked into the sky. No stars were in sight. The sky was full of clouds.

Troy climbed to his knees, then crouched in the pit. He lifted his head over the edge and slowly looked around.

The fog had thickened, blotting out visibility and muffling sound. He thought he saw a light sweep through the fog, then it disappeared.

Troy decided he couldn't stay there all night. He didn't know if vampires could smell blood or sense life. And he wasn't going to wait and find out. He fondled the cross around his neck and hoped it would aid him in some way. He also prayed the others were safe behind their crucifixes.

Troy concluded that he'd head for the nearest fence and climb out. He could wait in the woods across the road from the Blazer. Damn, Troy thought, he felt like he was deserting his brothers, but they should be doing the same thing. Damn them, they hadn't discussed what to do if they were split up. He cursed his own stupidity.

Troy quickly crawled out of the pit and sprinted across an open stretch. Headstones lined each side. Staying low as he ran, Troy headed for a cluster of trees. The fog swirled around him. His raging heart thundered in his ears as he strained to hear the beating of wings.

Troy reached the trees and jumped into the shadows. His breath whistled through his nostrils. Sweat beaded on his forehead. What he had seen boggled his mind. Terror clawed at him and he fought it with everything he'd learned while playing sports—willpower, visualization, and controlled body mechanics.

Troy heard a crash and then a shriek as if metal was being dragged across the ground. He whirled around, confused by the fog. What in the hell was that? Troy wondered. Where did it come from? It had sounded like a car.

Surveying the landscape, Troy concluded he didn't know where in the hell he was right now. He'd gotten turned around. The visibility lessened to twenty feet.

Whhummp. A muffled sound came from Troy's right. It sounded like the slamming of a car door.

"Hey!" came a hushed whisper with force. A hand touched Troy's shoulder. He jumped a foot and nearly screamed, then he saw Knives.

Troy could hardly breathe as he collapsed against the tree. Knives pulled him to his knees. "Pulmonary problems?"

"I . . . I nearly shit in my pants," Troy panted, still shaking.

"Color's not too good either," Knives said.

"Not . . . not surprised. I'm being chased by a God-damned vampire—something I didn't even believe in until about three minutes ago. He's chasing you too," Troy muttered. "Or hadn't you noticed?" Knives gave him a tight smile. "Seen anyone else?"

Knives shook his head. "I can't see anything. I didn't know you were around until you almost stepped on me."

"What are we gonna do?"

"Probably die," Knives said solemnly.

Troy started to snap a bitter reply when a scream ripped the night. "No! No! Stay away!" Shots were fired. The sounds seemed to dance in the fog, coming from everywhere.

"That sounds like Spider!" Troy said.

The shots rang again. "Follow the gunfire," Knives said. He took off running. Troy followed. They dodged through the trees and ran toward the struggle. Troy hurdled over a small headstone and dodged a squared piece of granite. A bush appeared out of nowhere. He leaped over it.

Funny, Troy thought, he didn't know what they were going to do when they arrived, but he couldn't desert Spider. Friends didn't leave friends to die.

"Halt, this is the police!" warned a voice.

"It's Glazier," Troy breathed. They saw a beam of light.

Troy and Knives burst into the courtyard. Illuminated in the haze of Glazier's flashlight, Spider struggled with Barton. The vampire grabbed Spider's arm and he dropped the gun. It shifted its grip and lifted their friend by his throat. The fountain was visible just behind them.

Troy and Knives leaped together as one. "Shove him in the water!" Knives yelled.

Surprising the vampire, they bowled Barton over.

The undead staggered back, throwing Spider in the water. Barton grabbed Knives and pulled him into the fountain. Troy's momentum put him on top. They landed with a splash.

The water was two-feet deep. Knives and Troy piled on Barton. "Hold 'im down," Troy gurgled, spitting water.

Water sprayed everywhere. A spotlight landed on them. The vampire grabbed Knives by the throat and threw him aside. He crashed into the center statue.

The undead tried to rise from the water. Piling on, Spider joined the melee. Then, J-Man splashed through the water. He carried a foot-long branch. "Gonna stake the bastard!"

Hands shot up and smashed Troy in the face. His head snapped back. He saw Glazier behind the beam standing dumbly at the edge of the fountain.

Troy had an idea. "Bill!" he shouted, "turn on the fountain!" Bill didn't move. Troy was struck again. He fell off the vampire's chest and sank into the pool.

As the undead tried to rise, J-Man jammed the branch downward. The vampire twisted. J-Man drove the makeshift stake into its midsection. Barton snarled and struck, driving Jay back.

Recovering, Troy wallowed in the water. "BILL! Turn on the fountain! FOR GOD'S SAKE, TURN ON THE WATER! RUN THE WATER!"

Bill moved. Waving the light around, he ran to a column of stone and searched. He found nothing. His eyes scanning the ground and trees, he moved in a circle around the fountain.

Barton ripped the makeshift stake from his flesh and tossed it aside. It grabbed Spider's throat in one hand and J-Man's in the other. Their eyes bulged. Desperate hands raked at the vampire's arms, clutching at its steely grip.

300

Still on the move, Glazier desperately looked for some type of switch. He couldn't find anything.

The vampire sat up and shoved the two underwater, smashing their faces against the bottom of the fountain. Bubbles escaped from their lips and nostrils. Barton laughed.

Glazier spied a white stone bench. He ran for it.

Troy kicked at Barton's grinning face. He missed, not sure whether the undead had dodged or if his foot had passed through him.

The pressure was tremendous on Spider's neck. He was beginning to black out. J-Man's face began to turn red. His hands futilely scraped at the concrete floor.

Bill found the switch below the bench and flipped it.

Behind the combatants, a gurgling sound came from the jug. Then water shot forth, showering them. It struck Barton in the back. He screamed and grabbed at himself, freeing Spider and Wreck. They popped to the surface like corks. With heaving lungs, they sucked down air.

Starting to sizzle, Barton rose. Smoke poured from him. His face was ghostly white and twisted in a grimace of agony. His gnashing teeth drew blood from his own lips.

Having recovered, Knives dove at Barton's knees while Troy hit him high. The vampire collapsed, his screams lost in the churning water. Hands wrapped around Barton's throat, Troy struggled to keep the creature of night submerged. Knives sat on the vampire's legs.

Trembling hands clawed their way up Troy's forearms. They slapped at his face and feebly clawed at his eyes. Troy refused to let go — he would die first.

J-Man piled on top. He held Barton's hips down.

Troy watched through squinted eyes as water splashed all around them. It seemed to encircle them.

301

Beneath the surface, the panic in Barton's eyes heightened, then dimmed. The questing fingers slowed, weakly grabbing Troy's throat. Trembling, they fell away. Barton's jaw grew slack. Then the vampire began to dissolve.

Hair disintegrated, then flesh eroded. Skin disappeared, revealing bone. The eyes emptied to sockets. Bone grew pitted as if dipped in an acid bath.

Suddenly, they held nothing down. All they gripped was empty clothing. The vampire was no more.

Gasping, Troy turned to J-Man. "He's gone! We destroyed him!" He began to laugh hysterically.

J-Man joined in, joy touching their souls. Knives got caught up in the laughter, and the three friends roared and rolled in the water. J-Man began splashing and making waves.

Spider crawled over to join them. For the first time in a long time, he gave them a genuine smile.

Detective Glazier walked to the edge of the fountain and watched them. He thought they were insane. Then he noticed there were only four men in the fountain. "Hey, what the hell's goin' on here?!"

Chapter Sixteen
Flashbacks

The next afternoon the sun broke through the clouds, reaching down to touch the foursome in the maroon and gold bass boat as it cruised across South Holston Lake. Despite the magnificent surroundings, the mood was somber. Their encounter with the vampire had left them drained physically and emotionally.

Troy leaned back, welcoming the warmth of the sun on his face. Last night's adventure had chilled him to the bone and its frigid touch still remained. Troy pulled in the sun's heat and tried to burn away the terror, anxiety, and fatigue of the past sixteen hours.

The wind whistled through the cockpit as the boat carved through the placid lake. No one had said a word since they launched and the radio was silent. They only dimly noticed the mountains crawling by as if the boat stood still. A flock of ducks passed overhead, then disappeared.

Troy gazed around him. They had just passed the park, then a wide cove, and were now entering the snakish part of the lake which led to the 421 bridge. It was at least another fifteen minutes until they'd reach Cemetery Ridge.

J-Man casually steered his bass boat across the water. The Procraft was set low, seeming to put the surrounding water within easy reach. A gray one-hundred-fifty horsepower Evinrude outboard hurled them forward, whinning its mechanical song. Jay hummed as they cruised along, occasionally sipping from a can of root beer.

Knives and Spider prepared for the upcoming dive. Stephen messed with the straps of his buoyancy compensator. He tightened them, then started to work on his mask, wiping it with a defogging chemical. Checking the batteries, he flicked his flashlight on and off. Across from Knives, Spider strapped a sheath onto his leg. It housed a blunt-nosed knife. As if he couldn't keep his eyes off of it, Spider picked up the ornate jewelry box. He fondled it, turning it over and over again in his hands. The silver clasps flashed in the sunlight.

As Troy's mind wandered, the shore became a blur. He was in the graveyard again, replaying last night's nightmare.

He remembered holding the empty clothing in his hands where only seconds ago he'd held a creature of the night, an undead being . . . a vampire. The shock still touched Troy. One minute the undead was clawing for his throat with superhuman strength, the next it disintegrated under the pure, life-giving waters. The abomination was erased from existence . . . but there were others.

Despite the horror that thought carried, there was another, worse horror he couldn't shake. He remembered when Barton had turned on them and the bullets ripped into the vampire, but didn't wound it in the slightest. The terror had grabbed Troy then—a blinding, nearly unreasoning terror. Troy was so scared he'd plunged into an open grave and wanted to die. He just waited for them to bury him! He shook his head.

Troy was disgusted with himself. Even if it was just for a moment, how easily he had surrendered his life.

He had just waited to die. Troy cursed at himself and pounded his fist on the top of the aerator.

Now what? How many vampires were running around town? A hundred? A thousand? Didn't Aunt Jada see a friend who was supposed to be dead walking down the street in plain sight? Yes, but that was during the morning — that was during daylight. Legends said vampires died when exposed to sunlight. Were legends true? They had been accurate about running water.

What's the difference? Troy thought. Whether in daylight or night, there was little humans could do to combat vampires. Troy felt nearly helpless. What if, he wondered, vampires had Dillon? Deep in his soul, Troy was afraid this was true.

His arms ached from wrist to shoulder. Even now, he still hurt where Barton's fingers had dug in. Troy's bruises mapped the path of the vampire's desperate, dying hands.

Detective Bill Glazier, once a close friend, didn't believe them. He didn't believe any of them, not Spider, or Knives, or J-Man, or even his own eyes. Sadly, Troy watched it happen. Glazier shut down on them. His mind locked. Bill wouldn't allow himself to believe it. He couldn't handle it. Troy was surprised the others had — it was so incredible, so unbelievable. Maybe the wolf attack had primed them. Troy was surprised he believed it, but their survival depended on it.

No matter what his eyes had seen, and despite the fact he'd turned on the fountain to save them, Detective William Glazier emphatically denied the possibility of vampires. He wouldn't even let them discuss it in his presence.

Bill couldn't decide whether to report the incident or even what to report if he did. Troy could tell Bill was bewildered. He didn't even say anything about them taking the revolvers from the scene. They'd left bullets buried in the shack and scattered across the lawn. An investigation would show that. Troy suggested to Bill that he report nothing — they wouldn't believe him anyway.

Bill told them to drive to his house and that he would meet them there later. On the way, Troy started worrying about Silke. As soon as they arrived he tried to call her. There was no answer. He chewed his lip. "I'm gonna drive out to J-Man's. No one is answering the phone. I'm worried about Silke."

"Sit," Knives told him. "If she took her medication she's fast asleep and the phone probably won't wake her. Besides, you can't go alone. You're exhausted. You need at least a few minutes of rest or you'll be worthless. Those are doctor's orders." Troy bit back his reply. He would wait a few more minutes, then tell Knives to shove his doctorly advice. Troy watched as Knives grabbed a pad of paper and began scribbling notes.

They'd been at Glazier's for nearly an hour and not one of them had brought up the vampire. It was as if they were digesting the incident. No one wanted to talk about the possibilities.

Troy made more phone calls. Silke didn't answer at J-Man's place. Or at Mrs. Urich's. He felt the fear gnawing at the pit of his stomach. If anything had happened to Silke . . . Troy decided to call one more time, then drive out to the lake. But while he lay on the couch, phone to his ear, waiting for someone to pick up, he fell into an exhausted sleep.

Almost two hours later, Troy awoke when Detective William Glazier came home. He looked grim and determined. Bill told them Silke had asked him to visit the cemetery. No, he didn't know where she was right now. Troy cursed and moved to leave. Knives and Bill grabbed him and forced him to sit. They told him if something had happened to her it would already be too

306

late to help. The worst part was, they were probably right.

Over coffee, they had a late-night powwow.

Glazier wanted them all to come down and file statements. Plus, he wanted the revolvers. The detective had to follow procedure, especially because things around Bristol had been so strange of late.

Troy smiled, remembering the curve Jay Beck had thrown him. "Uh, Bill, we have a small problem. I seem to have mislaid the gun that Spider was using."

"You did? Where?"

"Someplace around here, with all the boxes and furniture askew, I lost it. I might have even left it outside." Glazier's eyes narrowed.

"Ya know," Knives said, "I'm glad Bill was with us from the start. If he hadn't driven through the gates, we never would've caught and killed the vampire." Knives looked steadily at Bill.

"That's blackmail," Bill accused. He ran a hand through his hair as if brushing fleas away. "I won't stand for it."

"We'd all pass lie detectors," Knives said simply. "It's very close to the truth. I believe if you hadn't crashed the gates, and turned on the fountain, we wouldn't be alive right now."

"In fact, the missing .38 is one you gave Denny for his twenty-fifth birthday," J-Man informed him.

Even Spider cracked a smile. Troy said, "Listen, Bill, let's be rational . . . and emotional about this. If we get bogged down, we might never find Dillon . . . and a lot more people might die. We've already lost two friends. We don't know what to do, but we do know we want to finish it."

Bill sighed. "This is going against my better judgment, but I'd shelve my guns away for a while if I were y'all."

"Might as well," Troy said, "they didn't do us any good."

"Shotguns work better on wolves anyway," J-Man told him.

Bill blanched, then his face tightened and he said, "I don't want you shooting up the area!"

"Only in self-defense," Knives promised.

"Troy," Bill asked, "can you explain what's going on?"

"Not really, but I'll try," Troy said, and he did. Troy mentioned his dreams, told them about his underwater nightmare, and how they matched. They discussed the graves and finding Traylor's body, his neck torn open. No one mentioned the jewelry box. They all agreed that running water killed Barton and silver bullets hadn't. Silver slew the wolves.

Bill listened intently as Troy told him about their TVA research and subsequent interviews. Their theories as to what was going on sounded like plots for B movies — aliens from outer space, mutants from Chernobyl, a bad batch of moonshine. In ridiculing the facts, their mood lightened. Even Troy had to laugh once or twice.

The next several hours blurred. Silke finally called . . . from the hospital. She was relieved to find Troy safe, but sobbed while telling him that Aunt Jada was in a coma and might not last the night.

J-Man rushed Troy to the hospital.

Troy found Silke in Mrs. Urich's arms. Her beautiful amber eyes were red-rimmed. Her long hair was tangled. She cried on his shoulder for a while, then with her full lips trembling, Silke finally told him the story as well as Jada's warning. Troy listened intently, stroked her, and bid her to rest. The doctor gave her a sedative.

Troy was strung out, but wouldn't let Silke see that. Melting in his arms, Silke deflated immediately after taking the capsule.

Not long after, exhaustion finally overcame Troy and he too fell asleep. They curled up on the couch. When Troy awoke, someone had taken off his shoes. It was mid-morning. The light streaming through the window did not wash away the memory of the preceding night. Troy's first thoughts: I'm glad to be alive! I'm glad Silke's safe.

After Silke had been awake for a while, he told her of their plans to dive today. In a quiet voice, Silke told him to be careful and again repeated Aunt Jada's warning to beware of Dillon, his best friend. Troy didn't tell her about the vampire, and she didn't ask. Troy wasn't sure she was ready for it.

With a wisp of a smile, Silke gave him her car keys. Troy kissed her, then departed. He felt awful leaving, but he'd go crazy if he stayed in the hospital much longer. Troy needed air and space.

"Here," Knives said, interrupting Troy's thoughts and pulling him back to the present. He handed him two capsules. "Take these."

"They won't affect my diving?"

"Won't affect your diving a bit, but they may save your life."

"What are they?"

"Full of questions today, aren't we?" Knives said. "You think I'm poisoning you?"

"Of course not. What are they?"

"Something I learned about during an experiment at school. You have to take both to be effective. They're good for eight hours." Knives handed him a small bottle filled with both white and blue capsules. "Take one of each every eight hours. I'll check on you every twenty-four hours."

"Tough to do from Richmond."

"I cancelled things for a while. What I couldn't,

309

other people are taking care of for me."

"Is that fair to your patients?"

"Hey, I have blood brothers to take care of. Besides, the chance to examine the undead up close could bring about a scientific breakthrough."

"Please! You've got to be joking," Troy said as he popped the two pills.

"Seriously. What flows in their veins? How do they live so long? Is that a function of drinking blood? Although I think that has already been disproved. A tissue sample may reveal some amazing results."

"This doesn't frighten you?" Troy asked.

"It's science and discovery," Knives said. "Vampires might just be a different species, and I—" Troy shook his head and held up both hands, palms away, to signal surrender—no more.

"Only Dr. Stephen Curran," J-Man said, "would see this as an educational opportunity."

Troy smiled in agreement. "This doesn't bother you at all, does it?" Troy asked Jay.

"I just hide it well," J-Man said over his shoulder. "I'm scared spitless, but you know me, I take the risks anyway. There's no other way to live. A person can be scared, but he doesn't have to give in."

Troy nodded. He too had decided not to surrender, to struggle until the last card was dealt. Absently, Troy played with the ring he held in his hand. Bright blue sparks danced as the sunlight played through it. The stone was so brilliant that the word *magic* skipped through Troy's thoughts. It had looked perfect on Racquel's hand.

Thinking of her wide smile, dark auburn hair, and green eyes, immediately carried Troy's mind back to their meeting in the hospital parking lot as he'd been leaving Silke. "Fancy meetin' you here," Racquel yelled to Troy as he headed across the street toward Silke's rental Bronco. She was on the far curb.

Lost in thought, Troy did a double take. "Oh, hi," he managed without much enthusiasm, despite the fact that she looked radiant. Racquel obviously had spent plenty of time in the sun—she was a deep bronze. Her dark auburn hair was pulled back in a pony tail and she wore sunglasses with white frames. She was dressed in all white.

"Ya don't look too thrilled t' see me," she said with a pout.

Troy stopped next to her. "How about 'surprised'?" he said.

She smiled. "Somehow Ah don't think you were goin' t' make our lunch date."

"I think you're right," he said simply.

"Ya look like hell. Must've been busy." She gently reached out and touched his swollen lip, "Nice. You nevah got like this when we dated. Nevah thought you'd be in a barroom brawl."

"Long story."

"Ah'm takin' ya' t' breakfast." She gently grabbed his arm, watched him flinch, then let him go. "Do you 'ave t' be somewhere?" Racquel said softly. Troy saw confusion and concern in her eyes.

"Not until this afternoon. I'm going diving with the boys."

"With the blood brothers?" she asked pointedly.

"Knives, Spider, and Jay."

"An interesting trio."

There was a long silence. Neither moved. Troy couldn't quite convince himself to just move on. He looked back at the hospital and thought about Aunt Jada's words.

"Well, how 'bout breakfast? Ah promise not t' bite."

Without turning, Troy quickly glanced at her. "Sure. I could use some caffeine to wake me up."

They took separate cars and met at the Krispy Kreme. "Still serves the best donuts in town," Racquel said.

Sitting at the table with a cup of coffee in hand, she said. "So, how didya get so messed up?"

"The other got the worst of it. Question for you," he said and Racquel raised her eyebrows. She'd taken off her sunglasses and her eyes had an almost hypnotic effect on him. The attraction was still strong between them. "Have you ever been on Cemetery Ridge?"

Her face brightened. "Funn'ah you should ask that a second time. You asked me 'bout this on the phone."

"My mind doesn't seem to be working too well. I should have remembered that."

Racquel patted him on the cheek. "Barroom brawlin' will do that," she said with a wan smile. "T' answer ya question—" She held up her left hand and wriggled her index finger. She wore a ring with a sapphire. "Ah was just thinkin' 'bout that place when Ah found this two weeks ago. Ah'd thought Ah'd lost it. Ah originally found it on that isle. It was neat t' 'ave somethin' from Wreythville. Why all the questions?" she asked.

"Could I borrow it for a while?" he asked. Troy couldn't look away from her jade green eyes.

"For a price," she said. A slight smile slowly touched her lips.

"Which is?"

"A picnic before you leave town."

"Deal."

They talked for over an hour. During that time, Troy wondered if he'd ever stop catching his breath when he saw her or be able to resist her charms.

Talking to Racquel was easy. He told her about his dreams and about all that had happened to him. Racquel was visibly upset by his first-hand account of the fire at Marader's dock. She had heard about Aaron and

Pete's deaths. Again, he didn't mention the jewelry box or Aunt Jada.

Racquel didn't understand why they were going diving again, and Troy couldn't fully explain it. He could tell Racquel wanted to dissuade him, but didn't. She probably knew it wouldn't do any good.

They hugged in the parking lot. Racquel felt vibrant in his arms and he almost kissed her. She kissed him on the cheek. Then she was gone, and his heart felt heavy for a moment. Then Troy thought about Silke and smiled.

He was somber during his drive to Marader's dock. He arrived around noon. No one else had arrived yet. Elle was working by herself. He stood on shore talking to her and watching the crew from the Rentzel Construction Company take a break. Most of the structure was complete.

"You were trying to hit on Dillon too?" Troy asked.

Her emerald eyes shining, Elle said, "Of course. I told you that you two look a lot alike. I find you both very attractive."

"On the day he disappeared, did you talk when he stopped in to borrow equipment?"

"Yes."

"About?"

"Dinner."

"How about something important, something that will help me find him?"

Elle furrowed her brow in thought. "He showed me a drawing. Said it was a sketch of the lake's bottom." She shrugged and said, "There wasn't much to it."

"Could you draw it from memory?"

"I think so."

Troy ran back to the car and found a paper and pen. He gave them to Elle. She sketched from memory. At the top was a circle covered with crosses — Troy thought

313

that might be the graveyard. Below it was a series of boxes. The top left one had a plus on it, looking like a church. Several times, Elle circled a box below the church.

"What's that?" Troy asked.

"I never asked. There might have been an arrow pointing towards it, too. I don't quite remember," Elle said. "Now, about dinner."

"Elle, I can't. I'm already interested in somebody."

"So?"

"Let's change the subject. You said you haven't seen Tom since early yesterday?"

"Right."

"Who supervised the construction?"

"They seemed to know what they were doing," she replied.

"I'm worried about Tom, the little shit. He was supposed to be at J-Man's last night and wasn't." Troy then bade Elle good-bye and walked to the edge of the dock to scan the lake for his friends.

A boat suddenly swerved near the dock, spraying Troy with cool water. J-Man sat at the wheel. Spider and Knives were in back. "Sorry," he called. "Thinking too much and miscalculated."

"What are you thinking about?" Troy asked.

"Dying. There's a lot of it going around these days."

"Every day," Spider said.

"Well, Troy, this is another fine mess you've gotten us in," J-Man said.

"Blame it on Dillon. I wasn't even in town when this started."

"But we're glad you joined our 'Return of the Supernatural in Bristol' party," Jay said with a laugh. "So, oh deep thinker, what are *you* contemplating?"

"Women."

Spider grunted and J-Man laughed. "Racquel?"

Knives asked.

"And Silke," Troy replied. He saw Silke's face in his mind's eye. Troy needed her strength to keep going.

Troy jumped in the boat. About a half-hour later they would arrive at their destination.

The boat slowed and the motor quieted.

"We're here," J-Man said. Troy stopped reminescing Their wake grew smaller and the white water disappeared as the Procraft cruised to a bobbing halt. Cemetery Ridge was straight ahead.

The sun beat down on them from a nearly cloudless sky. Red rock surrounded the calm waters. There was no breeze. The day was oppressively still.

"What are we looking for?" J-Man asked.

Spider was staring intently at the jewelry box when he said, "I think we'll know when we find it. Try and use intuition." He closed his eyes for a moment, then looked at Troy. "I feel a pull."

"Let's go with it," Troy said. He put Racquel's ring in his wet-suit pocket.

"Everybody into the pool," J-Man said. He turned off the motor and flipped on the radio. They needed something to cover the eerie silence.

Knives threw the anchor overboard. It splashed, then quickly sank, pulling the line from the boat. Finally, the rope quit spiraling out. Checking the remaining line, Knives said, "Looks like it's about ninety feet deep." He tied it to a grommet left of the bow.

Troy climbed to the back of the boat where he slipped into his black wet suit, buckled on his weight belt, and strapped on a knife. He checked the straps on his BC, then turned on his air. The gauge registered three-thousand psi. Sticking the regulator in his mouth, he blew out, then sucked in. He had a clean flow of air.

"Beats holding your breath like when we were little and only dreamed of diving," Knives said as he zipped

315

up the front of his wet suit.

"I don't even remember dreaming about scuba diving," Troy said. "I wanted to breathe water. Instead, I practice holding my breath." He gave an abrupt laugh and said, "At one time, I thought the only thing I was really good at was holding my breath. I remember lasting around three minutes several times." Troy shook his head.

Zipping his black wet suit up to his neck, Troy felt sealed in. He patted the pocket containing the ring. Then Troy suddenly changed his mind about wearing the sapphire. Without knowing why, he dug it out and slipped it on. Surprisingly, it fit perfectly—just as it had on Racquel's finger. The sapphire sparkled like blue fire.

The flash caught Knives's eye. "Where'd you get that?" he asked.

"From Racquel."

He scowled, then said, "Ah, the one she found on Cemetery Ridge."

"Yep."

"Why are you wearing it?"

"Feels like the right thing to do."

"No obsession like Marader and the jewelry box?"

"No. You want to wear it? I think one of us should."

"No thanks. But you should follow your intuition."

"I guess." Troy shook his head. First werewolves and vampires, now psychometry. His brain must be turning to mush. Still, the ring seemed to give him confidence and energy as if it were protecting him.

Troy looked at his friends. This time, each wore a wet suit. They planned on being along the bottom for at least twenty minutes and the bottom was probably chilly. Funny, Troy thought, he'd already been on the bottom near Wreythville, and he couldn't remember the temperature. Showed what state of mind he'd been in. They'd need flashlights too, he thought. He turned his on.

Troy stretched, then forced a yawn. The tension was evident in the air. Troy could feel it. His friends were worried. This wasn't a typical dive. They didn't know what they were looking for, or what was lurking at the bottom of the lake. Troy remembered the skeleton crawling from its grave, holding onto him, then shook his head. He tried to forget, focusing on the business at hand. "Anyone have a dive watch?"

"I do," J-Man and Knives said at the same time. Both faces were studies in concentration.

"Good." Troy played with his cross as he watched the others get ready. He tucked it under his wet suit.

Spider had placed the jewelry box in a mesh net. "Those look like something Marader would wear," Troy said, pointing to the neon green gloves Spider wore.

"They *are* his," he said stoically. Spider sat down and slipped into his tank. He buckled the yellow BC, then stuck his mask on his head. Water dribbled down the side of his face. He turned on his flashlight, then hooked it on his weight belt.

"How are we buddying up?" Knives asked.

"Spider and J-Man, you and me?" Troy suggested. "Spider and I have recently been down there."

Everyone nodded. "Fine by me," J-Man said. He stuck three bright orange tubes in the pocket of his orange BC.

"What are those?" Troy asked.

"Underwater flares. They came in handy once."

"I'd like an underwater crossbow," Knives commented.

"Really," Troy said. "But we shouldn't have to worry about the undead while underwater. Everyone have a flashlight that works?" The trio nodded.

"I came prepared," Stephen Curran said, holding a

silver cross aloft. "I even convinced Bob to bless it for me," he said with a smile. His blue eyes twinkled. "And just in case, an iron spike. I seem to remember that vampires don't like cold iron."

"Let's hope we don't need it," J-Man said. He put on his mask, then sat on the edge. "Everybody ready?"

Troy put on his fins, then slipped into his BC and tank. "I am," he said as he strapped in. Troy looked at the ring one more time. It seemed to be winking at him.

Knives pulled his mask onto his face. "Troy, I'm gonna keep a close eye on you."

"I'd appreciate that. My last trip wasn't much fun."

Knives nodded sympathetically. "Ready here. Everyone checked air? Anything taste funny?"

"Good here," Spider said. He finished fiddling with the strap on his fins. Black booties came up high on his ankles.

"Let's do it then," Troy said. He grabbed his mask and fell face first into the water. With a flat smack, the lake swallowed him up. Pointing his flashlight downward, Troy sunk into the green waters. As if made from crystal, sparkling bubbles swirled around him.

Knives and Spider rolled backwards into the water. They coasted down to meet Troy.

J-Man scissor-stepped off the edge, leaving the craft rocking.

A few feet below the surface, they paddled to stay near the anchor line, and regrouped. Sunlight cut through the water like cascading beams. Dark chunks of sediment floated by. The world was now bright green.

Each blew a little air in their BC and waited, equalizing the pressure in their ears, readjusting their masks, and testing their air. Troy squeezed his nose, then touched his ears. His head felt fine except for the throbbing along his forehead — his mask was too tight.

Taking it off, Troy loosened the strap. He put it back on, tilted his head back, and blew out through his nose, clearing the mask. As if alive, bubbles danced around him. Yes, his breathing was fine. He hoped that the drugs wouldn't affect him like last time . . . if it had been the drugs and the bad tank of air. It might have been real — or an omen. Troy shivered despite the warmth of the water.

Feeling good and ready, Troy gave a thumbs-up signal. Knives smiled and did the same, then he cleared his mask. In less than a minute, J-Man and Spider lifted their thumbs.

Troy pointed toward the bottom. After watching them nod, he let the air out of his lungs. Silvery bubbles erupted from the relief valve. Troy sank, leaving a glittering trail behind. His friends did the same. Four beams of light followed the anchor line and sliced toward the bottom.

J-Man sank faster, and Troy watched him go by. If he hadn't looked around for his friends, Troy would have felt all alone. Instead of surrounding him with sound, his friends' breathing seemed distant to Troy. His senses felt a little skewed.

Troy shook his head. Surrounded by water, it was easy to feel alone — just me, the hoarse sound of my breathing, and my thundering heart, Troy thought. Just to his right, Knives coughed, sending out a huge burst of bubbles and reminding Troy that he wasn't alone.

The water grew cooler and darker as they descended. Troy equalized about every five feet. His ears only rang once. With lazy kicks, the foursome headed deeper. The murk grew a bit more dense. Visibility diminished to less than twenty-five feet. Troy felt hemmed in, a feeling not unlike his dreams of being buried alive.

They pushed their way through candy wrappers,

plastic bags, and other trash floating atop the thermo-cline. Troy shivered as cold water wrapped around him. The water's visibility improved.

Troy still wasn't sure why they were doing this; yet, nothing else made any sense. They couldn't just sit around and let their friends die and people disappear.

Within the light, Troy could almost see thirty feet. He watched J-Man's long fins swish back and forth in a lazy manner. Then he stopped. They'd reached the bottom. Troy turned to look at Spider who pointed to the right with his left hand. In his other hand, he held the jewelry box.

Troy squinted, thinking that he saw a structure not far away. He pointed his light in that direction, but found nothing. While they paused, several fish came by to investigate. J-Man waved them away. One persistent crappie nibbled at his hair, and J-Man swiped at it several times before it left.

As Troy began to swim toward Wreythville, Spider grabbed him. Troy turned. Spider looked agitated. He shoved the jewelry box into Troy's hands. He took it, wondering what his friend wanted.

The box felt cool, but seemed to dance with electricity. Troy's hands shook and a cold chill crept up his arms. Without closing his eyes, he saw a dark two-story building with shutters and a copper roof. It was partly buried in the mud. The windows were black as if the houses were filled with oil. Feeling the pull of evil, a coy, incessant call, Troy shivered. Suddenly, he knew where they needed to go. It was there, waiting for them just beyond the church.

Troy looked at Spider who nodded and pointed. Spider's face was taut, his dark eyes grim. Troy returned the box to his friend, then began to swim across the bottom of the lake. Knives was on his right while J-Man and Spider followed behind.

Troy wondered if this was how it had happened with Dillon. He wondered if he might find his friend's body in the house of darkness. Troy shivered, his flesh squirming beneath the neoprene.

Yes, Troy knew where to go, but he didn't want to be there. Death called them to come and explore — to come and play.

He shook it off and swam forward strongly. They didn't have air to waste. Troy waved at Knives and pointed at his forearm. Stephen coasted along, holding up eight fingers. They were down eighty feet. To play it safe, they had a maximum of thirty-five minutes on the bottom.

Despite his coursing adrenaline and pounding heart, Troy forced his breathing to remain calm, in a slow and easy rhythm. He didn't want to gulp down all his air.

Knives waved and pointed. On the edge of the beams of light, dark buildings loomed ahead.

As they swam closer, Troy's light danced over a church. One of the front doors were open. The structure stretched up to the limit of visibility, and he could barely see the bell tower. He wondered if the bell were still in there.

They passed the church on the left and another building, a small stone structure on the right. Suddenly, the water grew much colder and more dense. It was harder to swim forward, and Troy wondered if he were somehow being pushed back. There didn't appear to be a current.

Out of the murk and into their lights appeared a foreboding structure. It was made of brick that once might have been white, but now was stained a greenish brown. The shutters were warped and looked as if some tremendous heat had twisted them.

They continued on. Troy noticed that the roof was made of copper, tarnished to green. A chimney sat atop it.

Troy did a double take. The shutters appeared to creep and move. No, he thought, it was an illusion; some type of pattern or shapes writhed in the surface. The shutters stood still.

Beckoning for them to enter, the nearest window stood open. They floated closer, shining their lights inside.

All of a sudden, there was a rush of water and Troy was pushed aside. A fin smashed into his mask, knocking it askew. Water poured inside, momentarily blinding Troy. He collided with Knives and they got entangled. Before they could separate, Spider shot by them and swam into the house. He disappeared into the darkness.

With a silent surge of water, the shutters closed. Spider was in. They were out. Troy thought he heard laughter cavort inside his head.

Chapter Seventeen
The House Below

As Troy blindly tried to disengage himself from Knives's arms and legs, he cursed and swallowed a mouthful of water. Troy coughed and sputtered. Had Spider gone crazy! Had the world gone crazy! What was going on? His friend would never race off, swimming into the house alone—too many strange things were going on. Spider would never have broken one of the primary rules of diving—never leave your buddy. Troy had to get himself straight first. He rearranged his mask and cleared it.

Then Troy knew what he had felt the moment they neared the underwater structure. He could feel it; something evil had drawn Spider inside, then closed up tight. His friend was trapped. Dread crept over Troy. Oh Lord, he thought, I don't want to lose another friend. I've lost two already.

Troy joined J-Man who was already at the window. J-Man pulled and pushed at the wooden barrier, but it didn't budge. Troy tapped him on the shoulders and motioned that he wanted to help. With wide eyes, J-Man agreed.

With fins pressed against the wall for leverage, the

men strained against the old warped shutters, which gave an inch, then slipped from their grasp, snapping back into place. Troy cursed, sending a stream of bubbles upward. In frustration, he tried to pound the shutter. His fist, slowed by the friction of the water, softly tapped the wood.

The trio looked at each other. Frustration was in their faces. J-Man and Troy tried again. They positioned themselves along the sides of the window, straddling it, then gripped the shutters. Again, the window covers moved, then seemed to twist free from their grasp. The shutters slammed shut.

Troy wanted to scream, but couldn't. For a moment helplessness overwhelmed him, dragging him low. He felt like quitting. Spider was as good as dead.

No! Troy told himself. He refused to let another friend die. He wasn't going to surrender! There had to be another way in!

Troy waved his flashlight around, searching for another entrance. Knives and J-Man understood. Lights guiding their way through the murk, they swam in opposite directions. Troy knew they shouldn't split up, but time was of the essence. Rules were made to be broken—or amended in emergencies, Troy thought as he swam down to the first floor.

His light scanned across the wall, searching for anyway to enter. He found another window, but it was also blocked. A cloud of dirt swirled around it. The shutters had slammed tightly. Leaving trails in the mud, the shutters had pulled through the buildup of sediment before shutting. Off to the right, the ground rose, climbing ever higher along the outside wall. Troy followed it.

His flashlight danced over the partly closed shutters on the next window. They trembled. As if still trying to close, the warped louvers shuddered. Troy almost smiled. The shutters were stuck in the mud!

Ignoring the chills along his back, Troy quickly swam over. He examined the window. The mud had piled up so high that the sediment prevented complete closure. Troy shone his light through the opening. It slid across counters, shelves, and a sink. A catfish lazily swam across the opening. The window opened into the kitchen.

Waving his light, Troy signaled J-Man. His friend flashed an okay sign, showing that he understood and swam toward Troy.

Briefly, J-Man scrutinized the window, then took off. He swam around the corner of the house, searching for Knives.

Troy waited, barely holding his impatience in check. He wanted to rush inside the building and locate Spider, but Troy knew better. That would be foolish. They need to stick together to survive.

Troy checked his air gauge. He had 2100 psi left. They'd been underwater for over ten minutes and on the bottom over five. He was using his air faster than usual—too much excitement. Troy visualized the calm surface of the water above. Not a breeze stirred it. All was silent. Troy's heartbeat and breathing slowed. He was in control once more—barely.

Seconds later, J-Man and Knives appeared at his side. Troy pointed inside and they nodded. Taking the lead, Troy swam inside. The hinges screeched and screamed as the shutter tried to break free. Troy wondered if they'd be able to get out. Soundlessly, his friends followed.

Without more than a glance around the kitchen, Troy swam for the door. He had to keep moving to stay warm. Upon entering the house, the water temperature had grown increasingly colder. Fish scattered, scared by his intrusion. The door swung both ways. Troy pushed through it. Even underwater, the hinges seemed to creak. Every sound was heightened and rattled in Troy's ears. Ignore it, he told himself. Only one thing was important: finding Spider and saving him from himself and whatever else this accursed place held. Troy shoved his fear into a far corner of his mind. He'd almost let fear master him in the graveyard. It would not do so here.

Troy paused, floating. His beam illuminated the long hallway that stretched before him. It ended in an opening. There was one door to the left and two to the right. The walls were empty, but the threadbare carpet crawled and shifted along the floor like some undulating creature's back.

Troy decided to head for the opening. He swam up to the ceiling and pulled himself along. J-Man and Knives came through the door. Each kicked away from the twisting carpet and followed Troy.

As Troy pushed himself along the ceiling, he strained his ears to listen. He didn't hear anything except for his breathing and the exhalation of his friends. The house was as silent and dark as a tomb. He continued to crawl along the ceiling. Time seemed to moving at a crawl, too, and Troy didn't feel he was making much progress towards the opening.

Suddenly, the ceiling came apart in his hands. Chunks of plaster fell, slowly raining on him. A white cloud of debris surrounded Troy as he began to sink to the floor.

Troy furiously kicked, working his fins against the water. The carpet seemed to rise up, reaching for him. Troy kicked harder, propelling himself to the ceiling and out of reach. Inside his wet suit, he began to sweat. Patches of fog appeared on his mask.

Troy passed through the hole in the ceiling, then shoved himself out through the open entrance. He swam out into a large entryway. Again, the temperature dropped.

Steps rose to a balcony stretching along the second floor. To his left was the front door. Under the balcony and to his right was a set of double doors. A mirror hung on the wall across from him.

Giving his friends room, Troy moved farther into the entryway. His light danced over the hanging chandelier, sending rays of light spearing throughout the expansive room.

The trio looked at each other. The same thought flashed through their minds and across their faces — which way to go? Where was Spider?

J-Man pointed up. Knives shrugged and shivered. The entryway was even colder. It felt like it was just above freezing. He looked at his hands under his light. A bluish tinge began to develop. Hypothermia was a threat.

Checking his gauges, Troy did a double take. He grabbed J-Man and pointed. It had only seemed a minute or two since he'd checked his air, but it must have been longer. Troy only had 1200 psi left. J-Man had 1100 while Knives had 1300.

Had it taken that long? Troy wondered. Confused, he looked back at the hallway. He shook his head. No time to waste.

Troy held up a hand, wanting them to wait before racing off to search the house. They didn't have time to risk getting lost wandering about. Closing his eyes, he reached out with senses other then sight. Spider would probably be where the nauseating sensation of evil was strongest.

Suddenly, he was shoved forward. Troy opened his eyes and stared straight at a set of double doors.

There was a rush of bubbles, followed by a heavy thud. Troy whirled around and saw Knives. Behind him, the chandelier lay piled on the floor. Troy looked at his friend, then the chandelier once more—it might have well crushed him. Troy saluted his friend. Knives nodded.

Troy still stood before the double doors. He reached out and touched the left doorknob. Nothing happened. Troy tried to open it and found it locked. Something, an inner sense or his link with his blood brother, told him that Spider was inside. Troy tried the right door. It was also locked. He waved to his friends for help.

Immediately, they were at his side. J-Man removed his knife from the sheath on his dive belt. Knives did the same. Troy didn't understand until they began working on the hinges.

There was a squeal and J-Man popped a bolt free. Knives hammered on his with the butt of his blade. Floating above him, Troy tried to jimmy one loose. It resisted his efforts, then suddenly the edge of blade cut through the rust and pushed between the pin and hinges. Troy smiled. It moved!

Diligently, he twisted and pried. He almost had it free when Wreck tapped him on the shoulder. His friend held two pins in hand and motioned to the door. Troy smiled.

J-Man pulled the edge of the door away from the wall. It trembled in his grasp. Troy swam above him and grabbed the top edge. Knives gripped the bottom. Together, they wrenched it from the jam and lock.

They tossed the door aside and surged forward. Troy kicked hard, then immediately halted. A black cloud writhed before him, blocking their entrance into the room.

It swallowed their lights like a black hole. The cloud radiated a penetrating coldness that made the trio shake uncontrollably.

Beyond it, Troy spotted a greenish light. He pointed ahead. Across the room, Spider sat at a desk. The glow illuminated his frozen features. Motionless, he stared down at the open jewelry box. Dark tendrils as well as a sickly emerald glow leaped from the box. The ebony streamers swirled around his friend. One lovingly wrapped around his neck, then tightened.

Despite his growing terror, Troy shoved off the frame and shot into the room. The cloud twisted, trying to block him.

An ebony tendril grabbed his arm, then another wrapped around his waist. Like predatory weeds, they attacked. They slowed him, but Troy struggled on, keeping his eyes on Spider.

The dark thread around Spider's neck continued constricting. Troy watched his friend's eyes bulge. Bubbles no longer escaped from the regulator. Spider's body trembled and heaved, but he made no motion to free himself. His arms were slack at his sides. Then a tendril ripped the regulator from Spider's mouth. He began to choke, but didn't move to save himself.

Troy saw that Spider was drowning and tried to claw his way forward. A third tendril wrapped around his leg. They squeezed, drawing tighter. The cloud slowly engulfed him. The pressure became unbearable. A numbing cold enveloped him wherever the black cloud touched him. It was swallowing him alive. Troy wanted to scream.

Suddenly the pressure shifted. Troy twisted to find Knives jabbing at the cloud with his iron spike. The ebony threads quivered, then thrashed about. A few strands released Troy to attack Knives. Like snakes, they wriggled toward the doorway.

Knives slashed at one, cutting it back. Others danced away. J-Man struck the flare and a biting, incandescent light filled the room. The cloud looked like a twisting black hole. A long cord of blackness slipped through the water and into the jewelry box.

The black mass gathered itself, pulling in all its tendrils except those attacking Troy, then some twenty pods shot out. A few coiled, others struck straight forward. Another set looped around from behind. They weaved in, darting about Knives and J-Man, who floundered, slowed by the water. Each touch left the duo even more sluggish.

Troy drew his knife and jabbed at the strands. They pulled away from the touch of his knife. He jabbed, parting another. Troy freed his waist, then a leg. Coiling tendrils darted back, attacking, but Troy slashed at them, driving them away. One by one, Troy worked himself free.

He kicked away from the mass, finally unrestrained. Troy turned to Spider.

His friend slowly fell forward, slumping over the table. As the black thread released Spider, a single bubble, then a second drifted toward the ceiling. Spider's face was expressionless and his eyes open, but dead. His face landed atop the jewelry box. The inky tendril shot toward Troy.

As it did, Troy dumbfoundedly watched the death of his friend. A wisp of gray-blue light escaped from Spider's back and hovered above him in the water. Slowly a ghostly mass took shape, then it took on human form.

The darting coil of darkness wrapped around Troy's left arm. A second followed, nearly paralyzing his forearm and wrist. His hand tingled and he dropped his blade. It sank to the floor. The tendrils moved up his arm toward his throat.

Troy couldn't take his eyes off the ghostly form. Spider's image floated above his body. "I'm dead," he said, patting himself with his ethereal hands to be sure. Words rang in Troy's mind. "And you will be too if you don't do something fast."

"What?" Troy wondered. His right hand twitched. It was still free. He brought it before his face. The sapphire was glowing brightly. No darkness attacked his right hand.

The rope of blackness wrapped around Troy's throat. It squeezed, choking him. It struck with such force, Troy's regulator popped from his mouth. Hissing and bubbling, it fell away. Troy gurgled.

"Troy, save yourself," the vision of Spider said. "I had to die to be able to help you. I now know things I couldn't know in life. This mass of negative energy is powerless against the ring. Hoyt created it for that purpose."

Troy grabbed the tendril with his right hand and it dispersed. The thread twisted around and tried to snag him again. Troy swiped at the undulating string. It danced away.

Troy grabbed his regulator and stuffed it in his mouth. He took a deep, gratifying gulp of oxygen.

Quickly, Troy shot a glance at his friends. They were buried in the dark cloud, unable to move. Only a few air bubbles left their lips. Their fingers twitched.

Troy looked back at Spider's ghost. It was gone! Maybe it was never there, but suddenly Troy knew what to do.

Troy swam over to the desk. As he floated above it, he removed the ring. Pushing Spider's head aside, Troy dropped the ring inside the box. There was a banshee wail and the greenish glow disappeared. The coils straightened and then snapped backwards, retracting. The jewelry box seemed to suck them up. Troy shut the lid, hoping to trap the evil within.

Although he was sure Spider was dead, Troy

checked. He touched Spider's neck, searching for a pulse, but found none.

With a heavy sigh, Troy turned to look at Knives and J-Man. His friends were moving. Once again, bubbles flowed freely. They feebly waved to him.

Troy swam to them. Sadly, he pointed to Spider, then made a cutting motion across his throat. They understood. The pain was in their eyes and their features were set hard. J-Man closed his eyes, but Knives grabbed Troy and motioned towards Spider, then up.

Troy moved to help. As he did, he checked his air gauge. He only had 500 psi left of oxygen. He had to head for the surface.

Troy looked over to his friends. Their air would be just as low. Knives had grabbed one of Spider's arms and J-Man the other. Before they left, J-Man pointed at the jewelry box. Troy shook his head. He felt it should stay here. Troy opened the center desk drawer and stuffed it inside.

Together, they urgently swam out of the house. Troy led the way, guiding them with the flashlight. It seemed like it took a long time to exit the house, and an eternity to reach the surface.

For the first twenty minutes above water they tried frantically to revive Spider. Knives claimed that the cold water gave them a chance to save him. They pumped his lungs free of water, then Knives started administering CPR. They took turns, but it was too late. He was gone.

They covered up Spider's body and rested. After shedding the rest of their equipment, they collapsed, overwhelmed by the loss of another friend. They felt his death deeply, as if a part of them had died.

Finally, they recovered enough to leave. "Damn it," J-Man groaned as he turned the ignition key. Nothing happened. He tried again. The motor didn't respond.

The boat gently bobbed in the water.

Knives stepped over the pile of equipment in the center of the boat and looked over his friend's shoulder.

Troy was still thinking about Spider's death. Had he really talked to Spider's ghost or had he just been hallucinating? Whatever, he thought, shaking his head, it had saved their lives. They'd escaped the dark tendrils in the house and surfaced with less than 100 psi. J-Man's tank had gone dry about forty feet down, and he'd had to use Spider's air.

Troy shivered. Most of the numbness was gone, but the chills still remained. He recalled the knowing peace in Spider's eyes, then let the image fade away.

"What's going on?" Troy asked.

"The goddamn boat won't start," J-Man responded. He flicked a switch and the radio came on. He tried another and the bilge whined. A third switch turned on the navigation lights. "We have power, the boat just won't start. It's probably something simple."

Knives looked up. The sun was still high in the sky. He scanned the horizon. Not a boat was in sight. "The lake looks deserted. I think all the troubles have scared even the fishermen away."

"Nothing scares fishermen away," J-Man said. He got up from his seat. "Not to worry, I can fix it."

"I hope so," Knives responded.

"Anything I can do to help?" Troy asked dully.

"No, I think I can handle it. Remember, I'm a jerry-rigger *extraordinaire*." He forced a smile. "I can fix almost anything mechanical." He then left them to find his toolbox and start fiddling with the motor.

Knives looked guilty. "I'm sorry I couldn't help Spider."

"It certainly was not your fault," Troy said, rubbing his arms. He was finally beginning to thaw out from the coldness. The sun felt luxurious on his flesh.

"I don't feel that way."

"We're all blood brothers. We can't help but feel that way," Troy said. Troy gently touched his throat, wondering if it had bruised. His lip felt fat from holding the regulator and his head throbbed.

"How do you feel?" Knives asked.

"Physically or emotionally?"

"I'm a doctor, not a psychiatrist."

"Like shit," Troy responded. His thoughts returned to the scene where Spider's ghost rose. He looked at his empty finger. What was the sapphire? What deadly secret did it keep locked in the jewelry box? What had Traylor released? Troy shook his head. All the questions made it pound. Who was Hoyt?

"I can't believe he's really dead," Knives said.

Troy shrugged, then winced. "He would say that it happens to all of us, eventually." He debated on whether to tell him about the vision. "We may be dead too if we can't find shelter by the time it grows dark."

At that moment the boat roared to life and J-Man returned. "What did I tell ya? Even the powers of darkness can't keep a good man down."

They all smiled thinly at one another and Troy wondered how long they would last.

Interlude Six
The Hitchhiker

"I don't believe this is happening. I can't believe this is happening. . . . Spider is dead," Bob St. Martin told Denny as they drove along a curvy backroad to J-Man's lake house. The houses were few and far between as were the patches of light that created silhouettes of the trees. "First Dillon disappears, then Pete and Aaron are killed and now Spider." Bob shook his head and looked at his arms and hands which were still wrapped in gauze. "It's unnatural. It's almost . . . almost as if the devil has touched this area and damned us."

Headlights danced across the trees and hills as Denny slowed a little to take a sharp turn. The tires protested, squealing slightly. "Bob, please stop saying that. You've said it at least fifty times since I picked you up," Denny admonished. "I don't want to believe it either, but that's the way it is. Knives wouldn't lie to us. You're going to be a minister. You know these things happen—people die. Don't go blaming it upon Satan, please. There's too much of that talk already in the papers. Damn yellow journalism." He stepped on the gas and the red Supra shot forward. For a moment, the trees became a solid wall.

"But something is wrong, dreadfully wrong. These deaths aren't natural," Bob responded. "Each death gnaws at my soul." Denny braked and then let the car glide through the S-curve. Gravel skipped up and struck the car. The rear slightly fishtailed. Denny cursed, then accelerated.

"You could try slowing down," Bob suggested as his hands checked his seatbelt. His dark eyes stared at Denny in the greenish glow from the dashboard.

As fixed as stone, Denny's face was set in concentration. "I'm in a hurry to get there."

"I'd like to get there in one piece, if you please. There's nothing we can do for Spider now," Bob said. Denny was silent, his jaw pulled tight.

The tires squealed, then Bob said, "Are you thinking that if you were there, this wouldn't have happened?" Denny didn't say anything, but Bob could tell he'd hit the nail on the head. "I'm sure J-Man, Troy, and Knives did their best to save him. They're his . . . were Spider's friends as much as they are ours. Even if a few of them are heathens," Bob finished with a small smile.

Denny let out a heavy sigh. "There's just so many strange things going on. I haven't felt right since that night at Marader's dock." Letting go of the wheel to throw his bandaged hands into the air, Denny said, "And J-Man has been borrowing lots of hunting equipment — guns, bows and the like . . . he even took some dynamite!" Just as they slipped into a turn, he grabbed the wheel. Bob was pressed against the door.

"I must admit, I want to talk to Knives. He had me bless a cross for him. I wonder what they've been up to?"

"Did you know Marader's also missing?" Denny asked. He rolled through a stop sign and took a left down through an undulating stretch of road. They were thrown back in their seats as Denny quickly shifted into a higher gear. Trees whizzed by.

"What? When?"

"They haven't seen him for a little over a day. He hasn't been around to supervise the construction of the dock and Elle hasn't seen him."

Bob shivered. "The Good Lord help us," he muttered, then began praying.

Kurwhump-wwhump-whump! Bob opened his eyes and looked up just in time to see a flash of white. Flailing arms and legs appeared and disappeared as if something had rolled up the hood and over the windshield. "What was that?"

Denny's knuckles were white on the steering wheel. "It looked like a b—"

SKREEEEEeeee! The scratching of metal nearly deafened them. It reverberated inside the car like a sour note in an echo chamber.

Denny jumped and took his foot off the accelerator. The Supra leaped forward. "Maybe we better stop," Denny said.

Bob looked up. It looked as if powerful fingers had ripped through the metal, carving long and deep indentations into the roof. "I don't think so."

Denny followed his eyes, then gasped as a hand appeared on the edge of the windshield. Strong fingers pried back the metal and rubber of the car's body. Denny stomped on the accelerator. The Supra leaped forward and slid through a turn. The back wheels cut into dirt and gravel, creating a cloud.

The hitchhiker's body bounced heavily across the roof but hung on. Bob saw two tennis shoe-clad feet banging outside the passenger window just before they scrambled back on top of the car. Mocking laughter carried to them, and they both looked at each other. "What in the name of God . . . ?" Bob gasped.

A second hand appeared at the edge of the windshield. Then a blond head appeared. Glowing red eyes peered into the car. The hitchhiker's smile widened, stretching from ear to ear in an unnatural, leering grin. He let go with his left hand and waved, his fingers dancing back and forth. Then his arm stretched back.

"It's Mara. . . ." Denny couldn't finish. He flinched and turned away as a flash of white streaked toward the windshield. The hand slammed through the safety glass. It buckled, then exploded as the inner protective coat was breached. Bob and Denny were sprayed with jagged debris.

Two more blows totally shattered the windshield, leaving a gaping hole. Like rain, chunks of glass were driven inside the Supra. Denny gasped as the fallout tore at his skin.

He opened his eyes barely in time to steer around a curve. The car slid and screeched. A face appeared at the hole in the windshield. "Hi guys, long time no see. Got room for one more?" Marader said with a full-moon smile. "I have gas money." He laughed in a hideous fashion that made Bob and Denny shiver.

The car hit a bump, bottomed out with a scraping sound, and then bounded into the air. For a moment, Marader's face disappeared. Suddenly, he was back. His eyes burned like red-hot coals and his smile was tight. His incisors were canine in length. "Oh God!" Bob moaned.

Marader's eyes were on Denny. "That wasn't nice . . . and I thought we were friends." His eyes flashed to Bob. "And God isn't going to help you . . . but I agree with 'do unto others as they would do unto you.' You're trying to shake me off . . . kill me." His hand shot inside and grabbed the wheel. With a yank, Marader tore it from Denny's grasp.

Laughing, Marader gave it a violent twist. The car shuddered, skidded along sideways, then shot off the road and into the trees. Cheerfully, Marader sang "Back in Black."

Chapter Eighteen
Wish Fulfilled

"When we got to the surface, we tried everything we could think of to resuscitate Spider," Knives told the burly sheriff as the group watched the ambulance pull away. The red lights flashed in kaleidoscope fashion, but the siren was silent since there was no reason to hurry. A police car pulled out of the driveway and followed. "We pumped his lungs free of water, gave him mouth-to-mouth and performed CPR for over twenty minutes which was at least five minutes longer than he would have survived despite the cold water he died in."

"Ah reckon' ya know all 'bout that, don't ya?" Deputy Sheriff McDaniels replied as he scratched his chin with the top of the pen.

"Yeah, and it didn't do any good," Knives said tightly. His eyes grew darker as if he were absorbing the total responsibility for Spider's death.

"Now let me see if Ah got this straight," McDaniels drawled. As he wiped the back of his hand across his mouth and cleared his throat, the deputy sheriff slowly looked from Jay to Troy and finally at Knives. "The four of ya gone scuba divin' 'n explorin' Wreythville." He said the last word with distaste. "Todd Adder, Ah mean Spider, split off on his own t' go explorin' by 'imself."

They all nodded. "I was searchin' the kitchen—," J-Man began.

"What didya say the name of the house was?" McDaniels said, flipping through his notes.

"It doesn't have a name," Troy corrected. "As far as we can tell, it was owned by a Hoyt Wilhelm."

" 'N y'all figured that out from information ya got from the TVA?"

"Right," Troy said.

"Wilhelm sounds European," McDaniels said.

"Not surprising. Wreythville was mostly populated by Bavarians," Troy told him.

"Germans and the like?" McDaniels asked. Troy nodded. "Really, that's unusual," the deputy sheriff replied.

"We thought so," Knives said. A slight breeze rustled the leaves, then chilled the guys who were still in their bathing suits.

"When I turned around," J-Man continued, "Spider was gone. I went searching for him, found Knives and Troy first, then we all went looking."

" 'N y'all found 'im floatin' in the library?"

"Yes," Knives said.

"Purty strange story iffin ya ask me," McDaniel said as they all watched a dark blue Cutlass drive up. The front end was damaged.

Troy shrugged while Knives said, "Drownings are always a little strange."

"Ya hadn't been drinkin' by any chance, 'ad ya?"

341

"No, the autopsy will show that," Knives said.

McDaniels hurrumphed, then said, "Iffin ya don't mind me sayin' so, Mr. Bane, 'tween bein' attacked by wolves, escapin' a burnin' dock, and now this, sounds like your a dangerous man t' be around. Makes a man curious as t' what your doin' in Bristol."

Troy's eyes grew steely as they turned from the figure climbing out of the Cutlass to McDaniels. "As I told Detective Glazier, I'm hunting vampires."

McDaniels leaned back and roared in laughter. For a few moments he couldn't say anything. Glazier walked over and looked questioningly at the stout deputy sheriff.

"I told him what I was doing in Bristol," Troy said.

"Looking for Dillon?" Bob asked. He nervously played with his moustache.

"Huntin' for vampires," J-Man said.

Glazier's eyes narrowed and his jaw tightened.

McDaniels slapped Glazier on the back. Still laughing, the burly man said, "Your friend sure 'as a strange sense of humor."

"Yes, he does," Glazier said quietly.

"Ya on the case?" McDaniels asked.

"Not officially, no. South Holston Lake is out of our jurisdiction, but I am curious."

"Please keep me posted if ya come up with anythin' new. Ah smell a skunk round heah."

"If anything new shows up, I will," Glazier said, staring at Troy.

"Bye, boys," McDaniels said, then walked over to his car. Quietly, they watched him drive away.

"I wonder what's keeping Denny and Bob," Troy

said to no one in particular, then turned to watch the moon rise over the lake. It wasn't quite full yet.

"I'm beginning to worry," J-Man said. "Oh, hi, Fluffy." He reached down to pick up the white cat that rubbed his leg. As he stroked it, J-Man continued. "They should be here by now. Denny's usually late," he checked his watch, "but not this late."

"Maybe they had car trouble," Knives suggested. He ran a hand through his hair, then rubbed his arms to warm them.

"His Supra is brand new, so I'd doubt it," J-Man said, shaking his head. "Ya know, it's cool out tonight."

"First Dillon, then Marader. Lord, I hope we don't have to add Denny and Bob to the list," Troy said with a heavy sigh.

"Marader's missing?" Glazier asked.

"We think so," Knives said. "We haven't seen him since yesterday morning, and according to Elle he hasn't been out to the dock."

"He could be shacking up with somebody," Glazier suggested.

"That's highly possible," J-Man said.

"Gentlemen," Glazier said expansively. "I think it's high time we had a heart-to-heart talk. There are too many people already dead. It's time for some straight answers. I want to know everything you know, suspect, speculate, or surmise, whether you think I'll believe you or not."

"Now that's more like the Bill Glazier we used to know," Troy said. His eyes were still far away. He was thinking about Silke. He hoped she was holding up all right. It seemed like ages since he'd talked to her.

Headlights came around the corner and up the short drive. "Ah, they're here," J-Man said.

"I don't think so," Knives told him. "That doesn't look like a Supra to me. It's—"

"An old Cadillac, Mrs. U's car," Troy finished. "What's she doing here?"

The car halted before them and Silke jumped out. Her hair bounced wildly as she ran to him. Troy's eyes widened in surprise, then he took a few steps forward. She leaped into his arms and they hugged each other tightly.

"Silke, what are you doing here?" Troy asked. "How's Aunt Jada?"

Silke was sobbing. "Fine," she said.

"I called her while you were getting cleaned up," J-Man explained. "Spider was her friend too." Troy nodded. He would have preferred to have kept the news from her for a while.

"Let's go inside," Knives suggested. "It's getting cold out here."

"Good idea," Glazier agreed. "I could use a stiff drink and some answers."

Jay carried the cat inside. The others followed. Silke still clung to Troy.

After locking the door and rechecking all the entrances, they settled around the kitchen table. J-Man poured Glazier a healthy shot of Wild Turkey. "I hope you're not on duty."

"I'm not." Bill waved to the shotgun on the kitchen counter, then the bow on the living-room couch. "Looks like you're expecting trouble."

"Wouldn't be the first time," J-Man said, taking a sip of whiskey.

"How about starting your tale from the beginning?" Glazier suggested.

"We could do that, don't you think guys?" J-Man asked. Knives and Troy nodded.

"We haven't really sat down and fully discussed it, let alone analyzed it, because everything is happening so fast," Troy said. Silke squeezed his hand. "Maybe if we had, some of this wouldn't have happened."

"I seriously doubt that," Knives said.

"Roll with it," Bill said.

"Well, it started with our night skiing escapade," J-Man began. "Did you watch the video?" Glazier nodded. "Did you notice something leaving the island, I mean flying from Cemetery Ridge when we panned across the water to catch the rising moon?" Bill shook his head.

"We think vampires killed Traylor," Knives said flatly.

"Why do you think that?" Glazier said, "His neck was ripped open, not punctured like the legends claim. It looked more like wolves attacked him."

"We can't explain that, but what we can tell you is that Traylor brought something up from Wreythville," J-Man continued.

"We didn't find anything."

"We know, we kept it," J-Man said.

"What! You kept evidence? Listen guys, I want that evidence in my hands, *now.*"

"We can't," Knives said.

"No more games."

"It's back in Wreythville," Troy said.

"I may have to arrest—"

"Bill," Troy said, raising his voice, "do you want

345

to hear the goddamn story or beat your chest?"

Glazier grew quiet. "I can always arrest you later."

Troy nodded.

J-Man continued. "Knives found a jewelry box. When we found it, it was already empty. There were strange markings on it. Dillon was supposed to do some research on it, but we don't know what he came up with because he disappeared after diving Wreythville. Dillon left the box with Marader who became very possessive of it, obsessed in fact. We let things lie until Troy showed up. None of us knew that Dillon had disappeared."

Troy took over the story. "Strange things happened almost from the moment I arrived; actually, I had weird dreams on the flight to Bristol—more like nightmares actually. All were connected to a graveyard that looks a lot like Cemetery Ridge back in the early 1940s.

"Silke picked me up and whisked me off to her aunt's place. Aunt Jada is supposed to be psychic."

"And she is," Silke said. "She warned us of an evil, an immortal darkness that was spreading throughout the area once more. In retrospect, it sounds like she was talking about vampires."

"Aunt Jada claimed to have seen a dead man alive that afternoon while she was shopping in Bristol," Troy continued.

"In broad daylight?"

"Yes."

"That doesn't fit."

"I know," Troy said. "Then, right after we left Aunt Jada's place, we were attacked by the wolves." Troy didn't tell him about Jada's warning about the dark-haired, emerald-eyed woman who was to be his downfall. "You were with Spider, Jambo, and I at the morgue where Tim Barton's body was stolen, just like Traylor's."

Glazier nodded. "That still doesn't fit a vampire's modus operandi."

"How do you know?" J-Man asked.

"It happened during the daytime."

"How do you know?" J-Man asked a second time.

"Point made. Continue."

"It was while diving Wreythville that I noticed the connection between that town and my nightmares," Troy continued.

"He went a little crazy," Knives said. "We thought it was a bad tank of air."

"A skeleton crawled from a grave on Cemetery Ridge and tried to kill me," Troy said. Glazier looked skeptical.

"Anyway, that night the wolves attacked us at Marader's. When we swam to the boat, they were only interested in pursuing Spider because he had the jewelry box."

"Marader was furious when Spider lied, saying that he'd lost the jewelry box," J-Man added.

"Why?" Glazier asked.

"I don't know," Troy said. "After the attack we flew to Knoxville to research the flooding of Wreythville and the construction of South Holston Dam. Records show a large number of unusual deaths on the project. We copied down a list of names, hoping to interview some people upon our return. I spoke with Jeremiah Corning who confirmed that strange things occurred during the project. Many of the workers thought the project was cursed. Supposedly, a dark lady lured men off into the woods and they never returned. Wreythville was avoided like the plague."

"Still rumors and speculation," Glazier said.

"That night at King College Cemetery, Tim Barton confirmed it. He told us he was touched by the Dark Lady," J-Man continued.

"You believe him? You'd believe a vampire?" Bill asked.

"So you believe he was a vampire?" Troy asked.

"I don't know what I believe."

"Did you find Phillip Barton's body?"

"Yes."

"And."

"It had puncture marks in the neck."

"Did it disappear?" J-Man asked.

"No, we submerged it under water."

"That fits," Troy said.

"So you still have the body?" Knives asked, his eyes alight with excitement.

"Yes."

"I'd like to examine it," Knives said.

"Down, boy," J-Man said.

"Barton," Troy continued, "confirmed the presence of vampires and their connection to Wreythville. I'd surmise that the vampires didn't want their home flooded."

"Why didn't they just move to another locale?" Glazier asked. He took a good-sized swig of whiskey that made his eyes water.

"Good question. I don't know. Maybe they couldn't," Troy replied.

"While they were at the cemetery," Silke interjected, "my aunt called to warn me, which is why I called you. During the call, she had a heart attack. I think something tried to kill her or scare her to death."

"Why do you think that?" Bill asked. "Anything to eat around here?" He scanned the kitchen counter and his gaze fastened on some corn chips.

"All her protective crystals had exploded," she said. Glazier rolled his eyes. J-Man retrieved the bag of chips from the counter, then walked to the refrigerator.

"Deciding that everything was connected to Wreythvill.," Troy continued, "the four of us — Spider, Knives, J-Man, and I — went diving. Before I dove, I spoke with Elle, who remembered a conversation she had with Dillon prior to his dive. She also remembered a map. Dillon had circled a box on the map.

"We took the jewelry box with us. Spider carried it. It led us to a shuttered house with a copper roof."

"Led you there?" Glazier said incredulously.

"Both Spider and I envisioned the house when we were touching the box," Troy responded. Glazier shook his head. "Spider swam ahead into the house and all the shutters slammed closed behind him."

"You're bullshitting me," Bill said. His face grew flushed.

"Bill," J-Man said, "just listen. It gets wilder." He set a bowl of salsa on the table. Bill began munching.

"We found an open window where the shutters had gotten stuck in silt. It was a really strange house. We got disoriented, but found Spider in the library. He was sitting over the jewelry box, just staring into it. All around him the darkness swirled.

"It wrapped a tendril around Spider's neck and began strangling him. Spider didn't fight back. We tried to help, but the darkness was too powerful. I watched Spider die.

"Then I watched Spider's ghost rise from his body," Troy said and everyone fell quiet. He hadn't told anyone about Spider's ghost and he wasn't sure how they would take it, but he couldn't keep it to himself any longer. "He told me that the darkness was powerless against the ring I wore, a ring that Hoyt had created."

"Ring? What ring?" Glazier asked.

"One I got from Racquel."

"She found it on Cemetery Ridge over ten years ago," Knives interrupted.

"About the time that Traylor found the jewelry box, the ring seemed to reappear among her jewelry." Troy said.

"Spider told me to use the ring on the darkness. When I dropped the ring in the jewelry box, it sucked in all the darkness. I closed the lid. The ring and the box now sit underwater, inside the desk in the library. I think that's a good place for it.

"Now Aaron, Pete, and Spider are dead," Troy said, shaking his head. "At the very least, Dillon and Marader have disappeared. That's all I know. Anyone think of anything else?"

"Just the fact," J-Man said, "that we checked our research notes when we returned. A fair portion of the population of Wreythville was of Bavarian descent. Our guesstimation from the addresses, and based upon the nearby church, is that we were in the house of Hoyt Wilhelm IV who was an art collector and jeweler. The house was originally built by the first Hoyt Wilhelm, an immigrant."

"I wonder if it's the same Hoyt that Spider mentioned," Knives said aloud.

"I wondered the same thing when we discovered the connection," Troy said.

"And you didn't mention it?" J-Man asked.

"I'm not even positive I saw Spider's ghost," Troy said. "The only reason I believe it is that so many strange things have happened and the advice he gave me was right."

"I hope he's looking for our friends," J-Man said. "I'm worried about Bob and Denny."

"Me too," Troy said.

"How about these dreams you've been having?" Glazier asked.

Troy scratched his head. "I've had five or six. They all kind of blend together—you know how dreams are. The last one I had while in the hospital. I was in the Wreythville Cemetery. I heard digging and I followed the sound. A corpse was exhuming another corpse, a female one. Before my eyes, she grew younger. She was gorgeous with long dark hair and green eyes. She pulled me forward, but I fell into an open grave and then dirt began tumbling in."

"Female sounds like Elle," Knives said.

"That's what I thought," Troy said. "Later that day when I stood atop a hill in King College Cemetery, I saw her again. She drew me closer and closer before I was interrupted."

"Could be Racquel. She had the ring," J-Man said.

"But that came in handy and saved our lives," Troy defended.

"The Dark Lady of which Jeremiah spoke," Silke suggested.

"The Dark Lady that Tim Barton told us about, I'll bet," Knives said firmly.

"You people are certified lunatics," Bill said.

"Bill, hear me out. I don't . . . didn't . . . believe in the supernatural either, but with everything that has gone on here lately . . . Well, you asked for the full story," Troy said heavily.

Bill sighed. "Oh well, I can get you good rooms at the mental hospital, but I must admit, before I do, I want to hear about the rest of the dreams. I may be able to write a screenplay."

Troy frowned. "In the helicopter on the way to Knoxville, I had the last of the dreams. It was night this time in the graveyard and I heard chanting. I stood on three graves with writing on them." Troy closed his eyes. "I didn't really have time to read them but—"

"Three of your friends have died," Bill said.

"Oh Lord," Troy said.

"Are you sure there were only three graves?" Knives asked.

"Fairly sure. I was more interested in following the chanting. A dozen or so dark-robed figures holding torches encircled a pool of some kind—blood or something. I . . ." Troy closed his eyes again, "vaguely remember . . . smelling chemicals."

"Chemicals?" Bill asked. He scratched his chin. "Traylor's girlfriend was a pharmacist."

"So?" Silke asked.

Bill spread his hands wide. "I don't know. I'm grasping for straws as much as you folks are."

"Chemicals?" Knives said. "Wasn't —"

An eerie howl abruptly ended the conversation. The sound paused for a moment, then the baying grew louder, more intense, as if coming toward them. The sound permeated the house and sank into their souls. Fear flashed in everyone's eyes as they looked at each other. Troy felt a chill dance through him. Silke threw herself into his arms and hugged him. Troy looked at Knives who nervously ran a hand through his hair, then smiled a bitter smile.

Determination flashed in J-Man's face as he retrieved the revolver from the coffee table. Troy untangled himself from Silke. J-Man double-checked their fortifications.

The lights flickered twice, then recovered and stayed on. "Déjà vu," J-Man said. He clicked the safety off the revolver.

"No," Troy said harshly as he got up and walked into the kitchen. From a kitchen drawer, he plucked a second .38. The howling was so loud that they could barely hear him. He clicked the safety off the handgun. "No one dies this time. This time we're ready." He joined Jay in checking the fortifications.

"But we don't have the jewelry box!" Silke said.

"Maybe it doesn't matter. Maybe we were wrong," Knives said. He stood and walked to the kitchen where he hefted the shotgun.

The howling became one long drone, occasionally broken by yips and yelps as if the wolves were snapping at each other.

Troy moved to the window and peeked between the stacked furnishings. "I don't see anything," he called to the others. "Nothing on this side."

"Clear over here," J-Man responded. "Last time they were as thick as flies on shit."

"I'll light some candles just in—," Silke began when suddenly the lights flickered and died. The house was pitched into blackness.

"Damnation!" J-Man said. "I don't like this."

"At least we're not on fire," Knives laughed nervously.

"Stephen, that's my line!" J-Man parried, surprised by his friend's untimely humor.

There was the crisp ripping of a match being struck, then a tiny flame glowed in the dark. Silke lit one candle, then two. She stood and moved to the mantel over the fireplace where several shaded tapers waited. Soon the room was illuminated by a golden glow.

"I'm going to check the back bedroom and the garage," Troy said. Searching, his hands fumbled around on the kitchen counter. "Where's the damn. . . ?" He then found the flashlight and turned it on. Its brilliant white beam cut a swath through the dim candlelight that held back the darkness.

"I'm going with you," J-Man said. He carried a bow and several arrows. The revolver was stuffed in his waistband.

"Okay, just don't poke me with one of those fletched stakes," Troy said as they moved toward the hallway that led to the garage. They passed the steps to the upstairs. Suddenly, the howling stopped.

The two looked at each other. "I wonder what that means?" J-Man asked.

"I—," Troy began. A heavy thud reverberated from upstairs. They looked at each other again. "Fluff?" Troy said unevenly.

"Don't kid yourself," J-Man said. "That cat would have to have swallowed a bowling ball to make that sound and I don't bowl."

"Got your cross?" Troy asked.

"Yes. You?"

"Of course. Never leave home without it."

With the flashlight guiding the way, Troy led the way up the stairs. The steps creaked under their weight. Whatever was upstairs, Troy thought, probably knew they were coming. His hand tightened on the revolver. The flashlight shook slightly. Troy heard J-Man breathing heavily. They reached the landing and the light crawled along the walls and steps. Troy breathed a brief sigh of relief when they rounded the corner unmolested and started up the second flight of stairs.

He kept the beam moving, searching for any surprises. It danced off the walls and hovered at the top of the steps. Troy held the flashlight high as his eyes looked down the long stretch of carpeted hallway. "Hall looks deserted." He listened closely. He heard voices downstairs. Then . . .

"Owww," came a muffled groan.

"I smell a trap," J-Man said.

Troy glanced quickly over his shoulder at his friend. When he turned around, a furry ball bounded down the hall. "What?!" Its green eyes flashing, it leaped down the stairs at J-Man. Troy's finger twitched on the trigger as his .38 followed the target.

He dodged the flying cat and J-Man caught her in one arm. "She's shaking," he told Troy. "Something scared her."

"I almost shot her," Troy said breathing hard. He shook his head. "Maybe whatever was moaning frightened her." He started back up the stairs. The gun felt heavy in his hand. He lightly fingered the trigger as he reached the top of the steps. Every nerve, every sense, was stretched taut, just waiting for an attack. For some reason, Elle came to mind . . . then Racquel. Troy willed the visions away. He had to keep his head clear.

Jay set Fluffy down and readied his bow.

"Owww," came the moan again. It was down the hall and to the right.

"It came from the study," Troy said as he advanced.

"Be careful," J-Man warned.

"I'm trying," Troy whispered. He quietly ran down the hall and jumped across the open doorway. His light briefly touched the room, then Troy was beyond the opening. "The window is open and the curtains are blowing in. Damn, I don't have enough hands to hold the flashlight, a cross, and the .38."

"Wolves don't open windows. Carry the cross." J-Man yelled over his shoulder, "Knives, we've got a hidden visitor up here of the two-legged variety."

"Cover me." Troy shoved the .38 in his pants and entered the room. His heart was hammering and sweat beaded in the palms of his hands. A cool breeze touched him and Troy tried to sense anything unnatural, but he felt nothing . . . wait, he did sense a familiar presence in the room. Maybe it was Spider's ghost. "Hello," Troy said, feeling a little foolish.

J-Man moved closer. He waited in the doorway.

Troy searched the room. The closet door was closed. Nothing was out of place. The bookshelf and chair were undisturbed. The file cabinets were upright. The desk was as it should be, but the desk chair was missing. Troy started to peek over the top when he snatched his head back, changing his mind. "Jay, I think something is behind the desk."

J-Man stood silhouetted in the doorway. "Be careful."

Troy didn't say a word. His hand itched to reach for his .38, but he didn't. It probably wouldn't do any good. Instead, he just held the cross out. Troy rounded the corner of the desk. Nothing jumped— nothing attacked.

All was silent as Troy's light shone on a crumpled body. The chair had fallen atop the dark figure.

There was a scuffling at the window. *"Troy! Look out!"* J-Man yelled. Instinctively, Troy fell backwards, dropped the flashlight, and reached for the revolver.

Kablam-blam! As Troy fired, he saw teeth gleam in the firing flash. They were long incisors. The vampire started to crawl inside the window.

Troy boldly held the cross out before him. The figure blanched, then laughed. As if in pain, it slowly reached out.

The air whistled near Troy's ear as an arrow shot by him. There was a dull smack, then a scream.

The vampire fell out of the window.

Troy rushed forward.

Still shaking, but with a snarl on his lips, Troy looked out the window. He stared toward the ground, but saw nothing. Then he heard a fluttering and saw a small shape, a bat, fly into the night. Its flight was irregular. "You wounded it. Nice shot, J-Man."

From right behind Troy, J-Man said, "Good Lord, guess who dropped in." Troy turned. J-Man had moved the chair and shone the light on the fallen figure. "Dillon is no longer missing."

Chapter Nineteen
Satan's Cult

They tried, but not even Knives could awaken Dillon — he was pale, thin, and obviously exhausted. Knives said it was all right to move him. While J-Man and Knives carried Dillon downstairs, Troy closed and locked the window. Confused, he waited a minute before following. Troy stared at the window. He knew it had been locked — they had checked all possible entrances prior to sunset, but there wasn't any sign of forced entry. With his own eyes, Troy had checked this very window. Then how, he wondered, did Dillon get inside? More and more was happening that he couldn't explain.

From downstairs came Silke's cry of happiness. Dillon must be conscious, Troy thought. He wanted to go downstairs, but something held him. His reporter's intuition spoke to him, but Troy couldn't figure out what it was trying to tell him.

After a quiet, thought-provoking minute, he gave up and turned to go downstairs.

Wavering before him in the darkness was Spider's ghost. The spirit floated a few inches off the floor. Although pale and transparent, the likeness was identical to Spider's physical form. His face was expressionless and his eyes were clear. Spider's wandering soul didn't say anything, nor did it move. "Why are you here?" Troy asked quietly. His friend's phantom didn't say a word, but his eyes showed concern.

"Are you here to help us?" Troy asked. Spider's ghost silently nodded. "I appreciate it. I could use the help," Troy said, not fully believing that he spoke to his friend's spirit—but with all the strange things going on, it wouldn't hurt to have spiritual help. His doubt—no, scorn—of the paranormal no longer existed. It had been beaten out of him.

"Are we under attack, is that why you're here?" The spirit didn't respond.

Troy shook his head. "Spider, you haven't changed a bit. And here I was hoping you'd be more talkative in the afterlife than you were while you were alive. Oh well." Troy headed for the door. "Come on, let's go downstairs and see what Dillon has to tell us." Troy walked pass Spider's spirit and into the hall. "Maybe he can shed some light on what's been happening."

When Troy reached the first floor, Dillon wore a huge smile and was still hugging Silke. His smile widened when he saw Troy. "Troy! Damn, you're a sight for tired eyes," Dillon said jovially.

360

Troy smiled back, but noticed that the joy didn't reach his friend's eyes. He wondered if Dillon saw Spider's ghost—if anyone could see Spider's ghost. Was Spider really there or had Troy finally gone over the edge?

"Good to have you home." Troy crossed the room and shook hands with Dillon. "You look like hell."

"I feel like hell," he responded. "I've been there and back. And it's no vacation resort." Dillon shook hands with everyone, and there was lots of laughing all around. Their relief was obvious—one they had feared dead, after so many had died, had returned, alive! For the moment, danger and death seemed far away, shoved back by Dillon's salvation.

Silke was so glad to see her brother that she forgot Aunt Jada's warning. Troy hadn't forgotten—maybe having Spider's ghost close by reminded him, but Troy sensed something different about his friend. He couldn't put his finger on it . . . yet. Of course, it might be all that Dillon had been through—surely Dillon wouldn't bring harm to them. They were blood brothers, after all.

From near the window, J-Man said, "It appears we aren't the only ones without lights. It's a local blackout."

"I'll call the electric company," Bob said, and picked up the phone.

"And we should call Mom," Silke told Dillon. "She's at the hospital with Aunt Jada."

"Our crazy aunt," Dillon said.

"She's not crazy and she's had a heart attack," Silke scolded.

"No one's calling anyone for a while, at least not from this phone," Bill said. "It's dead." Everyone was silent for a moment. "I can radio the station from my car," Glazier said and headed for the front door.

"Here," J-Man said as he tossed Bill a shotgun, "you may need this."

"Silver buck?" Bill asked.

"Yes, and I'll watch you with the bow in case we find something other than wolves," J-Man said. Glazier had a look of scorn on his face, but he took the shotgun anyway and headed outside.

"Dillon, I am so glad to see you! I was afraid you were dead!" Silke told her brother once more.

"As we all did," Knives added.

"With all the strange things going on, I'd given up hope," Silke said, beginning another round of tears. Dillon patted his sister and pulled her tightly to him.

They all heard cursing from outside. Seconds later, Bill came storming inside. J-Man barricaded the door behind him.

Bill paused from cursing long enough to say, "Someone broke into my car and trashed the radio!"

"We can drive to a neighbor's," J-Man suggested.

"We might be better of waiting until the sun rises," Knives said. "We don't appear to be in any immediate danger."

"I'd feel safer in the city," Silke said.

"Just as many strange things going on there," Bill said. "Personally, I'd like to hear Dillon's story before I go anywhere."

"I concur," Troy said. "Anyone disagree?" No one did. "Well, then, I guess we sit tight and listen to Dillon's tale," Troy suggested. "Why don't you start with what happened after you returned the boat?"

"I promise to tell you everything if you'll fix me something to eat and drink. I'm starved."

Silke headed for the kitchen. "I can listen while I fix you a sandwich."

"Sounds good," Dillon said, collapsing into a chair to relax. "Well, folks, I never returned the boat. Members of the Six Finger Cult must have, though."

"The Six Finger Cult?" Bill asked.

"Yes, it's a satanic cult operating in this area."

"Where's it located?" Bob asked.

"I don't know for sure. Somewhere not too far from the dam. I was still drugged when I escaped. I don't remember a whole lot, but what I do remember is hazy. Lord, I'm tired too. I've been running since before sunset," Dillon told them.

Troy looked over at Spider's ghost, which was hovering just inside the doorway. Spider was frowning. "Bill, hold off on the questions and let him start from the beginning," Troy said.

"Thanks. That will make things easier," Dillon said. He drank deeply from the glass of water that Silke handed him. J-Man gave him a shot of whiskey. "I was kidnapped from the boat right

363

after diving around Cemetery Ridge. This old couple approached me in a boat. The wanted directions and a cup of water. They seemed harmless enough." Dillon shook his head. "Next thing I knew, three guys jumped me and before I could break loose, they injected me with something. I must have passed out. I vaguely remember them asking me questions, then they put me in the other craft. When I awoke, I was in a damp cavern and still drugged. There were several other people there too. They also appeared drugged. I tried to ask what was going on, but they were too far gone.

"Sometime later, some hooded members carried me to the cult leader. I was so doped up I couldn't walk. Anyway, they took me to the new son of Satan, Mephisto Trask." Bill started to ask him a question, but Troy hushed him with a look.

"He explained to me that he was preparing this area for a visitation from the Lord of Lies. To partially open the gateway so that Satan would bestow him with further supernatural powers, Trash was to slay sixty-six people. When he slew an additional six hundred people, or a total of six-hundred-sixty-six by the winter solstice, Satan would arrive."

"Insane," Bill said. "How many have been killed."

"I believe there have been sixty sacrifices. There are six more tomorrow night, including Jambo," Dillon said. "Poor souls."

"Jambo!?" several voices said simultaneously.

"Damn, we have to do something," Bill said, his face flushed. He and Jambo had remained close even after Glazier had drifted away from everyone else.

Sensing that something was wrong, Troy carefully watched Dillon, then his eyes darted to Spider's spirit. Spider looked disgusted. Troy didn't know what to make of it. "How'd you escape?" Troy asked.

"Good luck and more good luck," Dillon said.

"Meaning?" Troy asked.

"When Trask discovered I was a journalist, he thought he had a brilliant idea. He'd keep me alive to chronicle his rise to power, which means I was forced to witness some hideous rites. He didn't want me to miss anything." Dillon closed his eyes and buried his face in his hands. "I saw some things I'll never be able to forget. I fear I'll never sleep peacefully again."

"And here we thought vampires were causing all the trouble," Bill said. He looked pleased that something as normal as a cult was causing the problems.

Dillon looked up, a tear rolling down his cheek. "Some believe they're vampires. Several of the rites involved drinking blood." Dillon wiped the back of his hand across his eyes. "They ritually rape their captives and even engaged in beastiality and necrophilia."

Dillon drew a long, ragged gasp.

"Explains the grave robberies," Glazier stated matter of factly. Even this, he could deal with.

Troy shook his head. It all sounded so neat,

but then why shouldn't it? He looked at Knives who also appeared uncertain. "You still didn't explain how you escaped."

"Well, I was kept so doped up I could barely move, so it was easy to convince Trask that I could hardly write," Dillon said with a short laugh. "I showed Trask my notes and he flew into a rage. He didn't want history to miss a single moment of his rise to greatness. The mad bastard has an ego bigger than Texas." He winked at Troy.

Dillon drank his whiskey, gasped, then continued. "Anyway, they reduced my dosage. They were celebrating today, since they have all the sacrifices they need."

"This is disgusting," Bill said. "We have to do something!"

"While the guards were partying, I slipped out and escaped. I ran around aimlessly for hours, I guess, then I found myself near Marader's dock. What happened to the place?"

"It's a long story," Knives said. "We'll tell you later."

"Anyway, no one was there, so I staggered here."

"Anyone follow you?" J-Man asked.

"Not that I know of."

"How come you didn't knock?" Troy asked.

"The lights were out and I assumed no one was home. I figured one of the second-story windows might be unlocked. Last week Jay mentioned having trouble with the lock on one of the upstairs windows. You better check it, J-Man. It was a simple breaking and entering."

Troy heard Spider's ghost moan. He looked over to see the spirit burying its head in its hands. "Isn't the sacrifice supposed to happen tomorrow night?" he asked.

Dillon nodded.

"Then wouldn't it be better to wait until daylight?" Again, Dillon nodded.

"I'm going to drive into town, tell the chief, gather up some officers and kick some butt," Glazier said. "Paybacks are hell . . . and sometimes fun."

"Just wait a second, Bill," Knives said. "Do you know where to take this swat team of yours?"

Glazier looked embarrassed. "Er, no," he said.

"Then hold off a minute. Maybe as Dillon's mind clears, he'll remember something."

"All I can remember is passing the dam," Dillon said.

"That's something," Glazier said sarcastically.

"Bill, be patient," Troy said icily. He didn't understand what was going on, but rushing off half-cocked wasn't going to help matters any. "Dillon, for Jambo's sake, try to remember."

"I'm trying," he said. Silke set the sandwich before him. He began to devour it.

In the meantime Troy told him all of what happened over the last couple of days, including the deaths of Spider and the Ackles brothers, as well as their confrontation with the undead in the cemetery. All in all, Troy thought Dillon took it pretty well.

Troy looked at Spider's ghost. Troy couldn't ever remember seeing Spider this mad.

"Now Bob St. Martin and Denny are missing," J-Man said. "They were supposed to be driving here. I expected them hours ago."

Dillon's head suddenly snapped toward J-Man. "What kind of car does Denny drive?"

"A red Supra."

"I saw it on the road on my way here. It was wrapped around a tree."

"Damn!" Bill cursed.

"Show us where," Troy told Dillon.

"Let's go," Dillon responded. They armed themselves and headed for the cars.

"You're driving too fast," Troy heard Knives say from the backseat.

"I'm just trying to keep up with Glazier," J-Man said as the Bronco bounced along.

"I'm surprised he's driving this fast," Knives said.

He watched Bill's car disappear around a corner. The red glow trailed behind the detective's car, dancing off the trees and road as if leaving a briefly illuminated path for them to follow.

There was a short silence between them as dark fears danced in their heads.

"Something doesn't feel quite right—not with Dillon or his story," Troy finally said.

"I admit he doesn't look quite right," J-Man said as his hands deftly turned the wheel to steer them through the S-curves, "but he has been held

368

captive by a satanic cult for over a week."

"He's been missing for a week, but I'm not sure I believe his story about being held captive by a Satanic Cult," Troy said.

"Why?" J-Man asked.

"There's too many holes in his story. I'm a reporter. My intuition tells me he's hiding something. There's more to the story than we're being told."

"Why would Dillon lie to us?" Knives asked.

"I have no idea, unless he's confused and doesn't know he's lying to us, or under the influence of something."

"So what do we do?" J-Man said.

"Well, at the moment, we don't know what else to do so we just play along. Dillon is still our friend. We have to help him."

"Agreed," J-Man said.

"And another thing," Troy said. "Spider's ghost returned."

"Damn!" J-Man said. "I thought maybe you were hallucinating the last time."

"Me too," Troy said, "but he's back. He was in the room when we found Dillon. He came downstairs with me and—"

"I didn't see him," Knives said.

"He was shaking his head through all of Dillon's story. Spider claims he's returned to help." Troy shrugged. "How, I don't know."

"I can't believe we're talking about ghosts," Knives said.

"Well, we were talking about vampires," J-Man laughed nervously.

"Maybe I can see Spider because I was so close to him when he died," Troy suggested.

"Look," J-Man started, "if you believe in vampires why can't you accept ghosts?"

"Well . . ."

"Jay! Watch out!" Troy pointed out the front window. Bob's car had quickly stopped in the middle of the road. Not paying attention, J-Man slammed on the breaks. Squealing the tires, he barely averted a rear-end collision.

They climbed out of the car and wordlessly walked toward Dillon who was standing in Glazier's headlights. In front of him sat the mangled remains of a Supra wrapped around two trees. Bill was walking around the car and shaking his head. He let out a long whistle. Silke leaned against the Cutlass.

Troy could feel it—everyone feared the worse.

"Yeah," J-Man said, "it's Denny's car all right."

"Nobody's home," Bob said as he surveyed the Supra. "Empty. No blood and no bodies."

J-Man, Troy, and Knives instantly relaxed, then grew curious. If it was empty, where were Denny and Bob? "Were they thrown free?" Knives asked.

"No, they didn't fly through the windshield, although the safety belts have been ripped from their anchoring. I've never seen that." Bill whistled again. "There are three holes, but none man-sized."

Troy felt a heavy weight lift from his heart. Then it was replaced by dread. If the car was empty, where were they? "Another mystery—more missing people," J-Man muttered.

370

"When will this end?" Silke whispered.

"Very strange," Dillon said. He leaned against the car.

"I'm scared," Silke said.

"Any tracks?" J-Man asked.

"I can't find any," Bob stated.

Silently, Troy surveyed the damage. The car had hit a tree head on, driving the trunk nearly two feet into the left side of the hood, then spun around and slammed into a second tree just behind the rear wheel well. The Supra had several pretzel twists in it where the frame had warped. The trunk had ripples in it like abused aluminum foil. The battery and a headlight had flown off to the right. Sparkling like early morning dew, glass covered the asphalt.

"No skid marks," Knives said. Flashlight in hand, he was searching the road. "They never braked. They hit these trees at full speed."

Troy began to move toward her when something caught his eye. "Check out the roof. These look like claw marks—ten grooves, in two groups of five."

J-Man ran a finger over the grooves. "They go clear through to the interior."

Troy nodded. "The top of the windshield looks like a can opener tried to pry it open."

"Wonder how these three holes got in the windshield? Looks like a shotgun blasted it," Bill remarked. He peeked inside the car. "Troy! Take a look at this."

Troy ran around to the driver's side. Looking at where Bill pointed, Troy examined the steering wheel. There were finger indentations in it.

"The work of a cult, wouldn't you say, Dillon?" His eyes burning, Troy turned to look at his friend.

"I guess they're storing up more victims for the second round of sacrifices," Dillon said.

"Vampires," J-Man said slowly, "not Satan worshippers."

"We have no idea where they are," Silke said. She took Troy's hand. "I feel so helpless. Troy, isn't there anything we can do?"

"How about Denny's dogs? They should be able to track him," Knives suggested. "They're hunting dogs."

"Could b—," Troy started to say, then Spider's ghost appeared. Silently, his friend's spirit wavered before him. As if worried about scaring him, Spider slowly reached out and touched Troy.

"I think I know where to look," Troy said. A vision of Jeremiah Corning came to him.

"Ovahflow spillway. Helped pour ceement. Lotsa caves ovah thar. Smelled strange too."

Chapter Twenty
Preparations

As Troy sat on the dock waiting for the others, his mind wandered. The boat was loaded, better yet, armed and ready to go, but the people weren't. Troy wasn't sure an amateur rescue attempt was a good idea, but he didn't know what else to do.

Absently, Troy's eyes flicked across the back of the lakehouse, looking for Silke and Dillon, then moved to the helicopter where Knives and J-Man completed the preparations. The metal on the copter gleamed brightly as it reflected the rising sun. Troy watched as they loaded several guns, two bows, dynamite, and other odds and ends. If only they had holy water, Troy thought. They could use all the help they could get.

While Dillon, Troy, and Silke approached by water, the twosome would approach by the air. They'd hoped for a three-pronged attack, but Glazier had failed. Only minutes ago, they decided that they'd waited long enough. Bill had been gone nearly ten hours. They no longer felt he was going to return with help.

Troy shook his head. He felt uncomfortable about what they were going to do, but he didn't see any alternatives. Despite not fully believing Dillon, Troy thought he was telling the truth . . . about Jambo. He couldn't let Jambo be sacrificed—too many of his friends had died already. They were going to have to rescue him with or without police support—with or without a cavalry. No one would believe a story about vampires—Troy wouldn't have believed it himself except he'd witnessed the horror first-hand. No, they were on their own.

Damn, Troy cursed. Glazier should have returned by now unless there was an accident or they'd locked him up in a cell because of his story. That wouldn't have surprised Troy any, but he had the uncomfortable feeling that Bill might never have made it to Bristol at all, just like Denny and Bob St. Martin never made it to J-Man's place. The sun had risen over an hour ago and there was still no sign of Detective Glazier and his troops. They had to do whatever they could to save Jambo—today. Tonight would be too late. According to Dillon, sacrifice was set for midnight, and since most of the cult members slept all day, the rescue attempt had to be made during the day. Troy felt his stomach do flip-flops.

With the deaths of Pete, Aaron, and Spider fresh in their memories, they couldn't let Jambo die. And what about Marader? No one knew.

Staring at the torn-up Supra, there was one thing

they knew. Something terrible had happened to Denny and Bob St. Martin. Dillon thought that the cult might have grabbed them. Troy couldn't help but wonder if the vampires had struck again. There was no sign of blood, but there was plenty of damage as well as strange holes in the windshield. Windshields didn't crack like that.

He wished they had more time to think, to plan. Everything was strange, dangerous, and moving much too fast.

Troy heard a door slam. He watched Dillon walk over to the helicopter. Troy cursed himself — he wished he knew what was different about his friend. It might mean the difference between life and death.

Troy hadn't explained about Spider's ghost touching him and how his dead friend had forced him to recall an important conversation from his past. No, he didn't want Dillon to know about Spider's ghost. Troy seemed so certain where to go, everyone agreed it was worth checking out. What fools we are, Troy thought. They weren't Ghostbusters. This was real life . . . and death.

Troy watched Dillon return to the house. Leaving the dock, Troy approached his friends at the copter. "You guys ready?"

"As ready as we'll ever be," J-Man said. "I have the Vampire Hunter's Starter Pack as well as accessories," he said with a smile. He reached behind the seat and held up objects for Troy to see. "Mallets, stakes, garlic bulbs, a bow and wooden arrows, and several sticks of dynamite. We also have the standard-issue silver bullets for werewolves."

"J-Man, please, this is serious," Troy said.

"What am I supposed to do?" J-Man asked. "I'm so scared I could shit my pants."

"Are you taking your pills?" Knives asked.

"Yes," J-Man replied. His face screwed up. "What are those things? They taste terrible."

"I didn't tell you to suck on them," Knives said. "Troy, are you taking yours?"

"Yes. What are they?"

"Trust me, you don't want to know."

"I'm not sure who I can trust," Troy replied. "I don't feel I can trust Dillon."

"We'll stay in radio contact," J-Man assured him. "Once you find what we're looking for, I can land this baby anywhere. With any luck, we'll be able to slay the vampires before lunch."

"Feeling cocky today, are we?" Troy asked.

"I'm gonna pay 'em back for Spider, Aaron, Pete, and whoever else they've killed."

"Our first priority is to save Jambo, and whoever else is being held captive by the Six Finger Cult," Troy reminded Jay. He nodded.

"Are you sure you want Silke to go along?" Knives asked.

"I don't want her to come, but she has a mind of her own. She's worried that it might be even more dangerous to stay."

"I can see that," J-Man agreed. "Here they come."

Troy turned to watch Silke and Dillon approach. Dillon carried a shotgun. His jacket bulged in vari-

376

ous places with ammunition. Silke's face was tense, lips drawn tight.

"We're as ready as we'll ever be," Dillon said.

"You said that you never saw any of the cult members carrying arms, right?" J-Man asked.

Dillon nodded. "That's right, but that doesn't mean they don't store arms someplace. Our biggest advantage will be surprise."

"Troy, did you bring the poisoned beef for the wolves?" Knives asked.

Troy nodded.

"Then I think we're ready to go."

"Aye," J-Man said, "time for takeoff. The next time you hear from us will be over the marine radio."

"Good enough," Troy said. He shook both their hands and headed for the boat. Silke slipped into his arm on the way.

"Good luck," Dillon said, shaking J-Man's hand.

"I hope we don't need it," Knives said. As he shook Dillon's hand, he said, "Don't let us down, we're blood brothers . . . and don't let anything happen to Silke."

Dillon's stare wavered, then he turned away. "I won't," he said as he walked toward the dock.

J-Man slammed his door and started the chopper. As the whirring whine grew, J-Man said, "Don't trust him with your life."

"I won't," Knives said. He shut his door, buckled his safety belt, and put on his headset. Raising a thumb skyward, he said, "Let's do it." J-Man's hands danced across the console, then they lifted off.

From the boat, Silke waved at the helicopter. Dillon untied the mooring lines and climbed in. "Ready when you are, Captain," Dillon told Troy.

Troy took the throttle out of choke and let it idle. He looked at his friends and wondered if this would be their last time together. "Let's do it." He put the boat in gear and they shoved off.

Chapter Twenty-one
The Rescue Attempt

As the maroon and gold bass boat glided acros
the calm waters, the fog-filled morning air whippe(
around the windshield. The trio lapsed into silence
each lost in thought. Behind the craft, their wak(
spread out, until the disturbed waters eventuall)
grew calm.

They passed under the 421 Bridge and left it be
hind. The houseboats were empty — no one doing
repairs, no setting out for a cruise. Troy steered fo:
open water and the trio of islands that sat in the
center of the lake.

The boat slashed through the scattered patches o:
fog which obscured the shore and stood like nebu
lous columns holding up the sky. All around them
the forested mountains sat silently. Troy felt some
thing unnatural in the quiet. It was a differen:
peace than normally accompanied a lazy morning
in the Smokies; there was fear and expectation in
the air. Something was disturbing the natural balance.

Using all the techniques he learned over the years, Troy breathed deeply and forced himself to stay calm. He tried to use the peacefulness of the lake to soothe his tense nerves, but the strain of the moment, of the past few days, still coiled like a tight spring within him. Why did he feel that today was Judgment Day?

Troy shook his head. He was looking for someplace that might not be, with a friend he couldn't trust, against creatures that were already dead. No, he absolutely did not believe Dillon. The longer he thought about it, the surer he became. He was positive that vampires and the Dark Lady awaited him. Would it be the dark-haired mistress of his visions, with her haunting emerald eyes? Would it be Elle or Racquel—but hadn't Racquel given him the ring that saved his life?

Troy looked at Silke. Her body was taut and her amber eyes were lost as if trying to see the future. Troy wondered what she was thinking, but although he loved her, he hadn't known her long enough to read her mind. What a beautiful woman, inside and out, Troy thought. Again, he wished she wasn't with them, but there didn't seem any safety anywhere. Not even in death. Who would have thought, Troy told himself.

Glancing at the shrouded shores, the shadowy trees, and boundless forest, Troy had a disturbing thought. As they moved into the larger basin of the lake, he couldn't see land, but he remembered what it looked like. The red rock was everywhere. Out of the water and exposed to the sun, tree roots stuck out and hung in the air over the lake. Brown leaves

380

created a blanket for the dying forest—no water, no life. The drought had caused all of this, even the return of the immortal evil.

"A good place to die," Troy said so quietly that only Dillon could hear. His friend looked startled by Troy's voice—or was it the words? Were those tears that Troy saw in his eyes, tears of regret . . . or deceit?

The radio interrupted Troy's thoughts. "Hello, this is J-copter to Procraft 1750, do you copy?" came J-Man's voice.

"Could you turn that up, please?" Troy asked.

"I'll get it," Dillon said. He turned up the volume, then picked up the handset. "This is Procraft 1750, you've got Dillon here. We read you loud and clear, J-copter. What's the news?"

Silke picked up a pair of binoculars and searched for J-Man's copter. As it flew by the backdrop of the mountains, it almost seemed to disappear. Since the copter played hide-and-seek with the low-lying clouds, it took Silke a moment to locate the whirling blades and dark blue and black body. When Silke did, she waved at them. "I've got them in sight."

"From our vantage point the lake looks totally deserted, which is unusual for a Friday," J-Man said.

"Probably due to all those frightening stories Bill mentioned reading in the newspapers," Dillon suggested.

"Be extra careful. Knives suggests that you use the trolling motor when you get near the spillway."

Dillon laughed. "You guys must be psychic. Troy

and I talked about that a few minutes ago."

"Great minds think alike," J-Man replied. "Anyway, we've decided to fly on ahead and make a pass or two over the spillway. The fog shouldn't be as bad around all that concrete. We'll contact you again in a few minutes."

"Make it one pass," Troy suggested.

"Make it one pass to be safe," Dillon relayed.

"Okay. J-copter over and out."

"There they go," Silke said, pointing toward the gigantic earthen dam. They could make out the top of it over the sea of fog.

A long pause ensued between the three. It was as if they'd lost their voices to the fog. Suddenly, they cruised into a sunny patch that warmed them. "I hope they're careful," Dillon said.

"They'll die if they aren't," Troy said tightly. He squinted and put on his sunglasses.

"On your mind a lot, isn't it?" Dillon asked, stroking his stubbled chin.

"Death?"

"Yes."

"I have good reason. There's a lot of it going around, and death's scythe has been very near on several occasions." Troy looked at Dillon out of the corner of his eye. He noticed that Silke was watching them both. "It hasn't been on yours?"

"There are worse things than dying," Dillon stated, looking away.

Troy felt anger rise within him. There shouldn't be games between friends, and he was getting tired of it. They'd always spoken frankly to each other before now. Troy knew something was wrong. "Like what, may I ask?"

"Like . . . like living an unhappy life, time passing on and living all alone. It seems to me you have a good reason to focus on staying alive."

Troy was confused.

"I can tell that my sister has finally worked her magic on you. Have you finally rid yourself of Racquel's shroud?"

"I think so. I love Silke," Troy said. Silke moved up behind him and hugged his neck, then kissed the back of his head.

"I'm glad." Dillon shifted in his seat and knocked a fin out of the side pocket. The buckle clinked off a scuba tank. Dillon stared at it with a furrowed brow.

"Troy, why did you bring scuba gear along?"

"Oh, I don't know for sure. It seemed like the right thing to do. I had the crazy thought that we might need to dive Hoyt Wilhelm's house again. J-Man's even carrying a couple of tanks."

"*What?* What did you say?" Dillon asked, his face drained of blood. "Whose house?!"

Troy tried to calmly analyze his friend's reaction. It was as if Dillon had seen a ghost—and Spider was nowhere in sight. "Hoyt Wilhelm. We think that the jewelry box came from his house in Wreythville. Why?"

Dillon started to sweat, then shake. His expression crumbled, then firmed. He put his face in his hands. "Because—"

"Hello again. It's the J-copter calling from the friendly skies over the South Holston Lake overflow spillway with today's host, Jay Beck."

Troy silently cursed. The interruption of the radio seemed to snap Dillon from his resolution to tell the truth. His face was now calm and stoic, although his eyes still darted like trapped beasts. Maybe it wasn't too late, Troy thought. "Hey, J-Man, can I call you back in a moment?"

"Sure. Is anything wrong?"

"No, I'll explain later."

"No problem . . . What did you say, Stephen? No, I didn't see anything leave the ground."

The hair stood on the back of Troy's neck. He didn't hang up the handset. "J-Man, what's going on?"

"Knives thinks he saw something . . . What?" There was silence and static. "Knives thinks he saw several things, maybe flying things, soaring through the fog below us. Could have been birds."

"Could have been bats," Troy muttered.

"I didn't see anything. I was checking out the cove. You wouldn't believe this fog."

"Jay, why don't you cruise back over here and fly above us?" Troy asked.

"Roger wilco . . . What, Stephen?" There was pause. "No, I didn't see it this time either. Check behind us. See anything?" There was a long pause and then J-Man's voice returned.

"No. Good. Troy, I think these pills that Knives gave us are affecting him. He's seeing things."

Dillon looked questioningly at Troy, but lost interest when J-Man screamed, "What in God's name was that?!" There was an agonizing pause.

"No fucking way. That couldn't have been . . . a bat?" Silence and static.

"Jay, keep talking!" Troy commanded over the headset. "What's going on!" There was no response. Troy wanted to shake the handset. He wanted to reach through and grab J-Man and make him speak.

Silence and then static.

"Man o' man," J-Man's voice returned. "I just saw the largest goddamn bat. Could have mistaken it for a damn pterodactyl . . . *Skrreeechhherwham.*"

"That sounded like metal being bent," Dillon said. "They're hit!"

Holy Shit!"

"Jay!" Troy screamed into the mike. He squeezed it so tightly he feared it might shatter in his grasp.

"We're hit! Troy, damn, we're hit! The rotor's broken! I've got power, but . . ." Silence. In a quiet voice, J-Man continued. "But very little to keep us aloft. We're falling like a rock."

"No, no!" Silke said. She buried her face in Troy's neck.

Troy looked at Dillon's face. It was still expressionless, but his words carried urgency. "Troy, forget being quiet. Haul ass! Let's get there!"

Troy rammed the throttle all the way forward. The motor unleashed a powerful, mechanical bellow. The boat fully planed, hunkered down, and hugged the water. Wind ripping at them, they streaked forward over the placid lake.

"I'm . . . I'm gonna try and ditch in the lake. J-Man yelled. "God, the land is rising up to meet us! Pray, Stevie baby! This is gonna be close!"

Troy tried to will the bass boat to go faster. The tach was in the red and the speedometer read fifty-two. He hoped, prayed, they would arrive in time to pull them from the water. Troy looked up and away from the radio. The dam was straight ahead.

"Come on baby, GLIDE!" Knives yelled.

Troy wanted to make the last cove on the left. He turned the wheel and the boat nearly skimmed along its side. The motor roared angrily. They carved through the water and headed down the cove to the spillway.

"See anything?" Dillon asked his sister. She peered through the binoculars. Silke shook her head.

"We're not going to make it! My kingdom for a tailwind!"

Troy felt helpless. Again, he wasn't going to be able to save his friends. They were going to die.

"Bye, Stevie. It's been fun." Silence followed by static.

"No! J-MAN! KNIVES!" Troy yelled into the mike.

"We'll be there in a second," Dillon said tersely. They rounded the first turn. The spillway was just around the next bend.

The next few seconds seemed to drag on toward eternity. Troy noticed that the fog was indeed heavier in the cove than on the open lake. It was no longer in patches—it was more like a ghost's blanket.

As they rounded the corner, Troy drew the throttle back. He thought he heard something. "Do you hear . . ." Troy began, and turned off the motor. It immediately grew silent and they glided along.

A sound softly finished echoing through the valleys and bounded off the mountains. It sounded like shearing metal and breaking trees. "They crashed on land," Silke said plainly. "They didn't make the water." Her jaw trembled.

"Damn," Troy muttered. He reached to restart the motor when he heard a second sound. It sounded like a fire. "Look!" Troy said as he pointed toward the shore. Black smoke was beginning to dominate the gray-white fog.

"Hurry!" Silke said.

Troy fired up the motor.

Even before they touched shore, Dillon jumped off the boat.

Splashing in the shallows, Dillon ran ahead. Troy killed the motor. As they cruised in, he tossed the anchor onto shore. Silke climbed out, slowed the boat, then wedged the anchor between two red rocks.

Troy was chomping at the bit and wanted to rush headlong into the woods, but didn't. Something inside warned him of the danger. "Here, take this," Troy said to Silke as he handed her a shotgun.

"I'm armed. Aunt Jada gave me this." She held up a large fire opal.

"Great, carry this anyway. Shoot, then wave your gem at them." Silke frowned, but took the shotgun. She stuffed shells in her jeans pocket. "Do you have your cross?"

"Yes. Don't forget to bring the first-aid kit," she reminded him. She cocked her head, listening.

As Troy slipped on his backpack, they could hear the fire devour the trees. The crunching and cracking sounded like a gigantic herbivore consuming the

387

forest for lunch. The drought had left things so dry the woods burned like kindling.

Troy hurriedly slipped several arrows into the pack. They stuck out the top. He removed the safety catch on his pistol and placed the .38 under his belt. He carried the bow. Then a thought struck Troy—he didn't see Dillon.

Silke voiced his concern. "Where's Dillon? *Dillon!*" she yelled.

"Silke, please!" Troy whispered.

She turned cold eyes on him. "It doesn't matter if someone hears me yell. They would have heard the boat."

"You're right. Let's go." Troy hid the keys in an empty cassette case in the glove box and then jumped out of the boat.

They climbed over the rocks and up the hill. Some of the rocks were very sharp. Silke slipped several times and cut open her knee. It didn't slow her, but Troy had to nearly drag her over the overhanging lip. "The dropoff is incredible. Damn drought." Troy smelled smoke as the wind shifted in their direction. "Dillon! Dillon, answer me! *Where are you?*"

There was no answer. The fog seemed to close in on them. The smoke wafted in their direction, slowly surrounding them in a dark cloud.

"Troy, I'm scared."

"I know. Me too, my love, but we can't leave." Troy began to move forward.

"I know . . . we're all kin."

"Stay behind me."

Suddenly, Troy stopped. He thought he saw a

flash of movement. No—was Spider's ghost moving ahead of them? Troy shook his head and squinted.

"Arrrrgh!!" came the scream, as if a soul were being ripped free. It came from straight ahead.

"Dillon!" Silke screamed. She rushed headlong into the woods. Branches and briars grabbed at her. A thorn bush ripped at her legs. She ignored the pain. She wouldn't be slowed.

Troy couldn't catch her. It was all he could do to keep up with her. Clumsily, he nocked an arrow.

"Oh!" Silke gasped. She stumbled, staggered, and then tumbled forward. She hit the ground hard. Troy heard the breath explode from her lungs.

He knelt by her side to see if she were all right; then he saw what she tripped over.

The body was slowly dissolving before his eyes. The vampire groaned one more time as it tried to wrench a wooden shaft from its chest. Blood poured from the wound and from its mouth. The undead's hands shook one final time, then its entire body shuddered. Limply, its hands fell to the side. Skin flaked off, the dust blowing away in the breeze. Bones were exposed. Hair fell out and surrounded the white skull. Lips disappeared and long incisors stood out prominently, gnashing in frustration and pain. In moments, all that was left was a skeleton with a stake stuck in its ribs.

Troy's mind raced. He looked around wildly. What had happened? Then he noticed a different smell with a hint of garlic. There appeared to be a trace of powder on the ground. What had happened? Where was Dillon?

Dillon would have to wait. He had to make sure

Silke was all right. Troy reached down and shook her. She groaned, but didn't awaken. Blood trickled from her mouth. "Silke. Come on, baby, wake up!" He shook her again, but this time she didn't even moan.

It reminded Troy of their car accident, but this time he couldn't leave Silke. There was danger all around. He didn't know where, but he could feel it. Where was Spider's ghost when he really needed help?

Besides the crackling of the fire, all was silent. Troy tried to peer into the fog. Nothing seemed to move. Where was Dillon? Had he found Knives and J-Man? Were they dead? Had Dillon led them into a trap? No, it was Troy who had suggested they come here. Spider had—

There was a crunching of leaves just ahead of him. Footsteps! He raised his bow and pulled back on the string. His breath caught in his throat and his heart hammered. He could see a shadowy form in the fog. "Dillon? Knives? Jay? *Answer, damn you!*"

Troy heard a laugh so dry that it reminded him of a winter wind rushing through dead leaves. The figure moved forward. Troy tensed, ready to loose the arrow.

"Hi guy!" Marader said as he stepped from the fog. "Fancy meeting you here." He looked at the bow. "Whoa, you hunting game?" He looked down at Silke. "She looks hurt. Do you want help?" Marader locked eyes with Troy.

Troy was already confused, now suddenly he felt dizzy. All around Marader's eyes the world spun.

Troy wanted to throw up. "We better take her to a doctor. She's bleeding."

Troy quickly looked down, then back up. Again, he met Marader's eyes. His friend had moved closer. Troy's knees felt weak, but he didn't fall.

"Troy, what's wrong with you. You look pale." Ever so slowly, Marader moved closer. He was within fifteen feet.

"What are you doing here?" Troy slurred. Even his lips and tongue were sluggish. His fingers were leaden, his hand heavy.

"Put down the bow," Marader said quietly, but forcefully. Unbidden, Troy's hands lowered. The bow drooped. "That's good." Marader smiled widely, revealing inhumanly long incisors.

Troy struggled to raise his hand. He screamed at himself and pictured himself raising the bow and firing. With trembling arms, he did . . . and fired. The string twanged and the arrow whistled. As the arrow flew free, Troy sensed something behind him. Suddenly, all went black.

Chapter Twenty-two
Captivity

Groggy, Troy found himself on his knees in the dirt. He opened his eyes and looked around, but everything was blurred, mingling with the heavy fog. Troy couldn't distinguish one thing from the next. He rubbed his eyes, but his vision didn't clear. The woods were silent. Had the fire gone out?

Briefly, Troy wondered where Marader was hiding . . . or was he even there at all? Could it have been a dream? He'd had plenty of those recently, even while awake. Marader had looked like a vampire, but it was daylight — that sounded like a dream.

Absently, Troy rubbed his neck. It was stiff and sore as if he'd been struck there. His skin was rough to the touch.

Lord, he was hot and thirsty. Although the fog was cool on his skin, Troy felt as if he'd been sitting in the scorching sun for hours. Sweat rolled off his forehead and into his eyes. His lips quivered. His tongue felt like sandpaper.

Troy just waited, working on his breathing and eventually his vision slowly cleared. There was a slim body before him, then he remembered. Silke! He scrambled

392

forward and came to her side. He vaguely noticed that the skeletal figure was gone.

Silke was pale. Troy touched her cheek, then her neck. Her pulse was strong—very strong. He tried to shake her awake, but she remained unconscious. Troy searched for bruises or cuts, but found nothing.

Hoping that a kiss would awaken her like some princess in a fairy tale, he kissed Silke. He brushed her lips, but then found himself being drawn to the fine lines of her neck—her warm, white, and vibrant throat. The exposed flesh and jugular vein called out to him.

Troy wet his lips. His throat was so dry and he was so thirsty . . . hungry. It would be so easy to assuage his need. He was sure Silke wouldn't mind. She would want to give him whatever he needed—yes, she would.

Leaning over once more, Troy buried his teeth in her neck. Silke jerked and moaned. Flesh parted and warm, red blood ran over his lips. Troy began sucking, drinking. . . .

"NOOooo!" Troy screamed and immediately sat up. His heart pounded so hard it threatened to leap from his chest. It thundered in his ears. He felt cold and clammy all over as sweat poured from him. Troy tried to stop shaking, but couldn't. He put his hands down on the bed to steady himself.

"Sleep well?" a familiar voice said, then chuckled.

Troy rubbed his eyes and they finally focused. His mouth felt filled with pebbles when he first spoke. "Marader, you sonofabitch, what is going . . . on?" Troy noticed the change in his blood brother for the first time. In many ways Marader looked the same, but there were subtle differences.

Marader was still muscular, green-blond-haired, blue-eyed, and tan, but that's where the similarities ended. Troy couldn't help but be fascinated by the changes—enthralled by Marader's presence. In the glow of the lanterns, Marader's tan seemed radiant, as if an aura of power surrounded him. His eyes were intense and incandescent, but seemed to have a watchful and analytical aspect that Troy had never seen before. Marader gracefully folded his hands as if patiently waiting for Troy to speak. Again Troy noticed a change: Marader's hands were elongated, inhumanly so.

Troy tried to shake off the mesmerization, but it clung to him. He kept reminding himself that no matter what changes had overcome Marader, he was still Marader — an irreverent blood brother, lusty wencher, avid partier, and waterskiing fanatic. These thoughts finally enabled Troy to speak. He wanted to say, "Why are you here?" but instead Troy said, "You've changed."

Without answering, Tom Marader leaned back in his chair and put his feet up on a nearby desk. Troy wrenched his gaze from his friend and glanced around the room. It was a struggle just to look away from Marader. There was an insidious, unnatural beauty about him.

Marader watched Troy with amusement as he checked out his surroundings. Troy patted the bed he sat on. He was in a cave. Several lanterns were scattered about the room: one on the wall left of the door, a second on the large table, and another on a rock shelf next to the bed. The room felt damp, but looked dry.

Troy looked closely at his blood brother. He sensed that Marader was no longer alive. Troy didn't know what to say. So many questions leaped to mind but he became tongue-tied whenever his friend focused his burning eyes upon him.

They played a silent waiting game. Marader, who had always been the less patient of the two, spoke first. "You're dying of curiosity."

Troy found that the words came easier once Marader had broken the silence. He kept reminding himself that even if Marader was a vampire, he was still Tom Marader. It kept him sane. "Dying no, curious yes. It appears . . . you're already dead."

"And love every minute of it. You probably will too," Marader said with a smile. He grinned so widely that he displayed his unnaturally long incisors. "It was a big shock at first, but I adjusted rather quickly," he said with a nonchalant wave of his hand. "In many senses, it's what I've always wished for. I'm going to live, party, and fuck forever—until the end of the world!" he said with a huge grin. His head rolled back and he ran his hands through his hair.

"Now, I'll never have to worry about getting out of shape. Without having to lift weights or work out, I'm stronger than any man or beast." His smile almost became shy. "And there's something about vampires that make us irresistible to humans. You are drawn to us like a moth to a flame," he said, gloating, "and if that doesn't work, I have the ability to hypnotize. I can have any woman I want." He rubbed his hands quickly together in glee.

"And the women vampires are insatiable, just how I like them. Just like the men, they live for the moment and are constantly searching to satisfy their lusts . . . their hungers. And me," Marader pointed to himself, "I'm always available. I never tire."

"You know," Troy said, "there was always a part of me that thought, no, wished, that you might magically transform into a decent human being by the time you were forty, but I was deluding myself. You are, and always will be, a degenerate."

"Thank you. Eloquently spoken like the fine writer you are."

"Where am I?"

"In caves, some used for construction in the forties, near the overflow spillway."

"How . . . how did this happen?" Troy asked.

"It happened in the back of Ms. Samantha White's Nova." Marader smiled at Troy's look of surprise. "Yes, I know, you and Knives always claimed that if I didn't calm down, I'd catch a fatal disease and, you know . . . BOTH OF YOU WERE RIGHT!"

"Excuse me if I'm a bit . . . overwhelmed," Troy said.

"Bullshit! It would be understandable, considering you're in a vampire's presence, but I know you too well, Troy. You're mind's working away, analyzing."

"You still didn't answer my question."

"How did it happen?"

"Yes."

"Well, I was giving Sam the ride of her life, pumping away, when she bit me. Her legs were over my shoulders, just the way I like it, when all of a sudden she had me in a lock. I couldn't move no matter how hard I struggled. She fastened onto my neck and nearly drained all the blood from me." Marader grew introspective and his eyes seemed far away. This gave Troy some relief. He didn't have to struggle as hard to maintain his own individuality.

"She told me to listen very carefully, that I was going to die, but not going to die . . . that she was going to bestow upon me a wonderful gift. Lying there, paralyzed from the loss of blood and on the threshold of death, all I could do was listen, think, feel . . . and obey. I could feel the blood trickle through my veins. My lungs were slowing, but still gasping for air. I waited for the legendary death rattle, knowing that it was all over, but it wasn't. My heart slowed from a panicked hammering to a slow, tired throb.

"When I felt I was through, Sam bit her lip. With

blood flowing freely, she kissed me. She told me, no, commanded me, to suck on her blood. Once I did, it was all I could do. I couldn't stop. Suddenly, I felt vibrant, as if I'd snorted cocaine . . . only better. She finally pulled away, leaving me weak. Sam told me that I would soon be a vampire, that I'd taken the first step — that I would live on blood, live eternally. Now, I can see in the dark and change shape. It's wonderful. I could look like whoever I want if I so desired, but I'm fond of my own shape.

"After my body had settled more into its new state, Sam took me out on my first kill. Actually, I had to stand by and watch her kill someone first. That was proof of my true commitment to being a vampire — standing casually by and letting someone be killed.

"Then I killed my first human. It wasn't very challenging. He was a derelict over near the Four-twenty-one bridge. Now I was totally committed. Don't shed a tear for him, no one will miss him.

"His death was an incredible experience, the ultimate experience, in fact. As I locked on his neck and drew blood, my heartbeat matched his. It was as if our life forces merged. The drumming of his heart increased, then suddenly slowed. Sam told me I must leave him before he died or I would die with him . . . that he would drag me down to death with him. I didn't want that, now that I have so much to live for.

"You know, I once thought that dying was no big deal. I had to kill someone in self-defense once, but I didn't think twice about it. Now I look at death in a different light. For vampires, death is the ultimate sensation. I never thought I'd say this, but it is better than sex. When I hunger, I think only of it. I never think of sex until afterward. Odd how things change!" Marader laughed.

"After my first taste of the death which brings life,

my senses changed. I had vampire vision—vampire eyes. Where once I saw only color and depth, now I can see the vibrancy and flow of life. I can sense it and taste it as well. While my flesh feels dead, all my senses are now truly alive. No, that's not totally true, I can feel the breeze brush my flesh, but the emotional feelings that are tied to it are gone. I find myself oddly detached sometimes, able to think about and feel many things at once, without becoming totally absorbed in any particular one . . . except death and the life that accompanies the drinking of blood."

"We could actually subsist on animals, but it isn't quite so satisfying. Sam mentioned that by drinking the blood of an animal, you can assert control over others like it."

"If your body is dead, how do you enjoy sex?" Troy asked.

Marader thought for a minute. "It's the energy that's released, the mingling of the life force which occurs. It is not too much different than drinking blood . . . two souls become one for a time, bent toward one purpose."

"Another question. Why are you telling me this?"

"I don't know. Maybe I just need to share the experience with someone—someone I know, someone I feel comfortable with. You knew what I was, now you know what I am."

For a brief moment, Troy felt a pang of pity, then the pity was gone. Marader was now an enemy of life, surviving by the death of others. "Maybe you just like to hear the sound of your own voice."

Marader laughed. "Could be. You always knew me well."

"It could be I don't understand. Won't you miss the sun?" Troy asked. Despite the length of Marader's soliloquy, Troy was still trying to clear his head. He'd been struck very hard from behind. Tenderly, Troy fingered a lump on his head. "You were a sun worshipper. You always wanted to be outside, tanning your body so you'd be a bronze god."

"Not too worry. Don't I look tan?" Marader waited for him to comment, but Troy only nodded. "Well," Marader stood up and paraded back and forth, strutting like a peacock, "we are the new breed of vampire. We can live in the sunlight, bask in it, if so desired." He raised his hands to the roof. "No longer will vampires fear the day. We can have our fun at night or in the light." He laughed at his own rhyme, then grew somber for a moment.

"I must admit I was a bit concerned for a while. Sam talked about the time she thought she saw her last sunrise. She spoke of it with reverence, but she also explained the joy at seeing it once more. Now we are no longer limited," Marader finished.

Troy was confused—vampires living in the light, sitting in the sun . . . and working on their tans? He shook his head. Vampires working normal jobs, mingling with the living, breathing human beings—it couldn't be so. That made the abomination worse than it already was. The legends would be false. No one would ever suspect. Your closest friend, your waterskiing or bicycling buddy, could be a bloodsucking vampire. The woman you met on the beach . . . Troy gritted his teeth. All he could mutter was, "I don't understand."

"Oh, I'm not going to try to explain all the particulars to you, I'll let Von Damme do that."

"Who's Von Damme?"

"For lack of a better word, he's the headmaster."

"Do you know a Hoyt Wilhelm?"

"No."

Troy was almost afraid to ask the next question.

With time and practice, he found it a bit easier to distance himself from the aura of enthrallment that surrounded Marader. "Are Silke, Dillon, Jambo, and Bill Glazier held captive here also?"

"Yes to Silke and no to the rest," Marader replied. Troy cursed. "I brought Denny and Bob St. Martin here myself. Bob is quite beside himself. He's been praying since he got here." Marader snorted. "As if the Lord—or Satan—really cared. I care not for morals; I am beyond that now.

"But, I do know Denny and Bob will be glad to have company. Unfortunately Dillon eluded us." Then Marader all but salivated as he said, "Von Damme has Silke. Soon she'll be a vampire and I can't wait. Her lusts will drive her right into my arms. I've always wanted her to wrap her lovely, long legs around me . . . Mmm-mmm." He closed his eyes, leaned back, and rubbed his crotch.

Troy's anger released him from Marader's thrall. He grabbed the oil lamp and threw it at Marader. It struck him in the middle of the chest. "Arrrh!" Marader screamed as fiery oil exploded, setting his clothes afire. Flames danced up and down his body.

"Never!" Troy screamed. His head still throbbing and the room whirling, he threw himself at Marader. He stumbled as he left the bed and crashed to the floor. Scrambling to his feet, Troy grabbed a chair.

"Damn you!" Marader yelled as he tore his burning clothes off his body. He looked like a human torch.

Troy smashed the chair over Marader's head. The impact shook Troy's hands as debris flew. Marader staggered back, still ripping at his clothes.

Grabbing a jagged chair leg, Troy leaped at Marader. Without appearing to move quickly, the vampire seized Troy's wrist. The makeshift stake stopped inches short of its goal—Marader's heart.

Troy kicked out and they crashed to the floor. Landing on top, Troy tried to drive the stake home.

It didn't move, held fast by Marader. At first slowly, then with ever-quickening speed, Marader forced the stake away from his chest. "Not today, not ever!" Marader yelled as he turned the chair leg away.

He crushed Troy's wrist and the stake fell to the ground. Marader held him tightly. Troy could feel the flames continue to burn. His own clothes started to smolder. "Fire won't kill me. It's only a nuisance. We have changed. Not only does the sun not affect us, but neither does fire. I let my old human emotions get ahold of me. They will soon be shadows, then they'll be thankfully gone."

Marader smiled tightly. "How I wish to make us true blood brothers. Yes, your blood has touched mine, but how I'd love to have your blood rush through my veins . . . and that time will come. But the time is not now." Marader forced Troy aside, then tossed him away. Like a rag doll, Troy flew across the room and collided with the cave wall. He collapsed on the floor.

Marader stood and casually finished putting out the flames. His flesh was scorched and red, but he was uninjured. "I think our chat is at an end. There is more I'd like to tell you, to lessen your confusion when the change occurs, but I don't think you really want to hear anymore." Marader laughed. "I don't think you'll adapt to your new state of being as well as I did. Oh well, *c'est la vie*." He shrugged. "I'll take you to Von Damme. He will decide your fate. You might become a true vampire, or you might become just the shadow of one, more like a zombie."

Marader crossed the room, grabbed Troy by the shirt, and yanked him to his feet. "Let's go."

All but dragging him, Marader led Troy from the cave room and through a hallway. Troy finally gained his feet and staggered along behind.

They walked through a long and twisted cave. Makeshift sconces held burning torches which were set far apart. They traveled through several short patches of light in the long darkness. "The torches are for your benefit," Marader said. "I can see in the dark."

The rough floor suddenly smoothed and they entered a wider cave that was well lit. Troy thought he heard music. It sounded like a violin, but he wasn't sure. Troy noticed that even the walls appeared to have been smoothed. The haunting melody grew louder. It seemed to strengthen and fade like a heartbeat.

They climbed a short set of steps then halted. The tunnel continued on and up, but to their left hung a red satin curtain. The music wafted from behind the curtain.

"Von Damme?" Marader called.

The music stopped. "Enter." Marader shoved Troy inside, but did not follow. The room was dark. Little light slipped through the gaps in the curtain. Troy shivered. An unnatural chill gripped him. He was in the presence of a powerful evil. Troy wondered if, at any moment, he would die only to be reborn as an undead—a creature of the dark.

Chapter Twenty-three
Darkness Walks in the Light

Troy stood alone in the darkness. Immobile, he stood waiting to die — waiting for the vampire to strike. After the echo of the music faded, not a whisper of air, not a whisper of sound disturbed the silence. The suspense clawed at him, but Troy held it at bay each time it returned . . . and it returned every few moments. All he heard was his own breathing and heartbeat. He tried to slow both.

This reminded Troy of being entombed — reminded him of his dream. He remembered cowering in the grave at King College Cemetery, waiting to die. Again, his weakness sickened Troy and he fought back. Troy would not give into fear. With each assault, he told himself, he was growing stronger.

Troy concentrated, not giving into his feelings of helplessness and despair. He understood the battle was mental and psychological, not physical. Troy wasn't going to die, not immediately anyway. Marader brought him here for a reason, he told himself. Von Damme, whoever that was, wanted something from him. Then Troy laughed softly — Troy wanted something too. His curiosity burned and he wanted answers — probably the same thing Von Damme wanted.

Troy's laughter broke the spell and a deep voice spoke

inside the room, "You are either brave and strong-willed, or foolish and weak-hearted."

Clearing his throat, Troy found his voice. With enforced evenness he said, "A little of both to be in this predicament."

The deep voice laughed. "That is as rich as it is true." Then there was silence. "I seek answers from you . . . and maybe more."

"I have a burning curiosity. . . ."

". . . which kills the cat."

"And sometimes people too."

"Yes, you are as Marader described you."

"The same could be said for you, Von Damme," Troy said.

Again, Von Damme laughed. "It is only right that you see your master."

"Master or superior?" Troy asked.

A match was struck and a tiny light touched the room. Troy's eyes adjusted as the shaded candle cast a golden hue throughout the room. "Master. I am Viktor Von Damme. You see, the vampire's true nature is to kill without prejudice. Since we ourselves are immortal and cannot die of age or disease," the tall figure said as he moved to a second candle and lit it, "we are like God. We can kill indiscriminately and with detachment. We revel at the end of life in a way that only vampires can, death bringing rebirth as a dying mother gives herself up for a newborn babe." After igniting a third, Von Damme turned and said, "We slay the rich and the poor, the sick and the healthy, the black, white, red, or yellow. We care not. We slay like the hand of God, although we are not connected to heaven. No," he said with a laugh, "we are not. Be we are no longer mortal; we are close to godhood. We are the masters of the planet!"

In the flickering light, Troy gasped as he eyed the impressive figure. Von Damme was far more fascinating than Marader. His aura captivated Troy to the point that he was speechless. Troy stifled the urge to bow. Although something inside rebelled, Troy told himself that Von Damme was the most beautiful and graceful creature that he had ever seen. The head vampire was enthralling.

Von Damme was easily over six feet tall with abnormally wide shoulders and a narrow waist. His skin was almost luminescent and his green eyes glowed with a cold, predatory heat. Von Damme's face was smooth and expressionless with high cheekbones and an aquiline nose. Troy sensed cruel arrogance behind the stoic facade. His moustache was blond, matching his short-cropped hair, and sat over thin sensuous lips. "Is this what you expected to see?"

Troy somehow found the words to answer. "I don't know what I was expecting to see. Something terrible."

Von Damme turned and raised the wick on the lamp, then lit it. The room brightened. The light caught a set of red gems sitting sternum high on his chest. The silver chain sparkled, but the two stones stared at Troy like fiery red orbs. Troy had to turn his eyes away from them. They had the quality of Von Damme's eyes, a hypnotic pull that made him listless. He fought the idea that resistance was futile.

Von Damme was dressed in a charcoal black suit with a gray shirt open at the throat. He waved his cane at a chair. "Have a seat, there are some questions I would like to ask you." Troy froze above the antique chair when Von Damme said, "Silke and I have had a very interesting conversation, but there are some things I would still like to know."

"Where is she?" Troy said quietly. He tried to contain his anger and rage. He knew it would do him no good — except it seemed to hold Von Damme's hypnotic power at bay.

Von Damme waved to his right. "She is asleep." There

was a figure buried under the covers of the bed. Troy vaguely noticed that the room was plushy carpeted and furnished. Tapestries lined the wall. It didn't look like a cave. "She needs to rest after her ordeal."

"You've killed her?!"

"No, she hasn't had the pleasure of receiving my kiss as of yet, although she is very beautiful. Do not concern yourself with her welfare. I already have a fine consort who would be quite enraged if I chose another," Von Damme said with a charming smile. "When the time comes, I might let you do the honors," he said with a chuckle.

"I want to —"

Instantly the gracious charm left and steel returned, "Sit." Before he was aware of it, Troy immediately sat in the chair like a dog obeying its master. "Sit still and listen. You will answer my questions."

Troy tried not to look into Von Damme's eyes, but he was constantly pulled to the gems around the vampire's neck. No matter how hard he tried to avert his gaze, it always returned to the burning orbs. It seemed that Von Damme's eyes mirrored the fiery red stones. Both glowed red hot and riveted Troy's attention. He could feel his will slowly slipping away. His body began to go numb.

Troy tried to close his eyes, but they refused to obey him. He attempted to turn his head but he could no longer move. Troy was paralyzed. Ever so slowly, he was losing contact with his body. His flesh seemed far away, as did sensation. Troy felt hollow. He was in Von Damme's power.

Troy harnessed all the energy he could find within himself and tried to look beyond Von Damme. He tried to picture a burning red sunrise on an ocean. He tried to feel the sand under his feet and smell the salt in the air.

Von Damme's voice brought him back. "Your friends

found a jewelry box. It was made of polished wood and held together by silver clasps. A cursive E was monogrammed in the top. Where is it?"

"At the bottom of the lake," Troy said in a monotone.

"What?!" Von Damme said with agitation. He let his attention slip and Troy focused on the sunrise once more. This time he actually felt the sand between his toes.

Von Damme no longer focused on Troy. He mused as if talking to himself, as if Troy were nothing to him. "No, that can't be true! Traylor opened it on the island and freed me! I left it there, then it was gone. One of your friends found it. Where is it? Marader told me you had it! It must be returned to me! Tell me more," he demanded.

The sunrise disappeared. "Four of us went diving. Spider Adder carried it with him. It led us to Hoyt Wilhelm's home. I left it in the desk drawer after it killed Spider."

"Yes, yes," Von Damme said. "I should have known, I should have sensed it—the dream I had was no dream. My fears are confirmed," Von Dammed mused. "It still withholds . . ." The vampire grew silent, then slammed a first into the palm of his other hand. "I felt as much . . . I do not feel whole."

Troy wasn't listening. He was searching again for the sunset. This time he smelled the salt in the air. The water glistened.

"You will dive once more and return it to me," Von Damme quietly commanded.

Troy began to sweat. It was as if an incredible force were pressing on his mind, making it difficult to think. Troy summoned a seagull in his mind's eye and heard it cry. It made him smile. Troy shifted his vision inward.

"You smile. Marader was correct, you are strong-willed. But I am stronger." In Troy's mind, the crashing of the waves grew silent and the sea breeze faded. "Silke mentioned several attacks on you. You were attacked by wolves, red-eyed wolves that appeared intelligent, is that true?"

"Yes!"

"Both at the dock and in a Landrover?" Troy was silent. His heart began to pound. "Answer me."

"Yes!"

"Hmmm . . . troublesome. I did not send wolves to the Landrover. I fear . . . Silke also divulged that you encountered and destroyed a vampire at King College Cemetery."

"Yes." Troy had lost the sunrise. The ocean and beach were gone. He stared directly into the burning orbs.

Von Damme stroked his chin. "I was afraid of that. Did he mention Elsa?"

"No."

"Did he mention any woman?"

Troy put together enough fragmented thought to pretend that it was Marader who stood before him—still a vampire, but someone he was familiar with. "Yes . . . the Dark Lady."

Von Damme chuckled. "Have you heard that name before?"

Troy transformed the green eyes to blue and the blond hair thinned. Von Damme's moustache vanished in Troy's mind. "Yes, from Jeremiah Corning. He worked on the construction of Holston dam."

"Ah, so you've dug up some history. Very thorough of you." Von Damme thought for a moment and then said, "Where have you heard the name Hoyt Wilhelm?"

"Nowhere. I found it in a listing of residents next to a map of Wreythville in the TVA library."

"You have told me what I need to know. Very soon you shall retrieve the jewelry box for me."

The transformation was complete. Troy saw Marader

instead of Von Damme. The charisma was still there — the power was still formidable, but Troy knew how to deal with Marader. "Go fall on a stake," Troy said through barred teeth.

"Indeed. You are strong-willed. If you hadn't already told me what I needed to know, I would have enjoyed a battle of wills, but I do not waste energy." Von Damme was thoughtful. He slowly walked back and forth before Troy.

"I had toyed with the idea of making you one of us, but I don't need the competition. Slaves, predators, like Marader, yes, — competitors like you, no. I have just revived my followers. Vampires are not a social lot, and the balance is very fragile. I don't need you to tear my work apart."

"Will I die when you drain me or will I become a vampire? I'd rather die," Troy said with conviction.

"You are curious?"

"Yes, of course, I'm a reporter."

Von Dammed laughed. "Ah yes, a reporter's nature is to seek out the truth — or at least a story, while the vampire's is to kill." He chuckled then said, "We are much alike, I think."

"Would I die . . . or worse?"

"It depends on several things."

"Like?"

"You are curious until the last moment?"

"Maybe I'm stalling for time."

Von Damme laughed heartily this time. "Ah yes, time. Mortals can be so amusing. Vampires are not concerned with time anymore than they are with political shifts. Well, I shall indulge both of us." He scratched his chin. "If I just drained you and let you die, and you were not exposed to sunlight for twenty-four hours, you would arise as a simple vampire. You would then have one evening to drink the blood of a living creature or you would die."

"A simple vampire?"

"You would be . . . a common vampire. You would live off the blood of others, be immortal, live in the darkness, and have tremendous strength and extraordinary senses. Alas, you would not be able to shape-change, assume a gaseous form, or influence the elements."

"You, I assume, are a special vampire . . . an uncommon one?"

"Of course, I am the most uncommon of them all," Von Damme said with pride. "I, who was once the most famous alchemist in Europe, was transformed into a vampire. A vampire who would create a new breed of vampire. The evolution of my race must move forward."

"And how did it happen? How were you turned into a vampire?" Troy still pictured talking to Marader. Sweat was pouring freely from his flesh. His brow was wrinkled from the strain and his head had started to pound.

"The vampire who drained me fed me his own blood, then taught me certain things. As I mentioned before, I can shapechange and influence humans, animals, and the elements. I can transform into vapor and not be harmed. Religious relics can injure an uncommon vampire, but crosses can destroy a common one."

"And you can survive the sunlight?"

Von Damme swelled with pride. "Yes, an incredible accomplishment that will raise my people above the common rabble of vampire. It strips us of one of our few remaining limitations."

"That's incredible!"

"Would you like to go for one last walk in the sunlight? It is not long until the sun sets and you will die."

"Of course."

"Then follow me and I will explain more fully."

Unconcerned, Von Damme walked past him and

pushed through the curtain. Troy hesitated, thinking about Silke, but Von Damme said, "Come!" and Troy found he couldn't disobey. He followed Von Damme.

They wound their way through several confusing passages. After a while, Troy saw sunlight stretch toward them, waiting to touch them. Von Damme walked calmly toward it. He reached inside his jacket and donned sunglasses. Troy had to shade his eyes despite the softness of the light.

Ahead, a figure stood silhouetted in the cave mouth, a slim female form. When she saw Von Damme, she moved toward them. The dark-haired woman met them. Without any emotion, she kissed Von Damme on the cheek.

"My dear," Von Damme said, "may I introduce you to my reluctant guest. This is Troy Bane, a sports reporter and enterprising occult investigator." Von Damme laughed at his own joke. "Mr. Bane, this is Ms. Terry Bray, my consort and salvation."

Terry smiled at Troy who blanched. Her blood red lips parted to reveal sharp, white teeth. Her tongue flicked across them.

"You killed John Traylor," Troy said.

Her blue eyes locked on his and Troy swallowed heavily. Despite the color of her eyes, he knew who he faced. The way she looked at Troy held him spellbound.

She was the most exquisite creature he'd ever seen. Terry Bray was tall and shapely. Her dark hair contrasted with her alabaster skin and her eyes danced like flaming sapphires. "I did not have the pleasure of killing him, Von Damme did. I was only the vessel," she said with a sweet smile, thick with innocence.

Troy felt confused and wanted to ask questions, but couldn't.

"Mr. Bane is witnessing his last sunset, then he is yours, my dear."

"Thank you, my lord, I am still famished," she said, waving to her left where a pale corpse lay on a rock, "but I thought he was to retrieve the jewelry box for you?"

"No, another who is more malleable will serve. Mr. Rentzel is impressionable. He shall do."

"What is Troy Bane's fate?" she asked.

"Feast and drain him, then leave him to die—to decompose in the sunlight. He would not make a suitable vampire."

"Pity, I think Christine would find him . . . entertaining."

"Be that as it may, he will pass from this world." Von Damme turned to Troy. "Enjoy your last few minutes of sunlight, Mr. Bane, and as you watch the light fade away, know that your life is fading with it. When the sun sets, you will be bestowed with the ultimate honor—a vampire's kiss." Troy was silent, his eyes still locked on Terry's crystal blue orbs.

"To ease your burning curiosity, for I would not want you to die unfulfilled, I shall tell you a short story." Von Damme smiled. "As I told you, I was a renowned alchemist who lived in Germany during the 1800's. While on a field trip to the mountains in search of components, I was bitten. I have survived for nearly two hundred years. For many of those years, I missed the sunshine. My mentor, Vladic, the one who made me a vampire, said the longing would fade. For reasons that I can't explain, even as the years passed, I missed the light . . . there is so much vitality, so much to feast upon during the day. The days throb with life, while life at night is furtive.

"After my relocation to America where your people were totally unfamiliar with my kind, I devoted myself to discovering a way to survive, to walk and live in the sunlight.

"It was actually a Native American that aided me,

showed me a way for my spirit to reestablish contact with the land, and thus, I found a way to bask in the light." He grew thoughtful. "Shortly thereafter I discovered that there were others who also wanted to prowl during the day and they came to me.

"Unfortunately, my fame and skill fostered jealousy in others and they sought to . . . imprison me." Von Damme shook his head. "Who would have believed that my discovery would band together such a solitary and predatory creature?" He gave a short laugh. "But it did. Many flocked to my side, but many did not. While it created a society of vampires, it also polarized it. We were to vote on a new direction for our existence, be pioneers, but the vote never came and war ensued.

"And I fear from what you and Silke tell me, that the battle has been renewed. There are vampires who think it is unnatural . . . *wrong* for creatures of the night to play in the light. What do you think, Mr. Bane?"

Troy barely pulled himself away from Terry's eyes. "Vampires are unnatural. You shouldn't exist at all." Troy's eyes flicked across the landscape. The light had become orange and the sky was fiery. The sun moved behind the mountains.

"Well said as a spokesman for mortals. I might have agreed with you at one time."

A question came to Troy's mind. It nagged him and wouldn't let go. "Were you imprisoned by Hoyt Wilhelm?"

Von Damme's face tightened and he clicked his tongue. "That is true, but," and the vampire smiled, "I had my vengeance. A simple curse prevented them from leaving this area. As long as I live, they can not leave Holston Valley." He laughed. "What irony! They imprisoned me because they can't slay me, then they are overwhelmed by the very element that would destroy them. They tried, but could not stop the building of the dam.

413

Entrapped, I sensed their futility and laughed. Such a rare jest, such a fine piece of craftsmanship. They had to bury themselves to survive.

Then his voice grew grim. "I only wish I knew how they were revived. I must question my followers. A betrayer has freed my nemesis and set him upon me."

Von Damme looked at the sky. The sun was gone and violet and indigo were intruding upon the orange and scarlet rays of fading light. "Mr. Bane, I must admit, it has been a pleasure, but as they say, all good things must come to an end. The sun has set and your time is up."

Troy wanted to run. His mind screamed at his body, but it refused to obey him. Troy squirmed under Terry's gaze. She smiled and licked her lips.

Von Damme spoke once more. "Terry, it is time to go to work."

Chapter Twenty-four
A Clash of Darkness

As Terry grabbed Troy's hand, Von Damme turned and walked to the cave entrance. Marader exited, passing Von Damme as he entered. Troy's blood brother waved at him as Terry led him up a slope and toward a clump of bushes. "Have fun," Marader called.

Terry's grip was firm as she led him up the dirt path toward the outcrop. "Such a pity to slay you instead of transforming you," she said. "A fine specimen of masculinity like you should be preserved for all time, but," she smacked her lips, "if anyone has to have the pleasure, it might as well be me."

Troy's mind was lost and his will was gone. The air seemed thick and heavy. Darkness had closed in, oppressing him. A gentle breeze caressed him as if whispering farewell. The crickets played a sad melody. As they ascended, he vaguely noticed that the sky had darkened, smothering all signs of light except for muted pink and hazy indigo — sunset and death.

Using all the mental techniques he had mastered, Troy tried to fight, but there was nothing tangible to grapple. Terry's enchantment fully surrounded him, preventing Troy from making a move without her command. He could barely think. Troy was a zombie and deep inside it infuriated him, but the anger seemed too far away to touch, to stimulate him. He couldn't tap into it and drive himself to freedom.

Although Troy knew he was being led to his death, he followed obediently, like a lamb being led to slaughter. As one foot followed the other, he couldn't believe it was going to end like this.

Troy's legs were leaden and he slipped several times during the ascent, but Terry's strong grip kept him upright. Thoughts of death—of Aaron, of Pete, and of Spider—flitted through his mind. Yes, he would soon join J-Man and Knives. Troy briefly wondered about Dillon and Jambo. What would happen to Bob St. Martin and Denny? Would they end up like Marader? What would happen to Silke?

Troy's mind began to race. What would happen to Silke? To Silke . . .

Troy mentally searched for a crack, a weak place to exert his remerging but floundering will, but he couldn't find anything. His mind was sluggish and his body refused to respond. He couldn't run, he couldn't scream, and he couldn't cry. All there was left to do was die.

"Sit," Terry commanded. She pointed to a large boulder. Troy did as he was told, his vacant gaze staring out over the lake cove. Mountains melded into the darkness. "Enjoy this sight. It will be one of the last you ever see."

Something wet touched his neck, stroking it. As if preparing the area, Terry's damp fingers caressed him. "Such soft and tender flesh. So fine and pliant . . . ready for my kiss." Her lips touched his neck.

A fluttering sound grew louder, then passed them, dropping into the valley. The first flapping sound was immediately followed by a second, then a third . . . then many. The sound was overwhelming.

Sharp pain jangled through Troy as Terry began to sink her fangs into his neck. Suddenly, she pulled away. "What??" she asked the night, her head tilted back. "Bats

416

. . . lots of bats."

To Troy, the scream of surprise and rage that came from below sounded distant. *"No!"* Terry denied in a harsh whisper. "It can't be."

Screeches pierced the night. Angry bellows echoed throughout the cove, dancing off the mountains and interrupting the peacefulness of the night. Flickering flames cavorted below like bouncing balls of fire. On the breeze, the acrid smell of burning flesh drifted to Terry and Troy.

"No!" Terry whispered again. She stood erect, her eyes locked on the struggle below. Terry moved to leave. Automatically, Troy began to follow. "Stay! Don't move until I return," she commanded. Troy took another step. In anger, Terry struck out. "DON'T MOVE!" Her hand moved with blinding speed.

The powerful blow snapped Troy's head back and sent him reeling. He staggered back. Beneath his feet, the dirt and rock crumbled. Troy lost his balance and stumbled over the boulder.

Arms waving, Troy crashed to the ground and tumbled down the slope. His shoulder clipped a tree trunk, and Troy howled in pain as he landed in a thorn bush. Each slash, prick, and gouge brought his body closer to awakening. He bled from hundreds of cuts.

Wheezing and coughing, Troy sat up. His head spun and his stomach heaved. Every nerve screamed at him. He tasted blood and dirt. In a daze, Troy realized that he had a reprieve. *He was alive!* He didn't know why, but he was alive. As he tried to stand, his body locked. Troy still couldn't move.

Frustrated, his eyes moved to the disturbance below. What had drawn Terry? What had saved his life?

The sounds coming from below were bone-chilling. Screams of agony and rage assaulted Troy's ears. He thought himself crazy when he smelled blood along with

417

the stench of burning flesh. Then his eyes adjusted and he made out the grisly scene.

Vampire battled vampire—males and females, young and older, lean and wide. The valley below was filled with them, as well as wolves. There were well over fifty. There were no weapons, although a few wielded torches. It smacked of barbarianism—of a prehistoric and primordial urge to war.

Several of the vampires were afire, burning like human torches. Their fiery forms lit up the night, creating ghostly shadows that strengthened, then faded as the vampires died. Fog rolled in from the lake as if called on to hide the immortal battle from mortal eyes. It reminded Troy of a riot . . . except there was no militia, no authority. Here, the supernatural warred . . . for what?

Several creatures of the night danced the waltz of death. Whirling and spinning, they grappled, driving for each other's blood. Long white teeth slashed, gnashed, and gorged. Wounds were ripped open and immediately healed. Blood flowed freely, spattering the combatants.

Other vampires were locked in a different kind of battle. They stood stock-still, held in each other's hypnotic power—a war of wills being contested. One such struggle ended when an engaged vampire attacked, driving a stake through immobile warrior of the dark. Time rushed forward, dissolving the flesh and crushing the bone of the dying bloodhunter.

Like a wave of reinforcements, a second set of bats approached. One bat, then another, landed. Flesh transformed, melting and rearranging like clay, and each bat stood up a vampire.

Watching the struggle, Troy was confused by the wolves. Many dotted the battlefield. Some stood frozen like statues, while others darted and howled. The beasts looked identical, teeth bared, hair raised, jaws slavering.

Again, Troy tried to stand but couldn't. Despite his attempts to escape, he couldn't help but be drawn to the battle below. Hand in hand, locked in combat, vampires rolled in the dirt. Just below Troy, a tall vampire held a slim female down. He drove a stake toward her chest, but she disappeared in a puff of smoke. A small cloud drifted away. The tall figure cursed.

Armed, several vampires ran from the cave. They carried spears and shafts. A few brandished torches while others hurled bottles.

The air wavered before Troy's eyes. A white mist appeared, then began to coalesce. A human form took shape and Troy thought his time was up — one of the vampire had left the battle to claim him.

Spider's ghost appeared. He stared at Troy, his eyes burrowing into his soul. His friend's spirit began to slowly move off, urging Troy to follow. "Time to go, you must stand and leave," Troy heard in his head.

"I can't," Troy whispered. "I can't move."

Below, the battle took on a different tone. Von Damme, his scarlet cloak flying about, entered the fray. He struck out with his cane. It flashed bright like the sun and many of the vampires crumbled, fading to dust. The attacking bloodhunters started to fall back.

Von Damme's forces pressed onward. Several hurled small, viallike objects. Some burst into consuming fire, while others froze their victims, encasing the vampires in gleaming blocks of ice. Death followed wherever the vials struck. Suddenly Troy made the connection between the vials and Von Damme's alchemy.

Thunder rumbled and several dark clouds rolled in. The wind increased, blowing and screaming.

A burst of blue-black light erupted in the center of the battlefield. Two men and a woman appeared.

"Dillon!" Troy whispered, his eyes locked on his blood brother. Dillon stood behind the tall, thin male with the dark hair and radiant eyes. The woman next to him was pale and shapely. Her long dark hair wrapped around her as if it were alive.

Spider's ghost reached out and slapped Troy. A shudder ran through his body. The spirit eyed Troy, then seemed to make a decision. Spider leaped into Troy's body.

Troy wanted to scream. He felt invaded. His body rebelled as Spider exerted his will. Troy began to shake, then he threw up. Sweat rolled from him, leaving him dry.

Suddenly the pain and feelings of violation were gone. Troy raised his head and opened his eyes. Spider stood before him.

Troy straightened. He felt wrung out, but once again he was in control. "Let's go," Troy whispered.

Spider moved across the hill. Troy climbed out of the thorns and followed. His legs wobbled, but Spider's ghost moved at a pace he could match. With each step, Troy felt his strength return—as did the fear. Hostility and death surrounded him. It could strike from the darkness without herald. It could paralyze him with a word or a gesture.

Troy tried to shake off his fear as he staggered across the slope. They headed for the swaying trees. The wind lashed, pushing and pulling at Troy. Thunder rumbled, then cracked. Lightning flashed behind him.

Troy had broken into a trot. He was regaining his balance despite the wind and slope. The dirt was hard beneath his feet, and as rocks rolled down the hill and twigs snapped, Troy knew he was making too much noise. He just hoped that the struggle would keep the vampires too busy to notice him.

Climbing over a pile of rocks and pushing through bushes, Troy finally reached the thrashing trees. Leaves whirled around them. Dirt kicked up and small rocks flew.

Like a pale mist, Spider hovered just inside the forest, waiting for him. With a nod, the ghost took off through the trees toward the shore. Without a glance backward, Troy followed.

Starting to run, Troy followed. He jumped over logs, stumbled through depressions, and dodged rocks. Suddenly, the forest calmed, growing deathly quiet. The trees quit moving and it was silent except for the pounding of Troy's footsteps and the harsh exhalation of his breath.

For a moment, Troy wondered if he were the only creature alive in the forest. The crickets and the frogs seemed to be in hiding. Not a mosquito searched him out. What had happened? Was the battle over?

Troy leaped over a rock and ran down a short slope. He could sense the water just ahead. Where was Spider leading him? The boat came to mind.

Then a cold chill crawled up his back, over his shoulders, and clutched at his heart. Something was after him . . . he could feel it. There wasn't a sound. It was too unnatural. . . .

Troy threw himself forward. He knew that making noise didn't matter. The vampire was following his life force. Troy closed in on Spider's ghost. The spirit sensed the danger and flew ahead ever faster.

Troy stepped in a hole and twisted an ankle. It screamed in pain, but he ignored it. Even if it had been broken he would have gone on.

The silence seemed to mock him, as if waiting to explode with laughter when death caught him . . . one more time. How many times had he been lucky . . . how many times had he avoided death? Once? Twice? Three times? . . . more. The accident, the burning dock, the graveyard, and Hoyt's home flashed before his eyes. Terry's teeth came to mind and again Troy felt the pain at his neck. He slapped his hand against his throat as if to ward it off.

Lungs heaving, Troy pushed himself ahead faster. Branches slapped at him, trying to slow him. Troy ignored the pain; he ignored the needs of his body. He focused on only one thing—reaching the boat.

Did he hear the soft lapping of waves? Was the shore near?

Just behind him, so quiet that he barely heard it, came the sounds of flapping. A bat was close. A vampire was near. Death was here.

Troy prayed for a weapon, anything to protect himself so he wouldn't die helplessly like some farm cow. He had to get to the water. He had a chance if he could confront the vampire while standing in Holston. Yes, the water of life was his ally.

Suddenly, Troy broke through the bushes. Where was Spider? Then he saw it. Just below and floating in the water was J-Man's boat. It was just where they'd left it! Troy scrambled over the rocks.

As he began to descend, Troy felt it. The enchantment clawed at him, calling him back. Troy struggled onward.

A blow struck him in the back. Reeling, Troy staggered forward. He tripped and fell down the slope. He rolled several times then came to a stop. He was only a few yards from the water.

Troy heard a cold laugh behind him. His quick glance caught the slim figure and dark hair. Terry had returned. Troy crawled forward. The water—possible salvation was only a few feet away. The rocks bit into his hands and knees. His crystal necklace dangled from his neck.

Terry grabbed his collar as Troy reached the water. His fingers touched it, then he was yanked away.

Her other hand digging into his shoulder, Terry spun Troy around to face her. The vampire's eyes narrowed and her smile was wide. Her long tongue caressed her teeth and lips. "Hello again, handsome," she laughed. "I haven't forgotten about you. I'm still so hungry."

Troy hurled himself backward, hoping to pull her into the water. She didn't budge, but her smile grew broader. "Your luck has run out."

Her mouth open, Terry leaned forward. Then she saw the cross. She cocked her head, then roared in laughter. "Such a pretty trinket. I hadn't seen it before," she said as she reached out to caress it. "I am not a common vampire," Terry said. She crushed it in her hand.

"Another myth exploded by the truth," she told him.

Again she leaned forward. "Ahhhhhh!" she gasped. Troy felt her jerk, then shudder. They both looked down at the wooden shaft protruding between her breasts.

Her grasp grew weak and her eyes closed. The flesh dried, then fell away in clumps. Bones began to rattle. "No! NO!" she cried in desperation. Then all she could do was moan.

She collapsed, letting go of Troy. He rolled free and into the water.

Chapter Twenty-five
Surprise Reunions

Half in and half out of water, Troy lay on the shore. Sharp, shalelike red rocks poked into him, but he was too tired to move. The pain was minor compared to what had just happened. His neck throbbed, his flesh screamed as if flayed, and his ankle burned.

Troy knew he should be wading through the water, rushing to J-Man's bass boat and escaping to freedom, but he couldn't. He'd been emotionally, physically, and mentally twisted, and now he was exhausted. All the adrenaline, all the energy, had been drained from him.

Sluggishly, Troy lifted his head and stared at Terry's skeleton. It lay just a few feet away. Even in the dim light, the bones appeared to be bleached as if the sun had dried them. It should have amazed Troy, but he'd been amazed and terrified enough in the past five days. He no longer had it in him to be awed.

Stealthy footsteps approached. The lake was so quiet Troy swore he could have heard a raindrop fall. He watched as tennis shoes stopped next to the skeleton. "You were to be my kill," a familiar voice said quietly. The tone chilled Troy.

He rolled over on his side and looked up. "Dillon!" His best friend no longer looked like himself — Dillon looked more like Marader, except he looked sick. He was sweating, adding a sheen to his pale, luminescent skin. Against the darkness of the woods, it gave off a dim, eerie glow. Dillon's eyes were radiant and wild, darting about without ever focusing. His elongated hands were at his side. A bow was in his left.

Wary, Troy inched farther into the lake. "Saved me for yourself?"

"Yes . . . *no!*" Dillon said. His right hand clenched and unclenched spasmodically.

"I think I'm too tired to fight you," Troy said wearily as he continued to slowly slide into the water.

Dillon laughed harshly, then coughed. "You, my friend, will never stop fighting. I know you well. There's too much competitiveness in you. Please don't lie to me, can't you see I'm dying?"

"Dying or undead?" Troy asked.

"Soon to be undead. I'm on my way to being . . . a vampire. Just what every kid wants to be when he grows up." Dillon laughed harshly, which was more like a wheeze, then he coughed. He turned and spat, then said, "I can . . . I can feel my humanity slipping away. My body is dying, and my senses are changing. I see you as energy, as life," he sighed. "You are a very bright light.

"I can feel the hunger grow and soon it will consume me. It intensifies by the second," he said. His eyes focused on Troy, burning into his brain. "As of yet, I am not a full-fledged vampire, but soon I will be."

Troy stood up and took a step back into the lake. He was now waist deep. His muscles tensed. It was kill or be killed. "Am I am your initiation, your feast to celebrate your new unlife?"

Dillon smiled wearily. "You were supposed to be my first kill, my first feast of human blood. I have already been bitten, infected, just a short while ago. I've been fed vampire blood. I am to be an . . . uncommon vampire.

"Terry wasn't supposed to be here," Dillon continued. "I saved you not for myself, but because I wanted to save you. I didn't want to see you die." He wiped the sweat from his brow, then squatted. "Even as my humanity slips away,

I still have some . . ." he closed his eyes, "control. I remember what we were, what we are. We are blood brothers, we are the best of friends. Your blood is already in my veins. I cannot slay you. If need be, I'll find another . . . victim." He lowered his head. "Lord, help me, I can't help what I've become, and its nature is starting to exert itself." Dillon started to cry.

Troy instinctively started to move forward, then stopped. "How can I help?" He noticed that Dillon didn't have an aura of enthrallment about him . . . yet.

"Leave! Find help. Do what you must!" He waved his arms about, creating briefly glowing streaks in the night. "Do whatever needs to be done. Next time you see me, be ready to slay me, for I may be ready to suck your blood or even worse, make you a vampire," he growled at Troy.

"What about Silke? I love your sister!" Troy pleaded. "What are you going to do about Silke?"

"Whatever I can. If it's any consolation, I will kill her before I let them turn her into a vampire. I love her too much to let her become what I have become." His eyes seemed far away. "Lord help me."

"Goddammit, Dillon, I can't leave her!"

"You must. Alone, you can't save her. There are at least thirty vampires left alive. Find help. I don't know where. We have Jambo. Bill Glazier is dead."

"Von Damme has Bob St. Martin and Denny. J-Man and Knives are dead. No one will believe me," Troy said hollowly. He felt helpless.

"I am sorry. I don't know what to tell you," Dillon whispered. His face was twisted in anguish. A tear rolled down his cheek.

"I don't know what to do." Standing in the water with the darkness growing deeper and talking to his dying friend, Troy felt very alone. Not a whisper of life moved in the woods to offer comfort. Was everything dead or dying? Troy wondered.

"Leave. Save yourself. Time is short."

"Yes. It appears to be over." Troy's mind worked furiously. There had to be something he could do to save Silke and his friends. He clenched his fist when he thought of Von Damme or Marader touching her. His soul felt sick — there was nothing he could do.

Troy turned to leave, wading to the boat, then twisted around. "Why did you lie to us, lead us into this? You led your sister and your best friends into death!"

"I'm sorry," Dillon said sadly. "I had no choice. I was under the power, the thrall of Hoyt Wilhelm. You understand. You have felt it. I can see it in your eyes." Troy nodded — he did understand. "He broke me, then molded me. I am his . . . puppet. I had to find Von Damme."

"Good Lord, why? And why bring us?"

"There's a struggle between two vampire factions. Von Damme wants to enable vampires to live in the sunlight. Hoyt Wilhelm feels that's . . . blasphemy," Dillon laughed at his choice of words. "Blasphemy . . . I am blasphemy and abomination." He was silent for a moment, then continued. "Wilhelm feels it taints the nature, the very essence of the vampire . . . race. This struggle started in the late 1930's. Hoyt and Elsa trapped Von Damme's undead life force in an amulet." Troy nodded. He remembered the necklace that sat like two fiery red eyes on Von Damme's chest. "Then they sealed it in the magical box we found. Elsa tricked him, gave him the amulet as a gift. Von Dammed loved . . . or, rather, coveted her.

"In a sense, the box and amulet became Von Damme's coffin, safely buried below the waters . . . until John Traylor and Terry Bray found it and freed him."

"Tonight, the factions fought," Dillon continued. "For the first time in history, so I'm told, vampires have banded together and fought against each other, spilling each other's blood, committing the only atrocity a vampire can commit — killing one's own kind.

"Both sides agreed this must not continue. Later tonight, there is to be a debate and a vote. We will listen to both Wilhelm and Von Damme, then the majority vote will decide our fate. I suspect it will be a long and heated evening."

"I think," Troy said slowly, "that Von Damme still wants the jewelry box. He seems to still be linked to it. Do you think if I destroy it, I might destroy him?"

"Yes, it is possible. If you destroy Von Damme, the secret of living in the sunlight will be lost with him. With Von Damme dead, his curse will be released and the vampires will disperse throughout the land like the predatory individuals they are. They will no longer need to create more vampires, because they won't need, won't want, the strength in numbers. We vampires are very selfish."

"Then it appears that is what I must do. But Silke . . ." Troy took a step toward shore.

"Leave!" Dillon commanded, and Troy felt his hypnotic power. It wasn't overwhelming, but forced him to step back. Dillon ripped the anchor from between the rocks and threw it at the boat. "Leave, and do what you must. Leave before your luck runs out." Troy turned and waded to the boat. "And if I never see you again," Dillon said softly, "remember that as long as I lived, I was your friend." With that, Dillon turned and disappeared into the night.

Troy stifled the urge to follow. He knew what he had to do. As Troy climbed aboard the boat, he pushed off, sending the craft slowly out into the cove. He found the keys and stuck them in the ignition. As he prepared to leave, Troy had to keep pushing Silke's face, her pleading eyes, out of his mind. He hated to leave her, but he didn't have a choice.

Troy changed his mind. He stifled the urge to fire up the motor and take off, escaping as quickly as possible. Something inside told him to move quietly. Troy pulled the throttle back into neutral.

Moving to the front of the boat, he pushed the trolling motor over the side. Troy adjusted the foot pedal to steer him straight toward the dam. He flipped the "on" switch, and with a soft hum, the Procraft slowly pulled forward through the cove.

Convinced that he must destroy the jewelry box, Troy checked his equipment. As he did so, he kept his ears strained for the slightest sound. If he were attacked, it would come by air. He stifled a horrifying thought — vampires appearing from clouds of mist, altering their gaseous forms.

Troy set out a bag of garlic and a bow. He laid arrows next to it. From the glove box, he pulled a crucifix, although he doubted it would aid him, and an iron knife.

Riffling through the diving equipment, Troy found everything he needed. Nothing was missing. Even the underwater charges were there. They had already discussed the possibility of blowing up Hoyt's house. He hated diving alone, hated the thought of entering the chilling underwater dwelling one more time. Troy shook his head. With every thought, every motion, Silke's presence dogged him. Troy told himself he wasn't Rambo, he couldn't go charging in, blasting away, and save the day.

When everything was ready, Troy sat in the driver's seat and briefly looked around. Wisps of fog hugged the lake. The shore looked dark and foreboding. Each tree towered like a giant vampire, silent and waiting to feed. Troy shivered.

His eyes caught a movement on the bow, but when Troy looked, nothing was there. He moved to the front and turned off the trolling motor, then pulled it on board.

Something cool brushed him, causing him to shiver. Troy turned. Spider's ghost was sitting on the bow, staring at him. "What do you want?" Troy whispered. The spirit said nothing. "A lot of help you've been," Troy said bitterly. "No one's left but me."

Troy returned to the driver's seat and reached for the key. Spider raised his hand, motioning for him to wait — to be patient. Troy was indecisive. What did Spider's spirit know that Troy didn't?

Something bumped the boat. Troy caught his breath. Afraid, he started to turn the key. A cool breeze froze him. He looked up. Spider was leaning over the windshield staring down at him.

Again, there was a thud against the side of the boat, like a log or body bumping against it. Troy thought it too obvious to be a vampire.

With a splash of water, a hand appeared and grabbed the side of the bass boat. A second hand appeared, then a masked face stared at Troy. Thin, curly hair was matted above the scuba mask. A tank bobbed behind the figure. At first, due to the darkness, the two didn't recognize each other.

The figure smiled around his snorkel, then spat it out. "Taxi?" J-Man asked quietly.

Troy was so surprised and happy, he had to slap his hand across his mouth to stifle a cheer. Next to J-Man, a second head surfaced. The figure grabbed the side of the boat, then pulled his mask back. "Surprised to see us?" Knives asked.

Troy nodded, grinned.

"Same here," J-Man said. "We were afraid you were dead."

They slid around to the back of the boat. Twisting, J-Man slipped out of his scuba tank and handed it to Troy. Knives did the same as J-Man set his fins on the stern, then climbed aboard. Troy helped him in, then gave Knives a hand. Troy noticed that both his friends had sustained injuries. J-Man did move stiffly and his eye was blackened.

"God, am I glad to see you guys," Troy said, giving them each a hug.

"Never thought you were this emotional," J-Man said with a wan smile.

"Coming close to dying several times sort of changes your perspective on life and how you handle it," Troy responded.

"I suspect so," Knives said dryly.

"We're glad it was you in the boat," J-Man said. "We didn't know who was in it, if anybody. As we were swimming to it, I was afraid that the motor would kick in and the boat would disappear."

"I would have if Spider's ghost hadn't distracted me," Troy said.

"Seeing ghosts again?" J-Man asked.

"That and vampires, lots of vampires. Shoot, I hugged you guys to make sure you weren't ghosts, not because I was glad to see you," Troy said with a smile. "You know, we should get the hell out of here. There's a vampire war going on."

Knives and J-Man looked at each other. "Oh?" Knives said. He wiped at an open cut on his brow. "Is that why all the vampire-related weaponry is out? Not worried about Satan's cult anymore?" Before Troy could speak, Knives continued, "Where are Silke and Dillon? I have a feeling I won't like the answer."

"You first. How the hell did you survive the crash?"

As J-Man toweled off, he began his tale. "Well, as you know, we were patrolling the area over the dam. We're not positive, but we think a giant, I mean, prehistoric-sized, bat attacked and screwed up the rotors. We dropped like a rock."

"No, we didn't," Knives whispered. He picked the bow. "I wish my night vision were better. Anyway, Jay somehow guided us close to shore. We struck treetops, ripping open the fuel tanks, and tearing off the tail."

"That's in nontechnical jargon," J-Man interrupted.

Knives continued. "The cab crashed into the lake and

431

promptly sunk."

"I'd hit my head pretty hard, so I barely knew what was going on as the water poured in," J-Man said. "Knives grabbed the scuba gear and hooked us up. By the time we were submerged, we were breathing off the tanks."

"When we surfaced," Knives continued, "we couldn't see anything because of the fog and the smoke from the fire. We waited for a while, just listening. I didn't think it was wise to call out.

"Then, we thought we saw Dillon heading in the direction of the dam. We tried to follow, but we lost him. We never did see the boat.

"We waited around, hoping for a sound or sign. I didn't want to just blunder in, but nothing happened until a short while ago."

"Yeah," J-Man said, shaking his head. "We heard all sorts of screams, then saw fire and flashes of light. We were swimming closer when we saw my boat. The motor wasn't running, so we thought maybe it was adrift. We decided to take a chance."

"Everything we do nowadays seems to involve taking a chance," Troy said as he moved to the front of the boat. He adjusted the trolling motor to straighten their course. "Just sitting here and talking, we're taking a chance." Troy let out a long breath. "Death could descend upon us at any moment." Troy then proceeded to tell his story.

They both cursed, but neither appeared surprised when informed about Marader. "I was afraid of that. Damn," Knives said.

Troy continued, telling them about Von Damme and Terry. When he was finished, J-Man let out a low whistle. "So that's the story."

"I wondered how you got all those scratches," Knives said. "It looks like the Torture of a Thousand Cuts."

"So those screams were vampire killing vampire?" J-Man asked.

Troy nodded. "And now they're debating their future course, according to Dillon."

"Our crucifixes don't work against vampires?" J-Man asked.

"Not against uncommon vampires. Terry crushed mine and Von Damme, even Marader, was unfazed," Troy said.

"Well, what do we do now?" J-Man asked.

"I was going to blow up Hoyt's house and destroy the jewelry box," Troy said. "That's what Dillon and I discussed. We hoped that Von Damme's link was still strong enough that destroying the jewelry box would slay him. I didn't know what else to do."

"That won't help Den, Bob, Jambo, and Silke," J-Man told him.

"I know, but rushing in and getting ourselves killed won't help them either," Troy countered. "There are other people to think about. We can't let Von Damme loose vampires on the world."

J-Man shivered. "The destruction and terror I see. It would be even worse if word ever got out. Who would you trust? The prejudice would be worse than AIDS, homosexuality, race, or sex."

Knives stroked his chin. "I don't think anyone would believe us, now or later. I think going for help is pointless. Even I wouldn't believe us. Troy, didn't you say they'd be in debate?"

"That's what Dillon told me."

"We could sneak in and rescue the others," Knives suggested.

"That's crazy, I've been in a vampire's thrall. They're irresistible. They'd capture us and feast on us," Troy said, sounding dejected.

"Take these," Knives said, handing Troy several red pills from the glove box.

"What are they?"

"Well, they should help you resist the vampire's hypnotic gaze," Knives said. "They're stimulants, very powerful ones. The vampires shouldn't be able to hold your attention. Your mind and pulse will be working overtime. Take two. You'll be so wired you'll have to fight to slow your breathing."

"That might work," J-Man said.

"That's crazy," Troy said, but he was beginning to grasp at straws. He was no longer alone and he desperately wanted to save Silke. "I've been there, seen the struggle. There are at least twenty or more vampires, and maybe even magic."

"One problem at a time," J-Man said. "What about the other pills? The ones we've been taking."

"Rat poison and an antidote."

"What?" J-Man and Troy whispered.

"Remember that experiment I volunteered for in medical school?" Knives asked. Troy nodded. "Same thing. Your blood is tainted, poisonous, but you live because of the antidote. It doesn't purify your blood system, it just allows you to survive. But a vampire consuming your blood would get sick. Hey," he said spreading his hands, "it's the best I can do."

"There's not much we can do against them. We have garlic, some holy water, and bows." Troy shook his head and said, "I don't believe I'm going to do this. Hey Knives, I'm gonna need to tape my ankle first. I think I sprained it."

"Let me see it," Knives said. Troy lifted it up. Knives felt around. "Not too badly."

"I just want to kick some vampire butt," J-Man said. "Even if I die, I want vengeance for our dead brothers."

"Promise you'll kill me before letting me become a vampire?" Troy asked. They did, and Troy did the same. "Then let's do it." Troy turned the boat around. "This is crazy," he muttered.

Chapter Twenty-six
Dark Debate

Planning for a fast escape, the trio had used the trolling motor to land as close as possible to the cave. Instead of anchoring, they pulled the bass boat ashore. Now there was no turning back. The insane rescue attempt was on.

As the full moon began to rise over the mountains, Troy led his friends toward the cave south of the overflow spillway. The reddish orange glow of the moon washed across the waters, dimly touching the shore. The moonlight made it easier for the trio to see. They climbed up the slope and waited, searching for signs of danger.

The woods and lake were no longer quiet—they were vibrantly alive. Troy thought this was a good omen. Silence had always accompanied the presence of a vampire. It was a way of knowing danger was near.

Throughout the forest, the crickets and frogs blended to form a harmonious tone. It reminded Troy of background music, played without touching his consciousness. An owl swooped across their path and landed in a nearby tree. Its hoot called out a greeting to them. A soft breeze rustled the grass. The air seemed heavier than usual.

"I smell rain," J-Man whispered.

"You're hallucinating," Knives responded.

Troy looked up at the sky. Dark clouds were crawling

over the mountain peaks in the west and sweeping toward the rising moon. "Look, he's right," Troy said quietly. "We may get rain."

"Too little, too late," Knives said. Troy nodded. The drought had already helped release the eternal evil.

"The woods are alive," Troy told them. "I think it's safe. Let's go." Despite the taping, Troy's ankle throbbed heavily. As with all his injuries, he pushed it aside. Besides, there were enough drugs in him to keep him going even if he were near dead . . . Troy hoped.

Staying hidden in the tall grass, they snuck across the short plane. Furtive sounds came to them on the breeze, drifting down the cove toward them. The grass sounded as if it were whispering.

Then they heard the cry of the wolves, which sounded close and just ahead. "Wolves are guarding the cave mouth," Troy surmised. "We better head to the right and stay downwind. I hope the wind doesn't shift."

"They're howling at the moon like lost souls," J-Man said as he followed.

"That's fine," Knives said. "They soon will be lost to the world. I have a surprise for them." He patted his backpack.

Troy took a roundabout path, guiding them toward the ledge so they could scout the cave mouth from above. The howling continued. "Their barking at the moon should give us some cover," Troy said. In the past, Troy thought, howling meant death, but this time it might aid them — cover their sounds. As they moved up the slope, the orange light slowly became golden. Shadows deepened, crisscrossing in the heavy woods.

Using the trees, they pulled themselves up the hill. In a short time, they stood on the ledge where Terry had tried to drain Troy.

Crouching behind the boulder, Troy pointed to the cave mouth. "There it is." His friends looked over his shoulder.

"I'd guess about six wolves," J-Man said.

"Do we have enough meat?" Troy asked. He noticed that the wind hadn't changed and was thankful.

"Plenty," Knives said. "This should be good for at least a dozen."

"Are we ready to do this?" Troy asked. As he finished his question, the breeze became a strong wind. The trees gently swayed. The moon was now a dusty yellow. Dark clouds waited above, waiting to swallow the orb before it could shed its silvery light upon them. All around the shadows deepened, becoming black holes that seemed to suck in moonbeams but never lighten.

"Well, I'm scared witless," J-Man said. "Why else would I being doing this? But I'm ready to kick some vampire butt, even if it's just Marader's. Dam bloodsucker."

Knives began pulling the wrapped slabs of poisoned meat from his pack.

"Well, in case we don't have time to chat again . . ." Troy began.

"Are you getting sentimental on us?" J-Man said.

"Yeah, it's been a pleasure knowing you both, being your friend."

J-Man sobered for a moment, his eyes growing misty. "It truly has been enjoyable . . . except the time we got in trouble for setting the back porch on fire . . . and wrecking my parents' station wagon and—"

Troy stifled a nervous laugh. Knives grinned. "Well, it's better to burn out, then fade away," he said. "Take your pills." They did.

"How long?" J-Man asked.

"A few minutes," Knives responded.

"Will my head take off like a rocket?" J-Man whispered.

"No," Knives replied, "but time will seem to move at a

snail's pace. A snail on valium. You'll be very impatient."

They waited quietly, listening to the wolves howl and watching the moon rise. It was now ivory in color. Troy felt the wind shift. He was alarmed for a moment, then sighed. A strong wind came across the cove, striking them in the face. They were still downwind from the wolves. Luck was with them so far.

Troy's mind flashed back over the past week. He wondered if this was the culmination of it all. In his bones and in his heart, he felt that the end was near.

"It's working," J-Man said. "Never try this without a prescription from your family doctor."

Troy noticed his own breathing had accelerated, almost coming in gasps. He put his hand on his chest — his heart raced. Troy looked at his hands. They were jittery.

"Yes, the surge has arrived," Knives said. He began unwrapping the meat. It gleamed, looking slick in the moonlight. Knives handed out the slabs. "Let it fly."

"I wonder if meat throwing will ever be a sport on ESPN," J-Man muttered. Troy felt the uncontrollable urge to laugh, but stifled it. The danger, the fear, and drug were getting to him.

They stood and heaved the meat off the hill. The poisoned bait landed heavily below. When they were finished, the trio lay flat, listening and waiting.

Troy closed his eyes and focused on the sounds coming from below. He had to consciously slow his breathing and heartbeat. He felt like he was still moving although he was lying still — the drug was in full effect.

The howling paused, then briefly increased in intensity. Without any further movement to stir them, the beasts grew silent. There was shuffling as the wolves came to investigate. In the silence, the trio could hear them sniffing at the poisoned meat.

A whine carried to Troy's ears, then there was the

438

sound of gnashing and chomping as the wolves fed. The frenzied feast only lasted a minute. Suddenly, the wolves grew silent, then moved off. As if they'd eaten too much, too fast, a few seemed to walk unsteadily. Troy hoped that the poison was already taking effect.

"How long?" J-Man whispered.

"Less than five minutes," Knives said, "allowing time for their unusual body chemistry. How do you feel?"

"Like I'm flying down a steep hill in a wagon without any brakes," J-Man responded.

"Troy?"

"About the same. I'm having a hard time remaining still."

"Good," Knives replied. "That may save your life."

The next few minutes passed in silence between the three, but the land around them was lively. The full moon was bright and the wolves began howling again. The wind continued to increase. Troy thought he felt a raindrop or two, but it must have been his imagination. Instead, he found sweat.

As Troy shifted uncomfortably, his mind raced. He concluded that he'd gone mad, but wasn't sure what had caused it. Was he insane because of what was going on? Or was he insane because of what he was going to do? All he wanted to do was free his friends and get far, far away. He longed to spend time alone with Silke, out of danger and away from the horror. Troy knew it wasn't going to be that easy. This wasn't a fairy tale—unless it was one written by the Marquis de Sade.

"Let's go. They're quiet," Knives said. Until his friend had spoken, Troy hadn't noticed that the wolves had grown quiet. He'd been lost in himself, lost in his own world.

Without a word, the trio crept down the slope. They kept their bows out and their knives ready. Stressing the importance of staying quiet, they'd left the shotguns in the boat.

Nothing moved and not a sound came from the wolves as Troy, Knives, and J-Man neared the cave mouth. Troy nervously surveyed the area. Several forms had collapsed on the ground. He counted eight.

Troy leading the way, they quietly walked among the fallen beasts. They tensed, ready for an attack, but none came. The wolves were dead to the world—the poison had worked. They were barely panting, their tongues lolling to the side. Even with their eyes open the beasts didn't seem to see them. A few twitched. One whined.

Cautiously, they entered the cave. If Troy listened closely, he could hear a faint noise, but he couldn't name it. They waited a few moments for their eyes to adjust. Knives pointed ahead. They all spotted a faint light far along in the tunnel.

Troy shook. He wasn't sure if it were fear or the drug, probably both. He thought he smelled death in the air, but he shook it off. His imagination was running wild.

It appeared he wasn't the only one. In the peace of the passageway, Troy could hear J-Man's teeth quietly chatter. Troy stopped and softly gripped his friend's jaw. J-Man nodded. They both smiled tightly.

Feeling their way along the passage, they moved closer to the light. Again, Troy thought he heard a sound, but he couldn't place it. As he remembered, the tunnel didn't contain any side passages, although it did twist and turn. The trio never slowed, their pace as determined as if they were dogging a wounded prey.

The sound grew louder, almost like a buzzing. It rose and fell. Finally, as they passed the first torch, Troy identified the sound. It was the sound of voices. With each step, the voices grew more distinct.

Soon Troy recognized Von Damme's voice, then he could understand the words. "I repeat, I have the means, I have the knowledge to expand our horizons, to break through a limiting barrier. We can evolve. Our nature doesn't have to be stagnant. We can be more than we've ever dreamed.

"I don't know if any of you miss the sunlight, if any of you long for the day, but that desire is just a minor consideration — a bonus." Von Damme's words grew louder as the trio grew closer. There wasn't any place else to go but forward toward the voices. "This advancement of our species goes far beyond desire, it focuses upon survival — the survival of the vampire."

Ahead of the trio, light flooded the tunnel. Von Damme's voice was clear, no longer echoing. "We can be hunted during the day. We can be destroyed by the sunlight. Our weakness is well known by our legion of enemies — humanity. Those that live, flicker and die, leaving the world poorer for their existence. They are like ants unto us and we can overwhelm us by sheer numbers. During the daylight, we must run and hide like rats, fearing that we will be found and destroyed by our enemies."

Troy stood still. He feared that they'd have to pass through the debate to advance farther. Fortunately, he was wrong.

A large passageway turned to the right. A dim illumination showed that the perpendicular tunnel turned at least once. Just beyond it a large opening, like a window in the rock, spilled torchlight into the tunnel.

Quietly, Troy advanced. He tried to slow his breathing. His heart threatened to break free like a runaway train. Edging along the wall, Troy peered into the window.

The rough-hewn cave was enormous. Small stalactites hung over the throng of seated vampires. Torches burned on the walls, surrounding at least thirty of the undead. Von Damme paced back and forth before them. They were debating their fate. Troy thought he could identify the opposing factions on each side of the center aisle.

Von Damme continued. "We are invulnerable during the night and weak during the light. There should be no weakness. It is not the vampire's way to be weak. We are supreme beings. We are immortals, touched by God to do his bidding indiscriminately. We thrive not just to survive, but to act as a force of nature, a cleansing agent. Only we truly divine our purpose."

As Troy listened, he wanted to puke, but he was also enthralled. Von Damme was charismatic. The crowd absorbed his every word. Troy noticed that the master vampire no longer wore the amulet.

"We should not, must not, be confined to living and feeding only during the darkness. If we weren't meant to push back our barrier, destroy this limitation, I would never had been gifted. I would never have become a vampire. Fate, no, destiny called to me, an alchemist, to carry you forward into a more powerful future. A future filled with greatness and less limitation."

Troy looked for Marader or Dillon, but didn't see either of them. Knives tapped them on the shoulder. "Let's go," he whispered. "We don't know how long we have."

Nodding, Troy moved on. He ducked under the natural window and headed forward. Knives and J-Man followed.

They came to a crossroad—several passageways headed in different directions. "Which way?" J-Man asked. Troy racked his mind. He didn't know.

Suddenly, Spider's ghost appeared before them. He pointed to the left, then faded away as if he were never there. "Left," Troy said, heading down the tunnel.

"What changed your mind?" J-Man whispered.

"Spider's ghost."

They continued on for a short while until they heard voices. They paused. "Sounds familiar," J-Man whispered. They crept on.

"If I could, I'd kill myself," came a voice.

"It's a sin to commit suicide, Denny," came a second voice.

J-Man and Troy looked at each other. They both mouthed the words, "Bob and Denny." They rushed forward and found a heavy wooden door. A metal bolt had been thrown across it. Troy wasn't certain, but he thought it looked familiar. Had he passed this way before?

"Keep watch," Troy told J-Man and Knives. They positioned themselves on opposite sides of the door.

Troy lifted the bar, then opened the door. "Keep quiet!" He whispered, "It's me — Troy. J-Man and Knives are with me. It's a breakout!"

"Troy!" Bob said.

"Sssshhh!" Jambo hissed. Stumbling, he was the first to the door. His once hulking friend now looked thin, his face gaunt. Deep lines circled his eyes and cut into his jaw. His eyes were dull with disbelief.

Jambo stared at Troy and said, "Are you for real?" Troy nodded. "You're not a vampire like Dillon or Marader?" Troy shook his head and smiled broadly to reveal normal teeth. Jambo quickly hugged Troy, then stepped into the hallway. He rubbed his eyes, then smiled at the sight of Knives and J-Man.

Turning around, Jambo whispered, "It's for real guys. Let's go."

Cautiously, Denny and Bob came to the door. The light touched their grime-covered faces. Both had been injured in the car crash. Bob smiled, then winced. "My prayers have been answered. Thank you, Lord." Troy helped Bob outside. There were bruises and scratches on his face. He moved unsteadily, appearing lost without his spectacles.

"You don't look so hot," Troy told Bob.

"Neither do you. You feel all right? You look wired," Bob said.

"Compliments of Dr. Knives," J-Man whispered.

"Is there anyone else alive?" Knives asked.

Denny sadly shook his head. "Jambo was brought here only recently, by Dillon. Marader was here a while ago. He told us that we were lucky, that all the other captives were to become dinner prior to some big meeting." His lip broke open as he spoke, and Denny began to bleed. "Damn, am I glad to see you." He heartily shook Troy's hand.

"He said that they found the opportunity to turn a would-be minister into a vampire amusing," Bob whispered bitterly. With a bandaged hand, he gently rubbed a gouge in his cheek.

"They wanted me to build them a secluded mansion on some property I have out here," Denny said. "It was Marader's idea, the bastard."

"Let's get the hell out of here," Jambo said softly. His hands shook.

"Where's Silke?" Troy asked.

The three looked at each other. Denny responded. "Is she here? We haven't seen her."

"Let's go," Troy said, pushing Denny toward the way down. J-Man, you lead. Go to the boat. No stopping."

"I'll follow shortly," Troy said. "I've got to find Silke."

"I understand," Knives said. Without arguing, he shook Troy's hand and then followed the foursome.

Troy headed down the passage. He was sure that Von Damme's lair was ahead. Praying, Troy hoped that Silke was there . . . and still alive.

He quickened his pace. Troy shivered through the long stretches of darkness between the torches. His insides felt as if they were being jumbled in a Mix-master.

He constantly feared that something would leap at him from the shadows.

Love makes you do crazy things, Troy thought. He shouldn't be here, but he couldn't be any place else. Logic told him they had done the right thing. The vampires thought him slain and probably figured those in the helicopter had been killed. If they'd destroyed the jewelry box, but hadn't destroyed Von Damme, a rescue attempt would have been even more dangerous. He would have known they were alive. There hadn't been a choice.

He broke into a slow trot. The vampires wouldn't have to hear him to know he was near . . . they would sense his life force.

Troy came to a fork in the passage. He cursed. All the tunnels looked the same. Closing his eyes, Troy tried to sense Silke . . . feel the proper direction.

Picturing his walk with Von Damme, Troy tried to remember the area. He backtracked. With his mind, he pushed aside the red curtain and followed Von Damme. They had walked for a long time, twisting and turning, but never meeting up with other passages.

Troy opened his eyes, looking at the right fork. It was off to the side, shielded if one came from the other direction. Taking a deep breath, Troy took the left passage. As he moved off, Troy thought he heard footsteps. He paused, but didn't hear anything.

A short while later, Troy came to a halt. Just ahead was the red curtain.

Troy's pulse ran rampant. He was dizzy as he moved forward. A faint light framed the hanging cloth, highlighting the edges.

He listened for a moment. Nothing moved. His fingers trembled as he reached for the curtain and pulled it aside.

Nothing happened. Troy found he was holding his

breath, so he let out a long sigh. His body shuddered.

Boldly, he entered Von Damme's room.

Everything was as it had been. Several lit candles illuminated the room. Troy didn't see any danger, but he felt it. Was something hiding in the shadows? Did he hear footsteps coming down the tunnel?

Then Troy saw her—Silke! She was lying on the bed. A deep red glow illuminated her pale, frozen face. Von Damme's amulet sat on her chest which slowly rose and fell.

Troy wanted to call out her name, but his heart jammed his throat and he couldn't speak. Instead, Troy moved forward.

A vision of beauty, Silke appeared to be sleeping peacefully. Carefully, Troy pulled back the collar of his love's shirt. He had to know. Would he have to kill her? Had Dillon kept his promise?

There were bruises on her throat, but the skin appeared to be unbroken. Caressing her neck, Troy sighed. He leaned close to her ear. "Silke?" he whispered. "Silke, it's Troy. I'm here to take you away." Troy gently shook her.

There was a soft rustle of fabric. Troy turned to the entrance, but saw nothing.

"How touching," came the voice, "and how pathetic. The knight in shining armor returns to save the damsel in distress from becoming the Mistress of the Night."

Troy fingered his knife and slowly reached for the water bottle strapped to his belt.

Marader stepped from behind a tapestry and into the light. "I knew you would return, Troy. You're so predictable. I've been waiting for you. This time, there's no escape."

Chapter Twenty-seven
Flight

Troy let a deep breath escape as he faced Marader. Somehow, he knew that this moment was inevitable.

Even though Troy didn't hold the vampire's gaze, he could feel its spell reach out. The aura of power which had once overwhelmed Troy, now surrounded him. Like a silent siren, it called to Troy, urging him to relax, telling him that resistance was futile.

Troy's eyes jumped about, never fully focusing. Marader smiled. Teeth glinted in the firelight, but the smile didn't touch his eyes. They burned, pulling at Troy's soul. "I see that Dillon lied. Just like a journalist. Tsk, tsk. Oh well, there was probably too much humanity left in him. It will be gone soon.

"You fear me," Marader said. Troy nodded. "You should. I am your death."

"I guess it had to come to this, didn't it?" Troy told himself that he was still talking to Tom Marader — not a vampire, but an arrogant, phallic-oriented friend who would never mature. The drug assisted Troy in holding the hypnotic power at bay.

The enthrallment could only take hold if Troy's attention focused. Unfortunately, Marader's power had increased.

He slowly glided closer. "I gather you've already freed Denny, Bob, and Jambo."

Troy was silent. "TELL ME!" Marader commanded.

The words struck Troy like a sledgehammer. "Yes."

Marader smiled. A vein pulsed in his forehead. Unblinking orbs of blue fire bored into Troy's nervous eyes.

Troy felt his will slipping away. He bit into his lip, drawing blood, but the pain didn't help. Marader seemed to have grown in power.

"That's all right," Marader said. "All I want is Silke. Von Damme has promised her to me. That is all right with you, isn't it?"

"Of course," Troy said in a monotone. The aura was seeping through gaps in his willpower. Troy slightly averted his eyes, but they wanted to return.

Marader's wide smile split his face. "This is sweet." He glided closer, stopping before Troy. "Drop the knife."

Troy's fingers went limp, dropping the iron weapon. The blade bounced on the floor. "That's good. You should never have put your bow over your shoulder. Who knows, you might have gotten off a lucky shot.

"Now it's too late," Marader said as he leaned forward.

Mustering all his willpower and unleashing his

anger, Troy shoved the water bottle into Marader's face and squeezed. The water exploded from the spout.

"Arrrrhhh!" Marader screamed as the holy water scalded his face. Covering his face with his hands, Marader staggered back. Steam poured through his fingers and flesh began to ooze and curl. The vampire sounded as if he were drowning.

Troy bent to grab the knife. Behind him, the fabric softly rustled.

Marader spat. "You'll die slowly. . . ." The air whistled — *Thwaack!* "Urkk," gasped Marader.

Looking up, Troy saw Marader drop his hands from his decomposing face. He clenched the arrow that protruded from his chest. The air sang again, and a second shaft sank deeply, just right of the sternum. Blood erupted from Marader's mouth.

Shaking, he crumpled to the ground. Arrows skewered his back. His hands clawed at the dirt. Marader began to shrivel and die.

"Thanks," Troy said to Knives. "I'm glad you didn't listen to me."

Knives flashed him a smile. "I didn't see any reason to start now." Troy smiled weakly. "I checked on the vampires. They were still debating. Did you find Silke?"

Troy moved to the bed and stood over her. "She's out of it."

"Let's remove the amulet, then we'll carry her," Knives suggested.

"Sure," Troy said. He held her upright as Knives took an arrow and lifted the amulet from around her neck.

Knives wrapped the necklace in a pillowcase. "Let's go."

449

Troy tried to pick up Silke, but couldn't. He was too weak. "I can't."

"I'll do it," Knives said. He handed Troy the pillowcase, then bent over. Knives slung Silke over his shoulder. She groaned slightly. "Let's get out of here, fast!"

Waiting just a moment, he took a candle and dropped it on Marader's corpse. The clothes smoldered, but the dead flesh and rotting bones flared, immediately catching fire. "Good-bye, my friend. May your soul rest in peace."

They jogged through the tunnels, no longer worried about keeping quiet. "Did the guys get out?" Troy breathed.

"Yes."

It now seemed freezing inside the tunnels, but Troy was perspiring. He clenched his teeth to stop them from chattering. If only their luck would hold.

They reached the cell that held their friends. Knives kept going, but Troy stopped and closed the door. Then he set the crossbolt in place. He wiped the sweat from his brow.

As they neared the meeting hall, Troy once again heard a voice, but this time it wasn't Von Damme. "In conclusion, I urge you to vote against Von Damme and vote for yourself. Choose to follow the true nature of yourself—the true nature of the vampire.

"What he proposes will warp us, destroy the very essence of our being. We are masters of the night. We have no need for daylight, for the sun. There is no need to be tan, to frolic with mortals. They are our puppets, not our companions. We are power. We are immortal perfection. There is

450

nothing like us on the earth and we need not change," the impassioned voice pleaded.

The tunnel roared with thunderous applause and cheers. His jangled nerves overly sensitive, Troy covered his ears. Ahead, Knives got down on his knees and crawled under the window.

The caverns and tunnels once more grew silent.

"I have proof of the reason we should evolve, should change with the times," Von Damme said. "If I may, I will present my proof." There were scattered cheers of encouragement.

Irresistibly drawn, Troy glanced in through the window. Carrying a basketball-sized crystal ball, Von Damme walked toward the crowd. The clear orb seemed to pulsate in his grasp, then it began to glow and hum. "I will show you why we must adapt."

A rock struck Troy. He turned to see Knives motioning him to follow. Freeing himself from the collective enchantment and the fascination of the debate, Troy moved on.

He'd just slid under the natural window and taken several steps when a blinding flash of light surrounded him. It was as if a small sun had exploded inside the cave. As the intense light died, a wave of heat swept through the tunnel.

Dazed and sweating, Troy continued on. Groping, he staggered toward the exit. Screams assaulted his ears. It was followed by laughter. Troy stumbled and fell to his knees.

"YES! That's it, DIE!" Von Damme shouted in triumph. "If you are not ready to adapt, to be part of a grander, greater breed of vampire, then die in this captured sunlight." The warm light filled the caves. "If you cannot live in the light,

451

and you have chosen not to, then it is time to die in it. You poor, small-minded, and misguided souls, I'll shed a tear for you all . . . all but Hoyt."

Troy couldn't believe his ears. Von Damme had just destroyed his opposition, killing half the vampires! Rubbing his eyes, Troy climbed to his feet and fled as quickly as he could. The vampires might not be distracted much longer.

Through blurred vision, he spotted Knives ahead. They'd almost reached the exit. Troy rubbed his eyes. His vision was clearing. With a burst of speed, Troy caught his friend as he stepped into the night.

"What the hell was that?" Knives asked as they passed by the dead wolves. A strong wind whipped about them. Leaves in the trees snapped like pennants over a ball park. The moon was nowhere in sight, and the darkness was thick. The air was pregnant with rain.

Troy motion for Knives to keep going. Their eyes were slow in adjusting to the darkness, so they moved blindly toward the boat. The rocks tried to trip them while the foliage seemed to reach out and grab them, slowing them down.

Troy swiped at a bush in frustration. He could now dimly see the shapes close by. Worry about finding the boat when you reach the lake, Troy thought as his head pounded. The tall grass tore at them.

"It's not much farther." The wind caught Knives's last few words, but Troy got the gist of it. They finished crossing the long plane and started down the first slope. The loose rocks made it slippery footing.

"I hope J-Man is ready to haul," Troy said. He wiped the sweat and dirt from his eyes. He turned, finding that they'd left a trail of dust behind them.

Knives suddenly went down in a heap. "Owww," he cried out. Silke fell from his grasp.

Troy stopped. Knives was sitting, holding his ankle. "Sonofabitch! I think I broke my ankle. Damn! Damn! Damn!"

"We can't stop!" Troy said, knowing better than to ask if he could go on. "I'll carry Silke. Hop, skip, or whatever. It's not much farther."

Knives nodded. His face was ashen and his eyes wide. Troy helped him to his feet. Troy's own ankle began to hurt.

Knives groaned as he put weight on the ankle. He bit his lip.

Troy gathered up Silke and put her over his shoulder in a fireman's carry. In his current state, he could barely walk.

Knives hobbled along beside him, using his bow for support. They seemed to be making a lot of noise. His heart beat so quickly that it almost hummed, never resting between beats. Troy began talking to himself, telling himself to be calm. They were almost there.

They pushed their way through the tall, dry weeds and crossed the second plane. Just down the slope to the shore and they were home free, Troy thought.

Below them was the lake. "Where's the boat?" Troy asked. Panic touched his voice. He didn't see the boat anywhere.

A raindrop spattered on his cheek. "Rain," Troy said simply.

"I see it!" Knives said. He pointed to their left. "Come on." Knives hobbled across the ridge.

Troy spotted the boat. J-Man was waving at them from below.

Suddenly, Troy heard a flapping like drying laundry caught in high winds. The bats had arrived.

Troy didn't turn. He ran diagonally down the slope. The boat was only a few yards away.

"Come on!" J-Man yelled.

The flapping grew louder. A bat began to squeak as if chastising them.

Troy staggered and plunged forward into the lake.

He heard the furious sound of splashing behind him.

Denny and Jambo pulled Silke aboard. J-Man fired up the boat and the motor started with a bellicose roar.

Troy grabbed the side of the boat and hauled himself up.

"Let's get out of here!" Knives yelled.

Troy and Bob hauled him up. Even before Knives was in, Troy yelled, "Go, baby, *GO!*"

Suddenly the air was filled with squealing and squeaking black shapes. The flapping sound was deafening. A cloud of bats descended upon the boat. White teeth gleamed and red eyes glowed in the darkness.

J-Man shoved the throttle in reverse. They pulled away from shore.

A bat landed on the back deck and started to transform. Jambo smacked it with a paddle, sending it flying into the water.

Troy slapped at one as it nipped his shoulder.

"Go, Jay!"

Far enough from shore, J-Man jammed the throttle forward. The Procraft hesitated, then leaped forward. The bow jumped into the air as they raced off.

Screeching in anger, the vampiric bats pursued the boat across South Holston Lake.

Chapter Twenty-eight
Divers Down

"They're right behind us," Denny said as he put down the binoculars. Even in the darkness, he'd been able to spot the bats. Their red eyes and beating wings made them stand out against the black storm clouds.

Rain spattered across the windshield. The huge drops exploded, portending an intense downpour. Rumbling thunder carried through the valley like kettle drums of the gods. Lightning flashed ahead of them, illuminating the clouds in an eerie green glow. "Looks like a storm of Biblical proportions," Bob muttered, then began to silently pray.

The boat raced from the cove and reached open water. Their windbreak disappeared and the waters grew rough.

"Even if—when—we do reach land—," J-Man began, then hesitated as he braced for a jolt. The wind ripped across the surface, creating whitecaps that thrashed and churned. "When we reach land, the vampires will be on us."

"We're probably safer on water than land," Troy agreed. The wind stung his eyes as he stripped. He reached for a wet suit and was thrown across the boat and into a side panel. Troy cursed and rubbed his head.

"So we wait for daylight?" Jambo asked, hanging onto the side of the boat. The Procraft leaped into the air and landed awkwardly, jerking everyone about.

J-Man cursed. "I'm gonna have to slow down some. I don't wanna capsize this sucker. Damn! Damn! Damn!"

"Jambo, sunlight won't make a difference," Knives said. "It doesn't bother these vampires. Remember? They're a new breed. Troy, what do you think you're doing?"

"I'm going for a night dive to Hoyt's house. Kaboom," Troy muttered. As a huge wave struck, the craft thrashed mightily once more. A wall of water landed inside the boat and drenched them.

Troy sputtered, unable to finish what he was saying. The boat jerked about so much that he was having trouble getting into the wet suit, let alone carry on a conversation.

"I'm going with you," Knives proclaimed. Lightning flashed.

As Troy pulled his leggings on, he said, "No, you're not. You have a bad ankle and can't swim to save your life. Look at these waves." Troy waved at the water.

"Then I'm going," J-Man yelled over his shoulder. "I can swim and I've already been there." As the boat hit a wave, it shuddered and wobbled.

Again, J-Man eased back on the throttle.

"They're gaining on us," Denny told everybody. Even without binoculars, everyone could see the tiny, bouncing pinpoints of red grow larger.

"No, Jay, you can't go either," Troy said as he stretched the neoprene past his waist. Jambo crawled over to help him. "We need you to pilot the boat. No one survives a wreck like you do. You're lucky."

"You can't go alone," J-Man protested.

"No one else has been down there, and I don't need to take care of someone who's freaking out," Troy said. The scattered drops became more frequent, stinging as they struck.

"I plan to set the charges, then resurface and swim to Cliff Island. I'll wait there to be picked up . . . or to die," Troy finished. Another wave slapped the boat and doused Troy and Jambo.

"You'll never make it in this water," Knives said.

Troy tugged on the suit. "I'll try to travel underwater for as long as my tank allows."

"That might help, but you're not going alone," Knives said firmly.

Several bolts of lightning shot from the sky and struck the shore. Flames erupted as several trees caught fire. The thunder cracked like exploding cannons, followed by the ripping of wood. In seconds, the shore was aglow as the dry woods birthed a budding inferno.

"I'll go. I'm the next best swimmer. I'll go," Denny said. His eyes were still glued to the binoculars. "They're getting closer."

"Bullshit!" Jambo spat. "I can outswim your

458

ass."

Troy adjusted the collar and zipped up the front. "J-Man just slow down near Cemetery Ridge, don't even stop. I'll jump out. You just keep going. If everything works out, come looking for me near Cliff Island first, then search the water for my body."

"I'm going with you," Denny proclaimed. "I owe Von Damme. He threatened my family, talked about the things he'd do to Karen if I didn't do as I was told. Destroying him . . . it is the only way to ensure her safety. I'm going with you." He gave Jambo the binoculars. With a determined look, Denny pulled out a second wet suit.

Troy thought about it for a minute. He didn't really want to go alone, but was afraid that one of the others might get squirrely. Two, however, had a better chance of succeeding than one. "Okay, Denny. Let's do it."

Suddenly, the sky opened wide and unleashed a deluge. Heavy rains pounded down. Each drop seemed like a .22 bullet. The winds increased, howling as if to herald the end of the world.

"We could use a good prayer," Jambo said, sliding down so that his knees rested on the floor and his elbows on the back seat. He looked through the binoculars and found their pursuers. "Hey, the rain is slowing them down!"

"Thank God for small favors," Denny breathed. He pulled off his pants, then underwear.

Lightning struck nearby, its thunder causing everyone to duck. Troy felt a small charge run through his right hand which rested on the windshield frame. Denny looked at Troy. "Keep dressing," Troy told him. "Wear an extra-heavy weight belt. We want to sink like rocks." He slipped into his BC and tightened the strap.

"I think we're getting close," J-Man yelled. He steered left and suddenly the wind decreased. The waves were only a foot or so in height. They'd reached the somewhat protected bay where Cemetery Ridge waited. "All right!" J-Man said and eased forward on the throttle.

"I think I see it," Knives said, his nose pressed against the windshield.

"Then we're close," Troy said as he strapped the knife to his leg. Denny clasped his weight belt and adjusted his BC. "Any questions?"

"I'm to set a charge in the entryway while you set another charge in the library where Spider died?" Denny asked for confirmation.

"Exactly," Troy said as he pulled on his fins. "We'll enter through the open window on the bottom floor. That goes through the kitchen. We'll go down the hallway which leads to the entryway. The library is to the right." Troy tested his flashlight, then leaving it on, attached it to his belt. Denny did the same.

"We're here," J-Man said. He pulled back on the throttle and they slowly circled Cemetery Ridge as the duo finished preparations. "Tank time," Troy said.

Denny blew through his regulator, then drew a breath. "I'm ready," Denny said, his voice a bit shaky.

Troy tested his regulator and nodded, "J-Man,

charges?"

"Here," Knives said. He gave one to each diver. Denny stared at it. "Just set the timer. Maximum is fifteen minutes."

"I know, I know," Denny said nervously. "These look familiar."

"They should," J-Man laughed. "They're from Rentzel Construction." He slowed the boat down a little more.

"They're here," Jambo said.

Troy glanced up. He could make out the bats. They seemed to be laboring and some flew unsteadily. Their squeaking cries reached his ears and fear clutched his soul. The red pinpoints became bobbing orbs of fire. He stuffed the pillowcase holding Von Damme's amulet inside his BC.

Troy's stomach twisted. A cajoling call reached him. "We're here," Troy said. "Good luck, my friends." There was no time for sentimentality. He grabbed Denny and pulled him into the water.

Troy tried to hit the surface on his back, but landed awkwardly. Tightly clenching his regulator between his teeth, Troy struck the water on his side. His mask leaped off his face, but he grabbed it.

The water just below the surface churned, throwing them both off balance. Denny had landed better and already had his flashlight in hand. Equalizing as they went, they both sank quickly into the watery darkness. They left the agitated waters behind and slipped into the calm, silent world.

Troy unhooked his flashlight. Placing thumb and

461

forefinger together to form a circle, Troy put his hand before the beam. Denny responded in kind, informing Troy he was okay.

Troy didn't waste the energy or air trying to swim to the bottom. There was no reason to hurry. They were safe from the vampires. Although the new breed could survive sunlight, moving water still destroyed them.

Troy looked at Denny. He was examining the charge and appeared to be doing fine. Troy closed his eyes and tried to relax. The drug still propelled him forward and his heart still jackhammered.

Yes, Troy could feel it—the darkness of Hoyt's house called out to him, invading every part of his body and soul. Troy honed in on the chilling siren. Von Damme's amulet tugged in the direction of the call. Yes, it was as Troy thought. He would have no trouble finding the mansion.

It would only take them a few minutes to set the charges. Everything would go without a hitch. Fifteen, no ten minutes later, they'd be near the surface when the house exploded.

Troy prayed that would take care of it. He opened his eyes and pointed the light downward. The bottom seemed to be rushing up to meet him.

They landed softly and Troy pointed in the direction of Wreythville. Denny followed as Troy swam off.

Flying above the storm-wracked water in his bat form, Von Damme cursed the rain. He strove against the winds and ignored the intense pain as the driving droplets pelted him.

How could destiny be thwarted? Von Damme wondered. Were the elements conspiring against him? The bulleting rains had slowed them down, tearing at them and giving his enemies time to reach Cemetery Ridge. Water was still their bane. From a distance, he bitterly watched as the two divers dove into the lake. He sensed what they were trying to accomplish—they were going to try and destroy the jewelry box!

Von Damme cursed as the craft pulled away. He was no longer interested in the boat—he had to stop the divers!

Screeching, Von Damme commanded the bats to follow the boat. He would personally take care of the divers—he wanted his amulet back!

Von Damme hated the thought of submerging himself in water, but he would if it meant survival. A potion he carried would allow him to make the necessary transformation, but it would only last a quarter of an hour, then the waters would destroy him.

Von Damme hovered over the spot where Troy and Denny disappeared. He began the change.

"They're here!" Knives yelled. He thought it was futile, but he picked up the bow and nocked an arrow. As he readied to fire, he prayed for luck.

"Hold on!" J-Man yelled. He jammed the throttle forward and the boat shot ahead, throwing everyone to the floor except Jay.

They raced toward the oncoming wall of vampire bats. Several hovered in their path only to splatter on the windshield. J-Man could hear the crunch of breaking bones. Other bats swerved and then circled around to follow.

As J-Man glanced over his shoulder, he saw a huge bat hanging behind them. A dim greenish glow surrounded it, then intensified. He suddenly realized that the bat was changing shape!

J-Man turned to say something to Knives but couldn't; his words stuck in his throat. Standing between them, undisturbed by the storm, was Spider's ghost. He smiled briefly at J-Man, then pointed at the glowing form which hovered over Holston. J-Man didn't understand until the spirit made a motion as if drawing the string on a bow.

"Knives! Switch places and give me the bow!" Knives looked startled as he picked himself off the deck, but quickly moved to comply.

They switched places. "Now turn this thing around," J-Man said calmly as he nocked an arrow. He hoped the rain would continue to slow the bats and that the wind wouldn't change direction.

"What?!" Everyone but J-Man exclaimed.

"I have to slow that down," J-Man pointed. Knives saw the green mass and understood. He whipped the boat around. They headed for the pursuing bats once more.

"Duck!" Knives yelled. He gunned it. The Procraft bounded and leaped over the wave crests. They powered through the screaming bats.

One swooped in and attached itself to Bob. "Help!" Jambo dumped a bucket of water on it. The bat shuddered as it began to change shape.

464

Jambo ripped it off. It grabbed him and they both fell into the water.

"Keep going!" J-Man screamed. "We're all dead if you stop!"

The craft shot toward Von Damme.

"Slow down as much as you can," J-Man told Knives as they neared. With the boat rocking drunkenly, he knew Lady Luck would have to guide his aim for him to score a hit with a wet arrow, but he would give it a try. J-Man squinted and took aim. The string drawn tight, his hand quivered.

They drew closer and closer. The bats circled and returned. Their screeching combined with the rolling thunder and howling winds sounded like a symphony written for Judgment Day.

The vampire bats drew closer. Incisors drooled in anticipation.

J-Man took aim. He couldn't believe his eyes. The hovering creature's form flowed like liquid. One moment it was a large bat, then its wings and furry features grew more humanlike. Torn clothing draped about Von Damme. The glow cast a ghastly aura about the master vampire.

Von Damme reached inside his clothing and pulled out a vial. He put it to his lips and drank deeply of the bitter liquid, then he let out an inhuman scream as if his soul had returned to discover what his flesh had become. Von Damme's body shuddered.

J-Man tried to gauge the rocking of the boat. "Jay! They're here!" Knives yelled. His hand was on the throttle, poised and ready to drive it fully forward.

The screeching bats descended like a black cloud. J-Man let the arrow loose. It flew true toward the humanesque pterodactyl.

As the wooden tip buried into Von Damme's left wing, he wailed in pain. He hovered for a moment, then plummeted toward the water. Just above the surface, he changed shape once more. Becoming more streamlined, Von Damme plunged into the lake.

"Go!" J-Man screamed. Knives reacted and the boat bolted forward like a wild mare.

Chapter Twenty-nine
Damme'd

Troy was disoriented. The water was numbingly cold and the darkness so thick it seemed to cling to him. He felt smothered. His muscles were stiffening, nearly paraylzed.

Knowing they must hurry, Troy motioned for Denny to follow. He pushed off the window sill and swam inside. His light danced around the kitchen, but found all as it had been.

Just prior to entering the hall, Troy turned to make sure that Denny was following. Denny gave him a thumbs up.

Troy carefully tapped the floor with his exploration stick. Earlier the carpet had undulated like something alive; now, nothing happened. Did he only imagine the carpet trying to grab him the last time? He reached out a little farther and struck the floor once more. Again, the carpet remained still. Shaking his head, Troy pushed off and headed for the ceiling.

Without a second glance at the floor, Troy swam

along the ceiling. He used his hands as well as his fins to propel him down the hallway. He avoided the hole in the ceiling and quickly reached the entryway.

Troy was amazed at how rapidly he'd traveled the hallway—last time it seemed to take forever. As he waited for Denny, Troy surveyed the room, letting his light scan the fallen chandelier, faded tapestries, warped bookshelves, and shuttered windows. His beam reflected off the upstairs mirror. Nothing stirred . . . but each time his light moved on, the darkness swallowed everything behind it. Troy wished his could wipe the sweat off his cheeks. Paranoia threatened to overcome him, rampaging across his sanity.

As Troy drifted farther into the entryway, a sudden chill assailed him. He swore that he could feel Von Damme approaching. But, dammit, he was underwater! How could that be? How could any of this be happening?

A second light entered the room and Denny appeared. Troy waved at him and swam to the library doors.

At the entrance to the study where Spider had died, they briefly consulted each other with pantomime. Knowing what must be done, Troy swam into the room. Memories of the last time he was there came flooding back.

Denny moved to bookshelves recessed in the wall of the entryway. With trembling fingers, he removed his explosive charge and set it on a shelf. Denny rubbed his hands. Despite what Troy had told him, Denny couldn't believe how cold it was in the house. His hands were growing numb . . . and the darkness seemed to be coiling and alive. He felt the specter of death looming over his shoulder. Trying to keep his mind on the work at hand, Denny set the charge for ten minutes.

Inside the study, Troy floated over the desk. He tried to push the thought from his mind that this was where Spider had died. Troy wondered if his friend's spirit would rest in peace once it was all over—once the house was blown to smithereens.

Again, a biting chill spurned Troy on. He opened the desk drawer and removed the jewelry box. It sent a warm wave through his body. The silver clasp and hinges glinted attractively and the engraving on the top seemed to swirl. It was up to its old tricks again, Troy thought.

He took a deep breath as his hands caressed it. Oh, how he wanted to open it! The urge was almost irresistible.

A muffled crash stirred him from his reverie. Troy felt the house shudder, and a feeling of dread overwhelmed him. Fighting it off, he attached the charge to the jewelry box. He quickly set the timer for ten minutes.

A scraping sound reverberated through the house. Denny! Troy swam for the door. Without thinking, he carried the jewelry box with him.

His light questing, Troy drifted into the hallway. His beam touched the shelves. The bomb was there, but Denny was gone.

Oh, Lord help me, Troy thought. Fear coursed through him like a drug.

His light caught a movement to his right. Troy

whirled, expecting the worse. The beam glittered off sparkling pieces of glass. Like a slow-motion waterfall, a cascade of debris sank to the floor.

Troy followed the debris to its origin. His light exposed a once-shuttered window now shattered. The boards were smashed and bent inward.

Sucking in a deep breath, Troy made a decision. He'd take the bastard with him. Troy turned the timer to three minutes.

Sorry, Denny, wherever you are, Troy thought. If Von Damme has bitten you, you're better off buried in a watery grave—we both are. Time ticked away.

Troy sensed a movement to his left and turned. The beam illuminated his worst nightmare.

A red cloud filled with bubbles rolled from the hallway and up toward the ceiling. A dark shape shot toward him through the bloody swirl.

The light illuminated Von Damme's contorted face. As if ready to explode, eyes bulged above gill-like slits. His lips were pulled back in a snarl. Blood streamed from his mouth.

Flailing, Troy tried to get out of the way. Panic struck, overriding thought.

Troy fumbled with the jewelry box. Just as he got it open, Von Damme grabbed him with webbed claws. Pain shot through Troy's ribs and right arm. He wanted to scream, but couldn't. He dropped the box.

Locking both arms around Troy, Von Damme squeezed tightly. The air exploded from Troy's lungs. Bubbles battered Von Damme's face, and he laughed, the sound warbling.

Trapped in a bear hug and unable to draw a breath, Troy gasped. Sharp pain shot through his lungs. He struggled futilely to break free, but Von Damme was too strong.

Death was only moments away. The seconds ticked away on the timer. Von Damme turned Troy around, handling him as if were a puppet.

The master vampire's green orbs locked on Troy's eyes. Von Damme's gaze held him immobile. Troy wanted to struggle but his body wouldn't respond. He was too tired and his will was almost gone.

Leering, Von Damme reached inside of Troy's BC. The master vampire removed the amulet, then placed it around his neck with a sigh. He was almost whole again . . . now it was time to feed — time for vengeance!

Teeth open wide, Von Damme leaned forward to bite Troy. Meanwhile, the jewelry box landed on the floor below and opened. Escaping, the black mass erupted from the tiny chest.

It shot up and surrounded Von Damme. The vampire stopped his attack and his arms went slack.

"Yes! Yes! Come to me!" Von Damme screamed.

Free, Troy shook his head. The paralysis was gone. He was free! The clock ticked in his head. Two minutes more?

Troy started to swim, but his eyes caught the ring gleaming in the beam of his fallen light. The sapphire called to him, urged him on. Troy bent over, reaching for it.

"Yes! Yes!" Von Damme continued. He staggered back as if drunk. The dark, bloody waters churned. The current carried the ring away. It slipped from Troy's clutching fingers.

He reached for it again. The water twisted and the sapphire danced away, disappearing in the darkness. Troy grabbed the flashlight. Part of him was screaming for him to escape—the bomb was going to explode!—while another voice told him to grab the ring, that he couldn't survive without it.

Troy tried again. He touched metal, then the ring was gone. He heard the timer ticking away—a minute and a half?

The darkness seemed to be receding as if Von Damme was absorbing it. "YES! I AM WHOLE AGAIN!!" His wild laugh warbled underwater.

Troy saw a blue spark! Light flashed off the sapphire. Troy snatched at the cavorting ring. It slipped away. He tried again and snatched it.

Von Damme grabbed Troy from behind. One hand slipped around his neck, knocking the regulator out of his mouth. Bubbles exploded around the combatants. Von Damme's right hand pawed at Troy's mask.

Troy clutched the ring and prayed. He grabbed Von Damme's hand.

Von Damme laughed, then bit into Troy's neck. Pain ripped through his body. Troy thrashed about, elbowing the vampire, but Von Damme didn't move. Firmly attached to Troy's throat, the master vampire feasted, drawing blood from Troy's jugular.

Troy felt his life draining away. He was growing

weaker and dizzy. Would he drown before he died? Troy abstractly wondered.

"ARRRGGH!" Von Damme sputtered. His teeth ripped free from Troy's throat. His tongue danced between gnashing teeth as he gagged on tainted blood. Von Damme coughed and sputtered.

Troy weakly snatched the weaving regulator from the water. He missed once, then grabbed it and shoved it in his mouth. A cloud of blood surrounded his face and shoulders. With his first breath, Troy grabbed Von Damme's right hand and slipped the ring on his finger.

"NOooo . . ." Von Damme started. Then he was paralyzed.

The ring had worked! Troy breathed an abrupt sigh of relief, then he remembered the timer—less than a minute? He had to hurry.

Troy pulled Von Damme's arm from his throat and tried to swim away. He was jerked back. Troy turned. He had pulled Von Damme with him. Desperately, Troy tried to shake him free. Nothing worked. He looked over his shoulder—the vampire held his BC in a death grip. Von Damme eyes glowed with insane triumph. Time was running out.

Quickly, Troy fumbled with the clasp on his BC. The first seemed to be stuck, but his fingers were just clumsy . . . and moving in slow motion. Finally, the clasp parted. The next two came free easily. Urging himself to move fast, but stay calm, Troy undid his weight belt.

He grabbed the light, then took several deep breaths. Lungs saturated, Troy slipped free and

473

started his ascent. There was no time for anything else. Thirty seconds—or less? He didn't think he could reach the surface. It was at least eighty feet away.

As Troy hummed, bubbles slowly streamed from his mouth. He knew the air would expand the closer he got to the surface.

Good-bye Denny. Thank you, Knives, for poisoning me. God bless you, Von Damme, to true death, Troy thought.

He reached the broken window and shattered shutters. Troy pushed out into open water. The darkness swallowed him. He shot upward. The water grew warmer. But nothing mattered to Troy but reaching the surface.

He kicked upward through the darkness. Keeping his arms at his sides, Troy put every ounce of energy into the fins. Seconds ticked away with each escaping air bubble. His lungs burned and his head pounded. His fear screamed at him, "YOU ARE GOING TO DIE! DIE! DIE! Just like everyone else. Like Aaron, Pete, Spider, Bill, Marader, and Denny . . . YOU ARE GOING TO DIE!" Less than fifteen seconds . . .

Suddenly Troy wondered if Von Damme had somehow broken free of the ring's power and was chasing him. No! No! No! Think positively, Troy told himself. I will live! LIVE!

His lungs threatened to burst and all his air explode free, but Troy enforced discipline. He swallowed and the burning disappeared . . . for a moment. He thought about nothing else but kicking and slowly exhaling. Would the force of the explosion knock him unconscious? If so, he'd drown.

"Where is the surface?!" His brain screamed. "Where is the light?!" The darkness seemed endless. He swallowed again.

Why should I be different? Troy wondered. So many had died. Why should I live?

Troy's lungs screamed to inhale. But he fought his instincts. Swallowing no longer seemed to help. He had to make it; he had to know if Silke was all right.

The water warmed. Troy grew dizzy. His kicks grew weaker.

He heard the explosion. It cracked, then rumbled like an earthquake. He felt the water quiver, then roll. Desperately, Troy kicked even harder. Red swirls flashed before his eyes.

The water churned and thrashed. Troy was buffeted about. Stars shredded the darkness before his eyes. He was passing out!

Suddenly, he popped to the surface. He gulped down a breath. "Air! Oh, thank God," he rejoiced as a large wave battered him. Troy didn't care. The rain felt heavenly.

Chapter Thirty
Departures

Troy held his head in his hands as he sat on the bench in the hospital courtyard. He was oblivious to the pale glow that surrounded him as rain clouds parted and the full moon shone through. It was nearly dawn. Pink light swelled through the sky.

He shook his head. Only now during the respite did Troy have time to ponder it. J-Man, Knives, Bob, and he had spent the past few hours answering the sheriff's questions. Of course, he didn't believe their story, but he claimed he would check it out.

Knives had gone to check on Jambo and Silke's condition. So far, there wasn't any news.

Jambo had looked terrible when they'd pulled him from the choppy waters. Mouth-to-mouth had revived him. Troy hoped he'd be all right. So many died—there were so many funerals to attend, so many old friends to say good-bye to—Denny, Spider, Pete, Aaron, Bill Glazier, and even Marader. And what about Dillon? What had happened to him?

Would Silke be all right? Troy remembered the bruises on her neck. Would she be a vampire like her brother? Each minute away from Silke was torture.

When would they have news? How long did it take to run tests?

Troy looked up when Knives walked into the courtyard. Troy tried to stand too quickly and almost blacked out. Knives rushed to his side and helped him sit back down.

"Easy, my friend, you've lost a lot of blood," Knives said.

Troy rubbed the bandage on his neck. "How's Silke?"

Knives smiled. "All the tests are negative. She's going to be just fine. The blood tests showed nothing unusual. Those are just bruises. She's not a vampire."

Troy smiled with relief. "Thank God. When she's better, and the police will let us leave town, I think we're going to spend some quiet time recuperating far, far away from here."

"I don't blame you."

"In the meantime, we have friends to bury."

"Yes," Knives said sadly.

"How's Jambo?"

"Doing just wonderful. Luckily, he has the same constitution as he does appetite—a horse's."

"Great. I was worried. He looked terrible when we pulled him out of the lake."

"Fortunate for us that the vampires suddenly disappeared," Knives said, "or you both would have drowned."

Troy nodded. "I guess when Von Damme died, they split. Who cares? Von Damme is dead. I can feel it."

"But there're still vampires in Bristol. Dillon . . ."

"I'm too tired to think about that now. I just want to thank you for poisoning me," Troy said with a wry

477

smile. "It saved my life."

"What are blood brothers for? Hey, you look exhausted. Why don't you follow J-Man's example and go crash on a couch? You won't be able to see Silke until this afternoon."

"I think I will. Just give me a minute," Troy said, looking up at the sky. "I just want to bask in the sunlight when it comes up."

"Sure," Knives said. He stood and headed back inside.

Troy didn't know how long he'd been sitting there when he noticed someone was standing nearby. She stood in the shadows for a moment, then slowly moved toward him. At first, Troy thought it was Elle, but it wasn't.

She was tall, lithe, and shapely. Standing out starkly against her white dress, the woman's dark hair cascaded over her shoulders. Her emerald eyes held Troy's gaze. She was the woman of his dreams, the dark woman of his nightmares. He'd seen her before with Hoyt and Dillon during the battle of the vampires. She was the Dark Lady of rumors.

With grace, she slowly walked over to him, pulled her skirt taut against the back of her lovely legs, and sat. The dark woman's eyes left Troy. She smiled.

Troy was mesmerized by her cold beauty in the morning light. He knew he should be afraid, but he wasn't. Maybe he was too wrung out to feel much of anything.

There was a second presence coming up behind him. Troy sensed the power, but there was also familiarity. "Hello, Dillon," Troy managed. "Have you changed your mind?"

Dillon chuckled. He walked around and sat next to the Dark Lady. "No," he said with a smile. "I came to

478

satisfy my curiosity before I depart. I wondered how y'all fared. How is Silke?"

"She's fine," Troy said, then added, "She's alive . . . normal."

"Good." Dillon breathed a sigh of relief. Troy thought he saw a tear in his eye, but then it was gone. "And you?"

"I'll live. I can't say the same for Denny. Von Damme got him before I blew the bastard, Hoyt's house, and the jewelry box to kingdom come," Troy said bitterly. He saw a question in Dillon's face and said, "I stuck a sapphire ring on his finger and it paralyzed him."

Dillon still looked confused, but the Dark Lady nodded. "I will explain later," she said quietly to Dillon.

"Troy, this is Elsa."

"The Dark Lady and the owner of the box," Troy said. She nodded.

"Now that Von Damme is destroyed, the curse has been removed. The remaining vampires are leaving."

"How many are left?"

"Very few. Many died when Von Damme perished."

"Where will you go?"

Dillon shrugged. "New York City." He smiled slightly as he said, "I can put my curse to good use there. I can't control the need to feed, but I can choose my victims. Gangs, pushers, rapists, and other vermin will be ripe for the picking in the Big Apple.

"I don't like what I've become, but I'm not strong enough to kill myself. Maybe I can do some good with this curse, maybe I can become a cleansing agent." Dillon looked to the sky. It was no longer dark, but tinged with rose colors.

"Well, we must go. The secret of living in the light died with Von Damme. There will be no new breed of vampire." Dillon stood. He stuck out his hand.

Troy stood and shook his blood brother's hand. "Two short questions."

Dillon nodded.

"How did you survive Von Damme's . . . light explosion during the debate?"

"I wasn't there. I was out feeding. He spared Elsa because he'd always wanted her. Despite what you might think, vampires still feel. It's just . . . different. You will never understand. It is just another state of being."

"Why did you bring her with you to see me?"

"I thought you'd run if you saw me," Dillon said, smiling. "I needed something to capture your attention . . . and I know that beautiful women have always caught your attention. I am glad Silke has done so.

"Love her, take care of her, and please tell her I have died. Will you promise?"

Troy nodded. Despite that his best friend was a creature of darkness, he didn't feel rage. Troy only felt a profound loss so strong that he couldn't speak.

"Thank you." Again Dillon looked at the sky. "Good-bye, my friend." With that, he and Elsa disappeared into shadows.

A moment later, Troy heard the familiar flapping as the two bats left the courtyard. "Good-bye, my friend," Troy finally managed to whisper.